THE ART
OF REGRET

THE ART
OF REGRET

A NOVEL

MARY FLEMING

SHE WRITES PRESS

Published October 2019
Printed in the United States of America
Print ISBN: 978-1-63152-646-6
E-ISBN: 978-1-63152-647-3
Library of Congress Control Number: 2019906679

For information, address:
She Writes Press
1569 Solano Ave #546
Berkeley, CA 94707

Interior design by Tabitha Lahr

She Writes Press is a division of SparkPoint Studio, LLC.

For David

PART I

ONE

FOR MANY YEARS, in what might have been the prime of my life, I lived and worked on the rue des Martyrs. This narrow market street, which begins its climb at the northern edge of the banking and insurance district and ends in the skein of streets that wraps around the Sacré Coeur at the heart of Montmartre, is not on the tourist circuit and has no pretensions to Parisian grandeur. Behind and above its modest shop fronts are forgettable lives. Lives like my own, which I had reduced to a box, a one-room apartment on top of a one-room shop. Though the two were once a unit, at some point and for some reason—to make more space, to rent the shop and studio separately—the connecting stairs had been disconnected and my room could only be reached by an enclosed stairway in the courtyard. It's not unusual in a city with a long history. Buildings change their function and configuration, and one structure is squeezed in front of, behind, or beside another. It's just such quirks that have made Paris Paris, a city of endless layers and perspectives, a city of story upon story.

Though my story began in New York, the firstborn son of two Americans, it was moved across the Atlantic with a mother and a brother, minus a father and a sister, when I was eight. There on European soil the story reluctantly remained, until near the end of a resentful adolescence. Unfortunately, the long-awaited return to the United States of America, via a small college, proved a disaster, and back the story came to Paris, where it drifted into young and not so young adulthood. By the time it had settled on the rue des Martyrs, I had hoped that that was where it would end, the unremarkable tale of a not-so-proud bicycle shop owner.

One October morning in 1995, I pulled up the orange security grille to Mélo-Vélo. No matter how carefully I coaxed it, the clang of juddering metal scraped my nerve ends. It seemed such an offensive start to every day, I was thinking, as I walked to the back of the shop and assessed my morning's work, a bicycle that had spent the last twenty years in a basement. The airless tires were cracked, the handlebars rusty. Cobwebs draped every spoke, and the leather saddle was speckled with mold. The wheels squeaked and wobbled. A complete overhaul was in order, but for Camilla Barchester, the name I had noted on the repair slip, it might prove to be worth the trouble. I turned the bicycle belly up on the repair stand.

The Tibetan chimes jangled while I was contemplating which bit of the wreck to attack first. It was Madame Picquot, the concierge, with the morning post. Though I had long ago made it clear to her that I was not receptive to morning chatter, that I had no interest in the secrets and rumors, the scandals and grievances that scurried through the building and up and down the street, that I wished she'd just drop my post at the bottom of the stairs to the studio, she passed by the shop every morning to deliver my letters in person.

"*Voilà, Monsieur Mic-fa,*" she croaked. "Registered letter. I saved you a trip to the post office and signed for it. *Ca va?*"

"Yes, thank you."

Normally, since I received little of interest, registered or otherwise, I would have been in no hurry to look at my correspondence, but for some reason—perhaps a fundamental lack of interest in the task at hand—I went straight to the counter and looked at my misspelled name: "Monsieur Trévor MACFARQUAHAR." If my name is systematically shortened when spoken in French, it is lengthened when written, unfailingly adorned by superfluous vowels and unnecessary accents, and forever a reminder of my general square-pegged existence in a round world.

I sighed, ripped open the envelope, unfolded the slim sheet of white paper, and in the few short paragraphs saw my life crumbling before me. The letter, from the insurance company who owned the shop and studio apartment, informed me that when my lease ran out on the shop the following June, it would not be renewed.

How can they take my shop, ruin my plan for living, I wondered as I stumbled outside, almost immune to the cool, clear morning and the beehive domes of the Sacré Coeur, dog-tooth white against the uncompromising blue sky. I walked numbly to my corner café, Le Rendez-Vous des Martyrs, and plopped down at my usual spot in the corner. The morning sun slanted down the side street over small round tables and wooden bistro chairs. The honeyed glow illuminated the interior, almost masking the sticky ochre of yesterday's nicotine and *frites* oil that clung to the walls. Almost, in fact, managing to make the place look charming.

Jean-Jacques, the waiter, purposefully wound his way through the tables and chairs toward me, tray propped on his left hand, white sleeves rolled to the elbow. He wiped the table briskly with a wet cloth. "*Ca va?*"

When I didn't answer, he poked my shoulder: "*Ca va?*"

"No," I said.

"What?" Silence. "Come on, spit it out."

"I'm being dumped."

He sighed with a knowing nod.

"By an insurance company."

"Ha!" He laughed. "That's a good one."

"Could I just have my coffee? Please?"

Still chortling, he wound his way back to the bar where the other regulars were gathered. Marcel, the rotund, retired mechanic who stopped here several times a day with his wife's poodle Caline, was on his first glass of white wine. A group of Polish construction workers who had recently gutted a nearby building, leaving only its façade standing, were silently sipping coffee. And a couple of concierges on their morning rounds were chattering. Like Marcel's dog, they were looking for crumbs. None of them wanted to miss any neighborhood news, not least my own concierge Madame Picquot, who at that moment tottered in on bowed legs so skinny they looked drawn on her short, round body by a child. Hands in the pockets of her pink housecoat, she listened to Jean-Jacques at the bar before slipping Caline a cube of sugar and teetering out. By evening, the whole street would be *au courant*.

"What do you mean by an insurance company?" Jean-Jacques asked when he came back with my double espresso.

"I'm being evicted," I said, licking my cigarette paper. "From my shop."

He shook his dark head: "I've been telling you you're in the wrong business. Who wants a bicycle? They have no sex appeal. You need to be selling something fashionable. Computers maybe. Think about it. The insurance company could be your biggest customer." He shook his head and shrugged. "Well, I guess it's too late now."

"Thanks, Jean-Jacques."

"No problem."

Too late now. Back at the shop, Jean-Jacques's words clanged through my head as I savagely screwed and unscrewed bits on and off that bike. Though some might consider an eviction notice a mild inconvenience and others even a welcome development—the chance for change—for me that morning, it appeared nothing short of a full-blown catastrophe. A mortal blow to my life in a box, my overall plan for living.

The letter was a niggling reminder of another ugly fact. Mélo-Vélo was not, by any stretch of the imagination, a thriving enterprise. As Jean-Jacques had so promptly pointed out, bicycles were not even popular, much less sexy. If I lost this lease, I would not be able to buy another. I would have to sell out, change the course of my life, and that prospect caused a panic to rise up from my gut and flutter around my heart in a most uncomfortable manner. I didn't want to change. At thirty-seven, I'd finished with all that.

By noon, both the front and back wheels were trued and tightened and clicking smoothly when I spun them. I had changed the brake pads and inner tubes and tires, removed the rust and crust, and cleaned the leather seat with saddle soap. Except for a dirty little lock hanging on the baggage carrier, the bike looked not gleaming but respectable. I rolled myself a cigarette and waited, but by one, closing time, still no Camilla. Of course not. It was that kind of day, I said to myself as I locked up the shop and headed out the back door, into the courtyard, and up the enclosed staircase that led to my blue door.

The rectangular room, with two shuttered windows giving onto the street, was a contrived study in minimalism. There was a mattress on the floor. Various crates served as book shelves and low tables, though I did have a real table, with one chair, for meals. In the corner was the kitchen area, with a sink and two electric heating plates on top of a small refrigerator, which usually preserved more film than food. In a side niche I had built a rudimentary bathroom and put up some shelves. The wood-planked floor was bare, and the walls were white, with simple molding along the ceiling. My only concessions to pleasure and decoration were a television that sat on a crate and a stretch of cork matting on the wall where the occasional photo was pinned.

While I ate reheated rice left over from the night before, I turned on the TV news, which spent almost the entire half hour on the government's attempts to reform the social security system and the unions' resistance to the proposed changes. Since the unions never agreed with the government, I didn't see any reason to pay attention to this particular case. In fact, I couldn't quite grasp why the journalists were acting as if the Bastille were about to be re-stormed.

I rolled myself a cigarette. I thought about Camilla Barchester. She had begged me to hurry with her bicycle, had promised to be there by noon to retrieve it. Today this struck me as yet another offense, another piece of evidence that the cards were always and would forever be stacked against me.

———

That afternoon, not a client in sight, no more repairs to attend to, I was seated in the comfortable chair I had tucked away at the back of the workshop, reading. Rabbit Angstrom was just about to croak on the basketball court when the Tibetan chimes chimed.

"Sorry I'm late," she said breathlessly.

"No problem," I mumbled, though her arrival at the climax of the story—of the entire saga—was no longer welcome.

"I really am sorry," she repeated.

Camilla Barchester was tall with very fair skin and light brown hair that fell in loose curls past her shoulders. Pretty in that English sort of way. Confident too, in her manner of speaking. I could tell that she was what my mother would call a *nice* girl, from a *good* family. It was partly her accent, partly her perfect nose and soft but unflinching blue eyes that had no bone to pick with the world they looked out on.

"Here's the bicycle," I said.

"Brilliant," she answered in those rounded, flutey tones of the upper-middle class, and I refrained from asking, despite my general irritation, why the English find everything brilliant and why all girls seem to be called Camilla. She walked around the front wheel. "It looks great. Jean's mother *should* be pleased."

"Do you know the combination to the lock?" I asked, feeling unsteady in my rusty English. At that time in my life, weeks could go by when I wouldn't speak it, and mother tongue or not, disuse made the words roll around in my mouth, turning uncomfortable somersaults before tumbling forth.

"I have no idea what it is," she said.

"This one won't help you much anyway," I added, pulling at the flimsy coiled wire. "I'll cut it off, if you want."

Camilla Barchester hesitated at my simple question with its multiple implications. I saw that it addressed a tentative place at the edge of this Jean-person's family circle and her right to make decisions from that edge. After a moment she said, with a dismissive wave of her hand: "No, just leave it. I'll buy another one. The cheapest you've got."

After she'd paid, I wheeled the bicycle outside and set her off in the right direction. I watched her go, thinking that I liked the idea of an English girl. Especially a pretty one who buys cheap locks, indicating a short stay in Paris. An interlude of fun and games before she heads back to England and gets down to the serious business of finding a (*nice*) English husband. Except for damn Jean, she embodied the perfect confluence of criteria for what I will call a Casual.

My life, though ordered and narrow and frequently plagued by prolonged bouts of What's-the-pointism, did have its distractions. I am, after all, a man, and one blessed with a face not unattractive to women, despite its being attached to a bicycle shop. While the general picture is pleasing enough, it is my mouth, tending to tightness, that clinched the deal every time. I *looked* as if I suffered, and women, I had discovered, generally melted at the sight of a male in emotional pain, a man who had perhaps not quite achieved his full human potential. They thought we could *talk*, that they could save me.

At that particular time, I had two Casuals. One was Paulina, a Brazilian photographer whom I'd met through an old acquaintance. The other was Jennifer, a Canadian dancer. I did not consider having more than one woman cavalier, much less immoral, because I was honest with them right from the start about the conditions of our arrangement, that is, I was not interested in anything but the stated Casual Relationship that included no exclusivity clause. Furthermore, any attempt to attach strings would be met with scissors.

Of course, this strategy didn't always work as well in practice as it did in theory. There were those who at first accepted the rules of the game, then became impatient with, intolerant of them. They would want more. They would try on strings for size. And just as I had promised at the start, that would be it. Snip, snip, over. There were times, too, when I would feel myself slipping, losing my own firm footing on the solid rock of independence. But that was one of the advantages of multiplicity. In the case of growing affection, I would lean more heavily on another, until I regained my equilibrium. Because I was convinced that love was not and never would be my line of work.

Luckily I never had much trouble replenishing the stocks. Besides a loose group of people from my past, I had the active social life of my brother Edward and his wife Stephanie. Though I didn't think much of my brother, his wife was, to my critical eyes, a goddess. They often asked me to caulk up a hole around the table at one of their many expat dinner parties, and it was like fishing in an overstocked pond. There were always a few women who, like the fair-skinned Camilla, were in Paris for Adventure. Who were ready to throw caution to the wind. Generally they were on post-collegiate binges, final flings before settling down to real jobs in real places like Chicago or St. Louis or Detroit. The few who had come with more serious motives, like making Paris home, I steered well clear of.

But I did make it a point never to steal a woman from another man. Therefore, with all my scruples intact, I silently watched Camilla Barchester disappear around the corner, on her way back down the hill, to short-term Jean.

TWO

ONE SUNDAY A month my mother, Helen Stanford McFarquhar Harcourt-Laporte, produced and directed The Family Lunch. Family being, at this stage: my mother and myself, Edward and Stephanie, and their three children. And, much as I still wished otherwise, my stepfather, Edmond Harcourt-Laporte.

Each lunch followed the same story line. Edward, Stephanie, and children would arrive at twelve thirty for a drink. After closing Mélo-Vélo early, I would arrive about one. As a concession to my late arrival, lunch would be served at 1:20. We were always walking out the door by three, give or take the five minutes it often took to find a child's lost shoe or toy.

My pleasure in attending these meals was perverse. They allowed me to observe my unenlightened family's bourgeois rituals with scornful amusement or anthropological curiosity, depending on my mood. Because I of course had successfully left all that behind by becoming a bicycle-shop owner on the rue des Martyrs.

Sunday mornings were the busiest time at the shop, since weekend touring cyclists were my main customers. But the morning before October's Family Lunch was eerily quiet. Except for a quick and dirty repair on a chain, I had nothing to do but sit and contemplate the emptiness and remember the halcyon days when I was just an employee, when the shop belonged to Nigel Jones. The days when Mélo-Vélo, Nigel's 1970's conflation of *mélomane* (music lover), with bicycle (*vélo*), had been a hub for English and American expats under thirty, a lively, happening kind of place.

A few years after I'd started working for him, Nigel, an overweight, semi-alcoholic chain-smoker, dropped dead from a heart attack at the tender age of forty-four. His only family being a mother in Wales, he had decided, without telling me, to leave the lease for the shop in my name. Since I was actively seeking the route of least responsibility, I did not view this legacy as a favor. In fact, I'd wanted to sell straight away. Partly out of respect for Nigel's wishes but mostly out of inertia, I didn't. I held on.

Since his death seven years earlier, it had been a steady downhill ride, during which I'd made no attempt to change course. I liked to *say* I was a shop owner. It was the doing I found less appealing. Tinkering with bikes was okay, but I could hardly call it a passion. As for salesmanship, I actively disliked it and did not connect with the customers, much less try to encourage new ones. I had changed nothing, from the paint on the walls to the manual cash register, and the place was a little tired around the edges, to say the least.

Closing early, I pulled down the orange metal grille on Mélo-Vélo, winced at its clatter, and gave my obligatory nod to the Sacré Coeur. I had identified closely with this architectural outlier since first spotting it on the horizon at age nine. With its beehive domes it looked as if it belonged on another continent. Like me. Later I saw a deeper meaning: the two larger cupolas represented my parents, the three smaller ones the three children. I identified too with its stone that changes color according to the light. Today, cold and grey, it looked like wet concrete. I wondered why I'd bothered to lug my camera along.

In comparison, the street to the left looked prosaic and provincial as the late shoppers rushed to fill their baskets before the apples and lettuces were packed away. It was hard to imagine the street had once been a Greco-Roman thoroughfare. It was even harder to imagine Saint Denis, first bishop of Paris, with his two pals Rustique and Eleuthère, freshly decapitated, walking up the road, carrying their heads in their hands. But that's what the legend says, that the three martyrs-in-the-making walked up this street and past Montmartre, a full six kilometers, until they dropped at the site of what's now the Basilica of Saint Denis, burial place to the kings of France.

The métro was conveniently on the same Porte de la Chapelle–Mairie d'Issy line as my mother and stepfather and even my brother. In fact, it was the same line that I'd taken to school, first with Edward and my mother or Lisette the housekeeper, and later by myself, almost every day of my Paris youth. By that measure, I hadn't actually moved very far away, but as I emerged from the rue du Bac station that day, the contrast with the rue des Martyrs was stark.

Here in the *7ème arrondissement* on a Sunday, most of the residents had fled the city for their country houses. Of those who remained, not one ugly, unkempt person was in sight. In the *faubourg Saint Germain*, the less well-endowed physically could afford to cover up unfortunate features and the ravages of time with cashmere, hair dye, and plastic surgery. The grandeur carried over to the architecture: Haussmann resplendence on the boulevards and eighteenth-century stateliness in the back streets, where *hôtels particuliers* had housed the old, old aristocrats, the ones dubbed by a king, before Napoleonic upstarts began nudging into the nobility with their pushy, bourgeois ways. The *hôtels* still stood, but over the centuries many had been taken over by the government and transformed into ministries, thereby assuring their survival and lending a regal aspect to their bureaucracy that the French alternately love and hate.

Some families, however, had held on, and it was in just such an eighteenth-century building that I had spent the bulk of my childhood. My stepfather's father, who was not an aristocrat but the banker for one, had bought an apartment in a *hôtel particulier* from the duc de Coursault after the war, when money was scarce and help was needed to keep the place up. By the time my mother, Edward, and I arrived on the scene, Edmond's parents were dead and he was living in its spacious rooms all alone.

For as long as I could remember, nothing at the rue de Verneuil had changed, not even the code on the grand door giving access to the courtyard: B1207, birthday of the now-defunct duc's long-dead horse. Inside, under the porte-cochère was the concierge's loge, where for the last thirty years, Monsieur and Madame Morales had been the building's *gardiens*. Heavy, uneven paving stones still bumped across the courtyard, and the doors to the former coach houses, now garages, still sagged slightly. Even some of the potted plants and shrubs that dotted the edges seemed to have been there forever.

And on the left, attached to the wall, was my mother's bicycle, the one bought the only time she had ventured up to the rue des Martyrs, not long after I'd taken over Mélo-Vélo. She'd chosen a secondhand Raleigh with three gears. "There aren't many hills in the 7th," she'd said with an embarrassed shrug, "and I like its sturdy English look." Then, feeling guilty for not choosing something more expensive, she'd insisted on buying multiple accessories: a basket and luggage rack, a rearview mirror, and—despite my assurances that such a high level of security for a rusting, used heap of metal was unnecessarily cautious—an expensive, indestructible Kryptonite lock.

Our building, with its long windows and smooth façade, stood at the back of the courtyard. I took the steps of the wide stone staircase two by two and pressed the polished brass doorbell, next to which the letters "H-L" were discreetly printed. From the other side of the reinforced door, I could hear the flat soles of my mother's shoes slapping over the wide herringbone parquet.

"Hello, T," she said, opening the door and offering up each of her downy cheeks to me for a kiss. "You're here a little earlier than usual. Would you like a quick something?" Though she had lived in Paris for thirty years, Helen Stanford no-longer-McFarquhar Harcourt-Laporte had retained much of the Wall Street lawyer's daughter. The "quick something" of a Long Island cocktail party, the steady, slightly splayed step, and the good bone structure of well-established New York society.

"I just need to wash my hands," I said, holding them up. "I didn't quite get all the grease off."

Her eyes fluttered, almost imperceptibly. "All right," she said stoically before turning back to the living room and calling in French now: "Trevor is here."

I walked by the guest WC, with its scalloped bar of rose hip soap in a porcelain dish and its white linen towels, ironed by the fierce hand of Lisette into rigid rectangles, to the pockmarked enamel laundry sink in the pantry, with its solid bar of no-fuss *savon de Marseille* and a brush.

As I scrubbed, Lisette called from the kitchen: "*Trésor*, is that you?"

I dried my hands, walking toward her at the stove. She put down the wooden spoon and wiped her hands on the old white apron as she pulled me to her ample bosom. "How's business?"

"Thriving," I answered.

"Good, good," she said, picking up her spoon again. "Lunch is almost ready."

As a boy I'd spent hours with Lisette in the warm kitchen, sitting on a stool and listening to her chatter as she prepared supper.

Over the years she had become plumper and plumper, so that now, with her short, round body, her tripled neck, and bulging eyes, she resembled a pug dog. She was the one person in the house I didn't want to irritate or disappoint.

With my hands scrubbed, if not spotless, I approached the family circle. Just before I entered, the sun flashed through a crack in the clouds and illuminated the living room. It shot through the old glass cabinet containing some of the boxes my mother collected. My camera was there, on the entry hall table. I grabbed it, pulled off the lens cap, put my eye to the viewfinder, and adjusted the shutter speed, then the aperture, just as the sun disappeared. I pulled the camera from my eye. Missing these moments was like watching the train leave the station while I stood dumbly on the platform. I could regret them for weeks. At least no one had seen me. I laid the camera down quietly.

The living room was a high-ceilinged rectangle with three large windows looking over a garden that belonged to a building on the parallel rue de l'Université. The floor was warped and the oak planks creaked unpredictably, even the parts covered by an expansive Persian carpet. The furniture was a mixture of English and French, mostly antique, but with a few comfortable sofas providing a splash of Americana comfort. And strewn across end tables, laid out in that damn glass cabinet, were the boxes my mother had been collecting since she was married the first time, to my father. She picked up one box on every trip she took. Large and minuscule, round and rectangle, wood and enamel, French and American, even Chinese, they were everywhere.

"Brother," said Edward as I walked in. "How's life in the chain store on the hill?"

"Probably better than life in the stock-ades," I answered.

"That would surprise me," Edward answered, his arms closing across his chest, glass of white wine in one self-satisfied hand. Everything about my brother suggested success and prosperity, from his quick eyes and cocky smile to his slimly cut tweed jacket with the double vent and the ironed jeans, crease front and back. Mostly European but, like my mother, with some carefully selected American elements: today country shoes from L.L. Bean, to sustain a transatlantic image.

"Though I have to say," he continued with that slightly foreign accent he cultivated in both French and English, "that since you insist on living like *un petit bourgeois*, you should at least have considered a *boulangerie*. Bakers make packets of money and retire to large, ugly houses they build for themselves in the country."

"They work too hard," I said. "And I'm not interested in country living."

I turned my back on him. Really there were times when I wondered what we shared besides a métro line and a mother.

"Hello, Stephanie," I said as I kissed each of the ever-so-slightly hollowed cheeks.

"Trevor, hello." Her low voice rumbled, purred. Her snug black trousers allowed full appreciation of her long legs and perfectly rounded rump. The green eyes, deeply set into her gingery complexion, smiled back at me. A hand ran through the straight and shiny gold-red hair. Gorgeous.

I turned reluctantly to my stepfather, greeting him in the same chilly, brisk manner I always addressed him. He was my mother's, not mine, and that was a message I had communicated to him relentlessly over the years, even long after he'd given up trying to win my favor. Edmond Harcourt-Laporte, known to Edward and me as BP, nodded but averted his grey, inscrutable eyes, his aquiline beak. He couldn't stand the sight of me.

"Time to call the children," Mother said. It was, of course, exactly 1:20. Stephanie disappeared toward the back of the apartment, where their three children, aged eight, six, and three, were playing in our old bedrooms.

We proceeded across the creaking floor into the dining room next door and the large oval table, laid in its silver and porcelain splendor. The extra leaf was in; this was the first lunch where the children would be joining us, instead of eating in the kitchen. Matthieu and Henri came running in from the back, jumping and howling. Stephanie sauntered in with Caroline, who looked just like her mother.

"Come and sit down, boys," my mother said steadily above the ruckus. "You know you're not allowed to behave like wild animals in this house."

My mother, though allergic to discord, had not wholeheartedly embraced her daughter-in-law. Beautiful though she may have been, Stephanie lacked breeding, an element that in my mother's eyes was as vital as the air she breathed. Without it, one produced wild, ill-mannered creatures like her own grandchildren. Her role, one might even have called it a crusade, was therefore to care for them regularly and counteract Stephanie's slack regard for discipline and decorum.

Indeed, the boys did calm down; they were used to bending to Mother's authority. Caroline stuck close to Stephanie. She was dressed in a skimpy dark skirt. Like her mother's black trousers, it showed off her long legs nicely.

Lisette made her stout way among the children and adults, with the platters she then placed on the warming tray at the large oak sideboard. She clucked and scolded that the soup would get cold, that the meat would dry out.

"I really think the children would be better off in the kitchen," said Stephanie to my mother. "It's what they're used to."

"No, no, it's time that they learned to sit still. To endure adult conversation," answered my mother. "That's the way it is here in France."

So we all sat down at the well-armed table and this first cross-generational experiment in dining. Under the soup bowl was a flat

plate for the main course, always a roast, green vegetable, and potatoes. There were side plates for bread and later cheese and salad.
The heavy and ornate silverware, my mother's grandmother's, lay
gleaming and straight. Two forks on the left, two knives and a
soup spoon on the right, and a dessert fork and spoon crossed at
the top. Two silver candlesticks, elaborate things with long, loopy
arms, waved about over the table. What a production.

"*J'aime pas la soupe*," Henri whispered to his father.

"Just eat three bites," Edward answered, echoing our mother's
litany to us as children. Henri looked to his mother for sympathy,
but her face was firmly planted over her own soup bowl. He grimaced and picked up the oversized spoon in his fist.

My mother sighed.

Edward said to him: "No, Henri, not like that." And he plied
the child's fist from the spoon, adjusting his grip to the polite norm
between thumb and forefinger.

"Trevor," Stephanie looked up suddenly, "do you have any
children's bicycles? Caroline has outgrown that thing I bought for
her at the Bon Marché." While the rest of the adults spoke French
at the table, a practice that had begun when we'd first moved in—
to help Edward and me learn the language, and out of respect
for Edmond—Stephanie spoke and was spoken to in English by
everyone except her own children. They went to a French school,
the same one Edward and I had attended, and were only exposed
to English at home. Though they understood their mother's
tongue, they refused to speak it.

"*Maintenant elle est à moi, la bicyclette,*" piped in Matthieu
as he tossed a proprietary look of triumph at his sister. Just as Caroline looked like her mother, little Matthieu resembled Edward.
The curly hair, the confident round face, the light hazel eyes. He
had his mother's freckles, but that was about all.

"I have a few children's bikes," I said. All I could concentrate on, with her looking at me, was how utterly beautiful she was. The rounded forehead, the slightly ski-sloped nose, the strong, pointed chin. Those feline eyes.

"Maybe we'll come up and see sometime."

"Don't forget C-h-r-i-s-t-m-a-s is coming soon," Edward said. His jaw muscles were grinding, always the telltale sign that he was perturbed.

But as we moved onto the main course, a mischievous smile replaced the tense jaw. "What do you shopkeepers think of the new government?" He paused and wiped his mouth on the white cloth napkin. "They're trying to make it easier for small businesses."

"That's what they always claim," Edmond answered for me. "Then nothing ever changes but the number on an impenetrable form that takes months to fill out." Politics always got him going, while family matters, from the children's manners to my aloofness, he left to my mother. "But they're better than the Socialists, that much I'll concede. Fourteen years of Emperor Mitterrand would have ruined us, if he hadn't done a complete turnaround two years into office. Fortunately for the country, all he really cared about was his own grip on power."

"At least the Juppé government is addressing the social security issue," said Edward. "It's scandalous, these *régimes spéciaux* where train drivers and other state employees can retire at fifty or fifty-five. Before long, no one will have to work at all."

"Whatever his plans, the prime minister is an egghead," I said. "As a well-trained bureaucrat, everything he does looks fine on paper, but it won't work in practice. BP is right about small businesses." I threw a look his way. From time to time, I still liked to toss him a bone, make him believe we were on the same side. "You know that no French worker has ever given up one single acquired right, and why should he? The whole system is based on the battle between the haves and the have-nots. The elite looks out for its own, and the rest of the population scrabbles for whatever it can get through confrontation." I paused, irritated at my brother's silence. "If the people had more real power . . ."

Bingo.

"More power!" He lifted his quick and springy frame slightly from his cushioned chair. Though not quite as tall as his wife, he was just as athletic. "Every time a reform is proposed, your dear workers take to the streets, and after two days, the government has conceded and given them everything they want. If that's not power, I don't know what is." He pointed angrily at no one in particular. "I say fire them. Then they'll have something to demonstrate about."

Mother cleared her throat and began sawing vigorously at her meat.

"It is true," she said, "that in this neighborhood, with all those ministries, there are so many demonstrations, it's hard to keep track of who the people are and what exactly it is that they're complaining about. I try and ignore them."

"They're like spoiled children," Edward said haughtily.

"If that's the analogy you want to draw," I answered, trying to control my voice. He too knew exactly which buttons to press. "If you insist on portraying the workers as childish and spoiled, then I'd say the grown-up leaders are decadent, irresponsible, selfish, and ergo, unfit parents."

"The point is," Edmond said calmly, "change in France always occurs through conflict." Mother looked at him gratefully for intervening. "In many ways, nothing has changed since well before Louis the sixteenth lost his head. The titles have evolved, but the dynamic has remained the same: instead of a king, we have a regal president. Instead of a ruling aristocracy in the king's court, we have bureaucrats, the highest achievers in the country, running the place. And meanwhile, the people form their own impenetrable

factions." As so often with Edmond, on abstract issues he got right
to the point, straight to the heart of the matter. Even I, the only
family member who voted Socialist, had to agree with him here.

By now, little Henri had finished his potatoes. The meat and
beans sat cut and untouched on his plate, and any proud pleasure
he may have felt at sitting with the grown-ups was long gone. He
had descended from his chair and was rearranging the large reference books that had been used to raise his stature at the table.
And he was doing it ever more loudly. "Come sit on my knee,
Henri," Mother said to him. He obeyed immediately, settling into
the crook of her arm and inserting his thumb firmly in his mouth.

"Has anyone seen the Cézanne exhibit?" she went on.

"I have," Stephanie piped up. "It was too crowded and disor-
ganized. I could hardly see the paintings. They really do a better
job of logistics at the Met."

"I dow-n't know about zat," said BP in his heavily accented
English, but one that had been influenced by English-English. "Last
ti-me I was z'ere, I 'ad to wa-it twenty minutes to recuperate my
coat." Every meal, you could count on it. Stephanie would make an
anti-French remark, and she would be immediately contradicted.
I felt sorry for her. The French drove her crazy. Her mastery of
the language was halting and her accent atrocious in a family that
slipped from one tongue to another with amphibian ease.

And so the meal see-sawed on, through the cheese and
salad, into the lemon meringue tart. After art, the subject tipped
to films. Edward and Stephanie began to disagree heatedly about
Ken Loach's *Land and Freedom*. Stephanie loved it; Edward hated
it. Mother and Edmond hadn't heard of either film or director.
Loach was too gritty and working class a director for their tastes,
Edward's obviously too. Mother changed the subject to Prin-
cess Di, who was promising to tell all on television. Stephanie
had an opinion on that too. So Mother turned to the house on

Long Island, where we spent our summer holidays, where she and Edmond still went every August. She wondered aloud if now weren't the right time to sell, but since she'd been asking the same question regularly for the last ten years, Edward and I got up to help Lisette clear the table. The children had been released as the Camembert was making its rounds. My mother judged their presence a success. No one else cared to comment.

Right on schedule, just before three, Lisette arrived with a large jug of freshly squeezed orange juice. It was the sign that The Family Lunch was drawing to a close. Mother had adopted this French trick and had been using it on her dinner guests for as long as I could remember. Once we'd grown up, she simply carried the ritual over to us, dispensing with her family just as casually as she did friends and acquaintances. Which today was particularly fine by me. She had recently imported the American phobia for smoking and banned it in her house. Possibly it was just a way to avoid the pain I incited by rolling my own. In any case, I was dying for a cigarette.

As Edward helped little Henri with his coat, he tugged too hard, and the child started to cry. It added to an existing tension in the air that I could not quite identify. Earlier I had attributed it to the children's presence at the table, but that should have dissipated. It was Edward. He had seemed edgy and preoccupied all through lunch. It was unlike him to be impatient with his children. Then Stephanie, who was always slightly peevish at the rue de Verneuil, sent us looking for Matthieu's sweatshirt, and I forgot about it.

In the courtyard we ran into Antoine de Coursault, his wife Chantal, and their children. He and Edward had been classmates and friends since early childhood. Antoine and Chantal also lived in the building, having moved from the smaller apartment under the eaves into his grandparents' much larger flat when they'd had their third child. Number four, it appeared, was well *en route*, but that was to be expected. Anything less in this neighborhood was substandard, as I had keenly felt while growing up, when it had been just my brother and me, five years apart, like two gaping teeth. Childbearing was still viewed as a competitive sport down here in the *7ème arrondissement*, and this was one game Edward and Stephanie would have trouble winning.

As I was thus musing, the procreators planned a walk to the Tuileries gardens. On the street, Antoine turned to me: "Do you want to join us? I haven't seen you in an age." He had an ingenuous smile and blue eyes that reminded me of Camilla Barchester's in their candor. Even if I could never think of anything to say to him, it was impossible to dislike him.

"Trevor can't stay down here for more than three hours or he turns into a pumpkin," said Edward.

"Says the pumpkin's brother," I answered. "Maybe another time." I looked at Stephanie, and she looked uncomfortable with Chantal, who was the daughter—of course one always knew these things—of a count and countess. She had a maiden name that flung back several centuries and strung across a whole line of text. For all her husband's natural friendliness, she was a small-hearted snob who would have disapproved of Stephanie even more than Mother did. I wondered, since I only got invited to their expat dinners, how she fared in Edward's Paris world, with her halting French and brash American opinions.

Outside the building, they turned right to cross the bridge, and I turned left to walk off lunch another way home.

Home, I toss out lightly.

This short word has multiple implications, can be, has been, the source of countless questions and complications in my life.

Does it mean, for example, my ur-home, New York, where I was born to Gordon and Helen McFarquhar? My memories from that time are circumscribed to our Upper East Side apartment and my school, with snatches of Central Park in between. But didn't it leave deeper marks on my psyche than those in my conscious mind? In writing these lines, I have remembered my father, bent over his desk, grading papers or, briefcase in hand, about to leave for the university, where he was an assistant professor of English literature. I remember my mother crying over the chopping board, while I remained unconvinced that the culprit was the onion. Or with a book. So often with a book and I'd have to poke her shoulder to get her attention.

What about the house in Connecticut, where we spent weekends and the long holidays of an academic? It was there that both my sister and my father were violently removed from the picture. Those two deaths, occurring when I was six and seven years old, were, are, and will always be the cornerstones of my existence, the bricks and mortar of what make up me. Doesn't that, on some level, constitute home?

Throughout my childhood, I certainly insisted that the United States of America was where I belonged. I proclaimed, *ad nauseum*, to anyone who would listen, that the second I had my *Baccalauréat* in hand, I'd be on the plane, gone for good. For good, it turned out, only lasted the nine months of a freshman year at the small American college in the middle of nowhere that I'd insisted on attending. After a month with my ice hockey roommate Brett Bourne and a couple of fraternity parties, I'd already started charting my flight back.

So what about France, Paris, the rue de Verneuil, where I lived from eight to eighteen? Officially the flat belonged to BP, the man Mother inflicted on us not long after she dragged us to this foreign country, simply, from what I could tell, because she'd studied French and had spent a "fun" year in Paris. He certainly solved, and too quickly to my mind, all her single-motherly problems.

She also inflicted the name on us. BP, short for *Beau-Père*, stepfather, and a constant source of embarrassment and irritation. The initials sounded—still sound—stupid, and I avoided using them whenever possible. Besides, he was anything but *beau* to me. I never tired of reinventing his name: Bird Poop, Bat Puke, Bug Piss. Later, once my French had caught up with my English, there was *Boudin Puant, Bâtard Pusillanime, Babouin Pustulleux*. Et cetera. Though his only real sin was not being my father, for that I could not forgive Edmond Harcourt-Laporte.

The rue de Verneuil had too many complicated associations for me to call it home.

That left me with the rue des Martyrs, which like St. Denis, I was now climbing. Intact in body if not in soul.

THREE

YOU MAY BE wondering why I was so antagonistic to those perfectly pleasant people in the last chapter, my family. Well, it all comes back to those two deaths. The first occurred when my sister, four years old, was walking down a narrow sidewalk in the town near our Connecticut house. She pulled away from the hand that held her, jumped one little step to the side, and was run over by a car, flattened like paper. A year later my father fell to his death from the roof of our house while trying, it was said, to fix the television antenna.

Actually, it wasn't really said, and that was the problem. I did not discuss either of these events with any member of my family. Not with Edward, who was too young to remember, and not with my mother, who obviously did. As a result, it was as if they—and therefore our previous life—had never existed. It's fair to say that I never asked, but that wall of silence was too thick, too high. This meant that all the thoughts, all the feelings, all the half-remembered things stayed trapped in my brain. Like birds in an overcrowded cage, they flapped wing against wing with nowhere to go. The outward manifestation of this imprisonment was antagonism.

So why, you might then logically wonder, did I bother to see them at all? My chosen path of least resistance? An addiction to displeasure and perversity? An insatiable desire to antagonize those whom I resented?

Late one afternoon the week following the family lunch, while I was changing the crumpled back wheel on a racing bicycle, the Tibetan chimes knocked together. I had just removed the free-wheel from its axle. I stuck my head around the corner of the workshop, free-wheel in one hand, free-wheel remover in the other. There was my sister-in-law standing just inside the door. She wore an off-white jacket with a belt tied tightly around her thin waist. Her hands were in her pockets, and she looked like a model about to take off down the catwalk.

"Stephanie," I said, putting down the equipment and wiping my hands on a rag. "What are you doing here?" We kissed.

"Don't you remember? I wanted to see your children's bicycles."

"Right," I said. "Has Edward sent you up here so he won't have to ruin his weekend?"

She smiled her big smile, the one that made her full lips part, exposing a line of teeth, perfect but for a slight crowding of the two incisors. That smile turned her large mouth into a slice of ripe fruit. "No, no. I'm here of my own volition. Christmas isn't far away." She put her hand on the saddle of the bicycle she was standing next to. "So show me what you've got."

I pointed toward the only two children's models I had, on a platform at the side. "I'm afraid this is it."

She pointed at the flashier one and said: "This one looks fine." Then her eyes moved around the room.

"Not what you expected?" I asked.

"No, not really," she said. "I was expecting something a little less crowded. Something, I don't know. Sharper? It looks a bit dated, even for a bicycle shop."

"Since I inherited this place from Nigel Jones, 'a slobby Brit,' as he called himself, I haven't done anything but keep it open. So it still carries his distinctive early seventies' mark."

"Which explains the orange peace-and-lovey sign outside?"

I nodded. "And the Tibetan chimes over the door."

"That's incredible," she said, looking indeed as if she didn't believe me. "You've never repainted or even rearranged?"

"Nope," I said.

"Why?"

"Because I feel like I'm just passing through. Like the place really still belongs to Nigel Jones."

"But he's dead. And you've been here for years, haven't you?"

"Ten." I nodded. "Seven since Nigel died."

"Wouldn't you call that a bit more than 'passing through'?"

"I don't know," I said.

She shook her head in disbelief. "Well, before you get completely swallowed up in this time warp, would you like to go for a drink? Since I came all the way up here?"

"Sure," I said. "But what about the bicycle?"

"I told you. This one."

I waited for her to ask about price or readiness or something, but she kept looking around. "Have you got your car?"

"No," she said hesitantly.

"Then how are you going to get it home?"

"Good question," she said. "I hadn't thought about that." Then she brightened: "You could come to dinner a week from Saturday. And deliver it, if you wouldn't mind?"

"I guess so." I shrugged.

"Perfect." She smiled. "Now let's get you out of here. I have to say it's a little creepy."

"Let me just wash my hands."

As I stood at the sink at the back, scrubbing the resistant

grease, I wondered what this was all about. Christmas was still six weeks away. Why hadn't she come by car, instead of expecting me to schlep it over there on the métro in ten days' time?

It was almost dark as we walked up the hill. The Sacré Coeur had not yet been lit, and it loomed like a large cloud on the horizon. I decided not to take her to the Rendez-Vous, where Jean-Jacques would subsequently pepper me with questions.

"Sorry about the *ambiance*," I said as we walked in. "My neighborhood's not long on beauty and charm."

"That's okay," she answered, pulling her long arms out of the off-white jacket, exposing a pale-blue cashmere sweater. "Though it's true that when I came up from the métro, it almost seemed like another city." She sat back in her chair and ran her large hands over the top of her head, smoothing loose strands.

"Paris is lots of different cities," I answered. "Like any metropolis, I guess."

"I confess I haven't done much exploring. Too busy having babies." She shook her head and sighed. "When I do get out, it's never beyond the center. You know, to the cinema or an exhibition. Except when I take the car to go riding or play tennis, but that's outside of town completely. I should be more adventurous, not fritter my life away on culture and sports."

The waiter came to take our order. He was as brusque and unpleasant as the café itself. I ordered a beer, Stephanie a kir.

She was tapping her strong fingers, one after another, lightly on the table. Usually she wore a great rock of a diamond. Today there was only the gold wedding band, so slight it looked as if it would break if she pulled too hard on the reins. "Where do you ride?" I asked.

"Maison-Lafitte. The stable is pretty good, and I can ride in the woods too. I try to get out there twice a week." Then, abruptly crossing her arms on the table and leaning forward toward me with those intense green eyes set back on either side of her finely freckled nose, she said: "Were you and Edward ever close?"

The sudden change of course made my tongue, which was licking a cigarette paper, freeze in midair. "We've always been five years apart," I answered.

"I mean have you always been actively hostile?"

The crusty waiter slapped our drinks on the table, spilling my beer.

"Do you mind if I smoke?"

"One more cigarette in here won't make much difference." Stephanie's eyes moved around the hazy air, then back at me.

I struck the match. We sipped our drinks.

"I think hostility is too strong a word," I said, exhaling smoke. "Sarcasm and in more inspired moments irony seems a better way to characterize our relations."

"Call it what you will, there doesn't seem to be an overabundance of brotherly love between you."

"True," I said, shaving the end of my ash on the edge of the ashtray.

"Edward says it was the name thing," she said. "That wasn't really it, was it?"

"Let's say it was the last straw."

"But it's just a name."

"A rose is a rose is a rose, right?"

"I changed my name when I got married. It doesn't *have* to mean something profound."

"Well, sometimes it does." I took another sip of my beer. A large drop from the sloppily served glass trickled down the side of the glass and fell on my lap. "A name is who you are."

"You have to admit that McFarquhar is hard enough to pronounce in English, much less French," she said. The line of her long chin extended even farther when she was trying to win a point.

"Lots of things in life are difficult," I said, stubbing out my cigarette. "And when you have a complicated past, as Edward and I do, a name carries even more weight."

"I'm sorry." She leaned farther forward, hand on my arm. "I'm not trying to be contentious. I was just interested. In what happened. Edward's never very good with details."

"It was the whole thing. When getting French nationality, he decided to change his name to Harcourt-Laporte *and* be adopted legally by Edmond. A name, as you say, that was so much easier to pronounce." I started to roll another cigarette. "Never mind the complications involved in the adoption process. I've always believed that even then, when he was still a teenager, it was done with an eye on taking over the family firm." I still couldn't talk about it without outrage. "The legal relationship would obviously prove helpful."

"Did anyone put pressure on you, when you got your French nationality, to change names, be adopted?"

"No way," I said. "I took French nationality as the path of least resistance to my mother's nagging. At that time, I believed that as soon as I had my *Bac* in hand I'd be on a plane for the US, never to set foot in France again."

"Things often don't turn out as you expect, do they," said Stephanie vaguely, looking into her wine glass, fiddling with the stem.

"No, not for some. For others they do. Edward, for example. He walked right into his stepfather's shoes, and Mother could claim at least half a victory on the second family front."

"Well, she *acts* as if the victory were complete."

"Mother is exceptionally gifted at seeing the sun when it's nowhere in sight." Stephanie looked at me but didn't reply, so on I hammered. "Just because Edward says he has no memory of our father, of his very early years in the US, does not mean those facts don't exist."

"He feels like Edmond did the job of a father, and he wanted to recognize that."

"He was denying his real father, denying our family history." A woman from the next table looked up, startled by my rising voice. I mumbled: "You can't just rub out your past."

"His experience is different from yours. If that's the way he feels..." she trailed off, tapping her fingers again on the table. Finally she said, very quietly: "I don't know why I'm defending him."

"Well," I said, "he is your husband."

Now she sat back in her chair, letting her arms drop to her sides. She sighed, leaned forward again, and took a sip of wine.

"What I was really trying to figure out is this: once you lose closeness, can you ever get it back? It seems to me what was there in the first place should be retrievable."

"In my experience, love can turn to hate, but reversing the process is virtually impossible. It's like trying to rebuild a demolished building with the same broken bricks."

She nodded, looked around vaguely, then: "It just seems that Edward and I have started existing in two parallel worlds." She shrugged her shoulders. "We argue about everything. Especially the kids. He's so conservative."

"That's nothing new," I said, sticking a piece of métro ticket as a filter into a third cigarette—this conversation was really riling me. "I mean, that can't come as much of a surprise."

"No. But until recently, we joked about our differences."

I nodded, trying to think of a way off the subject of my brother's marital relations, but on she went.

"When I met Edward, I was seduced by the whole French thing. He was so different from all the other guys I knew. He dressed better. He actually spoke in complete sentences. Yet he was American, which made him seem safe. Then I met your family, and you all *seemed* so welcoming and kind. And since my mother had died not long before we met, I had no family of my own to speak of. I got swept away."

"You believed in fairy tales, you mean."

"I guess so." Stephanie shook her head. "Though it's not like me. I'm not a romantic person."

"Come on. Your life can't be so bad. Three beautiful kids. All that riding and tennis. The busy social scene."

"Your sarcasm is not appreciated," she said, her full mouth bunched into a knot of displeasure.

"I was being serious."

"Well, it's not my kind of fairy tale," she answered grimly. "It sounds like fun, I guess, but what's the point to all that tennis and riding, of going to movies and exhibitions and lunches with women I don't really even like? What am I accomplishing?" She paused. "That's what I wonder while I wait for Edward to come home from his busy, productive day. By ten o'clock I've already eaten and am ready for bed." She paused again impatiently. "I thought the French didn't work the long hours of us Puritanical Americans."

"Edward is, as you said, American," I said. "Sort of."

"Exactly. Sort-of-not-really. And he works for the most French institution I can imagine." She paused. "He says I should get a job."

"Why don't you? I thought a law degree was like a magic wand in the professional world."

She moved her fingers up and down the stem of her wine glass, then started tapping the table again. "I seem to have lost the confidence necessary to throw myself into that world. For the first time," she added, with a look of disbelief in those round green eyes, "something seems beyond me. That's what having babies in a foreign country has done to me." She looked at her watch, then said, suddenly all business: "Speaking of which, I've got to go. Let me get this. You've had to sit here and listen to my complaints about your brother for the last half hour." She unzipped a large black handbag, spread it apart, and searched the bottom for her wallet.

"Never mind," I said, pulling the francs out of my pocket. "This is my territory. You can return the favor another time."

"Thank you, I will." She smiled, rezipping her bag, putting on her jacket, and tying the belt tightly around her waist.

Out on the street she said: "Thanks for listening to me." And she leaned into me for a hug, American style. Besides the fact we had never embraced in such a way before, the hug lasted just that little bit longer than it might have. And her hands went up and down my back in a way that excited the wrong part of my body.

She pulled away, saying: "You won't forget to come, Saturday after next, and you don't mind bringing the bicycle?"

"No. I'll see you then."

"Bye," she said, turning with a wave. "And thanks again."

I watched her red-gold head, her athletic, almost masculine walk, until she was swallowed by the darkening street. It was a particularity of Stephanie to be intimate one minute and distant the next, as if she only came in two temperatures, hot and cold, running from separate taps. It was one of the first things I had learned about her, when Edward brought her home for Christmas, not long after they were engaged. They'd met in New York, where he was working for a year after business school and she, though a couple of years older, was attending law school.

On New Year's Eve, under pressure from Mother, I had accompanied them to a party in Senlis, at the Coursaults' château. Just before midnight, my soon-to-be sister-in-law, whose dancing I had been admiring, pulled me onto the floor. As the year changed, we kissed. Quickly, but on the lips. Later on the way home, squeezed in the back of Edward's Renault 5, Stephanie slipped her arm under mine and took my hand. Like the kiss, I put that gesture down to soon-to-be-sisterly affection. Even if she did stroke my hand with her finger. The next morning she hardly looked at me.

As I walked back to the shop, I put this hug down to Stephanie's hot-cold taps and turned to more disturbing elements of the visit. Being reminded of my brother's name change and adoption still worked on me like salt to a raw wound. But learning that all was not well between Edward and Stephanie was also unsettling. I couldn't get it out of my mind as I pulled down a new wheel from the ceiling where they dangled. In my immutable worldview, Edward's life was seamless, a smooth fabric of solid job, beautiful children, and spacious, well-furnished apartment, home to a perfect marriage. Weren't he and Stephanie as solid as that large diamond she usually wore on her finger?

Apparently not. Spinning the sparkling new wheel, now mounted onto the sleek frame of the racer, I thought it really was better to stick to inanimate objects, machines that could be made to work. Then I turned to my next repair, patching a punctured inner tube.

FOUR

MY BEST AND, since I'm trying to be honest here, only real friend is Cédric Mérei. We met in the school courtyard, shortly after my arrival in France. Though when he first approached me, as I leaned against the wall, hands shoved deeply into my lonely pockets, I could not understand a word he said, our communication quickly went deeper than language. Cédric's mother, Genviève Montsard de La Roquemare, came from an ultra-Catholic military family, but his father, Matei Mérei, was a Hungarian Jewish intellectual who had been Geneviève's professor. Though the couple had not stayed married long, Geneviève's family never forgave her. Cédric was ostracized on his mother's side and somewhat estranged on his father's. He too was an outsider; we were made for each other.

By this time, he lived about an hour from Paris, near the town of Vernon, where he taught French literature at a private *lycée*. He was married to Viviane Ledoux, a painter. Their house, Hautebranche, was a refuge for me, a place where complications and burdens could, for a short time, blur into the background. And that's where I was headed the Sunday after Stephanie's visit.

Once again closing early after a quiet morning, I ran through the scurrying shoppers to the Gare Saint-Lazare. There was a fine, cold drizzle falling, one that looked set to stay forever. The station was really gloomy that day. The dingy light filtering through the nineteenth-century iron and glass made it seem imprisoned in a cloud. After I'd bought my ticket, I took out my camera, put it on a low setting, and tried to capture the milky air against the wrought-iron skeleton but had trouble finding a focal point, until a black-clad punk crossed the scene—and I thought I'd really gotten a good shot. Until a few years later when I came across the photo in my archives and saw it was not quite as successful as I'd remembered—the figure was too small—but that's memory, isn't it. Only reliable up to a point.

The train was not crowded, and I stretched out across two seats, well away from anyone else. But no sooner had I pulled out my book than two American tourists found their way right across the aisle from me, their rainproof jackets swishing as they settled into the seats. They acknowledged me with timid, fellow-traveler smiles. I responded with a stony stare.

"Oh, look, Harry," said the woman. "There's a tray table, just like on an airplane. Isn't that nifty? It's perfect for our picnic." And they proceeded to unload goods wrapped in plastic from two plastic shopping bags. The whole business made an insufferable noise. "I'll cut the bread and slice the cheese," she continued her banter.

Harry, who was helping himself to a handful of potato chips, answered with a nod. They were an overweight, elderly couple with matching jackets that looked as if they'd been bought especially for this trip, and I quickly fit them into one of my prefabricated boxes: middle-western Americans from Kansas, or maybe Nebraska. He once upon a time sold either used cars or insurance to farmers; she was a homemaker, an organizer of Tupperware parties and potluck suppers.

I looked out the window. The urban knot was already unfurl-
ing into the countryside, or what was left of it. The church spires of
the old villages were being asphyxiated by concrete. Row after row
of Monopoly houses and vast shopping centers surrounded them,
eating away into the fields like a fast-spreading disease. The only
part of the scene that didn't change much was the Seine, which still
wound its way through the landscape, steadily making its way to
the sea. The train crossed and recrossed it, ran along beside it, then
moved away, in a flirtatious dance. I could have watched it forever.

When we were boys, Lisette would take Edward and me
across the Seine to the Tuileries to play. As we crossed the old
footbridge at the end of the rue de Solférino, from which I first
saw the Sacré Coeur looming outlandishly on the horizon, she
would slow down and lower her voice, telling us the people in
her Breton village called Paris Satan's city. They said the spirits
of the corrupted souls who had died lived at the bottom of the
river. "That's why the water turns and twists so," Lisette would
say, her bulgy eyes going even bulgier. "That's why it's often so
muddy and brown. It's all those tortured spirits writhing down
there, suffering for their sins." The spirits arose, she would tell us,
from their subaqueous hell at night, and floated through the city
in search of new recruits among the living. At which point, even
in the middle of winter, she would fish out the gold cross she wore
on a chain around her neck and kiss it.

Although she always ended by telling us these stories were
just village lore meant to keep the many Bretons who immigrated
to Paris in line, she still kissed that cross, and the stories haunted
me, frequently giving me cold-sweat nightmares. In my dreams I
would see people I knew—classmates and their mothers or the
short-tempered baker—all green-skinned and dripping in slimy
algae. They always came at me with a mad, hungry look in their
red eyes, and they would chase me and chase me until I could feel

their cold, slimy fingers, the ends of their long nails scraping my back as I tried to make a slow and ineffectual escape. The result of these nocturnal terrors was that I wouldn't cross the Seine alone until I was almost twelve. The idea of those gruesome souls roiling the waters of the river always stopped me dead in my tracks.

Over time my associations with the river changed. Childish terror turned to adolescent fascination as I read *Siddhartha* and walked the banks with Cédric. Then the frenetic swirls and eddies, the inexorable movement toward the sea, seemed to contain all the questions of existence, and, if you looked long and hard enough, all the answers. Both hope and fear, earthly knowledge and divine mystery lay within its banks. Fortunately, I'd grown out of that phase too, though the next—sitting for hours at the water's edge thinking about absolutely nothing while recovering from an accident—wasn't much better.

"Excuse me," I heard from across the aisle. "Do you speak English?" she mouthed the words loudly and slowly. "Because Harry and I were wondering . . . are we really on the right train for Gui-ver-nee?"

"Betty's a worrier," Harry said apologetically after swallowing a mouthful of his sandwich and wiping his mouth on a small napkin.

"Yes," I said. "Vernon station to Giverny. By bus or taxi." I looked back out the window.

"I told you we were saying it wrong," Harry said. "It's got a soft G. How come you speak English so well? You American?"

I nodded.

"Are you going to Giverny too?" Betty added hopefully, careful to get her G right this time. She was wiping crumbs into her hand from the tray table that had so impressed her.

"No."

"Where you heading?" Harry again. He unfortunately seemed to have lost all interest in his sandwich.

"To visit friends."

"Where d'ya live?"

"Paris."

"So you live here," Harry continued piecing his puzzle together. "But you're American."

I nodded.

"So you must be bilingual."

I shrugged affirmatively.

"Isn't that wonderful. You're so lucky," Betty said, tearing off one more chunk of baguette before putting it back into her green, plastified Harrod's shopping bag. "This bread is so good I can't stop myself," she added with a coquettish lift of her thick shoulders and pinch of her flaccid face.

"We're doing our first European tour," Harry said. "Just came over from London two days ago. Great pubs." He grinned while Betty rolled her eyes. "We're here two more days, then we take the train to Italy. Where are you from in the States?"

"New York."

"We're from Philadelphia. How long you lived here?"

"Since I was a boy."

"Whatcha do over here?" No matter how curtly I answered him, Harry would not get the hint.

"I have a bicycle shop," I answered.

"Oh, that's interesting. We're retired now," he continued with his unsolicited flow of information. "But Betty and I," he put a hand affectionately on his wife's ample knee, "we were social workers. Now we stick to our hobbies. Can't get Betty out of her rose garden. And I sing. For weddings, confirmations, anniversaries. That kind of thing. I'm really looking forward to seeing Italy. Italian songs are my favorite."

So Harry and Betty had devoted their lives to helping the poor and dispossessed on the East Coast, not to selling cars or insurance or Tupperware in the Midwest, and they now spent their time singing and gardening rather than watching television and attending community picnics. Though it wasn't surprising my scenario had proved incorrect, given that my lived experience of the US was limited to Augusts on Long Island and the short, disastrous year at the college, seeing Harry and Betty in the softer, dappled light of their real lives, rather than the harsh glare of my assumptions, made me resent their intrusion into my train ride even more. I preferred them to remain as I had invented them.

"It must be wonderful to be bilingual," Betty went on. "We wanted our daughter to study in Italy. She inherited her father's voice, and we thought it would be nice if she could understand all those songs. Unlike her father." Now she squeezed Harry's hand.

"I get the gist," he said with a defensive look at Betty. "It's the emotion that counts anyway."

"Actually," I said, looking straight at their attentive faces, "it's no big deal having two languages. No different from riding a bicycle," I paused, changing the comparison, "or knowing how to swim. It's just something I can do."

They sat in silence for a moment, stunned, perhaps, that I was actually able to assemble more than four words together at a time.

"Sounds to me," Harry said, looking down at his lap, "like you don't know how lucky you are. Betty's right. It does bother me not getting all the words, and the meaning under the words, of the songs I sing." He looked up at me. "I've always believed the more you know, the richer your life is."

I shrugged. We were arriving in Vernon, and the conversation I never wanted to have in the first place was thankfully coming to an end.

As I was rolling a quick cigarette on the platform, Betty lumbered down the steps of the train. Not seeing me, she said to

Harry: "Why would a nice-looking young man like that, at home on two continents, be so sour?"

"Beats me." Harry shook his head. "But what a pill. Let me take that bag for you, Betty."

I turned and walked quickly toward the underground passage that led to the station parking lot, indignant and embarrassed. A pill. What did they know?

Cédric was huddled against his car waiting for me with a gently mocking smile on his uneven face, as if everything about me amused him in a pleasant way.

"It's about time you decided to come see us," he said as we got in his old Volvo station wagon, which even in the cold smelled of dogs. He and Viviane had several; it was hard to keep track of the numbers.

"You know what a busy life I have."

"Yeah, right," he said, releasing the hand brake and moving into first gear. "Anyway, I'm glad you didn't wait any longer. The train drivers are threatening to go on strike any day now."

"They're always threatening to go on strike."

"But this time their precious *régime special* is being threatened."

"I guess losing the right to retire at fifty is something to strike about."

Cédric shook his head. "It's impossible, really. There's a teacher at my school who wanted to do the opposite, to put off his retirement for a couple of years. Because he loves his job and the students love him. His request was rejected."

"*Vive la France*," I said. "Speaking of jobs"—I looked out the window as we crossed the Seine, its wooded banks here crowding down to the water—"I was recently informed that I'm being evicted."

"What?" Cédric looked over at me. His long nose wasn't quite straight, and one side of his face was a bit higher than the other. It made him look perpetually uncertain.

"From my shop. I have to be out by next June, when the lease runs out."

"Are you going to look for new space?"

"I can't afford to buy a new lease. The shop keeps losing money."

"Maybe a forced departure is just the break you need."

"I know, I know, that's undoubtedly what the whole world thinks," I said.

"Most of the world couldn't care less." Cédric laughed. "And it's beside the point. The shop fell in your lap. It would be no bad thing for you now to stand up and let it drop. You're no shop-keeper, Trevor. *That* is the point."

"My life is fine as it is. I don't need anything else."

"Tcha," he said, his hands lifting from the steering wheel.

Unlike my mother and my brother, Cédric did not object to my employment status out of snobbery. Rather, he objected because he was a great believer in True Purpose, and according to him, my calling lay elsewhere, in the little black box that sat on my lap. Once upon a time I would have agreed with him. Once upon a time I too believed that a Nikon FM2 was my savior. Right up until three days before an exhibition of photos of the low stone-and-brick wine warehouses at Bercy, in the east of Paris, before they were torn down and replaced by a new sports stadium and a new Ministry of Finance. But largely thanks to a careless and fickle woman, any idea for salvation came crashing, literally, to a halt.

"Here we are," said Cédric as he turned into the courtyard. I hadn't even noticed our climb out of the valley, through fields, wood, and village. Thinking about her, about that time and the show that never happened—it obliterated my senses.

Hautebranche, originally an ancient peasant dwelling, was a mishmash of styles and building materials. With windows of different shapes and sizes, it had been added onto over the centuries. The house now seemed to meander over both space and time.

The front door was so low I had to duck to enter, but inside was a large room that went all the way up to the rafters. Three dogs leapt toward us from their pallets near the fireplace. They danced and wiggled as if they hadn't seen Cédric for several years. All three were abandoned mongrels rescued from the animal shelter.

Viviane was in her green apron behind the counter that partitioned the kitchen area from the rest. Her thick glasses had fallen down her nose while she worked over a bowl; a strand of her hair had fallen across her face. She was not a beautiful woman, but that somehow added to her aura, making her more appealing.

I went around the counter and kissed her hello.

"Sorry," she said, turning her face toward me, a small whisk still in hand. "If I stop now, the mayonnaise will separate."

"I wouldn't want to be held responsible for that," I said.

"Do you want a glass of wine, Viv?" Cédric asked as he took beers out of the refrigerator for us.

"I'm all right," she answered.

"Trevor is just about to be separated from his shop," said Cédric as he pried open a bottle. "Evicted." He took a swig of beer.

"Oh," she said, pouring some more oil into the bowl. "Well, maybe that's no bad thing."

"Yeah, yeah," I said. "You two and your echoing words of wisdom."

"If that's what you call the truth," said Cédric.

"Well, we'll see," I said, sipping my beer. "Is there anything I can do?"

"Nothing," said Viviane. "Is that what's been keeping you away? Shop troubles?"

"No," I answered, settling into the deep, sagging leather armchair next to the fire. "Just this and that." I started rolling myself a cigarette and thought about This. I had seen Paulina just before she had gone home to Brazil for a photo shoot. The sex had been great. I found it often was, pre-departure. Often post-return, too. I was already imagining one hand on each of her firm, round buttocks, my mouth on one dark nipple. I indulged this little fantasy, since I was cooling on That, Jennifer. Besides a tendency to hysteria, she was beginning to want more than I was willing to give.

"You'd better be careful," Viviane said, with her annoying ability to read my mind. "One of these days, some this or that is going to get you."

"You know I'm not the marrying type," I said, leaning forward and lighting my cigarette from a flame in the fire.

"I don't necessarily mean 'get' you in that way," she said, tapping her little whisk on the bowl, "though you never know. What I mean is that thinking you can plan and predict human behavior—or anything else for that matter—is a dangerous game. And living free of strings is impossible."

"Except for the odd tug, I've been all right so far."

Viviane shook her head and looked at me with what I'd like to believe was fond reproach. "Let's eat," she said, untying her apron.

The three of us sat down at one end of the long wooden table, which was laid out with silver, cloth napkins, and Italian dishes. Nothing matched, but the silver was solid, not plate, and the crockery heavy and hand-painted. We helped ourselves from a steaming bowl of crayfish.

"I got a strange visit in the shop the other day," I said, cracking open my first shell, extracting the delicate pink flesh and dipping it into the mayonnaise. "From my sister-in-law. Stephanie."

"Good heavens," said Viviane.

"I thought your relations stayed as far away from your shop as they could," said Cédric.

"She came up looking for a bicycle for their daughter Caroline. So she said. But then we went out for a drink, and it seemed her real purpose in coming was to talk about Edward."

"And?" said Viviane.

"He's busy and distracted. Not coming home until late, eating at the office."

"What?" said Cédric. "She's just now discovering he works long hours?" He scooped some mayonnaise onto his plate. "I find that hard to believe."

"She said she feels dissatisfied, bored."

"I have to say," said Viviane, pushing her glasses back up her nose, "the few times I've met Stephanie, she's always seemed bored and dissatisfied."

"I've been thinking about it." I paused and took a sip of wine. "And I think he's having an affair."

"Edward?" Cédric raised an uneven eyebrow. "Did Stephanie say that?"

"She hinted at it. Sort of."

"Huh," said Cédric.

"I don't know about that," said Viviane.

"It makes sense," I said. "He's got everything else. Money, kids, spacious apartment. And Edward the Conqueror isn't happy unless he's exploring new territory."

"You're always looking to disapprove of or dislike something in your brother," Cédric said. "Just because he's driven to succeed doesn't mean he's going to cheat on his wife."

"He's already got a beautiful woman," Viviane said, standing up. "And he cares too much about family for that." She picked up the bowl of empty shells. "If you want my opinion, she'd be the more likely candidate for an affair."

"I agree," said Cédric, pouring more wine.

"You two always agree," I grumbled.

While Viviane was getting the next course, I asked Cédric: "No other visitors this weekend?" Someone always seemed to be dropping in on them. If it wasn't a local, it was a friend from

Aix-en-Provence, where Viviane had grown up and where they'd met, where they still went for their summer holiday.

"It's been quiet," said Cédric. "We've been thinking some calm might help. You know," he half whispered, glancing up to make sure Viviane hadn't heard.

The one blight on their lives was that they had not been able to have children. Though both had been tested and nothing had been found missing or awry, it just hadn't happened. It made Viviane desperately unhappy, which in turn made Cédric gloomy. No matter how many dogs they got, the missing children meant the house never felt quite full.

Viviane returned to the table with a fish stew, its tomato sauce giving off vapors that made my mouth water all over again.

"Real, wonderful food. Delicious," I said, ladling it onto my plate. "What a treat after my reheated rice. How goes the painting, Viv?"

"These short, dark days are hard."

"You should see what she's working on now," Cédric said. "It's a large canvas, with a close-up of a case of quince. You don't see the case, just giant, heavy fruit, one on top of the other. It's great."

"If only the Paris art market agreed with you." Viviane laughed, but her lack of success was a sore point. "Buyers are not interested in a quince that looks like a quince."

"Tastes change," I said.

"Maybe," she said, stacking the plates, standing up. "You can taste the real thing for yourself. I've made some syrupy quince jelly to pour over our *fromage blanc* for dessert."

"My mother said the jar you gave her was really good," said Cédric. Viviane smiled vaguely.

"You'll see," I said. "Someday."

At the end of the meal, Viviane went back to her studio and Cédric to his office to correct papers. I cleaned up.

Melancholy was on some level at the core of my friendship with Cédric and Viviane. But they fought back, finding comfort and satisfaction in their work, their house and garden, their animals. In pursuing their True Purpose. Viviane was nevertheless undermined by feelings of failure, on the professional front and even more on the personal. There was this gaping, terrible hole in the canvas, the missing children. It seemed to taint everything. So wasn't it better to keep one's expectations low? Hadn't I chosen the right path? Okay, I wasn't a great shopkeeper, but I wasn't trying to win an award from some sub-branch of the Chamber of Commerce. The job was easier because it meant so little to me. Just like the Casuals. Nothing gained but nothing lost either, right?

"The pot's clean, Trevor." Viviane was at my shoulder. She put her empty coffee cup on the counter. "Are you going for a walk?"

"It's awfully dark out there." I peered out the window. "But yes, why not."

"Would you take Fyodor? I took him this morning with the other dogs, but he can always use more exercise."

"As long as he isn't prone to existential crises or epileptic fits."

"Not as far as I know, though Cédric thinks he would have pleased Dostoevsky, with that broad forehead and those bushy whiskers."

"He won't run away, will he?"

"No, he's so grateful for being taken in, he never strays far." She gave him a little kiss on the end of his nose, a rub of his uneven ears, before returning to her studio.

"Come on, Fyodor, it's just us now," I said, drying my hands. He wagged his tail. I envied his simple needs. Food, exercise, a kiss on the snout. Or I envied his ability to be content with such simplicity.

The road that ran through the village was quiet. No cars passed, no birds sang, no dogs barked. The only sign of life was smoke curling out of chimneys, lights shining from the inside out.

I paused outside one house, looked in the window, and saw a man intently tinkering with something at a table and two women sipping tea or coffee on a sofa. Lives viewed from this angle always seemed cozy, pleasant, fulfilled. Everything that mine wasn't. The warm inner light made the cold, damp outside air feel sharper, and I walked faster to try and create more heat. The dog bounded along, headed down a farm track that led around the edge of an empty field. I followed.

At the end, the woods were very dark, and I was afraid of late-afternoon hunters. Calling and whistling for the dog, I turned back. Just then, there was a great honking-whirring noise overhead, and I looked up to see a huge V of wild geese. There must have been fifty of them, wings batting the air relentlessly as they pushed south. Though their formation expanded and retracted, it never lost the three points of that V. And all the while that frantic honking, which seemed partly an announcement of their passage, partly a warning to anything that might try and get in their determined way, and partly rallying cries to one another. As if, like teammates, they were cheering each other on while they pushed hard to get just that bit farther by the end of the day. Even the dog was looking up, ear cocked, at these willful creatures. It was one of those moments—like a full moon on a clear night or the Seine in the morning before any boats have disturbed its mirror calm—that I wished would never end. That I wished I could catch like a ball and hold onto forever.

Capturing a moment, fixing it so it couldn't be forgotten. Despite a loss of faith in True Purpose, I had never stopped taking photographs. An uncontrollable compulsion, a celluloid-alcoholic urge to pull my camera from the cupboard and capture things I found fleeting or sad, sometimes beautifully sad, always took hold of me. The trouble is, the photo is so often missed or impossible. Today it was already too dark and those birds could never be captured on film, or not through my 50mm lens, anyway. They would only have been remembered as meaningless black dots on a grey background. That inability to capture the migrating geese— or any number of moments like it, such as Mother's boxes in the sun—left me feeling defeated and hollow. As if everything, ultimately, came to naught.

Back at Hautebranche my mood persisted. Through a bowl of soup and a film on television. Up the steep back staircase to the tiny room, hardly more than an alcove, where I always slept. Not even the soft bed under the eaves, nor the bull's-eye dormer window with old, colored glass in a lead frame, could dent my dense gloom. I spent most of the night huddled near the small bedside lamp, reading, finally falling asleep, just as I heard Cédric beginning to stir.

When I woke up, he'd left for school and Viviane was back from her morning walk with the dogs and in her studio. The empty kitchen and living room felt cold, and I went back upstairs with a cup of coffee to take a hot bath. It didn't help, didn't counter a crushing sense of being out of synch. With my friends, who had plunged back into their True Purpose. With the whole world, that was busily doing something, while I soaked glumly and numbly in a tub of hot water.

FIVE

THE FOLLOWING WEEK, I never left the rue des Martyrs. I stayed in my box, hobbled by What's-the-point-ism, a state best described as the inability to see the purpose of any occupation, other than staring at the ceiling. Or the television screen. Or a book. I did read, for hours and hours during insomniac nights. French, English—it was all the same to me—as long as it was fiction, a genre so much more gratifying than real life. What a relief to plunge my mind into the slings and arrows of other people's misfortunes.

During such periods I would wonder why suicide is considered a cowardly act. After all, wouldn't the world be a better place without me? Wouldn't sparing everyone I knew from further interaction in fact be an act of kindness? Even when I tried to rally, counting a blessing or two, they accumulated in my head but left the rest of me unconvinced, unmoved. Nothing could sway me from the certainty that the best course would be to remove myself from the planet. The trouble was I couldn't bring myself to pull the trigger, pop the pill, or make the leap, so it seemed to my downcast eyes during these bouts that the real act of cowardice was *not* being able to end it all.

Midweek I did speak to Casual Paulina on the phone, but that only made matters worse. She had just returned from Brazil, where she'd been taking pictures of rain forest devastation around the Amazon. She was full of earnest enthusiasm for saving the trees and for her photo project, and the more she talked, the more pathetic and doomed my own life appeared. I postponed our encounter, wondering if, with Jennifer on the snip list, maybe even the Casual angle of my program for living was about to collapse. It wouldn't be surprising.

Last chapter I let a black-haired, blue-eyed woman slip into my mind and onto the page. Jacqueline, blight of my life, especially once she'd tired of my loins, was her name. Child of two psychiatrists, student of psychology, I had met her in front of a notice board at the Sorbonne, where I was studying English literature, perversely mostly in French, after my disastrous stint at the small American college. I can't remember what she'd asked me, but after a short conversation, we went to a café for lunch. She ordered a Camembert sandwich. For a good fifteen minutes she didn't touch it. Then she proceeded to pull the sandwich to pieces, nibbling at the soft white part of the bread and the soft white part of the cheese, leaving a heap of bread crust and cheese rind in her wake. Where it would end should have been obvious to me right then and there.

Instead, I was bewitched by her small person and strong opinions, by the fact that she was so different from anyone else I knew, most notably from my family. Her intensity on the subjects that interested her was fierce and engaging. She could talk for hours about films, books, and music, but also—and this was completely virgin territory for me—about feelings and the psyche. All this fervor pushed me to confide in her, to tell her things I'd never even told Cédric. And so it happened that during one of our endless discussions in the *chambre de bonne* where I was living at the time on the rue de l'Université, I told her about my father and my sister. Her response was: "That's why you say you feel an almost superstitious connection with that building." And she pointed toward the Sacré Coeur, perfectly framed on the distant horizon by my window. "You see your family, intact. The vertical tower is your father. The large dome is your mother, the three smaller ones represent you and your brother and sister. The only trouble is there's a fourth small dome—you just can't see it. I'm afraid," she'd sighed, crossing her arms across her flat chest, "your Mecca is an illusion."

My bigger illusion was that I could in some way save Jacqueline from herself and her numerous neuroses. She was convinced that her psychiatrist parents had had her as an experiment for their work, a tool for improving their understanding of the human psyche, right from its seedling start. Whatever her parents' intent, they had produced a bundle of self-obsessed insecurities. She demanded constant reassurance, and her emotional needs were insatiable. Nothing I did was ever enough. I spent my life apologizing.

For a couple of years, though, it was okay. We went to the cinema a lot, we talked and talked. I was having regular sex with someone other than myself, and that seemed pretty cool. I was happy enough at the Sorbonne, studying literature, especially since on the side I was taking photos. But after I'd graduated and just before the show of my Bercy photographs, I had an accident for which I'm afraid to say Jacqueline was directly responsible. Besides the canceled show and a subsequent loss of belief in True Purpose, it resulted in my developing a firm belief that Love was not and never would be for me. Now, maybe even the casual variety was doomed.

By the time I got to Saturday, I was feeling like a ghost. The shop was quieter than any other weekend day I could remember. It was as if the place had already been reclaimed by the insurance company, and I was just a specter floating around inside. Except for the thoughts in my head, I did not exist. At one point, remembering the proverbial tree falling in the forest, I spoke out loud to myself for confirmation. I can be heard, therefore I am.

When the phone rang, my blood turned icy, my heart pumped in my ears. I stared at the grey object, terrified. But I answered it, just as irrationally terrified of what would happen if I didn't. It was Stephanie reminding me about dinner and the bicycle. Like an automaton, I said okay, I'll be there, either because that was the passive path of least resistance to which I had grown so accustomed. Or because I'd done a lousy job dismissing the bourgeois values, such as personal responsibility, with which I'd been raised. Anyway, I rationalized as I wheeled Caroline's new bicycle into the street, wishing I were still flat-backed on my mattress, I'll get a check, which might me make me feel less of a ghost.

The rue des Martyrs was always dead quiet in the evening. A small grocery store, run by two Algerian brothers, was open until midnight, but otherwise, metal grilles were pulled down on all the shop fronts, with café chairs stacked inside dark windows. In my still delicate state, I imagined the ghost of a headless St. Denis appearing at any moment—I pushed the bike faster to the métro. Underground, I entered a stormy, choppy sea of humanity. As the evening news had announced, the first train drivers were going on strike; the transport system was beginning to clog. I squeezed onto the platform with the bicycle, and the crowd shifted irately to make room. An angry woman next to me grumbled about my "heap of metal." When an already loaded car finally arrived, I barely managed to push my way in. The doors closed hard on my back; more passengers complained about having to share precious space with a vehicle that should have been above ground, rolling itself to its destination.

I was the last to arrive, but after parking the bike in the front hall closet and walking into the living room, I wished I were even later. Days, months, years later. Standing next to the fireplace with a glass of red wine in her ringed hand was Jennifer, about the last person in the world I wanted to see.

But my policy was to face the music when it was blaring in my ears. I shook hands with four other guests, then walked right up to her at the fireplace and kissed her, like a friend, on both cheeks. "Hello, Jennifer."

"I haven't heard from you in a while," she said, stepping back from me abruptly.

"Yes, well," I answered and turned to the woman with an amused smile on her face standing next to her. "Hello." I offered my hand. "Trevor."

"Béa. Béa Fairbank," she said with an English accent similar to Camilla Barchester's. "I'm a friend of Jennifer's," she added. I nodded warily. In my experience, the friends of the offended could be more vindictive and vicious than the offended themselves.

"Béa's painting me," Jennifer said through clenched teeth, a forced smile. Posing as a live model for artists was how she paid the bills.

"Ah," I said as Stephanie placed a hand on my shoulder from behind: "Sorry not to greet you at the door. What can I get you to drink?"

"If you'll show me where it is, I'll get it myself." I turned to Jennifer and her friend. "Excuse me."

"Don't count on it," said Jennifer.

Various bottles were laid out on a table. I poured myself a glass of white wine, but it was too dry and I added a little *crème de cassis* to sweeten it up, spilling a drop of the sticky red liquor on the white tablecloth. As I was trying to dab it up with a cocktail napkin, there again was Stephanie at my back. "That's not how to make a kir. Look," she pointed, "all that heavy *cassis* is globbed together. You have to put it in first." She was right; the *cassis* hung like blood in the glass.

"Doesn't matter." I shrugged. "Cheers."

"Cheers," she said, clinking her glass against mine, that ripe fruit-slice smile opening up on her face. She gestured to the closet where I'd put the bicycle. "Thanks so much for lugging that thing all the way over here."

"No problem," I said.

"And don't let me forget to give you a check for it before you leave." She put her hand on my shoulder.

"Okay."

"So," Stephanie said, turning to the room, "we're going to eat in just a minute. Drink up." She and Edward had much the same farmer's approach to social events as my mother: feed and water the guests, then let them quickly back out to pasture. "Dolores," she called to the Filipina maid as she strode toward the kitchen.

In order to keep my back to Jennifer, I turned to the two couples sitting on the sofas. I recognized them from another party. They were church people, and I assumed from their intent, exclusive huddle that they were hotly discussing church business. It struck me that Stephanie had made a mistake. Dancing Jennifer, with her ringed fingers and sexy prowl, would not mesh with the church folk. Neither would her friend the painter, who was dressed in a flowing, *après-yoga* outfit. Out of the corner of my eye, I saw the two of them still standing by the fireplace in their own intense huddle, probably smoldering over my hard heart and cruel ways. Jennifer had her shapely back to me, but it looked rigid and angry. The painter was looking sympathetic.

Stephanie clapped her hands to call us in to dinner.

"Where's Edward?" I asked, suddenly realizing I hadn't seen him.

"On the phone." Her eyes narrowed and her mouth tightened. "You sit next to me," she added more cheerfully, patting my chair back.

It was a squeeze, with nine people around the sleek table made for eight. Perhaps Jennifer, who commandeered the seat on my other side, had insisted on coming with reinforcements.

"We're destined to be together, one way or another," she said as we sat down.

Edward entered looking distracted. Stephanie looked at him, and her fine nostrils flared, but he did not look back at her.

The table arrangements were lopsided. The churchgoers flocked together at one end, with Edward, while I had the disturbed females at the other. The chatter and insouciance on their side made the silence in our corner even weightier. We proceeded with our slices of smoked salmon. I turned to the painter, the only woman at my end not fuming. "Do you live here in Paris, or are you visiting from Britain?"

"Mostly I live in the south of France. But I move around a lot." She looked me straight in the eye but no daggers. "We have friends in common, you know."

"We do?"

"Viviane and Cédric."

"Really? What's your name again?"

"Béa Fairbank. I've known Viviane and Cédric since the summer they met in Aix-en-Provence. I couldn't make it to their wedding, and now I mostly see them down there, when they come south in the summer." She paused. "I've heard about you, though." The wry smile implied she'd heard quite a bit. I didn't say anything, just rolled my eyes, and a most extraordinary laugh emerged from her. One that started deep down and exploded in many bright pieces when it reached the surface. Her eyes glittered. What a shame she was on the chubby side.

"I've just bought a bicycle for Caroline from Trevor," Stephanie said, emerging from her gloomy silence.

"Sometimes I think I could use a bicycle, but I move around too much," said Béa.

"He's got anything you want, I'm sure," added Jennifer with a proprietary edge. She reached forward to pour herself more wine. "But just stick to bicycles, is my advice to you, Béa."

"Careful what you say about my brother-in-law," Stephanie said with her fruity smile. She put her hand on my thigh under the table, then removed it.

The meal went on, through the stuffed guinea hen that had obviously been prepared by the butcher, the wild rice, which must have been bought at an American store, the cheese and salad, and the bakery-bought chocolate cake. Dolores the Filipina maid continued to move in and out, clearing plates, replenishing platters. But it was like two different parties, with Edward and the churchgoers babbling about the shocking number of face-lifts in Paris, while Stephanie on one side lavished me with attention, and Jennifer on the other threw verbal darts at me. Fortunately, as the meal went on, the wine dulled their tips, and by dessert Jennifer's missiles were as soft as warm wax. Béa, on the other side of the table, said little. She observed the scene of the two women and me. Stephanie ignored her, and Jennifer spoke pointedly to her, when Stephanie was speaking to me. All through dinner, Stephanie kept glancing at Edward, and he never once looked back.

Jennifer settled in an armchair and threatened to go on to cognac. I pulled up a straight-backed chair and told her what I should have told her weeks before: that she wanted more than I could or would give. That, as I'd warned from the beginning, this meant the end. I avoided phrases like: "Don't take it badly" or "We can still be friends." Experience had taught me such words of comfort were taken to be patronizing and had an explosive effect. Instead, I spoke softly and firmly, and in her drunken state, that approach fortunately appeased her. Dissuading her from a cognac, I fetched her a verbena tisane, and by the time I returned with it, Béa was at her now quietly teary side. I took refuge with the churchgoers: Diane, Leslie, and Don. Guillaume, Diane's French husband, had stayed in the dining room to smoke a cigar with Edward.

"So remind me, Trevor," Leslie said as I sat down next to her, "what work you do." She and Don, sensibly dressed, community-minded people, worked at the Embassy, I remembered.

"I run a bicycle shop," I answered, already regretting my move to the sofa. I wanted a cigarette, and smoking would not be a crowd-pleaser here.

"You don't see many bicycles in Paris," Don piped up, with a hairy hand propped on his perma-press khaki knee. "Where do you drum up business?"

"Here and there." I shrugged.

"Here and where?" asked Leslie, just short of mockery.

"The few you do see on bikes *never* wear helmets, that's for sure," said Diane. "I've had ridiculous arguments with Guillaume about the children wearing them in the park."

"Crazy." Don shook his head.

"It depends on your point of view," I said.

"And what is your point of view?" Leslie asked.

"Besides looking silly and ruining the hair, helmets don't fundamentally protect you."

"Well," she said, "they protect your head, where injuries do the most damage."

"I mean that what's going to get you will get you, whether it's a bicycle accident or a cancer or a falling meteorite."

"Ah, I see," she said. "A fatalist. I guess you don't work the law of averages into your calculations. The fact, for example, that your chances of being mowed down by a French driver are considerably greater than the possibility of your getting in the way of a stray heavenly object."

"To me," said Don, leaning back on the chair that looked too small for his simian body, "it's just plain stupid. Especially, as you say Leslie, with the way people drive here."

"Exactly," said Diane, as if finally, someone had understood what she had to put up with, day in day out.

"The incredible thing to me," said Don, "is how rules and regulations *generally* are just thrown to the wind in this country."

"Well, it's not for any shortage of restrictions," added Leslie. "Our children are having real trouble adjusting to that at school—and the school is supposed to be bilingual. We incorrectly assumed that also meant bicultural."

That was it. They were off, launched like a rocket into the wide open space of French Bashing. Leslie and Don, having been in Paris only a year, led the attack, at moments with a viciousness I found most un-Christian. Diane, married to a Frenchman and, minus long summer vacations in Vermont, probably stuck here for life, veered from commiseration to explanation to mediation. She was keenly involved in several volunteer associations promoting better understanding between the two countries. No wonder she found the inability to reach an agreement with her French husband on the utility or futility of bicycle helmets so troubling.

At some dinners I leapt into these debates with vigor, contrarily defending my adopted country tooth and nail. But tonight, after a morose week and a four-course meal sitting between Stephanie and Jennifer, I didn't have the energy. I listened as they hammered the French school system—how inflexible, unwelcoming, unencouraging, unimaginative it is—in bored silence.

Stephanie plopped down next to me and started telling me about a book she'd just read and that she thought I'd like. I was surprised. Even though we often discussed books, she was an inveterate French Basher and was usually only too happy to jump into the fray. But not tonight. The book, I remember, was *Independence*

Day. She looked at me playfully and said: "The main character is rather like you." Her hand alighted on my knee. "Disaffected. A bit cynical but basically endearing."

I felt my face go warm. I looked furtively at the churchgoers to see if they'd heard, but they were entirely absorbed in the unforgiveable shortcomings of the French. "Sounds like I should read it," I mumbled. I did not tell her, as she continued to talk, that my mother had already passed on *The Sports Writer* to me, that I'd already spent several hundred pages in the company of the dysfunctional Frank Bascombe and was now beginning to feel more like a literary type than a human being.

The evening wound down, ending in a general discussion about the strike that was simmering and the shameful laziness of the French worker. "It's downright sinful," said Don. I stood up and said I was leaving; Stephanie said: "Not before I pay you. My checkbook's in the back. Come with me and I'll give you the book, too." I followed her down the dark corridor, past the sleeping children, to my brother's bedroom. "Let's see," she said, eye running over the messy desk. "Here's the book," she said, handing over Frank Bascombe's latest adventures. Then she leaned over the desk, rustling papers. Her hair slid off her shoulder and across her face. Her firm torso that showed no trace of motherhood was outlined in the orb of desk-lamp light. I put my hand on her back, felt vertebrae and rib cage. Without flinching, she said: "Here's the checkbook." Her pen didn't miss a loop. When she'd finished, she straightened, and my hand slipped off but not before it brushed her left buttock. She smiled at me, looked me up and down, then folded the check and stuck it in the pocket of my shirt, with a little pat at my pounding heart. "Here you go," she said and pulled me into one of those hugs again. "Thanks again."

I took my leave as if nothing had happened, or ever would. I said good-bye to my brother and chastely kissed his wife's two cheeks. I walked down the stairs with the churchgoers. All the normal motions, performed in a trance. The chilly walk home did not knock me back to my senses, nor did a restless night's sleep. Not even the light of the next day, when I went to see Jennifer, so that I could tell her again, while she was sober and I was not under the gun, that our short interaction was over. Not a single question about what had happened with Stephanie in her bedroom reached my conscious mind. Only the memory of her backbone and rib cage. Only the tingle, at her hand on my arm, the smile on her face, the outline of the firm stomach, and the hair falling.

I wasn't depressed anymore. I was on drugs.

———

Monday morning I lifted my head from the pillow, then let it drop back down, while I once again replayed the bedroom scene in my head. But when I got to the check in the pocket and the pat at my chest, the reverie came to an abrupt halt. Money reminded me that today was the day I was meeting Monsieur Petitdemange, my bank manager. It was the day that my accounts would be spread out like tagged pieces of evidence at a trial, exposing my insolvency, my failure.

I got up and marched heavily into my sort-of bathroom, letting the hot water of the shower douse me and douse me again, imagining it was Stephanie touching me all over as I jerked off. It didn't help. As I got out and dried myself, the bank visit still loomed. I wiped a circle clear on the foggy mirror, started shaving, and cut myself. The corner of the Kleenex I used to stop the blood on my neck wouldn't stick, and I had to pick up sodden bloody scraps from the floor as I got dressed.

On the radio, the only news was the transport strike. Train service was completely halted, they said, and the métro was at a virtual standstill. As for buses, there were still a few, but nothing you could count on. Out my window, the rue des Martyrs was a solid line of cars, with frustrated drivers hooting for someone to move forward when there was no place to go.

Once I got down to the street myself, I joined the solid mass of foot soldiers. All those who usually traveled underground had surfaced. People walked briskly, without any exterior sign of annoyance at the change in their routine, at the need to take a long, cold walk to work, rather than a crowded, warm hurtle underground.

At the Rendez-Vous, where I stopped for breakfast, Jean-Jacques said: "You should have seen the traffic this morning. It's going to be bad. I'm taking over the room out back and camping there." Usually Jean-Jacques took an early train in from the suburb where he lived because, like most café waiters, he couldn't afford the city.

The strike was splashed across the front page of the newspaper someone had left on my table. "Another 1968?" the headline asked ominously. It was not only the train drivers who were unhappy. Students wanted more teachers and better conditions at the universities. The entire public sector, meaning a whopping one-quarter of the French workforce, was up in arms at the government's attempt to reform the heavily indebted social security system by requiring *fonctionnaires* to pay into the system for forty years, like the private sector, instead of their current thirty seven and a half.

The shrillest cries, however, did come from the train drivers, the ones who had gained the right to retire at fifty, in the days when driving a train was hard work, not merely a matter of pushing buttons. Technology had changed, but not the laws or the drivers' expectations.

"Who," I heard Jean-Jacques say to Marcel at the bar, "except some elitist politician is going to agree to work more years? I mean, who would want to put off the good life, except a power-hungry, money-grabbing elitist?" Marcel nodded sympathetically but didn't say anything. Although he found life without the garage dull and tedious, he felt obliged, as a member of the working class, to agree on principle. It was the same for a majority of the French nation, working class or not.

However, what preoccupied me most that morning as I ate my bread and butter and drank my coffee was not the latest chapter in this interminable tale of class struggle. What worried me as I watched the endless stream of people flowing by the window was that I would have to walk with them to the *7ème*, where I still had both my professional and personal accounts. I'd stayed at my family's branch because when Mademoiselle Lafarge had been our bank manager, there was a certain tolerance for overdrafts, especially given that the rest of my family maintained plump sums in their accounts. But Monsieur Petitdemange had marshalled in a new era of austerity.

At the end of the morning, I trudged south with the hoards, feeling like a farm animal on its way to slaughter. I waited for Monsieur Petitdemange in a bright blue chair opposite a bleak brown desk. He was late, but I knew from previous meetings that he would keep me waiting. It helped lend an air of importance to his lower-management existence. The office in which I sat was a box separated from other box-like offices by flimsy partitions. The furniture was sparse and functional. There were no windows. The only adornment was a painting, a landscape that looked expressly designed to offend no one.

Monsieur Petitdemange finally arrived at a brisk and breathless clip. After shaking my hand, he sat his short, harried body at the desk, pushing his bulbous shoes forward so they stuck out the other side. My feet instinctively recoiled under my chair.

"So," he said, folding his hands on my red folder. The cuffs of the bright blue shirt that protruded from the black, four-button suit jacket covered half of his small hands. Monsieur Petitdemange glanced at the only other object on his desk, a folded copy of *The International Herald Tribune*. He never failed to make at least one reference to this expat paper. Checking my watch, I wagered today it would take seven minutes.

"The last few months, I'm afraid," Monsieur Petitdemange sighed, "have been less than satisfactory." I wondered by what artificial means—gel, grease, spray—he got that hair to curl so implacably to his head. "In fact, the situation is becoming untenable, Monsieur Mic-Far-Car, and I must demand what you propose to do about it." Instead of looking at me, he fixed his eyes intently on a corner of the ceiling.

Finally forcing his gaze back to the task at hand, he opened my red folder and spread his fingertips around his temples, as if even the idea of consulting my account gave him a severe headache. "Your file indicates that when you inherited this venture, you had over two hundred thousand francs in your account. Your balance at the present moment is," he went on, snatching up the top sheet of paper with a flourish, "on the wrong side of zero. Firmly in the red."

I nodded slowly while considering whether now was the time for him to know that the whole messy business would soon draw to a close. That I was being evicted and the money from the deposit on the lease would cover my overdraft. "Monsieur Petitdemange, I can promise you that the *situation*, as you call it, will change in the next several months."

"You are referring, I suppose, to an upswing in the French economy," he began. "As predicted in this morning's '*Erald Tribune*.'" I looked at my watch—only five minutes—I'd way overestimated his restraint and was disappointed in myself. He touched the paper lightly with his right hand and again gazed thoughtfully at the ceiling, perhaps this time in search of the H he'd snipped off Herald. "But I fail to see," he continued, stretching back in his chair like a replete cat, "how that will affect your prospects, Monsieur Mic-Far-Car. You run a bicycle shop."

"I expect my circumstances to change. That's all I can tell you at the moment." Then he looked at me for the first time, I think trying to assess whether I was a liar or a nut.

Our conversation went back and forth in much the same manner for several more minutes. He got his calculator out and tried to prove that any significant change in my "*situation intenable*," as he called it, was impossible. And I kept assuring him, without providing any evidence, that a solution was at hand. Finally he looked at his own watch and said: "All right. I'll give your miracle until February. Then I will be forced to take drastic measures." From previous meetings, I knew Monsieur Petitde-mange was sounding tough so he could bring the meeting to a close. Arguing with the likes of me was not worth cutting into his lunch hour.

What I had managed to mask better than anything else, I thought as I stood in the security space of the bank, waiting for one door to close so the other would open and release me, was my own panic at this financial uncertainty. I didn't used to live like this. As a young man, I took care of my finances and always made sure I had enough money. According to how much came in, I would calculate how much could go out. It was the days before cash machines dotted every corner, and I would go to the bank on Monday to withdraw whatever I could afford for the week. Never a centime more. Inheriting Mélo-Vélo had been like marrying a spendthrift woman. Though I still spent almost nothing on myself, the shop bled money or at least didn't make enough to keep it—and me—afloat.

In this way, I reasoned with myself, as I made my way back up the crowded rue du Bac, I'll be better off once Mélo-Vélo is gone. It'll just be me again. This whole *situation intenable* is merely another reminder that attachments, even inanimate ones, equal trouble.

That's what I was thinking when I spotted Stephanie. Her perfect red-gold head stuck out above the crowd, and my eye gravitated toward her as it would to a glint of light. She had just walked out of the dry cleaners. Over her left arm, she held reams of plastic; with her right she was rearranging her wallet in that yawning black bag. Today it had a riding crop sticking out of it. People flowed around her.

"Stephanie," I said. The face with the long jaw and pointed chin turned toward me. Her first expression was one of annoyance, but when she saw it was me, the chill melted and the fruit-slice smile exposed her line of white teeth, two front incisors slightly overlapping.

"Trevor," she said, readjusting the dry cleaning that was slipping from her arm, "what are you doing down here?"

"A meeting at the bank."

"Monsieur Petitdemange?" she said, her nose wrinkling in amusement. He constituted one of the few subjects we could laugh about as a family. Edward did a particularly good job of imitating his folded hands on the desk, his references to the *'Erald Tribune*.

"The one and only," I said. "Let me help with you that."

"Thanks," she said, handing me the whole package of cleaning while she finished settling her wallet in the bag, which she then zipped up and put back on her shoulder. "Where are you headed now? Do you have time for a bite of lunch?" The two of us were standing like two tall pillars, while annoyed pedestrians made their way around us on the narrow sidewalk.

"Sure," I said, shrugging my shoulders. There was so much human traffic that we walked most of the way to the rue de La Planche single file. She led; I followed with my brother's suit and my sister-in-law's silk shirt and her blue cashmere sweater, wrapped in plastic, over my arm. The blocked streets somehow blocked my brain. I didn't think about what I was doing. I just walked, looking at the back of Stephanie's head, at the straight, shiny hair with the blunt tips pulled into a tight ponytail. At her black bag with the riding crop sticking straight up in the air.

Stephanie punched the code into their building, using several fingers, as if she were at a keyboard.

"Phew," she said as we squeezed into the elevator, which was so narrow I had to stand at an angle. We were face-to-face under the bleak white light. The inner metal doors clunked closed and we jerked upward. "In the States, this piece of junk would never pass an elevator inspection," Stephanie said. "I'm always amazed when I get to the top in one piece."

As the elevator moaned, I could feel Stephanie's presence, as if it had tentacles that were touching me all over, and was thankful for the dry cleaning plastic shield. By the time the metal inner door clunked open at the fifth floor, both heart and penis were pounding. Backing out of the narrow elevator, I held the outer door for Stephanie with my body and felt her brush past my excited nerve ends.

She opened the front door and I followed her inside. It was dead quiet.

"Sorry it's a bit of a mess," Stephanie said as she kicked a toy fire engine out of the way. She took off her jacket, then sat on a chair so she could pull off her worn leather riding boots. "Dolores couldn't get here this morning. Your mother took Henri. I have to go pick him up after lunch."

"The other two stay at school for lunch?" In the back of my mind, I'd imagined the kids would be here. That we wouldn't be completely alone. When I was a boy, Lisette picked up Edward and me at eleven thirty and whipped us home on the métro, to the hot lunch that sat ready and waiting in the oven.

"No, some other mothers and I share feeding the children. On Mondays, Caroline and Matthieu eat at Odile de Chauvignac's house. Her daughter and Caroline are best friends, but Odile still insists on calling me *Madame* and *vous*. Even though I've purposely slipped in a friendly *tu* from time to time, she won't take the bait. But what should I expect from someone who was appalled to learn that Madame Villeneuve uses potato flakes for her mashed potatoes instead of the real thing? What would she do if she saw the boxes I pour the soup out of? Or that Dolores pours. I usually give her lunch duty." She stuffed long wooden trees into her riding boots and headed for the kitchen in her socks. "You can hang those clothes in the front closet. I'll get going on lunch."

I hung up the dry cleaning in the large closet, where the bicycle for Caroline still stood, then looked around the room. I did not remember ever having been here during the day, when it was empty. The place looked different, distorted in a way. The ceilings seemed lower and the windows larger, the apartments across the street closer. I'd never noticed the childproofing chicken wire along the iron railings of the narrow balcony. A few beleaguered geraniums lay in tilted pots along the bottom. Inside, the edges of the furniture looked sharper, the glass tables reflected the light from the windows, and the just off-white carpet gleamed.

I went into the kitchen, which was right off the entry hall. In most Haussmann Paris apartments, built when everyone had full-time hired help, the kitchen is way in the back, at the end of a long corridor. But at great expense (so Mother had informed me), Edward and Stephanie had changed the order of things, converting this large room into kitchen, breakfast room, and playroom. Their bedroom had been the kitchen. It now looked more like an American apartment.

"Is some leftover Chinese food all right with you? I'm afraid it's all we've got," Stephanie said as she opened the large two-door refrigerator.

"Just fine," I said, looking out the window onto a narrow shaft that was covered with a net to keep out pigeons. Maybe burglars too. I turned away from the window.

The kitchen area was a vast expanse of counter space, white cupboards, and shiny appliances. Stephanie moved around it gracefully in her skin-tight riding britches and stocking feet. She swept from fridge to microwave, counter to drawer, as if she were taking part in a choreographed dance.

"Would you like a glass of wine?" she asked, punching buttons on the microwave. "We've got red and white."

"Red," I said.

"Why don't you open it," she said. Our hands touched as she passed me the corkscrew, then our eyes met, and we continued the lunch preparations in silence. I opened the bottle of Bordeaux with my brother's state-of-the-art corkscrew. Pop went the bottle. Beep, beep, beep, went the microwave. Stephanie put two glasses on the counter. I poured while she re-stirred the stir-fried vegetables in their plastic container and reinserted them into the microwave. I put knives and forks on the table while she got plates.

"Not very elegant," Stephanie said as we sat down with a series of plastic containers between us. "But it's lunch and I'm always starving after I ride." She scooped herself some vegetables and rice while I negotiated a heap of noodles onto my plate, then some pork. "Is the food all right?"

"It's good," I lied. Some of the noodles had stiffened, as if stricken with rigor mortis, and they were only hot every other bite. I took a swallow of the wine. "So how are things with Edward?" I asked because I didn't know what else to say.

She put down her fork and wiped her mouth with a paper napkin she had grabbed from a holder on the table. "We had a terrible fight the other night when, as usual, he came home at ten." She finished chewing. "The kids had already been in bed for over an hour, and I'd had two glasses of wine while I waited, starving, for him. When he came in, he looked as if he didn't even know where he was. He could have been in an airport for that blank stare. He did notice that the table was set, but all he said was, 'Oh, sorry. I had a sandwich at the office.' Then he sat down in front of the television with a cigar and a glass of wine." She paused for a minute, taking a sip from her own glass. When she looked up at me, her green eyes were round and bright, and her full mouth gave an uneven smile, revealing a piece of black Chinese mushroom stuck next to her overlapping left canine. "I lost it. I put myself between him and the television and screamed that he was never home, and even when he was, he might as well not be, for all the attention he gave me. He told me he was tired, stressed at work. I said, 'What about me?' He said, 'You're always edgy and critical and unhappy.' He said, 'I'm just trying not to rock the boat. To give you space.'"

She looked down at her plate and began stabbing the food, vengeful jabs at bamboo shoots and soy sprouts. "Where do I fit into the picture? The guardian of his offspring? His housewife? I can't live like this." The fork clattered onto the plate and she looked straight at me, her round eyes steady as a cat's. "It's as if we have nothing but our three children in common anymore. Sometimes I wonder why we ever got married in the first place. What was I thinking?" She shook her head, and her now loosened hair fell forward. She slowly swept it back, then let both hands fall on the table.

"Isn't this what happens to all people with small children?" I asked lamely.

"No," she answered. "No, it isn't. Not to the other mothers at school. All they want to do is to have six children and spend their days mashing potatoes. Not to the American women I meet through all those associations. They seem happy in their little gaggles. I just don't fit." The tears now filled her eyes.

I got up and went around the table, putting my hands on her shoulders. "Paris is a big city. You just have to find something else to do, different people to see."

"I know, I know," she said, dabbing her eyes with the paper napkin.

She stood up too and then, despite all my pretensions to a clean and uncluttered life, it happened. Before reason could trump desire, the delicate features of her face were tucked into my neck as if she were a small animal that needed protecting. Her shiny hair brushed smoothly against my cheek while my hands ran over the soft grey sweater, under which her ribs and muscular back were once again all too palpable.

We accomplished the irrevocable act on the floor of her American-style kitchen-playroom, on the unfolded futon that was already covered with stains from the three small children, my niece and nephews. Pillows and toys were tossed aside, riding britches and jeans lying in a crumpled heap. All around us was a mess, as it was bound to be.

SIX

———

THE STRIKE WAS indeed the most determined protest movement France had seen since 1968, and that was saying something.
Mai '68 was still referred to with wide eyes and reverentially low
voices. Not quite a repeat of the Revolution itself but almost. In
this case, there were no decapitations, no hurling of paving stones,
but the country—with no trains, no métros, no buses—ground to
a halt. Roads and streets in and around every city were an endless
stream of idling engines, manned by frustrated and angry victims
of the strike who honked their horns and flapped their arms like
trapped geese. Meanwhile, the sidewalks were an unbroken mass
of moving human traffic, as all the underground travelers surfaced
to make their way as best they could on foot.

At first, the government did nothing. The prime minister
stayed locked in his office, convinced he was right. It all made
sense on paper, after all. But if he thought he could outsit the
strikers, he should have known better. French workers are a stubborn and determined lot, especially when riled. They are able to
outsit anyone, particularly with public opinion behind them. And
despite everyday life being rendered miserable, the majority of the
population continued to support the strikers. As Jean-Jacques had

said: "Who in their right mind would want to work *longer* hours, *more* years?"

Maybe that solidarity explained the unusual atmosphere of struggling camaraderie during those three weeks. Paradoxically, despite the endless inconveniences, normally grouchy Parisians, at least those who weren't stuck in cars, had never been so patient and forbearing, so polite and attentive to one another. Even the most modest employees spent hours getting to and from work. Those who lived outside the city formed car pools, previously an unknown concept to the individualistic French. Still others hitchhiked for the first time in their lives.

That being said, unnecessary activity was reduced to a minimum. Movement anywhere, anyhow, was a lumbering chore. Dinners were canceled, appointments were put off, museums closed early, and shops were empty.

Most shops, that is.

Every crisis benefits someone. In a matter of weeks—actually days—the status of bicycles rose from the untouchable world of shabby hippies and the fractious proletariat to the heady heights of latest Paris chic. Mélo-Vélo was almost as busy as the streets themselves. My entire stock of cycles was quickly depleted, and the accessories rack began to look as bare as the shelves in a third-world country. Repairs streamed in so steadily, I started turning people down. Seeking help was against my precepts, but during those three weeks, I broke every rule in my hardcover book.

My savior came in a most unexpected form.

Just as everyone on the street had known that Mélo-Vélo was struggling, everyone now knew that its fortunes had reversed. There was a new interest in my shop, even from Madame Picquot, who had taken to popping in several times a day to gauge the buzz, provide a bit of unsolicited advice to me or to a customer.

One morning when I was at the Rendez-Vous eating breakfast and drinking my coffee, over she swaggered on her stick legs.

Forgoing any pleasantries, she said: "There's a young man over there." She threw her head in the direction of the bar. "A Pole. He's a friend of those construction workers who are always around. He's looking for work. Maybe he could help you out."

I looked at what appeared to be a boy staring anxiously in our direction. "He doesn't look old enough to buy a drink."

"Good. Then he won't come to work drunk." She jammed her hands into the pockets of her housecoat. "From what I've seen, you're not managing very well on your own. But do as you like." She shrugged her shoulders, then turned and swaggered past the bar and out the door.

I had to take her point. I couldn't keep going as I had been the last ten days. So I sighed, stood up, and walked over to him at the bar.

"I hear you're looking for work?" He bobbed his head up and down eagerly. "Why don't you come sit down. Do you want a coffee?" He shook his head and followed me back to my corner.

The boy sat nervously, large hands in his lap. He had dull brown hair that was very straight and thick, like a brush, as if no matter how long it got, it would still stick straight out of his head. He had clear blue eyes and pale skin, a broad nose and high cheekbones. An open and honest face, at least. "What's your name?"

"Piotr."

"How old are you?"

"Twenty-four," he said. I looked doubtful. He nodded vigorously. "Twenty-four."

"Have you ever worked in a shop? With bicycles?"

Now he looked pained. "I work farm. Family."

Maybe Piotr was of legal working age, but he hardly spoke French. He'd never even worked in a shop. How could I hire this man? Then again, I thought, he wouldn't annoy me by talking too much, and if he grew up on a farm he must know about tools and machinery. Since he was undoubtedly an illegal immigrant, he'd also be easy to get rid of once the strike ended, or at the latest, come eviction time. I agreed to take him on.

We walked back from the Rendez-Vous in silence. I opened the orange metal grille and took him straight to the workshop so he could begin on the backed-up repair jobs. I showed him the tools, which were scattered about because I hadn't had time to arrange them on the wall. He nodded while I explained slowly and deliberately, and within half an hour, I had him replacing brake pads and fixing punctures. With his large hands, he was clearly in his natural element. And the minute he started a job, he was completely absorbed by the task. The rest of the world disappeared. I could see it in his face, feel it in the room. It reminded me of my former days in the dark room, before I got photos developed by professionals, where I could spend four hours and think only one had passed.

With Piotr helping me, I could turn my attention to what was really on my mind.

After our romp on the kitchen floor, we saw each other every weekday, despite the strike. While others were sitting in traffic or demonstrating in the streets to hold on to their social security, I, in my ever contrary fashion, was on the move and throwing my own personal security to the wind. I would close for lunch and be at the rue de La Planche twenty-five minutes later. Pre-Piotr, that only gave us about an hour together. It was too rushed. So on the first day he worked for me, I showed him how to ring up pumps and reflectors and left at noon. It didn't even cross my mind that he might rob me blind, this Pole I'd known for three hours. I was obsessed, possessed. More time with Stephanie was all I could think about.

Our love nest was their maid's room, on the top floor of the building. Usually it housed an American student in exchange for babysitting in the evenings and on weekends, but conveniently, the last one had recently returned homesick to the States. Every day I would run up the six flights of service stairs, where Stephanie, wrapped in a grey silk gown, waited for me. We were at each other before I took off my coat. I liked to feel her firm body through that thin silk, to pull it off her shoulders and let it fall in a slippery puddle at our feet, while I stayed fully dressed. Once naked, Stephanie would take off my clothes, item by item.

She was irresistible, a picture of athletic perfection. Long arms and legs, rounded by well-exercised muscles, broad shoulders, and thin hips. From the back, it could almost have been the body of a young man. And it was her back I liked the best, the way her shoulders tapered to her waist. The way the muscles and ribs showed when she bent over or lifted her arms. The way a golden parabola, remains of her summer tan mark, dipped into the white skin. I liked to run my hand over the usually unexposed areas, the small of her back and buttocks, round and firm and perfectly feminine. Not surprisingly, she was as athletic in bed as she was on the tennis court. It was like a daily trip to the gym, and I quickly became addicted to the exercise. It brought me running back, day after heady day. It kept my mind whirling, my body aching with desire until our next encounter.

Of course, what added to the exhilaration was the lustful pursuit of forbidden pleasure, but I wasn't thinking about that, either.

After our workout, we would sit tucked up in cushions and quilts, eating the sandwiches Stephanie had bought at the bakery and sipping red wine straight from the bottle. And talk. Or she did. She needed to talk.

"Your mother doesn't like me," she said, with a smile hovering between irony and anger, "because I'm a bastard."

"What do you mean?" Until then, I knew almost nothing about Stephanie's pre-Edward life, as it was yet another subject avoided by my mother.

"During Mom's last year at college, she had a one-night stand with the pianist at a local bar. She let things slide until it was too late and moved to western Massachusetts to ride out the pregnancy. The plan was then to move to New York, get a job as a journalist. But life with a child was harder than she'd imagined, and it never happened. We stayed in Great Barrington, living in the guardhouse of some rich New Yorkers in exchange for caretaking. She did finally become the horticultural correspondent for a New England magazine. But no big New York career."

"You have no idea who your father is?"

She shook her head. "None."

"Did your mother tell you anything about him?"

"After a one-night stand in a bar where she'd had too much to drink? She told me she couldn't even remember his face. Only his hands. His large pianist hands."

"Doesn't that—I don't know—drive you crazy?"

"My mother and I were very close. Our unit always seemed enough. I mean, sure, sometimes I wondered. I got the hands, I guess." She held hers up. "But not the musical talent. Maybe he had green eyes. My mother's were brown." She pulled her knees to her chest under the cover, wrapping her bare arms around them on the outside. "Anyway, that one night in my mother's life frustrated her ambitions, and she was determined that things would be different for me. She pushed me to be the top of my class, to be competitive in sports. Luckily, I loved school, loved working hard and doing well. I had the confidence she believed she'd lost." She sighed. "Anyway, I ended up in New York, just as she'd hoped. First Barnard, then a year as a paralegal, then NYU for law school. She died in my last year. Wasted away before my very eyes with colon cancer.

And I had nobody. She'd worked so hard to make me independent I'd never realized how dependent I was on her. It had always been just the two of us, revolving in our little world. We had no close family. She, too, was an only child and had had strained relations with her Midwestern parents since she was a teenager. My arrival didn't help. I hardly ever saw them. And I've never had intense female friendships. There was always Mom. Then suddenly, there wasn't. I was devastated. Edward came along at my most vulnerable moment. His timing was perfect."

"Just like his serve in tennis," I said.

She smiled and started picking at a ragged fingernail.

"At the time, he seemed just the right mix of exotic and stable. And he came equipped with the family that maybe, I suddenly thought, I'd always been missing."

"And isn't that what you've got?" I asked.

"I suppose. But it's more complicated than I'd imagined. I'm not leading the career life I was brought up to lead. Instead, I'm married with three children and living like a rich expatriate housewife. Not even *like* one—I *am* one. It's ghastly."

"Just because you're rich and have children doesn't mean you can't work, if that's what will give a sense of independence. The kind of life you lead doesn't restrict you to charity work at the church, you know. You don't have to be like what's her name the other night."

"Diane." Stephanie rolled her eyes. "The biggest problem," she said while continuing to pick at her nail, "is that I've lost my self-confidence. Just like my mother, except three times over. Thank God she's dead, or this would have killed her."

"Most people would say you have the perfect life."

"My mother would have said people like the two of us weren't meant to live a family life, surrounded by lots of children and in-laws." She paused, now tearing the nail right off. "I can't stand sitting at home, waiting for Edward to finish his busy day, with its meetings and accomplishments. He's out there doing something, and I'm just treading water. I might be two years older, but he's way ahead of me on every other front."

"You're not in competition," I said.

"It's hard for me not to compete, and with Edward I always feel the loser. Another first in my life." She paused, stretched out her long legs, and put her head against the cushion behind. "You remember the first time I came to Paris, before we got married?"

"I certainly do."

"At the beginning of that visit, everyone seemed kind, and your life so civilized, so wrinkle-free. Your mother said all the right things. Edward treated Edmond like his real father. Even the fact that you were clearly a black sheep didn't *seem* to trouble anyone."

"My mother excels at keeping up appearances. That's why she's so happy in France."

"By the end of that trip, my first impressions had already begun giving way to a more complicated reality. Do you remember my holding your hand in the car that night?"

"How could I forget."

"Well, I was *already* feeling insecure." She shook her head: "Naive, naive me. Earlier that evening Edward had told me your mother was worried about him marrying me. She said to him: 'You go to New York and bring back an orphaned older woman from the middle of nowhere? She won't make you happy. Your backgrounds are too different. You don't see it now, but you will. The differences will surface.' Edward had replied: 'Mother, this is a different age. Stephanie's got beauty and brains. That's enough.' To which your mother—I can just see her lifting that long, whiffy nose of hers into the air—replied: 'What's wrong with beauty, brains, *and* breeding?' She actually said that." Stephanie threw her arms in the air; the duvet fell from her naked torso. The nipples of her smallish breasts turned upward in the most enticing way. "Can you believe it?" She pulled the covers back up.

"Absolutely," I said, sticking my hand under the duvet and caressing her breast. "But I'm surprised at Edward's tactical error in telling you. He's usually a better strategic thinker."

"But he'd decided I was all right," she said. "And he's almost as big a snob as your mother. He kept telling me she'd change her opinion once we were married and living in Paris. I didn't know what to think. But I should have. All the writing was on the wall, and I skimmed over the words instead of reading the fine print. An unforgivable mistake for a lawyer."

We sat for a few minutes in silence. I moved my hand from her breast to her taut, flat stomach, to her crotch. It was a sticky filament, the Harcourt-Laporte web, and Stephanie had been lured in by what she believed to be a delicate but safe mix of the foreign and familiar. She—and funnily enough Edward, who really should have known better—hadn't seen that our America was not the same as hers. From what I had witnessed on Long Island, the country was hardly a classless society, and those occupying the upper rungs of the solid social ladder did not take kindly to intruders from below. Stephanie may never have been ostracized for her unconventional status in her Great Barrington public school ("Who would have dared tease me? I was the strongest person in my class until I was fifteen."), but it would have been different at my private school in Manhattan. The parents would have talked, the children would have listened.

Stephanie was lured in by that timeless attraction to the apple, in this case the shiny, seductive French variety, offering a mix of tradition and beauty and refinement. Though I'd seen couples take a fatal grab at it time and again, I'd thought Edward and Stephanie, such sure-footed winners, immune to it. But for whatever reasons—Stephanie's inability to cope with a large, extended family that was considerably more foreign than familiar, or my mother's dislike of her, which had become more pronounced once the children were born—things were falling apart. Another Experiment in International Living was in trouble.

"Time to go," Stephanie said. She was right. It was already well after two. But Piotr would be there to reopen the shop. I dug my hand deeper into her crotch.

"In a minute," I said.

"Okay," she said, rolling on top of me, which was the position she not surprisingly preferred. After exploring every corner of my mouth with her tongue, she sat up straight, eyes closed, head bent, hands caressing her own breasts while her pelvis pumped down hard on me. Holding her small waist, I pulled her down even harder. Our orgasms were quick and simultaneous, and it seemed, as we lay interlocked afterward, her face breathing warmth into the crook of my neck, as if something very profound had happened, as if our bodies were fused forever.

When we did get up, she was all business, assuming the professional persona she claimed to have lost. Hot tap off, cold tap on. It was as though we had been discussing a legal brief, and she were now slipping on a suit coat, rather than the silken bra. I half expected her to grab a briefcase on the way out the door, but all she did was bend over to turn off the electric heater.

———

I was, during the strike, constantly running. Every day there was a ceaseless flow of customers and repairs, a trip to the rue de La Planche and back, then more customers and repairs. In the evening, exhausted, I'd drink a beer, eat, watch television, and read a book. And then I'd sleep, like death.

Why, you might have been wondering, was I running rather than riding? Why in the course of this narrative have I not once taken recourse to one of the two-wheeled vehicles so readily at hand?

Well, that brings us back to Jacqueline, the black-haired, blue-eyed one I met at the Sorbonne. In those days I rode my green Raleigh racer, bought from Nigel upon my return from the US, everywhere. It was like an extension of myself. Then one day, about two years after she'd mutilated that sandwich, Jacqueline borrowed it for her "cousin." When she returned it, she informed me that she'd had to lower the saddle and the handlebars for him ("He's small, like me."). In an unusually thoughtful gesture, she had raised them again before returning the bicycle ("See how nice I am?"). Except she hadn't tightened those handlebars quite tightly enough.

The bicycle accident happened three days before the show was supposed to open. It left me with a broken right shoulder, three broken ribs, two deep, wide cuts on my head, and a severely scraped ear. For three weeks I was also in a coma. The doctors had begun to worry that even if I did wake up, my brain would have gone soft, leaving me at best a drooling half-wit, at worst an overcooked vegetable. Of course, I did wake up, only to discover that I'd missed my show and that Jacqueline's "cousin" was in fact a Polish filmmaker named Kazimierz ("Kaz") with whom she'd been carrying on for six months.

It had been like receiving two more death blows. Whether it was the injury to my head or my heart, these events on top of the deaths in my family left something broken in my spirit, made me lose any faith in True Purpose. Circumstances, it seemed, kept turning me down another path, a road stripped of passion and risk.

One night during the strike I was lying in bed, thinking about all the time I was wasting on foot. Wasn't this the moment to overcome the bicycle phobia that had descended on me after that accident all those years ago? Wasn't I feeling better now? Wasn't life intense and exciting again? Wouldn't that propel me forward?

Throwing on some clothes and a jacket, I went down my staircase to the courtyard. It was deadly still when I opened the back door to the shop and eerie at night, with the bleak street light coming in through the bars of the protective grille, making it seem somewhere between a prison and a tomb. I turned on a small light in the workshop and looked at the bicycles Piotr had finished repairing that day. There was a Dutch woman's cycle, with no bar on which to castrate myself, no gears, and back-pedal brakes. Like my first tricycle. Easy, I said to myself as I pushed it out the door and under the *porte-cochère*, its back wheel clicking lazily, unthreatening as a tired old horse. Once on the street, I turned right, up the hill. The domes of the Sacré Coeur, with the spotlights turned off, sprouted into the night sky like determined mushrooms.

I wheeled the bicycle toward a little park where I sometimes came and sat with a sandwich on a sunny warm day. It was closed at night, but I easily hoisted the bicycle over the low gate. Here no one could see my struggle. For a few minutes, I pushed and pulled on different parts of the bicycle, making sure nothing was loose. Eventually, I swung my leg over and for another few minutes, straddled its low, spongy saddle. Then I lifted one foot onto a pedal. My heart was racing and I was sweating under my jacket, despite the cold night. I put my foot back on the ground and pushed forward, using each of my feet as training wheels. This was easy. I could do it, couldn't I?

When I tried to push off, however, the front wheel wobbled, and I almost fell off in my panic. I tried again. And again. And again. I don't know how many times, but I couldn't do it. I tried reasoning with myself: if I'd done it once, I could do it again. That didn't work, so I turned to science, reminding myself that the physics of the thing was proven fact. When that didn't work, I tried ridiculing myself, repeating how silly and childish I was being. To no avail. Finally, I tried coaxing, goading myself, with visions of Stephanie's naked body, her intense orgasms. Even that didn't work. My mental block was as firmly in place as a prison door, and after almost an hour of aborted attempts, with the results degenerating the longer I kept at it, I lifted the bicycle over the fence and wheeled it back down to the shop, feeling exhausted, foolish, and resigned to my own two feet as my only source of locomotion.

And shaking, still shaking, in a cold sweat, even once I'd climbed back up the stairs to my room and lain down on my mattress.

It had been a Sunday. The photo show was set to open, with everything ready to go, and I'd decided to clear my head with a bike ride in the country, something I did often those days. I rode my newly returned bike up to the Gare du Nord and got on a train to Senlis, the town near which the Coursaults had their château. The train passed the Sacré Coeur and the jumble of Montmartre roofs that huddled around it, out to the *banlieues*, with their depressing postwar blocks. But soon I was in Senlis. I bought my standard picnic lunch on the main street and stuffed it in my rucksack, next to my camera.

Then I headed into the Ermenonville Forest. The huge old trees towering all around gave it a haunted, ancient feel. I remembered stories of the Coursaults hunting wild boar here, and they had spooked me, because I had not been in France that long and had mistaken their talk of *sanglier* for *sang*, blood.

Anyway, my ride that morning was mostly infused with a nervous excitement about the photo show. The cold damp of the forest was at first clammy on my skin, but I warmed up as I pedaled. At lunchtime, I emerged into a spread of open fields, near the village of Mortefontaine. The sun was warm, and I settled in a clearing between a field of young wheat and a field of bright yellow rapeseed flowers. I propped myself against a rusty, abandoned plow. The breeze cooled my sweaty back as I pulled off my rucksack and unloaded lunch. The mineral water was still cool as a mountain stream. I cut the baguette lengthwise and spread the chunky paté, slathering it over every centimeter of bread.

Sitting in that sunny field, my hunger earned but not yet sated, I felt exalted, fully alive. I put off the first bite of food, as one might delay an orgasm. The pleasure was that intense. When I did take it, expectation and fulfillment melted into a feeling of undiluted happiness. Under the cotton puff clouds and blue sky, with the balmy air lulling me, I remember thinking: maybe I've turned a corner. As I peeled my orange, carefully plucking off the pith that clung to the fruit like a chamois cloth, I counted my blessings. I was here on my bicycle. I had a girlfriend, I had a photo show, already hung and ready to go. What more could I want or need?

I ate half my Fitness chocolate bar, savoring the raisins and chunks of nut, thinking I'd eat the other half on the train ride home. I rolled myself a cigarette and smoked it while lying flat on my back. The little clouds slid across the sky. After smoking that satisfying cigarette right down to the filter, I closed my eyes and drifted into sleep. When I woke up I had no idea where I was. My head felt heavy and musty. I packed up my rucksack and pushed the thin wheels of my touring bicycle back out to the road. I dipped back into the forest. The first part was a slow downhill stretch, and I moved into top gear, allowing the cooler air to clear my head. This downhill cycling was almost as good as lunch, I was thinking, when halfway down the hill, there was a rut, really no more than a small dip. My front wheel hit it and jarred the bicycle. When I pulled on the handlebars to straighten my course, they came clean out of the fork.

It was an instant that lasted a lifetime. Those seconds of futile fumbling play over and over again in my head and still cause a numbness to creep up my spine. The front wheel fluttering like a panicked butterfly, while I try to stick the handlebars back in the fork, while I squeeze the brakes, the cable still connected but not of any real use. My head hurtling over the front while I cling to the handlebars is the last image before the scene goes black.

I lay on my mattress that night, stiff as a board and sweating.

If I was so crippled by the memory of the accident, by the world inside my head that I couldn't put faith in the simple, proven physics of motion, what hope was there for me?

———

A few days after my nocturnal terror, I walked into the shop from my daily romp with Stephanie and heard:

"It's not quite right. Haven't you got anything else?" I did not even have to look. Jacqueline. Dressed in her winter black wool rather than her summer off-white linen, with her short black hair and her pale doll's face. Though I shouldn't have been surprised—even Monsieur Petitdemange had come in search of a bicycle.

"We got no much," Piotr said. "Lot people want bicycle now."

"Hello, Jacqueline," I said.

"My bicycle got stolen," she said, flying past formalities, "and I need a replacement immediately. I'm going crazy." She put her hands to her head.

Paris is a small town, and losing sight of people you know is almost impossible. You're bound to bump into one another somewhere, sometime. I'd run into Jacqueline one day on the boulevard St Germain, just about the time Nigel died. Kaz was long gone; I think by then it was Alexis. Anyway, she had not completely disappeared from my life, and to her credit, she had bought a bicycle from me once, even before they became trendy.

"As Piotr said, we haven't got much. Everyone in the city wants a bicycle these days."

Piotr, relieved at being delivered from this peremptory woman, returned to the workshop.

"What? So now you have an employee?" she asked in the offended tone I knew so well. It was a tone suggesting that she should have been let in on the answer before she was required to ask the question.

"As you can see."

She peered at Piotr around the corner, looking him up and down. For Jacqueline, meeting new people was first and foremost a fault-finding mission. "Huh," she finally said. "*That's* quite a step for the Lone Ranger."

"Who knows what a good French strike will do to you."

"You sure haven't got much to offer."

"This is it," I said, pointing to three bicycles. "Do you want one or not?"

"Yes. But how much? I'm low on funds."

The first time she had bought an expensive new Dutch bicycle, shiny, sturdy, and black. "How did the other one get stolen anyway? You had a Kryptonite lock."

"I was running late one evening, and when I stopped at the supermarket, I didn't lock it. I was only going to be a minute, but then the place was packed. I got stuck at the end of a long line, with an old lady in front who took hours counting out her change. And when I got back, it was gone."

"You should get a cheaper bicycle if you're not going to take care of it."

"I don't need moral lectures, just a new bike. I guess this one will be okay," she said, pointing to the most expensive. "Can't you give me a good price, though?" She looked at me with those blue eyes that once upon a time made me want to help her, to save her from just the kind of stupid mistake as the unlocked bicycle outside the supermarket.

"This bicycle is already very reasonably priced."

"I know. But it's a bad time. My patients can't always get to their appointments and then they don't pay."

I hesitated. Another day I might have argued with her, but I just wanted her gone. "Ten percent off."

"A little more than that? Please?"

"All right. Fifteen." Piotr, who was wheeling out the repair, looked at me as if I were crazy.

"You're an angel," she said, fishing out her credit card. "You should come to dinner. Are you free tonight?"

"No."

Her attention had already shifted to another customer who was looking at baskets. "I should probably have one of these too. Could you put one on, quickly?"

She went shopping while I got the bike ready, and it was all I could do, as I made a few last adjustments, not to loosen the handlebars.

———

Ushering in the end of an era seemed to be Jacqueline's karma, and shortly after her unwelcome visit, the strike sputtered and died. Having extracted most of what they wanted from the government, the transport workers climbed back onto their trains and buses and revved their engines. Paris, like a knot being massaged out of a tense muscle, began to relax, to loosen up. Once again, half the population at any given time of the day was underground. Traffic still jammed, but for minutes instead of hours. There was little joy, however, in the return to normality. Paradoxically, the goodwill that had buoyed the stranded victims of the strike drained away as life settled back into its sodden winter sameness. The war was over and with it the romance, the adventure. The only challenge on the low, grey horizon, it seemed, was surviving the bleak winter months ahead.

With Christmas just over a week away, the decorations had gone up on the rue des Martyrs as usual. Food shops laid out their Christmas fare just like every other year: twenty choices of *pâtés* and *terrines*, mounds of lobster and *langoustines* and *langoustes*, all slit down the middle, piled high with mayonnaise and topped with sprigs of parsley. But shoppers were still scarce, and it was particularly hard that Christmas to imagine how all that food would get eaten.

Mélo-Vélo, while not as busy as it had been, continued to have more business than any other shop on the street. Even the press was talking about the new bicycle craze, and the mayor's office, in what was perhaps more an effort to powder the blemished face of government than a genuine concern for ecology, announced the creation of kilometers of bicycle lanes all over the city. But with the strike over, the crisis passed, I was back to worrying about the impending eviction. Should I try and renegotiate with my insurance company landlord? Or should I try to find a new place? If business kept up as it was, it was possible, but did I want that? If not, what did I want?

Furthermore, if I managed to keep the shop, what should I do about Piotr? Whatever he may have lacked in sophisticated language skills, he made up for with his hands. The long row of repairs cluttering the shop on his first day had quickly shortened, never to grow unwieldy again. His pleasure in the job even improved the *ambiance* in the shop; he immediately put customers at ease, and now that I was used to his discreet and able help, it would be hard to go back to the way things were before. In a short time, he'd begun to seem part of the place.

One thing was certain: it had been a long, hard month, and I decided we both needed a break.

"We're closing next week between Christmas and New Year," I said to Piotr. "I'll buy you a bus ticket back to Poland as a Christmas bonus. What do you think?" He had been cleaning a chain in a bowl of white spirit. Wiping his hands on a rag, he looked at me and went red in the face, shaking his head.

"Papers," he said.

"I always forget you're not supposed to be here," I said. "Well, you get the week off anyway and the bonus in cash."

"I have plan," he said, getting even redder. "I have friend. She come in Paris." Then he pulled the chain out of the solution, turned his back to me, and started working again. End of story.

That was the way with all of Piotr's communications—just a thread, for which the present tense sufficed. There was no fabric, no weave. And it didn't bother him one bit. Unlike me, who had gone through the same struggle with the French language but who, even once I had mastered the whole range of verb tenses, never stopped grappling at every turn with the past, the future, the conditional. Even the present.

⸻

After the strike ended, I went down to the rue de La Planche once. It was all different, start to finish. Instead of walking, I took the métro, and it was just another hot, noisy trip underground. The sense of urgency and adventure—the feeling that I was fighting my way through a war zone to a love tryst—had evaporated, and I may as well have been paying a visit to Monsieur Petitdemange. As the métro hurtled through the tunnel, the enormity of what I had done began to dawn on me for the first time. Strange times can make strange behavior seem perfectly normal, and incredible as it may seem, I had not really stopped to consider how uncon-scionable—not to mention perverse—it was to be sleeping with my brother's wife. With the restoration of order and routine, my judgment was returning, and what I'd done appeared unimagin-ably sordid. It was as if the act had been carried out by someone else. By the time I climbed the back stairs on the rue de La Planche, I wondered what on earth I was doing there.

Fortunately, Stephanie felt it too. She opened the door fully dressed, with an excuse instead of a kiss: she couldn't stay, she had to pick up Henri from my mother. By the time she'd phoned me, I'd left. It was the all-business, cold-tap Stephanie. The air in the room, which had always felt highly charged with our overexcited ions, was today as neutral as a waiting room. And cold as an icebox, since she hadn't even bothered to turn on the heater.

"But I did buy us some sandwiches," she said. "You can at least get lunch out of the way." The duvets and pillows that had made our love nest were folded up in the corner, and we sat on the edge of the stripped bed, eating our sandwiches. Neither of us spoke. Stephanie tore large pieces off the baguette with her teeth. She was in a hurry, either to get Henri or to get me out of there. I didn't feel hungry and nibbled the edge of my chicken sandwich. Finally, I said: "It's different now that life's back to normal." She nodded and finished chewing.

"I guess so," she said without much enthusiasm. "Edward's talking about finding another student in January. Of course, there's always your place," she said, smiling for the first time since I'd arrived. "Then I can finally meet that wife and three children you're hiding in there."

"I've told you. I'll let you in my room the day I *do* have a wife and three children." I shook my head vigorously. "Never."

"That's what they all say, just before they fall."

"I've fallen far enough these last few weeks, thank you," I said.

"Don't start feeling guilty on me," she said, popping the last bite of sandwich into her mouth. "I've enjoyed myself," she went on while chewing. "It's given me a much-needed boost. So please. No guilt." She swallowed the last bite, leaned over to kiss me, then stood up. "Sorry to be in such a hurry, but your mother's waiting." I stood up too, stuffing the rest of my sandwich in my pocket and following Stephanie out the door. She locked it, and we walked down the dingy stairs. Outside the back door to their apartment, we kissed again, but it was brisk and efficient, dispassionate.

The sun was shining weakly, and I remember feeling warmer outside than I had in the unheated room. An unrelenting chill and a half-eaten chicken sandwich, that was what I took away from our last meeting in the maid's room on the rue de La Planche.

SEVEN

WHEN I GOT back to the rue des Martyrs, I stopped at the Rendez-Vous.

"The usual?" Jean-Jacques asked.

"Yes," I said, but still with a bitter taste in my mouth from my trip to the rue de La Planche, I added: "No. I'll have a hot chocolate."

"You could use a bit of sweetening up," Jean-Jacques said as he passed his damp rag over the counter. "A little sweeter and you'd have women falling over bicycles for you."

"Sounds messy," I said, lighting a cigarette.

"I tell you, if you listened to me, you'd be a much happier man." Jean-Jacques shook his head and began unloading a tray of dirty glasses as he slid the hot chocolate in front of me.

"I'm not looking for happiness," I said. "I'm looking for peace. Now let me drink my chocolate and smoke my cigarette. In peace."

He shook his head and moved down the counter with his damp cloth, clearing drink spills, real and imaginary. Jean-Jacques was a believer in the Family Unit as the route to a contented and fulfilled life. Though he didn't claim to have a perfect marriage

("Monique can be a real hornet," he'd recoil as if still recovering from the sting), he considered that life without his wife and two children would be unbearable. In fact, he'd told me that for the first years of his career as a waiter, he'd lived alone in a small studio, probably not unlike mine. "I would have thrown myself out the window," he said, "if it hadn't been on the ground floor of the darkest, smallest, grimiest courtyard I've ever seen."

But for me, especially now that I was coming down from my Stephanie high, the notion of happiness seemed particularly nebulous. It could never be more substantial than the froth on my hot chocolate, never more lasting than an ephemeral pleasure inspired by sex, a good book or film, a walk at Hautebranche after one of Viviane's meals, or a photo that captivated me. Contentment would always wither, leaving me on a bare vine of anxious melancholy.

Which is where I dangled in the run-up to Christmas. But while I gloomed around Mélo-Vélo in the full throes of What's-the-Pointism, Piotr was in a state of restless agitation. As the day of his friend's arrival grew near, his usually placid progress through the workday gave way to frenzied activity. He tidied and rearranged the workshop and unloaded a shipment of accessories, carefully lining up lamps and pumps and reflectors, pert and efficient as a nurse. He was driving me crazy, but finally it was Christmas Eve, the day the friend would arrive by bus at the place de la Concorde. That day he did not come dressed to fix bicycles. Instead of his T-shirt and jeans, he was wearing a perma-press shirt and trousers; instead of sneakers, cheap grey shoes with a buckle at the side and toes that ended in an inelegant point. In an attempt to flatten his brush-like hair, he had put something on it that might have come from Monsieur Petitdemange's cupboard.

"Why did you do that to your hair?" I asked.

"Too . . . pow," he said, hands exploding over his head.

"The natural look suits you better, Piotr."

"It smell bad," he said, his pale, almost hairless cheeks turning red. He looked at the floor. I felt sorry for him, this poor young man who still believed in love. And so I asked him up to my room to rinse out his hair. We stuck up the "Back in 10 Minutes" sign and climbed my stairs. He was the first and only person to pass through its door since Cédric had helped me install the sort-of bathroom when I moved in. Piotr's pale blue eyes were cautious as I opened my door. He hesitated on the threshold. "There's nothing in here that bites," I said. Inside, he froze again. "Come on, then. The shower's over in that corner. Just take a towel from the shelf on the side." He followed my instructions silently.

While he was in the bathroom, I sat at my table and looked at the lone photo on my cork board. It was a color picture so dominated by grey it looked black and white. The subject was a lime tree, old and leaning, on the side of the road near Hautebranche, on a dark day. It had been heavily trimmed, amputated really, and the branches it had resprouted on one side reminded me of Piotr's hair. The other side was withered. It looked poised between life and death, the winner still undecided.

I looked around the room more generally. At the crates and the mattress, the small refrigerator with the electric heating plates on top. In the days of big-hearted Nigel, this room had been crammed with stuff. He hadn't lived here so used it as storage, usually for other people. When he died, it had taken me a full six months to track down the owners of the overstuffed, springless armchair, the croquet set, the electric keyboard, and the punching ball. The only thing I'd kept was a clunky grey dial-up telephone. It still sat on a crate, perfectly functional. Like everything else in the room. Piotr was wrong to think my room might contain evidence of some dark secret, some great hidden truth about me.

He walked out of the bathroom, his hair wet but springy, and looked me straight in the eye: "Robbed?"

For a moment I didn't answer. I looked around again myself. "Yes," I finally said. "I *was* robbed. But not here. It was elsewhere, a long time ago." Of a father and a sister, of *that* family, and even of its memory.

Off Piotr went to the place de la Concorde, hair sticking out with its natural candor. His absence left a gaping hole, making me aware how much he had become a part not just of the shop but also of my life. I'd allowed him into my inner sanctum; he'd not only witnessed my burgled life but also understood it instinctively. The afternoon hours crept by. Finally I closed early and went upstairs to lie on my mattress until party time.

From floor level I looked again at the photo of the amputated, struggling tree. My affair with photography had begun when I went to the US. Mother had given me some money as a graduation/going-away present, and on an impulse while visiting New York before classes started, I had walked into a camera shop near Times Square and bought myself a used Nikon FM2.

Putting that black box between my eye and the rest of the world was a revelation. It provided a shield between me and the world but also served as a tool for viewing and framing that world. For making sense of it. At the college I signed up for photography and discovered the dark room, into which I could disappear and make images appear on a hitherto blank page. Memory became tangible, an object I could look at with my eyes, hold in my hands, a reality rather than a figment. Photography had, in its way, given me a feeling of coming home.

From the perspective of my mattress, it occurred to me that even its frustrations—the missed or bungled opportunities—suited me. The tortured tree photo was a case in point. Before I could get my camera ready that day, a cyclist hunched over his racer, his bright yellow rain cape billowing around him, had passed in front of the tree. I'd missed the element that would have deepened the picture, multiplied its layers, made it very good instead of just statically okay. Photography is the art of regret. And since in my life generally I had cultivated regret to the state of an art, it was no wonder I felt at home in a form of expression that yes, preserves memory, but also causes constant, aching reminders of all that is missed.

———————

Christmas Eve, an extended version of the Harcourt-Laporte family and the one remaining McFarquhar gathered at the rue de Verneuil for dinner and the opening of presents. Edmond's sister, Clarisse, came with her three children, my stepcousins, and their spouses and children. Then there was Edward and Stephanie and their brood. It was a large gathering, and Mother had to put all the leaves in the dining room table. The children ate in the living room near the tree but away from the Persian carpet.

What worried me this Christmas Eve, of course, was seeing Stephanie with other family members present, her husband/my brother foremost on the list. Electricity between people is palpable, if you're paying attention. Wouldn't someone notice? I always believed my mother noticed lots of things. She just never spoke them aloud. And Edward—wouldn't he sense it, instinctively?

Lisette answered the door, her short round body wrapped in its formal serving wear, black dress and frilly white apron.

"Ah, *Trésor*," she wheezed, reaching up to kiss me. "I was just coming back from the dining room when you rang. There's some Christmas luck. You haven't been here since that dreadful strike began. All those people complaining, when they should be thankful. The French are spoiled rotten. They don't realize how lucky they are, how good their lives are." She wagged her finger at me. "Well, thank goodness it's over." And off she waddled to the kitchen.

Mother's Christmas was a carefully orchestrated Franco-American affair, an interweaving of what she believed to be the best traditions of each culture. The Christmas tree, which always stood in the corner of the room next to a window, was firmly in the American camp. It was huge, ordered specially from "my tree man." I don't know where her tree man got it, but no French person had ever entered the apartment on the rue de Verneuil around Christmastime without remarking on the towering conifer in the corner. When I was small and still excited by Christmas, I loved it. It reminded me of *The Nutcracker* that we'd been to see at the Opéra, and I imagined all sorts of exotic scenes taking place in our living room while I was asleep. But as I got older, the tree embarrassed me in its extravagance. I didn't see why we couldn't be more modest. It was dripping with quaint baubles my mother had bought over the years. Tasteful little white lights draped its thick branches, illuminating the large, sparkling star on the top. When we were small, Edward and I had begged her for some color, some blue and green and red lights, preferably flashing. "When you grow up," she'd answered, unmoved by our pleas, "you can have those dreadful blinking things, for all I care, but here it's white. And white." Then she'd attach another of her precious baubles to a metal hook and place it on a carefully considered bough.

All around the room candles had replaced electric lights, except for two or three discreet, low-wattage lamps strategically placed so no one would trip over a dark chair leg or a small child. The fireplace, rarely used, snapped and crackled with controlled flames. In this dim light the members of my real and imposed family were scattered. The children, Edward and Stephanie's with Step-Tante Clarisse's grandchildren, were buzzing about the tree, speculating on the contents of each present. Mother had forbidden them to touch, so they pointed and got close, then backed away, like visitors in a museum examining a precious work of art. The adults formed little groups, some standing, some sitting. Mother, in another solid American tradition, insisted on serving eggnog. Though I had overheard the French *cousins* complain about its sickeningly thick sweetness, a few polite souls held a glass of the stuff. I imagined them gathering before the party and drawing straws over who would suffer it that year, while the lucky ones sipped whisky or champagne.

"Hello, T," Mother said at my shoulder.

"Mother," I said, turning to kiss her. "My eyes haven't adjusted to the light yet. I didn't see you."

"I thought it was the Christmas spirit you had trouble with." It was Edward, who had crept out of the shadows on my other side. Mother's brow furrowed. Even on Christmas, all her sons could do was spar. Except this evening, wary of provoking him in any way, I didn't jab back.

"Edward, I've put you next to Clarisse again," Mother said. "I hope you don't mind. You cope so much better than anyone else."

"It's good," he said. "You've given me a challenge for the evening. I'll see if I can get a laugh out of her this year." Step-Tante Clarisse, widowed when her three children were teenagers, was a lemon-lipped complainer. Nothing was ever right; her list of woes was endless. She was always harking back to when "*cher Jean*" was alive, and it certainly seemed she hadn't enjoyed a single moment of her existence since his death. Edward, always tempted by a challenge, was the only one who could bear sitting with her for more than the first bite of *foie gras*. Even her very Catholic children and their equally Catholic spouses could only take her in small doses.

"Just say hello to her, T. Just speak to her for a minute," my mother said.

Step-Tante was sitting next to the fire, talking to Jérôme, a son-in-law. "Did you come straight from the garage?" she asked me after I'd leaned down to kiss her sallow cheeks.

"No. Motorists went home early today."

"It just looked as if you didn't have time to change," she said, looking at Jérôme, whose rather weak hand I'd just shaken. "Hasn't your mother ever given you a tie for Christmas?"

"Now, now Belle-Mère," said Jérôme, answering for me with a tense smile, "what's wrong with a dash of Bohemian chic at our family gathering?" After an awkward silence, Jérôme pressed on with the subject that really interested him. "You were saying we could, perhaps, use the chalet in February?"

"Well," said Step-Tante Clarisse in a drawn-out, put-upon voice. "I'll have to see with Audrey and Philippe. I may have already promised it to them. It's so hard to keep track."

"Excuse me," I said, turning away. "I'll let you finish your negotiation." Every Christmas Clarisse's children seemed to be vying for use of her one desirable asset, a ski chalet in high-end Méribel. Though not having been there herself in over twenty years, she kept it on for them, she said. And there, at least, was one thing Clarisse seemed to enjoy: watching her children squabble over who would get the chalet when.

"Such a disagreeable young man," she said loudly as I walked away. "So unlike his brother . . ." her words faded into the general din.

Then there she was. Stephanie in a red velvet dress, short and form-fitting. It showed off her figure perfectly, but of course she never wore anything that didn't. She had on high heels, which made her tower over Edward. Instead of desire, I felt a sinking heart. Her appearance jarred me. The heels were too high, too pointy. As for the red dress, it may have been festive, but it didn't go with her hair and skin coloring, and it was so short, that on second glance, I saw that it almost managed to make her long legs look chunky.

She hadn't noticed me, being too involved in conversation with Clarisse's son François, a stiff but brilliant civil servant. I watched her shift her weight from one pointed heel to another, watched her smooth her hair back on her head in what looked to me this evening like a flirtatious manner. Every gesture in fact seemed calculated, stagey. I had always seen her as the exquisite victim of my family, of her life in France. What had formed this crack in my vision? It seemed the three weeks of getting to know every inch of her physical body had also, without my being conscious of it, given me a more nuanced and certainly less adoring picture of her as a whole.

Mother began herding us through to the dining room and the enlarged oval table set for twelve. As usual, on the table were the spit-polished silver cutlery, the crystal glasses, the jugs of water and decanters of wine, all dimly glittering in more candlelight. Each place, with its name card indicating our seating, had a small serving of *foie gras* in front of it, the first in a long line of courses. It was the same menu every year. Next would come the seafood salad, then a turkey and its trimmings (Mother's only concession to American tradition on the food front), then mixed greens and cheese, and finally the over-rich *bûche de Noël*.

And just like every year, I sat next to one of my stepcousins and another of my stepcousin's wives, neither of whom I had a sentence in common with. One lived in Versailles; the other led a mirror existence in the *16ème arrondissement*. Both were full-time mothers. They spent the whole meal talking across me. During the *foie gras*, they discussed New Year's plans. During the seafood salad, it was a friend they had in common, though "friend" was a peculiar term, given that they took turns sniping at the woman, whose greatest sin appeared to be sending a babysitter to pick up her children at Boy Scouts, instead of coming herself. And for the next three courses, they talked competitively about their children's strengths and weaknesses in excruciatingly minute detail. Occasionally one of them would remember my presence and put a hand on my arm to exclaim: "Oh, this must be such a bore for a bachelor like you!"

But their chatter was just a background buzz in my ears. My attention was mostly focused on Edward and Stephanie across the table. Though he had coaxed a smile out of Step-Tante Clarisse, his jaw was grinding away and he looked as if his mind were miles away. Stephanie was between François the *fonctionnaire* and Philippe, *beau* but not very bright. Both men were fawning all over her and she was flirting back, splashing around that fruit-slice smile with affected abandon.

The meal finally ended. People regrouped, some staying in the dining room, others moving back to the living room. I opted for the sofa in front of the fireplace, where the children were preparing to roast marshmallows, another American custom my mother had chosen to import for the festivities. Leave it to her to come up with a dozen straight sticks, their ends whittled to a pencil point, in the middle of the city. After putting the older children in charge of the marshmallow roasting, she went off to attend to the next stage of her party, the serving of *digestifs*, coffee, and tisanes.

"Hello," Stephanie said, plopping down next to me on the sofa, crossing one overexposed leg over the other.

"Enjoying the family Christmas?" I answered.

"I always find roasting marshmallows in the middle of the city a bit much," she said.

"You looked entertained at dinner."

"You didn't."

"I didn't think you'd noticed," I said, immediately regretting the self-pitying tone. She fiddled with the large diamond ring on her finger. Its cold facets caught the light and twinkled. The feeling of fusion that had seemed so permanent when she was lying in my arms was completely gone. I felt nothing but a mild desire for her to move away.

"The women in this country are unbearable. At least the men can talk about something other than *les enfants*," she said affectedly through her nose.

At that moment her youngest *enfant* Henri started howling. His marshmallow had caught fire. Though his sister Caroline had blown it out, it was too late. The puffy white ball was now a charred and shriveled blob. "Oh, Henri," Stephanie said. "It's just a marshmallow." But he wouldn't stop crying, and everyone in the room was beginning to look. She stood up and grabbed his arm: "Would you stop it?" and that only made him cry harder. By now Edward was there. He scooped up his son and whisked him from the room, Henri still clutching his stick with the burnt blob at the end. Stephanie didn't follow. Instead she looked at me and shrugged her shoulders: "What do you expect, keeping children up until midnight. He's overtired."

My tension-averse mother began herding us around the tree to open presents. BP, the Beneficent Patriarch, sat in a chair, and the children handed him presents, which he distributed after reading aloud the name on the card. Not long into this ordeal, Edward reappeared with Henri, who had stopped crying but looked fragile. He was immediately handed a present, and the burnt marshmallow was consigned to history. Edward looked at Stephanie, but she didn't look back. She was hovering at the edge of the circle, behind Step-Tante Clarisse. It was dark, and all I could really see was her red dress. When she was called for a present, she came forward, then retreated into the shadows. With all the children, the distribution took forever, but finally it was over and I would soon be outside with a cigarette, my new sweater, and a gift certificate to the FNAC multimedia store. Mother had organized the children to collect the tossed wrapping paper. She looked tired and distracted and for once didn't even ask hopefully if I had plans for New Year.

I went to Mother and Edmond's bedroom to collect my jacket. While I was sifting through the pile of coats, Stephanie appeared at the door.

"I just had to tell you—to tell someone," she said, stepping toward me. "There's a lot more going on here tonight than you might imagine."

"There's always a lot more going on here," I said.

"Didn't you think Edward looked funny?"

"What do you mean?" I asked, beginning to feel uneasy.

"Tense, I mean."

"What are you trying to say? He doesn't know, does he?"

"No, no," she said dismissively. "Edward is about to merge Frères Laporte with another firm. Or get eaten by them. The other one is bigger."

"You're kidding."

"Of course I'm not kidding. Edmond is dead against it. He's never liked the buyer, but he's too far out of the picture to have any real influence. Edward says it's the only way they can keep going. And at least, you'll be happy to hear," she said with an ironic smile, "he'll be able to keep something of the name. Frères Laporte will become Laporte-Faucher."

I shook my head. "Why didn't you tell me about this sooner? It must have been simmering for months."

"Yeah." She shrugged. "But as you might remember, Edward and I don't communicate much these days, and I stopped paying attention ages ago. Anyway, it's been making him edgier and more preoccupied than ever and I've really just had enough," she said, her head slumping. I put the cigarette I had just rolled into my left hand. I put my right hand on the small of her back. The same part I had been so fond of caressing. And at that very moment, Edward's face appeared in the doorway. Though tonight I had meant this as a gesture of comfort, not lust, a man's hand does not find itself just above a woman's buttocks unless it has already groped the same area with less platonic intent. Edward's eyes flickered as he pieced together hitherto unconnected shreds of evidence. In a flash he knew the whole story. I removed my hand, and the three of us stood frozen, as if time had stopped. Of course, in a way, it had. Like a photo, this was an image that each of us would hold in our memories forever.

Though he said nothing, Edward's face crumpled. He pivoted and walked back down the hall. Stephanie plopped down on the bed and shook her head as she looked at the floor. She had a little smile on her face that still troubles me. Although it could have been a nervous reaction to extreme emotion, I have never been able to completely convince myself that the smile didn't hold a note of triumph.

I grabbed my jacket and skulked away from the rue de Verneuil.

PART II

ONE

I WILL NEVER forget the look on my brother's face. Nothing, not even the five years during which I didn't get so much as a glimpse of the real Edward, dimmed the memory of those features crumpling on his face like an aluminum can under a heavy boot heel. It would flash in my mind's eye in the middle of the street, appear in my dreams at night. And each time something close to panic would rise up and engulf me. Panic and bewilderment that I, who had held myself to be so morally superior—basically to the whole world—had been capable of such treachery. After the fact, I simply couldn't imagine that I had done what I had done.

I couldn't get the look on Stephanie's face out of my mind either. Edward's crushed can versus her upturned lips. I continued to wonder if she hadn't engineered the whole thing, if the affair with me hadn't been another attempt to win that competition she always felt they were locked in. To trounce him once and for all. Of course, on one level what else had I been doing but paying back my brother, trying to make him suffer, for changing his name, for generally enjoying his life.

Once or twice in the months following the scene in the bedroom I tried to contact Edward, but not surprisingly he wouldn't talk to me. Just as I wouldn't talk to Stephanie. At the shop, I made Piotr answer the phone; at home, I never picked up. It was Mother who first provided a laconic account of the *dénouement* between Edward and Stephanie. A short separation led to a quick divorce. Stephanie moved back to New York, leaving the children with Edward. "For the time being, they're better off here," Mother had said. "Because she will be alone and looking for work. She recognizes that too." Mother could no longer bring herself to say her former daughter-in-law's name; I don't know if or how she referred to me. Though she had never liked Stephanie and her predictions had proven correct, circumstances had taken any gloating out of her I-told-you-so sails.

As it turned out, the only "affair" in Edward's life at the time was the merger of Frères Laporte and Jean-Paul Faucher. Though he only stayed in the reconfigured firm for a few years—it was then gobbled up by an even larger bank—Edward, according to Mother, had carried off the deal admirably. Even Edmond had finally admitted it was the best solution, in this new world where small but good is usually not good enough. Where size and weight are what tend to carry the day.

After three rocky years, Edward's life got back on course. He went to work for an American investment bank with offices all over the world, and he got remarried to a younger French woman, Anne-Sophie. From the scant information I was fed, she seemed to combine all three of Mother's precious Bs: beauty, brains, and breeding. Besides coming from a large family of aristocrats (ten children, and so what if they'd fallen on hard times), she was working on an advanced degree in urban history. Although Mother didn't specifically say it, I assumed she was pretty. Edward couldn't have changed that much. Besides taking on three stepchildren, she produced one of her own in swift order, making them a reconstituted family of six. "Anne-Sophie still works," Mother told me, "but she's got her priorities straight. The family comes first."

Stephanie's childless return to New York was taken as confirmation of her inherent depravation by people who had known her in Paris. Stories emerged illustrating what an inconsiderate wife and an even worse mother she had been. Even I could see that she had not been the most maternal of mothers, but I had trouble thinking of her as totally heartless. Practically speaking, as Mother had pointed out, hadn't she in fact made the right decision? Wasn't it better for the children to have stayed here? The letter she sent me didn't really answer the question.

New York, September 12, 1996

Dear Trevor,

Since you never answered my phone calls, I feel the need to write. It has hurt me to think that you are just like everybody else in that cursed city. Judging me, despising everything about me.

Granted, I am not proud of the way things ended, but the marriage was doomed. In the end, the only thing Edward and I could agree on was that we should call it quits. I couldn't muster any love, and he couldn't summon any forgiveness. But no matter what all those dreadful people in Paris say about me, it was not easy to leave my kids behind. I did it because I had to get out of that place—me as the expatriate wife, the nonworking mother, the bumbling speaker of French—I had no positive identity. It was all wrong. I did what was best for the kids. At least for the moment.

I'm here in a one-bedroom apartment in Brooklyn, the only place I can afford right now. It's a pleasant street, tree-lined and cobbled. All the low buildings look safe and trouble-free. They open onto the street like a trusting child—just the opposite of the walled world of Paris. Though I know I'm in the right place, it's funny how those coded doors have left their mark. The eager overtures of my new neighbors make me uncomfortable. I don't like being called by my first name quite so quickly. Experience always alters you. Right now it's mostly left me feeling dulled, like tarnished metal.

I'm looking for a job and am hoping that will re-polish my outlook on life. I must say, when I put myself together in the morning for an interview, it feels right. Those Wall Street towers make me tingle in a way Notre Dame never could. A couple firms sound interested. Something will work out. And then I'll see about the kids.

So that's the way things stand with me. I hope at least you understand.

Love, Stephanie

"You would have thought," Viviane said, taking off her glasses to wipe her teary eyes, "that she could have put up with Notre Dame for a few more years. There must be plenty of American law offices in Paris." Viviane, her most desperate wish for a child still unfulfilled, could not fathom a mother's desertion, even if it proved temporary. How could this woman, who had popped out three children with no more effort than as many forehands in tennis, walk away from her perfect good fortune? Cédric shook his head: "She should have been born a man."

Whatever her appropriate gender, it was competition and high achievement that really made her tick. It was why she'd never had close women friends; it was what allowed her to leave her children in Paris while she pursued her True Purpose elsewhere. I guess. What did I know about marriage or motherhood? About family life? I finally wrote her a short card, wishing her well. It was all I could muster.

If the Harcourt-Laportes weren't going to forgive me, my friends took me back. "Affairs are no more or less than a symptom of a disease that is already festering," Viviane said. "Though you, Trevor, showed yourself to be just as sick as Edward and Stephanie's marriage."

"Exactly," echoed Cédric. "As if we needed any more proof that this perfectly balanced life you talk about living is a complete sham."

===========

While I continued to rent the room upstairs, Mélo-Vélo was taken over by a mobile phone store. Not surprising, given that portables were suddenly everywhere, addictive as a drug and producing similarly mindless behavior. "I'm just walking up the steps of the métro," I would hear people saying into their phones. "Now I'm on the sidewalk." Or "I'm standing in front of the cereal section at the supermarket. Coffee behind me." In one short year the barrier between the brain and the mouth had been removed completely, which to my mind begged the question of how technology could really constitute an improvement, a sign of progress, for the human race.

The paint of Nigel's orange storefront was stripped, revealing an even older façade underneath. Mélo-Vélo had previously been a restaurant, Chez Tante Louise. Maybe it was in that incarnation that the upstairs and downstairs had been disconnected. But I would never know, and now no one else would either, as the mobile phone company vigorously stripped that layer of paint too. But not before I preserved Tante Louise on film, even giving her a frame and a place on the bare wall of my cell. The new storefront was refitted with a metallic surface, painted a glossy brown. The inside, too, was completely gutted, then replastered, repainted, relit, and redecorated with functional, nondescript counters, fake wood paneling, and powder blue wall-to-wall carpet.

The transformation would have been more painful to watch if I hadn't been so busy getting the fish smell out of the new Mélo-Vélo. My profits had kept pace with the new bicycle lanes being built all over the city, and I'd decided to look for more space, to keep Nigel's legacy alive, since what else was I going to do? I found it on another market street: the rue de Seine, heart of the Left Bank and right down the street from the gallery where my photo exhibition would have occurred all those years ago. When I'd been a student at the Sorbonne, I'd often done my shopping there, with Jacqueline, on the way home to my *chambre de bonne* on the rue de l'Université. It was, in fact, no more than a fifteen-minute walk from the rue de Verneuil.

This once up-market street had fallen on hard times around then. One family-owned shop after another had closed—the cheese shop, the butcher, the *traiteur*—leaving boarded-up, peeling façades that I also catalogued on film. All that was left for shopping was a fruit and vegetable stand owned by the supermarket that kept changing names as it was gobbled up by ever-shifting, ever-larger chains. But it was still a street that got a lot of human traffic, and even if the rent was a bit steep, I took it. Contrary to the phone company, I left the blue mosaic façade with *Poisson-nerie* written in white tiles as it was. After Piotr and his Polish construction-working friends fixed up the interior in a similar fashion to the old Mélo-Vélo, I put up Nigel's old orange sign underneath the *Poissonnerie* tiles. The color combination wasn't great, but keeping the history apparent was more important to me than aesthetic harmony.

Though slightly smaller than the rue des Martyrs Mélo-Vélo, the new shop seemed roomier since I could spill out onto the pedestrian street. Every day I would put a line of bicycles out, running a huge steel cable through the frames so they wouldn't get stolen. Being more noticeable and better situated, we had more customers than ever. Despite the growing rage for huge sports stores that also sold and repaired bicycles, we managed if not to thrive, at least to make ends meet comfortably. Somehow down here on the Left Bank, the well-heeled population was still attracted to the neighborhood *boutique*.

Things changed for Piotr too. Not long after we moved to the rue de Seine, the right-wing administration, thoroughly disgraced by the strike fiasco, was replaced by the Socialists, and the new government instituted an amnesty program for illegal immigrants. "Clandestine aliens" who could prove they had a job and a stable living situation—the paradox of which made no one smile—could come out of the woodwork and apply for legal status, *une carte de séjour*. I did all the paperwork for Piotr, and he became a bona fide resident. Of course, helping him meant that I then had a legal employee who, under rigid French labor laws, would cost a fortune to fire. I did suggest—for his sake—that with papers, he could surely find a better-paying job. But he answered with a shake of his bristly head: "I'm good here." Then he turned back to work with the confident air of a man who was playing his cards right, who was holding on to his ace. And I reasoned with myself lugubriously, since I no longer had a family, why not adopt a struggling Pole.

During the legalization process, Piotr also got married to Wanda, the friend who had arrived by bus at the place de la Concorde that fateful Christmas Eve. She'd stayed, finding her own illegal job taking care of children and cleaning house. I went to their wedding service at the Polish church on the rue Saint-Honoré. After the ceremony, at the reception, I drank too much vodka, while a group of excited Poles told me in broken French what was wrong with their country and why they'd had to leave it for France. Passion for their homeland was as boundless as their capacity for vodka, and it contributed to the general good feeling of the wedding. By the time I wobbled home, even marriage seemed less of a doomed institution to me.

———

After Piotr's wedding, life settled into its new rut. The years ticked by, the century, even the millennium changed. As time passed, scars formed. After a year or so of living like a monk in my cell, my celibate state came to an end. Paulina and Jennifer were eventually replaced by Marlène and Marie, then Joséphine and Claire.

Work, women, weekends at Hautebranche. Hours on my mattress reading books. The main difference from my previous rut, besides the absence of my family, was that I now had to commute, a journey that I made on foot, right through the heart of the city: from the banking and insurance district, past the *Opéra*, in between the Louvre and the Tuileries, then across the pont des Arts to the rue de Seine. Sometimes on my way home, with nothing else to do, my eye would catch a courtyard, a passage, an unusual building, and I'd veer off course to have a look. Take a photo.

The only other time I'd explored the nooks and crannies of the city like that was the August I'd spent in Paris recovering from my bicycle accident. My family had gone to Long Island and Lisette to Brittany. The first couple of days I only left my bedroom to eat what Lisette had prepared for me. Then I began wandering the apartment, lingering at my mother and Edmond's well-stocked bookshelves, paying attention for the first time to the details of my mother's boxes, hoping to find in them some answers to questions about what went on inside that obsessively private but devoted person. She had stayed at my bedside day and night, Lisette told me, even getting the hospital to set up a cot for her;

I had opened my eyes from the coma to her worried face and her muttered, "Thank God."

Once I'd eaten through the contents of the small freezer, I was forced to venture into the streets. The search for an open *boulangerie*, never an easy undertaking in August, led me quite a way. Which in turn led me farther, for a bit longer, the next day. Paris is at her most seductive when the *Parisiens* are away, and I was drawn right into her ample skirts. The buildings themselves were making me feel better, so that even when the people were back and my physical injuries mostly healed, I kept walking. It was in fact during one of those urban rambles that I'd returned to Nigel's shop, where I had bought my now crumpled green Raleigh and where I now found a Help Wanted sign.

All these years later the beauty of the city was again proving salutary, therapeutic. The color of the stone or the uneven symphony of buildings jutting up around Montmartre; the sun reflecting in an incendiary orange off the wrought-iron balustrades or a glimpse at a bold cloud, its fifteen shades of grey exploding above a line of zinc roofs. Some visual detail always pulled me out of myself and improved my humor. And unlike that earlier time, now I was taking photos of what I saw, capturing some of that beauty.

Shortly after the move, the Rendez-Vous changed hands. The new owners were sour and taciturn and no one liked them. Jean-Jacques left and went to work at a restaurant in the suburbs, closer to home. Dogs were no longer welcome, so Marcel became a regular elsewhere. Madame Picquot and the other concierges, or what was left of them—every year another retired and was not replaced—often met now on the street. And I began frequenting a place near the new shop, the Relais des Artistes, named for its proximity to the Beaux Arts art school and the many galleries in the area. The Relais regulars were more intellectually inclined and refined, the interior more charming and the food better than the Rendez-Vous des Martyrs, I had to admit, but part of me still regretted the loss of the old place, the changes in the old *quartier*.

One day in early February, five years after my disgrace, I was on my way to lunch at the Relais. As usual, some homeless men were camped in front of the supermarket, where the greatest human traffic flowed and where they could sit under the overhang in bad weather. They lingered there with the ease of guests at a cocktail party. Though most came and went, Michel seemed a permanent fixture. I often chatted with him and gave him a coin or two.

He was at his usual post with two of his buddies. And a black-haired dog at the end of a leash. As I approached, the animal unfurled from its sleepy ball, jumped to its feet, and greeted me like a long-lost friend. "Where did this come from?" I asked.

"I'm babysitting," Michel said, his bad teeth grinning through his dirty beard.

"Don't let him watch too much television," I said, which gave them all a laugh.

At the Relais, I sat down in my usual seat near the back. "I've got a great *faux filet au poivre* today," said Alain, who owned the café with his wife Nicole. He talked too much and was always trying to sell me something. On bad days it could irritate me into buying a sandwich at the bakery for lunch.

"Did you know Michel's got a dog?" I asked.

"That won't last long," he said. Along with his big mouth, Alain had a big heart. He passed on leftover food to Michel and his friends, as well as letting Michel use the Relais as his postal address. "It's unbelievable." Alain would shake his head. "The guy gets all sorts of mail—including handouts from the government!"

"Says he's got a job babysitting."

Alain shook his head. "I'll get you that steak, rare, the way you like it."

I ate my lunch and read, then walked back to the shop. The dog was gone. "Finished work?" I said to Michel.

"Here's my paycheck," he said, opening up a new can of beer.

In the following days, the dog was with him more and more, until one day, it became a permanent fixture. Dog paraphernalia began to appear: a mat, a rubber toy, cans of dog food and bones from the Relais. Alain told me: "He's got some ridiculous story. Something about a rich lady and a nasty mother-in-law."

"Still babysitting?" I asked one evening a couple of weeks later. By this time of day, Michel was off beer and on to cheap whisky. He held a half-liter bottle in one hand and the dog's red leash looped through the other. By now the dog's black fur had turned ash grey, but it looked oblivious, wagging its tail from the filthy tartan mat at me.

"Permanently," he said with his head swaying slightly as he looked up at me. "She's mine."

"And how did this change of ownership occur?"

Michel took a swig of whisky. "She never came back."

"Who never came back?"

"The lady. The one who looked too *bourge* even for this neighborhood. Skirt, stockings, silk scarf tied in a knot around her neck. Certainly not the type you'd expect to stop and talk to me. Much less leave her dog with." Michel paused for more refreshment.

"And?"

"One day this lady asks me to hold on to the dog while she's in the supermarket, in exchange for a modest remuneration, enough for a nice big bottle of beer. So of course I say yes. Then a couple of days later, she comes back and asks me to take the dog for the morning. Says she has an appointment and every time she leaves the dog alone, it tears something up or leaves a mess on the floor. She doesn't look like the type who'd like a mess." He took another swig. "It goes on like this—her dumping the dog on me, paying me a little better each time. I'm thinking, I practically got a job here—first time in fifteen years. Except I don't have to go anywhere or do anything but hold on to this leash. She even starts talking to me a bit, in a nervous kind of way, looking around to see who's watching. She tells me the dog was a gift from her mother-in-law to her children, a 'surprise' Christmas present. 'A dirty trick, is what it was,' the woman said. Then one day, she never came back. I waited and waited, even attached the dog and went inside. Nowhere to be found. She must have snuck out the side door. So I go back out to the dog and look for a tag. Instead I find a little pouch with a five hundred franc note folded up in it. I haven't seen a bill that size for years." He shrugged. "And I never see the woman again."

"That's quite a story," I said.

"True, every word of it." He patted the dog's head. "Really, this is just what a guy like me needs. I've had much better luck out here in the street. People feel sorry for the dog, so they give me money. I should have thought of it myself."

"Crazy," I said, shaking my head, giving him a few coins.

That evening I made my way to the Bastille and an evening meeting with one of my current girlfriends, Claire. She lived on a small street off the rue de la Roquette. It was an area that had been working class, like the rue des Martyrs, until about fifteen years earlier, when artists and the trendy professional classes began to discover its warren of narrow passages, lined with potential studios and dramatic spaces for living. It was just the right amount of rundown plus charm to equal chic. Claire was a newspaper journalist I'd met through former girlfriend Paulina. She lived in a building that, despite the newly polished *tomettes* tile floor and renovated timbered staircase, had fallen lines everywhere. Nothing was straight, and everything was cramped, from the narrow, uneven steps, to Claire's helter-skelter apartment.

Until a couple of weeks ago, I'd been trying to ease off Claire. She was almost forty, and talk about her biological clock had been getting too frequent for comfort. But then things at work had picked up, and she seemed to have forgotten about the baby business. Once again, like me, all she wanted was some company for the night. As she opened the door, a thick mix of cigarette smoke and incense was released. She was talking on the telephone, so I cleared a place for myself among the magazines and newspapers lying on the black leather sofa. From there I could see more mess, down the narrow corridor that was lined with tumbling stacks of books. At first the disorder in her life and her inability to throw anything away had seemed charming; now it felt suffocating.

While she talked to a colleague about another woman colleague they both seemed to feel threatened by, I was thinking that I should have been spending this evening with Joséphine. The soft and comforting kindergarten teacher was what I needed, not Claire the thin and neurotic chain-smoker. February, with its short, dark days, is a nasty little month. Always depressing. Tidy Joséphine might have made me feel better. But it was too late now; I was stuck listening to complaints about a young upstart journalist who was using her feminine wiles rather than professional talent to worm her way into the good graces of their older, male editor. "She couldn't write her way out of a paper bag," Claire said not long before she hung up and curled her small-boned body on my lap. "Sorry," she said. "There's this new *girl* at work causing all sorts of problems. Thinks she's God's gift to the written word but spends most of her time striking attractive poses for our editor, who seems to have forgotten he hired her not to model for him but to string coherent sentences together." She kissed me and laughed. "Reminds me a bit of myself fifteen years ago." An arch comment that reminded me why I liked Claire.

Then she was off: "What shall we do tonight? I meant to pick something up on the way home, but I was still turning over in my mind the story I finished this afternoon. I'm not sure I got the conclusion right. There's a new Tex-Mex restaurant on the rue de Charonne. Our food critic gave it a good write-up, but I think it's very noisy. Or we could go Chinese—I haven't eaten Chinese in a while, but I'm not sure I can deal with MSG tonight. Or maybe we should go to a movie and grab a bite afterward at this wine bar I tried with my friend Gabrielle last week. That's probably the best idea," she said, leaning over the cluttered coffee table to rummage for another cigarette. "There's the new Woody Allen, which of course I have to see."

I rolled my eyes. "Like every person who lives in this city. What is it with all of you?"

"He's brilliant. And you're too critical. Have you got any other ideas?"

"No."

"Well, let's go. It's playing at the Bastille."

"Good idea, I guess," and I waved my hand in front of my face. "The smoke is driving me crazy."

"You converts are always the worst," she said, cigarette hanging from her mouth.

The winter of my disgrace I got a severe case of the flu and was in bed for over a week, too sick even to smoke, and when I got better, I never started again. Now, the smell of cigarette smoke not only irritated me, it positively repulsed me, and I complained about it often.

"Unbearable, actually," she added as she grabbed her bag and coat.

Perhaps. But what a pleasure it had been after several non-smoking months to start smelling the world around me again, whether it was the newspaper ink on the just-delivered stacks at the kiosk at Notre Dame de Lorette, or the crisp air on the edge of an autumn morning. For the first time, too, I realized how strongly

Mélo-Vélo smelled of rubber and grease, how that smell was a distinguishing feature, rather than a vague background presence.

This olfactory reawakening released long-forgotten memories of other smells. I remembered how the reigning odor at the rue de Verneuil was wax, which was not surprising, given how ardently Lisette pushed that foot-brush over the wide wooden floor planks, and food—a cake being baked for tea, a roast for Sunday lunch. I went even farther back, to our house in Connecticut, which smelled of old wood fires and sun-bleached fabric. When we arrived there for a weekend or holiday, the scent was like a greeting, a welcome. Just the opposite of our first Paris apartment, which was furnished and smelled foreign. That alien odor got mingled with the fear I felt at my new life, and to this day a whiff of a similar smell makes my stomach clench, my heart quicken.

Anyway, Claire's smoking annoyed me to the point that even the crammed cinema felt a relief.

"Remarkable," Claire said as the last credits to *Small Time Crooks* scrolled by and the lights came back on. "Woody Allen's brilliance never fades."

"The jokes are stale," I said as we put on our coats. "The Woody Allen character too. By now it all seems derivative."

"Well, you never like anything," she said, shaking her head. "So I refuse to take you seriously."

The wine bar was dark and rustic, with plain wooden tables and candles in green glass jars. Taped jazz played quietly in the background. After a couple of glasses of Madiran and a plate of *charcuterie*, I began to enjoy myself. Claire didn't eat much, but she smoked and drank with abandon. While the wine made me more talkative, it had the opposite effect on her. She slowed down and stopped gurgling like a mountain stream. I told her about Michel and the dog; she cited figures on the homeless and abandoned animals from articles she'd written on both subjects in the last few years. We talked about politics and a book she'd given me to read. Once she regulated her flow, Claire was a good conversationalist. She was smart and knowledgeable about an impressive array of topics. I went home with her.

But the next morning I woke up with my left leg tangled in her disheveled sheets and my right arm hanging over the edge of the bed. Claire, as always, had spread her small body diagonally across the mattress, and I was close to rolling off. My head felt heavy and in the wrong place as I lifted it from the pillow. I looked down at her, thin arms splayed, full lips parted in deep sleep. In the blurry half-light, she was delicately beautiful. But she wasn't that interested in sex and was only fun to talk to some of the time. I took a quick shower to wash off the smell of smoke on my skin and in my hair, and dried myself with a musty, damp towel. Claire slept on. She could never rouse herself before eight, and I could never lie still beyond seven. I slipped out the door. Though there had been no more mention of biological clocks, life with Claire was winding down.

It had rained in the night and the slick streets shone like sheets of ice under the artificial light. The air was sharp and quickly worked to clear my head as I walked through the dark streets to Mélo-Vélo.

The trouble with striking Claire from the list was that I would be left with only soft Joséphine, who seemed content with her life as surrogate mother for rotating classes of four-year-olds. She never spoke about the desire to have her own. To her, biological meant *biologique*, all-natural food. Herbal teas and pulses, yoga classes and weekend seminars for homeopathic healing. That was what made Joséphine tick. Going to bed with her was like rolling in feathers plucked from free-range chickens fattened on fertilizer-free grains. Just the opposite of Claire, but a little too soft and earnest.

While crossing the Pont Neuf on that chilly morning, I could just see the top of the giant Ferris wheel that had been put up for the Millennium on the place de la Concorde and which the owner was now refusing to take down, despite the city's repeated demands. My love life was just like that wheel: a woman got on for a few spins, pausing at the top to take in the view before being deposited at the bottom so the next passenger could climb on board. These were the exact circumstances of the life to which I'd aspired on the rue des Martyrs: predictable days, uncluttered with people, except on my terms. I'd even managed to rid myself of the family I'd found so tiresome and to become a solvent shopkeeper. Yet here I was, middle-aged and drying myself with somebody else's smelly towel. Creeping out the door to walk across town in the dark, to eat breakfast alone in a malodorous café. This predictable, independent life had brought me no inner peace whatsoever.

By the time I got to the Relais, the sun was beginning to appear on the horizon, and the sky was a deep blue-black. The rain had cleared the air, and it would be a crisp day, where the sun would shine at its oblique, uncompromising winter angle. Perhaps at midday there would even be a hint of spring nestled in the breeze. But the prospect of sun or the change of season brought me no joy that morning. I was beginning to think that nothing could.

TWO

MIDDAY, SANDWICH IN my hand, I was walking back to the shop, and I noticed one of Michel's homeless friends holding the dog at the end of the leash. He was pacing back and forth, as if he were the trapped animal.

"Where's Michel?" I asked.

The man stopped pacing. "He's in the slammer. And I'm stuck with this." He gave a tug at the leash; the dog looked up and wagged its tail. "Do you realize it's almost three, and I haven't had so much as a beer? Because of the dog." He gave the leash another tug. "But I can't take it much longer." He practically hopped from one foot to the other in laceless boots that flapped underneath blue-and-yellow-striped trousers, both too short and too tight. "There are limits to friendship."

"What happened?"

"Last night we were celebrating his monthly money, when these two strangers came up to us with their own bottle. They said they were Ukrainians, but who knows. One guy didn't speak any French, but he did all the talking, while his friend translated. It put me to sleep, but when I open my eyes, Michel has his knife on the guy."

"Michel carries a knife?"

"Of course. Anyway, he's screaming: 'Give me my money back!' The Ukrainian, whose hand is already bleeding, screams back in whatever language they speak there, while he tries to get free. Then the police come trotting up the street in their tight-assed uniforms and pull them apart. The French-speaking friend is long gone, so the police don't have much luck getting the story. Instead they have Michel on one side screaming about getting his money back, and the Ukrainian blabbering who knows what on the other. They haul them both off, each one still kicking and screaming like cats. And I get stuck with the mutt. What am I supposed to do with a dog? This is too much stress for me. You got a cigarette?" I shook my head, and he started patting his pockets. "Can you hold this?" he asked.

"Sure," I said, taking the lead. "How long do you think Michel will be in for?" I was still thinking about that knife.

"I don't know," he said, lighting a limp cigarette that he had pulled gingerly from his tattered corduroy jacket. "He's had knife trouble before. Well, I'll be seeing you." He exhaled, then turned and walked away from me.

"What about the dog?" I called stupidly. It was pretty obvious what-about-the-dog.

"I'll try and find out when Michel will be back," he said with a broad smile that exposed a line of remarkably white teeth in the tangle of his red beard.

I looked down at the dog. It wagged its tail, nudged my leg with its snout, and stared hopefully at my sandwich, but I was frozen to the spot. What was I going to do with a dog? After several minutes it finally occurred to me that Piotr would probably be delighted to take it. Since Michel had got the dog, he'd always stopped and given its ears a rub. He'd told me halting stories about his favorite animals on the farm. It would only be until Michel got out of jail anyway. I picked up its grimy bed and bowl and marched back to the shop.

Piotr was sweeping the floor with his back to us as we walked in. When the dog saw the broom it lunged, pulling me off balance. Muttering something in Polish, Piotr looked up at me with his pale wide eyes. "Michel's dog."

"I know that. How would you like to take care of it?" Piotr had put down his broom and was squatting next to the dog, rubbing its ears. "Just until Michel gets back," I said.

"Where's Michel?"

"In prison," I said casually, as if he'd gone on a short holiday.

"Michel?"

"He stabbed a Ukrainian. Or some foreigner." Piotr grimaced. "Don't take it personally—I don't think it was a Pole. The guy tried to take his money. Now what about you taking the dog. Wouldn't Wanda like that?"

Piotr's face dropped. "No," he answered. "Remember the cat?" My heart sank. Wanda had found a kitten in the street and had brought it home, lavishing attention on it. But the owner of their small studio lived right underneath them and watched their every move. He would hear nothing of a cat in his place, and they had to get rid of it. Wanda, Piotr had told me in the same flat voice, had wept like a baby.

"Well, what am I going to do with it?" I asked, beginning to feel desperate.

"Her," Piotr said. The dog was pulling on a rag while he held the other end.

"How about using it to guard the shop at night," I said.

"Not nice," Piotr shook his head. "And look." The dog now had complete possession of the rag and was looking playfully at him—looking, in fact, as cute and harmless as a stuffed toy. Watchdog did seem a bit of a stretch.

So that evening I walked it back to the rue des Martyrs, coaxing it away from smells, nudging it back to its feet when it lay down, with a resolute look of "Don't rush me" or "I don't want to go this way; I want to go that way." It whimpered all night, when it wasn't scratching itself. Michel had obviously had no reason to house-train the dog, and it left an unspeakable mess in a corner of my room, during the short time I managed to get some sleep. At six a smelly, wet tongue ended that fleeting state of bliss.

Later in the morning, after a tortuous walk back to Mélo-Vélo, I phoned the closest vet. It had continued to scratch itself with a vigorous, whooshing sound reminiscent of the foot-brush that Lisette used to polish the floors. And the messes it deposited were of a nauseating consistency. The vet, who seemed amused when I described the circumstances of my new charge, poked and prodded, looked it up and down, and confirmed the dog was home to a broad array of parasites—fleas, earwigs, intestinal worms—and had a staph infection all over its belly. After giving it three shots, she prescribed treatments that cost a fortune. She insisted that there be no canned food. "You're asking for gum problems later on," she said. I said: "There is not going be a 'later.' Not one involving me anyway," but I bought the *croquettes* she suggested anyway.

From that sunny afternoon in February, the dog nosed and butted its way into my life, demanding adjustment after adjustment to my calibrated days. In fact, I remember nothing about the month that followed except dog care. Pills that the dog wouldn't swallow until Viviane, whom I consulted urgently and frequently, told me to try sticking them in *Apéricubes*—small, individually wrapped squares of highly processed cream cheese. With cotton swabs for babies (extra-large ends), I cleaned the ears of black, smelly wax left by the earwigs, before dripping liquid down the Eustachian tubes, while she wriggled and resisted. But that was nothing compared to the baths for the staph infection. After the first treatment she was on to me, and I had to chase her around the room like a contestant in a greased pig contest to get her in the shower. Water went everywhere as I administered vast quantities of prohibitively expensive medicated shampoo onto the thick coat of fur.

But when I went back to the vet after a month, she nodded approvingly. The dog's various ills were cured; her black coat gleamed.

"She's a beautiful dog," she said, pulling up her ear. "I can't figure out why she's not tattooed."

"What?" I said to what I thought was a poor joke.

"Dogs in France have numbers tattooed into their ears for identification. Usually pedigreed dogs—and this one is a beautiful Labrador—have it done before they leave the kennel." She held the muzzle in her hand and looked her up and down. "Well, whatever happened, I guess she's yours now." She smiled.

"I'm just keeping her until the owner gets out of prison." I was holding her trembling body tightly so she wouldn't try and jump off the metal examining table. Just one visit with injections had made the dog quake when we got within a hundred meters of the vet's office.

"Turn her back to life on the streets? After all the time, care, and money? How could you?"

"Well . . . ," I started to say as I thought of the glass she'd broken, or the row of bicycles she'd felled like dominoes, breaking a pedal here, a bell there. Or the time in a post-bath frenzy that she'd knocked the lamp off the table, leaving the lightbulb shattered and the shade forever lopsided. Or her mine-sweeping tail that cleared my crates of all objects. Or the fact that what she didn't break, she chewed. And it wasn't just the proverbial shoe, though she got one of those too. She liked to live more danger-ously than footwear, and one day almost electrocuted herself on a wire. Another time I left her alone too long in my room, and to teach me a lesson, she knocked over my one chair and gnawed a leg, rendering it uneven and useless. As a result of the mishaps, I had dubbed her Cassie, because *casser* she did.

Wasn't I looking forward to giving her back to Michel, so that I could return to the ordered existence that she had completely disrupted? Because even once she got housetrained, she had to be walked three times a day; she needed a lot of exercise, meaning that my way to work now included a stop in the Tuileries gardens, where she could run free or with other dogs. Even once purged of parasites, I had to brush her because she shed. I had to feed her twice a day, change her water constantly, clean the floor where she drooled, which she did profusely, or sweep where she dragged her dirty paws.

But she was trouble I wasn't able to resist. The damn dog had worked her way into my heart with the skill of an Olympic fencer. The way she looked at me with her upturned brown eyes, exposing a heartbreaking crescent of white, so full of trust and devotion—they spoke to me in complete sentences. "You can't leave me here"; "Come on, let's play"; "You wouldn't forget to feed me, would you?" The way she followed me everywhere, nipping lightly at my leg to remind me she was still there. The way she rested her head on my foot while I ate supper. I fell for her every trick.

Except they weren't ruses. She sat there with her perfect head and gleaming coat, the picture of good breeding and beauty—you didn't need to be a dog expert to see that—but she didn't know or care about her looks, didn't use them or her abundant charm as tools of manipulation. She had no complex layers; all she required was food, exercise, and affection. This was a first for any female I'd opened my heart to, and that stupid dog (for brains she was not long on) barged right through all those doors I'd carefully closed and locked.

So when the vet continued: "You have to consider whether you want her sterilized. I could tattoo her ear at the same time, and then you would be the legal owner," I just nodded my head. I wrote a huge check. And afterward I carried her up the stairs, changed her bandages with the greatest of care, and watched her every move for three weeks, until the muscle tissue had grown back together again.

All during this time, Michel's friend—Claude was his name—would stop by from time to time in his tight, short striped trousers and laceless boots, never with much news. Only that Michel's past offenses meant he was in for longer.

"Don't you get at least ten years for knifing someone?" I asked.

"Not when it's hardly more than a scratch on the hand of an illegal immigrant."

Each time Claude came by, always lingering for wine money in exchange for his non-information, my heart give a little jump at the reminder that one day Michel would get out of prison. Now that the medicine and the operation were over, I'd settled into life with a dog. She kept me company walking to and from the shop and in the evenings, more and more of which I spent alone in my room because it was over with Claire, and Joséphine was away on a teacher-training course. At the shop, Cassie and Piotr got along like a pair of shoes. Every morning she awaited his arrival impatiently, then danced around him as if she hadn't seen him for weeks. Once she was calm and on the new bed I had bought, he'd get down on the floor and whisper to her in Polish, and Cassie would wag her strong, straight tail as if she understood every word he was saying.

———

Piotr may have loved the dog, but something else was wrong. Soon after Cassie entered our life, he'd started coming back from lunch with red, glassy eyes, smelling like fermented fruit. First he'd be half an hour late; then it sometimes stretched to a full hour. Many mornings he'd arrive looking ragged, his usually pert hair flat and unwashed, his pale face ashen as he leaned over Cassie's bed. I asked him several times in a significant tone if everything was all right, and he always replied, "Yeah, yeah, yeah." But one morning he was a full three hours late.

"Okay, what's up? If you're going to start showing up at noon, you have to tell me why."

"I sleep over."

"I guessed that. The question is why did you oversleep? Farm boys don't do that. The cows won't stand for it."

"Wanda wants to move. Back for Poland," he answered, hanging his head, stuffing his big hands in his pockets.

"And you?"

"She says one day she wants to make a baby. She says our baby needs Polish air, Polish ground, Polish grandparents. But what I do back there?" He threw his hands in the air. "In Poland, you make millions of zlotys and they are worth nothing. Nothing. Who wants Polish zlotys?" He looked around. "I don't go back there!"

Pushing past me, he grabbed a bicycle to repair. He hoisted it brusquely onto the stand, snatching a wrench in rough anger. I'd never seen Piotr anything but smooth-motioned and even-tempered, no matter how impossible the customer, how heavy the repair load. And I'd stopped noticing what a quiet worker he was until that day, when tools clattered, rubber squeaked against metal, and every few minutes he'd sigh and begin muttering under his breath in Polish. I had trouble concentrating on the books I was painfully trying to balance. Cassie rose from her bed and stood near him, looking at his impatient movements with her head cocked, her tail waving in perplexed sympathy.

"Maybe she just needs a visit," I finally said. "It's been five years." Members of their family had come to Paris, but they had never gone back themselves. "Sometimes a visit will cure you."

"Money. Time," he said, not even looking up.

"You need a break. Or you're going to end up like Michel or Claude." The screwdriver stopped. He stood up, then bent down over the dog. "Don't think I haven't noticed," I went on. "Why don't you take two months, in July and August. I'll even pay you what's not vacation time."

"Hmm," he said, turning back to work, but quietly. "We see."

Although he didn't mention Poland or Wanda again, over the next week, Piotr showed up sober after lunch every day but one. He came to work on time; his hair returned to its clean-brush pertness. The following week, he said: "We go to Poland, July and August. Thank you."

That same week, Claude came, dancing from foot to foot, now that he had real news: Michel was getting out of prison. "Soon. I don't know exactly when. They always say it's one day. Then it's not. They like to make us suffer." He looked at me expectantly. "He's already mentioned the dog."

"Oh," I said and handed him some money.

———

I decided to hide Cassie and tell Michel that I'd given the dog away because I couldn't deal with her anymore. Or I could say she'd run away. Then maybe he would knife someone else. Maybe he'd move to another begging station. At least I'd gain some time.

The obvious place to hide the dog was with Cédric and Viviane, and besides, a visit was long overdue. The weekend I'd planned to go in February I'd spent shampooing the dog and popping her pills, which meant I hadn't seen them since Christmas. In the meantime, they'd finally become parents. Adoptive parents, to a Russian orphan. Though she had held out for three more years—had kept hoping and believing—Viviane finally conceded to Cédric's adoption plan. The process itself had been endless and grueling. Besides voluminous paperwork, they'd been made to jump through hoops—interviews and signed statements from professionals—that no natural parent would ever have been subjected to. Finally the previous December, they'd been approved and told that a five-month-old baby was available. In January they'd traveled halfway across Russia to pick him up.

So Saturday afternoon, on another wet day in April, I left Mélo-Vélo in the hands of Piotr and took the train to Vernon with the dog and all her worldly possessions: bed, leash, food bowl, water bowl, and the rubber toy Piotr had given her. Cassie thought the Saint-Lazare station, where muzzled and unmuzzled pit bulls roamed beside their body-pierced, leather-clad owners, and the train, which was littered with scraps of food from previous passengers, was high adventure. She lunged right and left and generally infuriated me, until we sat down, and I realized her presence meant that nobody would want to sit next to me. As the train made its way to Vernon, doing its coy dance with the Seine while the city unfurled to the increasingly suburbanized countryside, I slumped in my seat and watched through the rain-speckled window. Cassie, who had exhausted the possibilities of finding food, was asleep with her head on my foot.

In my car was a group of older American tourists on their way to Giverny. They looked like East Coast people, from New York or Boston or Philadelphia. People who might go to Long Island in the summer. One woman wore combs in her hair and looked reserved, like my mother. Suddenly a great wave of longing for my family washed over me. Particularly for Mother, my only connection to the father and even to the sister I only remembered snatches of. But I even missed Edward and his unflinching ease in the world, his quick dismissal of the past—or had I destroyed all that too, just as my malevolent semiconscious had desired? Even Edmond I could have stomached. He was, after all, the owner of the rue de

Verneuil, and over the last couple of years, I'd found myself getting funny longings for that apartment with its creaking oak floors, its high ceilings, and large, ripple-paned windows. Even for Mother's oversized collection of boxes. And certainly for Lisette, whom I must have hurt very much with my unconscionable behavior.

My resentment had dissolved into a large vat of regret that I didn't know how to transform into something more solid. There was that looming temptation to call or to write, to try and make amends, but I could never get myself closer than a hand on the telephone, a letter unsent. An insomniac night of resolve always evaporated in the light of day. I'd been difficult enough to endure before my disgrace; who'd want to ruin their Sunday roast with me now?

Or should I say that I'd succeeded in creating yet another form of regret. Because as I've already mentioned, even before being ousted from my family, I was wallowing in the stuff. Regret for my early life, regret for my failed career, regret for my unsatisfactory love life. Regrets that I had carefully camouflaged with resentment and disdain, until I blew my own cover to smithereens. In the fallout, I'd left myself with almost no people, just memories of them. Yes, some of those memories had been preserved in photographs. But I'd discovered that memory on paper, in the absence of flesh and blood human beings, remains a visual exercise, a mental picture, a cold and lonely function of the brain.

The train pulled into Vernon, with Cassie once again all nervous attention. Cédric was there, an unusually broad grin on his mild face.

"What's the stupid grin?" I asked. "You haven't gone baby crazy, have you?"

"Fatigue, probably," he said, stroking Cassie's head. "Sweet dog."

"Thanks. In fact . . ." I started but stopped because Cédric was grappling with Cassie, trying to get her into the back of the old Volvo. "She's not used to cars," I said instead.

"I can see that," he said, holding her with one hand as he closed the back hatch with the other.

I threw all her paraphernalia in the back, next to the baby seat. The car was cleaner than I'd ever seen it.

"So now you've got a dog in your life," Cédric said, shifting gears to get us up the hill out of town.

"For the moment she's just a mission of mercy. I told you about the homeless guy Michel, who went to prison. His friend Claude came by the other day to say he'll be out soon, and he's already asked about the dog. I don't know what I'm going to do."

When Cédric didn't answer, I looked at him. He appeared not to have heard a word I'd said.

"You're not listening to me."

"Sorry," he said. "I'm distracted."

"Distracted by what?"

"I'm not supposed to say anything."

"Not even to me? Come on."

"Viviane's pregnant."

"She's what?"

"Pregnant." Cédric turned left from the main road, onto the narrow road that stretched across the fields. "The doctor says it's fairly common. Just when you give up hope and sign the adoption papers, bang, a baby of your own. If we'd only known years ago that all Viviane had to do was abandon hope."

"What are you going to do with two babies?"

"Just what anybody would do. Take care of them, watch them grow up. What do you think? We're going to pack André back to the orphanage in Russia?"

"I've been meaning to ask you. Please tell me it's not André as in Prince André."

"It's a nice name."

"I can't believe it. A dog called Fyodor is one thing but naming a baby after a character in *War and Peace*?"

"Why not? Besides, I like to think of him as a prince. It helps me forget that awful place."

"The orphanage?"

He nodded. "I mean, it was clean, and the people were perfectly pleasant. It was all the kids, especially the older ones. Their eyes. They were either angry or vacant or hopeless." He shuddered. "It would have broken even your hardened heart."

"But two kids. It's hard enough for me to get used to you with one child, much less another."

"Your saturation level on the number of children we have is somewhat beside the point, wouldn't you say?"

We turned into the courtyard of Hautebranche and parked next to another car. "There are other people here?" I asked.

"Didn't I tell you? I'm really in another world these days. A couple of painter friends and their model are visiting. As a matter of fact, the woman—English—says she's met you. Béa Fairbank?" I shook my head.

When we got out of the car, a cold rain was still coming down in that calmly persistent Normandy way. Everything dripped, from the branches of the still leafless trees, to the eaves under the undulating tiled roof. But through the wetness, birds were chirping. It was an odd note of spring in a still almost wintry scene. Cassie, once released from her car prison, went wild. She darted left and right, sent into a frenzy by the onslaught of new odors. When Cédric opened the front door, their three dogs charged out. She went low to the ground and began darting around in figure-eights, spinning herself in circles, until she finally landed under a bush, with the other dogs sniffing her from top to bottom.

Inside, everything was different. There were toys scattered

about; a large playpen dominated the middle of the room. There was no fire lit, no smell of cooking, just a vaguely sweet smell of baby on the slightly chilly air. Viviane approached me with the same silly grin Cédric had been wearing at the station, and a white-haired baby tucked around her waist like a monkey. When I leaned down to kiss her hello, the simian attachment grabbed a large clump of my hair and yanked with all its might.

"Ow."

"I'm sorry," said Viviane, trying to pry his fingers one by one away from my still inclined head. "He just loves hair."

"Good grip," I said.

"He's a strong little guy."

"Thank you," I said, finally able to pull away. "You look great, Viv." Which she did. Her face had smoothed out, as if she'd just dropped ten years.

"Actually, I feel great. Finally. Is this your new friend?" She put a hand down to Cassie.

"Here, let me," Cédric said, reaching out his hands to take the baby.

"No," she said, pulling him even tighter. "I'm going to put him in his pen for a minute while I get his food ready." Cédric turned away. His uneven face went even more askew when hurt.

"How's the painting?" I asked.

"I've hardly picked up a brush since we left for Russia. Isn't he amazing? So alert, such a sensitive nose." Little André did have startling eyes. They were bright blue and looked right through you. "They said at the orphanage all the babies have that wise old man look. It's because no matter what they do, they can't give each child the attention he needs. They said the look would go away. It's already faded." She wrapped her arms around him, kissed his forehead, then each cheek, then each ear. "We're making up for lost time."

"You can take the dog off the leash, you know," Cédric said. "I put the other dogs out back." I let her go and she began hunting around the room, checking their empty bowls.

"We're just having a cold lunch today," Viviane said. "Getting something hot on the table is too complicated with this little guy." She kissed him again and put him on his back in the playpen, then rattled a toy in front of his face and cooed at him while he pedaled his legs. I was beginning to wonder why they'd bothered with the enclosure, when he suddenly rolled over and crawled rapidly to the other side, plopping down on his rump and looking back at Viviane with a smile. "Can't keep him still," she said.

Viviane's doting on André as if he really were a prince was hard to watch. As was the way she barely let Cédric get near the child. "Aren't you worried about your painting?" I asked. "Now that you're getting some attention?" There had been one or two magazine spreads, with photos of her studio and paintings, the previous year. It had been a breakthrough, which before the baby had delighted and encouraged her.

"I'll get back to it. There's nothing wrong with channeling my energy somewhere else for a while," she said, putting her hand to her stomach and looking down at André who was intently turning a clear plastic ball filled with smaller colored balls around and around in his tough little hands. Even under her large sweater, Viviane's bulge was beginning to show. She suddenly looked right at me, through her big round glasses. "Anyway, since when did you start worrying about letting work slide?"

"Exactly," said Cédric as he popped the cork of the wine bottle from behind the kitchen counter.

At that moment the back door from the garden opened. I could feel the cool, wet air waft in too, overpowering for a minute the baby smell. The figure of a person, darkened like a puzzle piece against the milky light behind, stepped into the room. Suddenly Cassie lunged at the dog coming in behind the woman and turning abruptly back toward the room, hitting the woman at the back of the knees. They buckled, and she fell in a heap on the floor, bumping her forehead on the edge of a stool on the way. The baby gave a high-pitched cry. I ran over to help her up, get her to the sofa while Viviane ran for a cold cloth and an ice cube, and Cédric shooed the dogs outside.

"Wow," she said, lifting herself up on an elbow. A pink and blue lump was forming above her eye like a small egg. She gingerly put the ice on it.

"The dog's never been to the country," I said. "She's a little overexcited. I'm really sorry."

"Can I get you anything else?" asked Cédric. "That's quite a lump you're growing."

"No, no. I'm fine." She rested her head on the sofa-back.

I sat on a nearby chair. The dog was a liability. There was no way I could leave her with Cédric and Viviane, even for a week.

"Are you sure you're all right, Béa?" Viviane called from the kitchen area. "Do you need more ice?"

"I'm fine. Really."

"I'm Trevor, by the way."

"I know. We've met before," she said in English.

I shook my head.

"At your brother's." I still couldn't get it; she suppressed a smile. "I was a friend of Jennifer's."

"Ah," I said. That was an evening I was unlikely to forget, being the one where, after being a cad to Jennifer, I had first laid my hands on my sister-in-law.

"It was a long time ago, I guess."

"No, no. Now I remember. You were the painter friend. We talked about your knowing Viviane and Cédric." Something was different about her—I couldn't place it. "And remind me why I have never run into you before or since?"

"Until a few months ago, I was based in Aix-en-Provence. That's where I met Viv and Cédric, and that's mostly where I've seen them until now."

"That's right."

Cédric was in the kitchen, laying out some pâté and cheese on plates, and Viviane was fussing with André again. Béa pulled the ice from her forehead.

"The lump on your forehead seems to have stopped growing."

"Good. But I don't think I'll go running. I got hopeful that the rain was letting up." Her small person, stretched along the sofa, was dressed in dirty, well-worn running shoes, a baggy sweatshirt, and leggings. That was it. She'd been, well, not fat, but on the heavy side that night at Edward's. It was as if she'd melted.

"Jennifer never really forgave me," I said. "Have you kept up with her?"

"She went back to Canada. I think she's still dancing and waiting tables. I haven't heard from her in a while. To be honest, we weren't great friends. She just asked me to come with her to that dinner because she knew you were going to be there." She paused. "I'm sorry. I shouldn't have said that."

"Well, it's not surprising she wanted reinforcements. I was a total jerk," I said, feeling like one all over again. Shame leaves a stubborn stain.

"Here you go, Béa." Cédric put down a bottle of wine and some glasses. "The wounded first." Usually the coffee table had an assortment of yogurt pots with candles in them, a wine bottle with torrents of hardened wax tumbling dramatically down the side. But like everything else around the room, I now noticed, it had been cleared, baby-proofed.

Viviane came and sat down with André on her lap. "Come on, now, a little dessert before nap time," she said. He sucked greedily, his hands hovering around the bottle protectively. The stairs creaked, and a sturdy man with a beard appeared. "You missed the excitement," Béa said. "I just got floored."

"Ouch," he said, helping himself to a glass of wine.

The stairs creaked again, and a young woman appeared.

"Curt," said Béa, "this is Trevor." He had a wide hand, an overpowering handshake, and he smelled like pepper. "And this is Connie."

"Hi," she gave a little wave. She was very young indeed, with a fresh, freckled face and an upturned nose.

"Connie's modeling for us," said Curt. "Nice wine." He held up his glass.

"Just a little Côte du Rhône." Cédric shrugged awkwardly in English.

The whole atmosphere had suddenly gone tense, I assumed because of the language thing. Like most French people my age, Cédric and Viviane spoke terrible English. Like most Americans, Curt did not speak French. I'd experienced countless such social gatherings, where the failure to communicate left everyone feeling awkward.

"Here, Connie," Curt said. "Let me pour you some wine."

"Great," she said in that enthusiastic American way. "Your house is really cool," she said, looking around.

"Thank you," said Cédric.

Then silence. As always in these situations, where I should have been providing some cross-cultural emergency aid—saying something in French and English to put people at ease—I couldn't think of a thing to say. But this time I was saved. André was being patted on the back against Viviane's shoulder after his milk, and he let out a hearty burp. No need for translation; everyone could laugh.

"Let me get him settled," said Viviane in French. "Then we can eat."

There we were again. Silence. Cédric got up and went to the counter to cut some bread.

"So, Trevor, are you an artist too?" Curt asked me. His beard looked more like a couple weeks of planned neglect.

"No," I said.

"I thought you were a photographer," Béa said, pulling the ice away from her forehead and taking a sip of wine.

"Only the weekend variety." The blue egg on her forehead stared at me. "The rest of the time I run a bicycle shop."

"A bicycle shop!" said Curt, his eyes lighting up. Maybe out of interest, maybe out of mild mockery. I couldn't tell. But they were sparkly eyes, eyes that pulled you in.

"Cool," said Connie.

I looked from one to the other. "It's—"

"*Bon*," Viviane said, coming out of their bedroom, baby walkie-talkie in her hand. "Time for some grown-up food."

The meal may have been cold, but it was still exquisite. There were roasted red peppers with fresh goat's cheese and thyme and olives, a slab of *pâté de compagne*, next to paper-thin slices of country ham. There was a mushroom and *mâche* salad and a plump, soft Camembert next to a large piece of Beaufort cheese. Since I still didn't bother about the food I put in my mouth when I was alone, Viviane's meals continued to jolt me into awareness of what I was missing.

"Are you exhibiting much these days, Viviane?" Curt asked. He had a strong physical, almost animal, presence. "Béa showed me your magazine spread."

"Before André, yes," she answered in heavily accented English. "The Paris market changes. Some people like that apples look like apples." Better than Piotr but not by much.

"There was another magazine article," Cédric said, accent just as thick. "It was for fashion. With the studio, the garden, the paintings."

"I'd like to see some of the real thing, in your studio, before we leave."

"Yes, of course."

The conversation sputtered to a halt. We ate. I tried to think of something to say. Nothing in either language came to my socially deficient mind.

But Curt was an assertive sort. He didn't seem bothered by the language barrier. "Now that we've moved up to Paris, my agent Hillary keeps telling me I need an exhibition. She says the new economy has hit and people have francs, soon euros, to spare."

"If there's money, Hillary will be here," said Béa

"It will be better than in Aix-en-Provence," said Viviane in painful English.

"That's what Hillary said," said Béa.

"Come on, Béa, I'm lucky someone's thinking about the bottom line for me. Anyway, she says if the French invest their money in art, they don't have to pay taxes on it. Or the wealth tax. Something like that."

"Maybe," said Cédric, though of course he had no idea.

"The art market changes," said Viviane. While she was doing her best to describe it to Curt, Béa and Cédric started talking about something that had happened the previous summer in Aix.

I turned to Connie, who was sitting on my left.

"So what are you doing over here?" I asked.

"I finished college last year," she said, looking up at me with large green eyes, "and I'm over here doing what every other American in Paris does. Writing a novel. Nothing new," she shrugged. Having cut most of the food on her plate, she put her knife down, switched the fork into her right hand and took the first bite. This American method of eating, rather than the European practice of using knife and fork together, had always seemed unnecessarily

labor-intensive, fastidious, but today I found it added to Connie's freshly graduated charm. "I thought it would only take one
year, but it looks like I'll be here another. Which is fine by me.
My French still needs lots of work, and I'm having a blast. The
modeling these last couple months helps a lot. At least I can pay
the rent." She looked at Curt, who had just laughed.

Over the course of the lunch I learned that she was from a
large Irish Catholic family. In fact, she couldn't stop talking about
her parents, all her brothers and sisters. It was endearing. She was
perfect Casual material: young, pretty, and looking for fun, but
clearly planning to go back into the fold of that beloved family.

Cassie came over and nudged my leg. I looked around the
room. Viviane and Béa were now huddled in one corner, and
Cédric had taken Curt off for an architectural tour of the house.
His pepper smell lingered in my nose, even once I was in the
garden with Cassie.

It had turned into a magnificent day, the brilliant blue sky
illuminating the first signs of spring. Daffodil shoots had pushed
their way through the damp earth, and their delicate yellow flowers were just beginning to open. The tougher, broader tulips had
elbowed their way above ground too, but their red heads were
still tight pods of green. Along the wall a forsythia bush was on
its way out; yellow petals lay scattered at its feet. It was amazing,
I thought, how every year spring took me by surprise.

"It's a lovely garden, isn't it? Even at this time of year." I jumped.
"Sorry. Didn't mean to intrude on your solitude," said Béa.

"I didn't hear you coming," I said. "Still too stunned by the
sight of the sun, I guess."

She walked over to a line of rose bushes, all cut down to
spindly stumps. "There's just the first hint of a new shoot here. It's
amazing to think that in a few months it will be a huge, unwieldy
plant with an abundance of flowers." She had a low voice for a

small person, and that combined with her airy English accent gave her an unexpected resonance.

"Is this the kind of thing you paint?" I asked as the two of us looked intently at the reddish-green nub of a budding branch on the rose bush.

"I usually wait until the plant has something more to show for itself," she said. Then came the laugh, which I suddenly remembered from that dinner years ago. The thing that seemed to start way down and work its way up, before being released like a flock of birds. The kind of laugh that made you want to make a joke so you could hear it again.

Just then Viviane, Connie, and Curt came out. Viviane was carrying the baby, wrapped in a shawl, and Curt had a fold-up stool under one arm and his painting box in his other hand.

"I'm off," he said to Béa. "Any interest in joining me?"

"I think I'll walk," Béa answered.

"All right then. See you all later."

"Paint well," she said to his back as he walked through the gate.

"What about you, Connie?" Béa asked. "Are you going to come for a walk with us?"

"No, I think I'll sit here in this pretty garden and try to get some writing done."

"Well, good luck," said Béa.

"Can you help me get the pram out?" Viviane called from the shed.

"Don't you think this thing will be a little awkward once we get off the road?" I asked. "It barely fits through the door."

"The wheels have great suspension. It'll be fine. But what about you? Are you heading off on your usual solo stroll?" Cassie was already leaping around the three dogs.

"I'll come with you. You'll need some help pulling that thing out when it gets stuck in the mud."

We walked first through the village. At the edge, there were three new houses, their pale walls and roof glaring in the sunlight, the ground around them scraped raw. The three of us stood stricken, as if we were witnessing a car accident.

"Even here," I said. "From the train you see swath after swath of them."

"It breaks my heart," said Viviane. "Literally. I feel each new house as a physical blow."

"The trouble is," said Béa, "they will never blend into their surroundings. Old houses do because the material—the wood, the stone, the brick, even the earthen roof tiles or the slate shingles—comes from the land. In an old house, nature's elements have just been rearranged. But this is all manufactured. And cheap to boot." She crossed her arms over her chest and shook her head. "These houses will always look awful."

"I certainly hate looking at them. Let's go up the other way," said Viviane, pushing the huge pram toward a footpath across a field that rolled ahead of us to meet the huge sky, now a mixture of deep blue and bold, urgent clouds. "This is a good view. You can't see any buildings."

"You have to live with blinders on," said Béa. "Or you have to go further and further away." This small woman was full of opinions. I dropped back a bit, and they began to talk about the studio she was hoping to get at Montmartre. I watched their backs. Viviane was leaning forward into the pram as she walked, while Béa became more and more animated. Her hands flew up in the air; she moved up on her toes and back down again.

"So what do you paint besides roses?" I asked again, catching up with them.

"A bit of everything," she shrugged.

"But at the moment you're painting Connie?" I asked.

"Mostly. She's a really good model. Supple and patient. And that sweet face is surprisingly expressive."

"Careful what you say, Béa," said Viviane. "You might encourage Trevor to pounce on the poor girl."

"Come on," I said.

Béa gave me a wry smile. If there's one thing I know about women, it's that they share every detail of life with one another. No one's story is safe in their hands, and I therefore had no doubt that Viviane had told Béa absolutely everything about me. This made me feel uncomfortable and embarrassed. I was tired of people thinking badly of me.

"Let me push that pram for you," I muttered to Viviane as we started up a hill.

Near the top we entered the woods where the bare trees were still shiny and slick from the earlier rain. Little white flowers carpeted the forest floor. "Do you mind taking the pram back?" I asked. "I'd like to take a photo."

"Let me," said Béa, taking the handle. Her eyes had changed color from before lunch, in the house. Then they were light hazel. Now they were tinged with blue.

I squatted down, trying to get as close to the ground level as I could, to catch the flowers and the tree trunks in the light. Cassie stood by me, panting. I'd been afraid she might wander, but until now she'd flopped along with the others, never going beyond the invisible circle drawn by the other dogs, instinctively staying with the pack.

"Oh, no!" I heard up ahead. "I've never seen it so muddy," Viviane was saying when I got there. "I'm not sure I can get down this bit."

"It's likely to be just as slippery going back the other way," said Béa.

"I don't know," Viviane said anxiously.

"If you take the baby," I said to Béa, "I'll try to maneuver that pram down the hill."

"I can take André," Viviane said.

"You need to be careful," said Béa. "And I'm the one with the good traction," she said, pointing to her running shoes.

So Viviane took the baby in his shawl and handed him reluctantly to Béa. I took the pram and the three of us inched our way down the rocky, slippery path. My old shoes had long ago lost their tread and sure enough, halfway down the hill, I slipped. Grabbing onto a sapling with one hand, my other still on the pram, I couldn't move. Béa and Viviane, ahead of me, were now on level ground.

"Help," I said, trying to sound ironic.

Béa scampered back up the hill like a mountain goat: "Let me get your camera to safety first," she said, lifting it over my head and hanging it over a branch, while she took the pram from my hand so I could regain my balance.

"Thank you," I said, retrieving my camera. We picked our way downhill, pram between us.

"You were quite a sight," she said at the bottom, releasing one of her laughs.

"Let's go back," said Viviane as she cradled André protectively.

When we walked through the gate at Hautebranche, Connie was gone and Cédric was sitting in the sun reading.

"Where are the others?" asked Béa.

"I haven't seen them," he said. I helped Cédric move out some other chairs and a table, a plastic tarp and the playpen, and we had tea outside in our shirtsleeves. The garden walls trapped all the sunlight, heated the air as if summer were right around the corner. Connie wandered in, saying she'd decided, finally, to take a little stroll of her own. Then Curt came back, and the thick clouds came rolling along behind him. The temperature dropped too, and we had to hurry inside ahead of the next rain, which came down all through dinner and all night, needling the leaded panes of the bull's-eye window in my alcove.

I lay in the bed, watching the rain run down the colored glass. How silly I must have looked and how terrified I'd felt on that hill. The near fall had brought back all too vividly another fall on a hill with a camera. While I was stuck there, I saw that bicycle wheel, robbed of the handlebars, wobbling frantically. I saw my body flying forward toward the verge of the road. Viviane and Béa of course had no idea, but oh—I shuddered all over again, turned, and pulled the cover tightly around me—how relieved I'd felt when Béa had come to my rescue.

Béa, the small person with strong opinions. Jacqueline was a small person with strong opinions too. But they were very different. Jacqueline's pale doll face with the blue, blue eyes, the short dark hair, now even darker because of the hair dye she applied to mask the grey. Béa's hair, which appeared to be younger by several years, was light brown and tumbled over her shoulders. Her skin was softly toned and her eyes changed color according to the light. Jacqueline had a brittle laugh; Béa's was jubilant and generous.

At least they seemed different.

I turned over again. Why was I comparing these two women? Why was I thinking about women at all? During supper, I'd cornered Connie again. She'd babbled about her novel, offered more information about her family, and I quickly found her excruciatingly dull. But what should I expect? At twenty-two, she was twenty years younger than me. She was hardly more than a child—could have been *my* child—and there I was toying with the possibilities. What was I thinking? Interest in Connie was verging on the indecent. What kind of person was I?

Several words came to mind, none of them flattering. All, in fact, in a range between ridiculous and contemptible. How could anyone put up with me—I couldn't even stand myself.

Cédric took me to the train the following morning.

"I hardly recognized your friend Béa," I said as we drove past the glaring new houses at the edge of the village.

"What do you mean?"

"Didn't she used to be on the plump side?"

"I guess that's right. I've always thought she was incredibly pretty, whatever her weight. She's got the kind of beauty you don't notice right away. That always appeals to me."

"Her eyes change color."

"What?"

"They change color according to the light."

"Well," Cédric said, looking at me. "Whatever the status of her eyes, you're too late on this one. Unless you're planning another heist."

"I certainly am not. In fact, I'm giving women up. As a general policy."

"*That* I don't believe."

"You'll see. I am. I'm too old." A night's sleep had not removed the bad taste in my mouth from my even vague interest in young Connie. "What makes the boyfriend smell like pepper?"

"I wondered too. Viv says it's patchouli oil."

"In the year 2001? I thought that was hippie stuff."

"Who knows," Cédric said as we rolled in front of the station. "Viv also says he's a really good painter."

"And? So?"

"I don't know. He's okay. They haven't been together long enough for me to form a real opinion." He yanked on the parking brake. "Don't wait so long between visits next time," he said as I got Cassie out of the back of the car.

"I'll be back before the house gets too crowded. Count on it."

THREE

MICHEL'S RELEASE FROM prison got closer and closer, and I still had no plan for hiding the dog. With Hautebranche excluded as a possibility, where else could I look? Who else could I ask? My bleak personal landscape left me high and dry. I thus awaited Michel's return like a bankrupt man anticipating the bailiff's knock. Imminent dread hung over every day.

Finally one afternoon, with Piotr out to lunch, he came. I had just hoisted a bike on the repair stand for a gear adjustment when the Tibetan chimes chimed. I popped my head around the corner of the workshop, and there was Michel, with Claude looking on eagerly.

"You're out," I said, wiping my hands on a cloth.

"I am. And I want Leffe back." He leaned down to Cassie, who by now was dancing around him. She hadn't forgotten. "Hey, that's my girl."

"Leffe?"

"My favorite beer, when I can afford it. Anything wrong with that? That's my girl," he repeated.

"Not really," I said. "You've been gone a long time."

"And now I'm back. Where's the leash?" Claude was watching this exchange as if he were at a tennis match. "I want the leash and the bowl and the bed."

There was an awkward silence. Claude began his little dance, hopping from one foot to another in his laceless boots. "He's got the leash, I've seen it," he offered helpfully.

Still I didn't move.

But then I had an idea.

"Okay," and I went to get Cassie's leash. Michel was smiling; Claude looked disappointed that game, set, match had been settled so quickly. Michel attached the dog and tried to pull her toward the door. Cassie leaned back, legs stiff, paws firmly planted, just as she did with me if I tried to deny her a turn through the Tuileries gardens on our morning walk. The harder Michel tugged, the more the loose skin of her neck wrinkled her face in stubborn resistance. When he eased up for a second, she sat down and began scratching, sticking her back paw right into her ear with concentrated attention. Just as I'd hoped, she did not want to leave the person who had been feeding her the last months. Michel's face fell.

"She won't come with me," he said helplessly.

I shook my head. I felt sorry for him, but I have to admit, it was the supercilious pity of the victor.

"I told you. It's been a long time." I paused before moving into Phase Two of my plan. "But I'll tell you what." I paused again. "She was your dog, after all, and you should be compensated accordingly. I should pay you for the dog." He didn't say anything for a minute. He fiddled with the end of the leash. "Come on," I said more softly, "she's happy here. You won't have to worry about taking care of her, but you can see her all the time." The leash slackened. "How about five hundred francs."

"She's worth more than that," said ever-helpful Claude.

"The woman gave you five hundred," I reminded Michel.

"A guy in prison told me these dogs go for more like five thousand francs." Michel looked at me defiantly. I waited. He said: "I couldn't give her up for less than four thousand."

"Wow," said Claude.

"Come on, Michel," I said. "What are you going to do with four thousand francs? You'll have every Ukrainian in the country after you, and you'll end up back in prison." This reasoning seemed to make a dent; his face began to relent.

"I don't know."

"It's getting to be drink time," Claude said.

We haggled for a few more minutes and finally agreed on two thousand five hundred francs, which I would distribute in five installments, to discourage further thievery by greedy fellow drinkers.

Just as they were walking out, Piotr came back from lunch. "How much?" he asked.

"Don't ask," I said, shaking my head. "The amount of money I've spent on that mutt." Cassie wagged her tail.

"Five hundred?"

"Times five."

"You turn crazy," he said, pointing his finger to his temple. "You going to send us down the pipes." He leaned over and whispered into Cassie's ear.

"Don't try and get the dog on your side," I said.

"I tell her how stubby you are."

"Stubborn."

"Stubby, stubborn—you give too much money."

"It's my turn for lunch," I said. Piotr shook his head and went back to work. "Come on, Cassie." I walked to the café with the gleaming dog, now all mine, trotting along at my side. Two thousand five hundred francs seemed like a pretty good deal.

———————

With the dog officially mine, I felt something of a letdown. There was absolutely no edge to my life, not even the fear of Michel's release from prison. And it seemed that if I didn't give up on women, they would give up on me. When Joséphine returned from her teacher training, we'd gone out for sushi, and cold, raw fish just about summed up the flavor of our meeting. People always surprise you: for all her holistic wooliness, she didn't like dogs. So I couldn't spend the night, which, if truth be told, suited me fine. I was tired of Joséphine too.

Besides, who had time for women when there was the future of the planet to worry about? The weather over the last year had provided me, anyway, with all the proof I needed that the earth was angry and melting. Just before the millennium, a windstorm had ravaged the country, felling millions of trees and even blowing the *L'An 2000* countdown sign clear off the Eiffel Tower. How could a clearer message be sent? Since then, it had rained almost nonstop, causing disastrous flooding in the first months of 2001. It seemed to me that the Apocalypse was right around the corner, and all the population could do was shop. On Saturdays the rue de Seine was so crowded, I bought a sandwich at the bakery in the morning and ate my lunch at the back of the shop, as far away from the hordes as I could get. When I complained—okay, ranted might be a more accurate word—about this conspicuous consumption in a drowning world, Piotr would throw his hands up and say: "Good for us!"

One night as I was coming up the stairs to my room, soaked from another sudden downpour on the way home, the phone was ringing.

"Ah," said the voice.

"Edward," I said, panting and dripping water around me. Cassie shook and sprayed more water everywhere.

"I was just about to hang up. I've been phoning for three

days, and there was never any answer. You apparently still have no answering machine."

"No. I've been out a lot." I remembered several instances over the last days of a ringing phone that I hadn't felt like answering.

"Right." Pause. "It's been a long time. How are you?"

"Okay." Pause. Clearing of the throat. "And you?"

"I was hoping we could get together."

"I guess. Yes. If you want." I was having trouble breathing.

"Good. How about tomorrow," he said more than asked. "Five would suit me." And he gave the address of a café not far from the Champs-Elysées, near his office.

Why, I wondered, as I put the phone down and took off my soaked clothes, after more than five years of silence does he suddenly want to see me? And tomorrow, no less.

The rest of the evening, I careened from euphoria to panic. I drank more beer than usual and slept almost not at all, and when I did, had a strange dream that mixed Lisette's Seine monsters with the roiling brown water of the river's flooded banks. Specter-like forms of Edward and Mother and Edmond were walking in the Tuileries, and the water had risen so high, it was lapping right beside them. But they were oblivious, too busy laughing at me. They were saying what a silly person I was, and I was trying desperately to catch up with them and tell them I'd changed, I really had. And to beware of the rising water. But they kept just out of my reach.

The café Edward had chosen was one of the trendy new places that were beginning to pop up all over the well-heeled *quartiers*. They had sleek lines and cushioned chairs and waiters and waitresses who, with their slim-fitting black suits and catwalk ennui, looked more like fashion models.

A tall, slim, dark-haired waitress sidled over to my table, and I ordered a coffee. It was a quiet time in the café, and the background music, as well as its volume, had been selected for the benefit of the staff rather than the odd customer like me. I opened the newspaper I'd brought along but kept rereading the same paragraph.

Then my eyes were drawn upward, and Edward was walking toward me. He still had the same brisk manner, the agile step, but his light-brown curly locks had gone almost completely grey. I stood up. I couldn't think of a thing to say.

"My hair got your tongue?" he said, same ironic smile, though perhaps now somewhat tighter. Closer up, I could see he'd grown lines around the eyes. I felt guilty for them, as well as for the hair.

"Surprising," I finally got out, wishing my own head had at least a sprinkling of wisdom to show for itself.

"Better than losing it," he said. "And when you go grey young, you don't associate it with getting old."

"You always do see the advantage."

"And you the disadvantage."

My coffee arrived. Edward ordered a Perrier.

"So it's been a long time," he said, sitting back and crossing his arms across his chest. Same old compact posture on his smallish person. Same elegant clothes: a tailor-made grey suit and a Hermès tie with yellow gazelles leaping across it.

"Five years."

"Five years and four months." Same old mathematical superiority. We were silent for a moment. "The bike shop still going strong?" Edward finally asked.

"It's fine."

"You've moved up in the world, as I understand it."

"Or down, depending on how you look at it. Geographically, I've moved south. The rue de Seine."

Edward took a sip of his Perrier, then pulverized the slice

of lemon with the long spoon. "It's taken me a while to stand the sight of you, I have to say," he said.

"Understandable."

"There were times when I thought if I saw you, I might kill you. But then later," he said with a smile that sent the wrinkles spraying around his eyes, "there were moments when I was almost grateful."

"Oh, please," I said.

"Well, maybe not quite." He took another stab at the lemon slice. "Though I didn't realize it at the time, I had a bad marriage. Without your help," he paused and looked at me, with irony, pain, and a dash of disbelief on his face, "I may not have seen it until it was too late."

"No one needs help like that."

"It gave me a second chance while I was still young." Now he was wearing a look I'd never seen on his face before. I would almost have called it misty. "I got it right this time."

"Mother said you were very happy. But it doesn't change what happened. What I did, which was inexcusable." I fixed my eyes on the coffee dregs; I couldn't look at him. "For whatever it's worth, which I know isn't much, there isn't a day goes by where I don't regret it."

"Have you heard from *Maman* recently?" he asked very softly, turning the spoon, looking into his own glass.

"No." I shrugged. "I thought she'd probably given up on me too."

"Did you think of phoning her?" he asked edgily. "Do you ever think sometimes *you* have to make the effort? That someone might need *you*?"

"I'm an albatross around the entire family's neck."

"Come on, Trevor. Stop with the martyr business. You're no more a victim than anyone else." He paused, collecting himself.

"Look, I'm not here to refight old battles." He was now concentrating hard on that spoon and smashed lemon slice. "She's ill."

"Ill with what?"

He kept at that lemon, shaking his head slightly, as the words just wouldn't come out. "What else?"

"Cancer?"

He nodded.

"What kind?"

"Ovarian. They'll be operating on her early next week."

"So quickly? Since when have you known?"

"Only since last week. You know how she is. She wouldn't admit she wasn't feeling well and didn't go to the doctor. BP had been begging her for weeks, and she finally relented."

I shook my head, speechless.

"It doesn't look good," said Edward.

"It might just be an aggravation if I phone."

"What are you talking about?" He let go of the spoon abruptly and it clattered against the glass. Looking straight at me, hazel eye to hazel eye, more serious than I had ever seen him, he added quietly: "You're still her son. How could you *not* call?"

We parted on the sidewalk outside the café, right hands shaking, left grabbing the other's arms, closing a circle, a physical reconciliation of sorts.

"I'll call," I said.

He nodded and turned on the heels of his tasseled black loafers. His step was so light, so quick, his feet hardly had time to touch the ground. With his head leaning forward, even from the back it looked as if he were already thinking about the afternoon's meetings and phone calls. And for the first time I actually admired my brother's energy and intensity. His hurry. He was no student of literature, but he heard and heeded the wingèd chariot hurrying near nevertheless. Veering to the right, Edward cut across the street, timing his passage between two moving cars perfectly, and I lost sight of him.

It had rained hard while we were sitting inside, but by the time I reached the Champs-Elysées, the sun was out. The reflection off the wet pavement was blinding, and with my eyes half closed, I walked on the very edge of the sidewalk, oblivious to the hordes of shoppers on one side and the heavy traffic on the other. Edward's announcement had hit me like a board across the head. For better or for worse, wasn't she, like me, a survivor? It was my father and sister who had not made it. Not us. How could she be dying? She was only seventy. Mixed in with the shock at her illness was a strangling fear that she would in fact not want to see me again. That my presence would, no matter what Edward said, only increase her pain and suffering by reminding her of all the pain and suffering I had inflicted upon her and everyone else in the family.

Just as I reached the gardens of the Champs-Elysées, it started to rain again. Pour. The long stretch of chestnut trees, their leaves just beginning to unfold like little umbrellas, offered no protection. Water dripped down my neck, into my eyes. The wind blew and the rain came down at a vicious slant, but I kept walking. As I crossed the pont de la Concorde, the rain was needling the Seine, rendering water, land, and sky an opaque grey. The only relief was the red brake lights that dimmed and brightened in the creeping, dense traffic.

Too much had been turned upside down in the course of one short coffee. On top of news about Mother, my brother had practically *thanked* me for my treachery. What was I supposed to do with *that*?

By the time I got back to the shop, water squelched in my shoes, dripping from my cold body as from one of those melting glaciers. The familiar smell of rubber and grease, and the steady presence of Piotr and Cassie's excessive joy at my return enveloped me like a deep-seated armchair next to a crackling fire. I plopped down on a stool and stroked Cassie's velvet ears.

"What?" asked Piotr, turning from the repair stand. "You are white."

"I just saw my brother for the first time in five years. And my mother has cancer."

Not knowing what to say, he stood there with his large, dirty hands hanging by his sides like buckets. Finally, he turned to lift the bicycle he'd been working on off the stand: "You should go home."

I had been thinking about sitting on the stool in the kitchen with Lisette while she made dinner. By home I thought he meant the rue de Verneuil.

"Yes." I nodded. "I should."

———————

Three days after my drink with Edward, during which time I had thought about Mother constantly without being able to summon the courage to phone, I was down on the quayside with my camera trying to capture the sun lighting up the water and the underbelly of the pont de la Concorde. Between showers that spring, there were many complicated skies and dramatic shadows; I'd been taking a lot of photos. Footsteps pattered behind me and stopped. Cassie wagged her tail. I pulled the camera away from my face and saw Béa Fairbank, red-cheeked and out of breath.

"Hello," I said. "Every time I see you you're on the run."

"Every time I see you, you're taking photos," she said with that chortle of hers. "I'm beginning to wonder if this bicycle shop of yours really exists. If it isn't just a front."

"Oh, the shop is real. I promise."

"I hope so. It looks like I'm going to be in Paris a lot the next year, at least. I'm thinking of getting a bicycle. Do you have anything secondhand? I haven't got much to spend."

"Sure," I said, trying to remember if indeed we did have any used bicycles at the moment. They didn't stay around long these days. "What are you doing up here? I thought I heard Curt say you lived in the 13ème."

"Yes," she said vaguely. "But now I'm staying with a friend near Les Invalides," she said. "Until I can move up to Montmartre. The studio came through, but I can't move in until next month." Today her eyes were a blue-green reflection of the water. "Could I stop by your shop sometime to see what you have? Maybe tomorrow?"

"Sure," I said.

"Around midday?"

"Let me write down the address," I said.

She tucked the paper into the pocket of her green zip-up sweatshirt and took off again. When she rounded a small bend, she turned to wave, a smile on her face. Béa actually looked as if she were enjoying herself. Most people I saw running—everyone except the firemen who ran around and around the Tuileries, chatting effortlessly—looked miserable. I always wondered why they put themselves through such added daily torture. But here was Béa Fairbank, as if running were her natural element in the same way it was for Cassie, who looked longingly after her, tail still swaying.

The next day I waited for her, putting off lunch. "Midday" ended up being close to two. By that time I was grumpy from hunger, plus I was doing inventory on accessories, finicky work that I hated, plus it was about to rain yet again and the air was charged with particles. Had I phoned my mother, though she hung over my thoughts like the new wheels that dangled over my head from the ceiling in the shop? Of course not.

Then the rain began to fall in a solid, inconsolable white sheet. It was coming down so hard, the chimes were barely audible. I looked up at Piotr's "What can I do you?" Finally Béa, soaked.

"Not exactly good bicycle-buying weather," I said, trying to sound cheery.

"Forgot my umbrella, if you can believe it. Sorry I'm a little late." She smelled of spring when I kissed her wet cheek.

"The bicycle's outside, under the tarp."

"Oh," she said.

"Have you had lunch?"

"No. No I haven't." Water ran down her face. "But . . ." and she lifted the edge of a sodden sweater.

"The only towels we have are covered with paw marks or grease. But I do have a dry shirt. And probably a sweater."

"Are you sure?" she said.

"Of course." I walked to the back of the shop and handed my dry clothes over to her. "You can change here."

"Much better," she said, coming around the corner, her light-brown hair brushed flat back, making her broad forehead and strong nose more prominent. Her fair skin had a pink tint, which contrasted with the yellow-green bruise that was still visible from her fall. My shirt and sweater came way down her skinny legs.

We headed to the Relais huddled under one crooked umbrella. It felt comfortable walking arm to arm, protected from the rain by the flimsy umbrella. It crossed my mind that I could now have women as arm-to-arm friends. And maybe Béa, safely attached to Curt, would be a perfect start.

"It's like the Day of Judgment," she said, at a gust of rain and wind that almost blew the umbrella inside out.

"Somebody up there isn't happy, that's for sure," I said.

We sat at my usual table, over in the corner, by the window. Alain rushed over with a jug of *Glühwein*. His family was from Alsace, and often in bad weather, he spiced warmed wine with clover and cinnamon and orange peels. We both ordered, at Alain's insistence, the *quiche lorraine* and salad.

"This is a nice spot," Béa said, when Alain had left.

"It's okay. Just an old-fashioned café."

"Cheers," she said, holding up her glass in my direction, then taking a sip. "Delicious."

"Cheers." I held up my glass. "So you're settling in Paris for a while?"

"As long as this studio lasts. At least a year. And I'm really happy. This morning I got a call. I can actually move in beginning next week."

"What about Curt? Can two painters share the same studio?"

"No. Not me anyway. He's actually in the States right now," she said, looking hard at some speck on the table. Then looking up at me with a smile: "So you enjoy selling bicycles?"

"You've been talking to Viviane."

She smiled. "You just don't seem the shopkeeper type to me."

"Or to Viviane. Or to Cédric."

"Just because there's a consensus doesn't mean there's a conspiracy," she said, picking up her knife and fork, pausing over the plate that had just arrived. "In fact, I was surprised this morning to see you taking pictures of a bridge. The photos that Cédric and Viviane have of yours are all scenes of things falling apart. Tortured trees and crumbling walls, that kind of thing." She cut a piece of quiche and popped it in her mouth.

"It's the dog," I said.

"The dog?"

"Since I've started walking her in the morning, I get the early light and I find it irresistible. On the stone. The water."

"Now that I think about it, you were taking pictures of flowers in the forest too, that day we walked at Hautebranche. So you're slipping?"

"I hope not. I worry. It's so easy to take a pretty picture."

"From what I've seen, I think your photos are good." I

shrugged. To my silence she added in her low voice, with a gently mocking smile: "But you'd rather not talk about it."

"Not really." I shrugged again.

"I know what you mean," she said. "Art talk can get pretentious very quickly." She pushed more salad and quiche onto the fork with the help of her knife and looked out the window while she chewed.

So we talked about Cédric and Viviane. Over coffee, we lamented the melting world—she got even more agitated on the subject than I did. But I found her very easy to talk to; it was a nice lunch. This women-as-friends thing was off to a good start.

Back in front of Mélo-Vélo, the rain had stopped, but the green tarp over the bicycles was sagging with puddles of rain. It looked like a cadaver, old bones sticking through lifeless skin.

"Stand back," I said. Untying the rope around it, I grabbed two corners and flicked it like a tablecloth. Water went flying. "This is the only used bike we have, I'm afraid." I pointed, then fished a key out of my pocket and unyoked the pack. After a struggle I extricated an old Dutch bicycle, with its heavy frame, its back-pedal brake, and clunky back wheel. "Not exactly the latest in design and performance, but it's sturdy. It won't let you down."

"Just what I'm looking for," said Béa, taking the handlebars from me. "But how much is it?"

"I'll have to ask Piotr. In the meantime, give it a try."

"You remember," Piotr said as he unloaded a box of rear lights and hung them on the hook. "We get that bike for free when we sell the guy a new one. He say we do him a favor."

"So technically, I could just give it to her." I was thinking about Cassie knocking her over, how I owed her something.

"Technically, you do what you want. But I spend most yesterday morning fixing the bike. Half hour to get off that back wheel. No less than seven hundred francs," he called to me as I went back outside. Béa had just made a narrow, wobbly turn back toward the shop, but she straightened out before braking to a halt in front of me.

"Seems great," she said, putting one small foot to the ground.

"I'll tell you what," I said. "Why don't you take it for a few days, until you move into the studio, and see what you really think of it. The hill up to Montmartre is pretty steep. You may decide it's not enough for you."

"I'm quite sure I can handle the hill," she said. "It's the price I'm worried about."

"Five hundred," I said. "We got it on an exchange."

"Are you sure?"

"I'm sure. Just give me a call after you've moved in."

"And your clothes?"

"Keep them. I mean, until you've decided on the bike."

———————

That night I dreamed about Béa Fairbank on a bicycle. It was a glorious spring day in the country, kind of Hautebranche but not really. In the middle of a green field there was a cleared area, a circle. Béa was riding around this circle, wobbling as if she were in trouble. I was in the house, standing at a window in an upstairs bedroom. I wanted to go and help her but was unable to, though the reasons for my immobility were not clear. As I watched her wobble, then straighten out, she suddenly looked up at me with one of her laughs, and all my worry melted. She didn't need my help after all; she was only trying to show me how easy it was to ride a bicycle, to reassure me. I sat down in a chair and leaned my chin on the window sill, content just to watch her go round and round on a spring day. When I woke up, all the warmth and green of the dream, of Béa's laugh, were still with me, and they stayed with me throughout the morning.

At midday I went to the bank, still the branch near the rue du Bac. As I was waiting for a teller to free up, I got a glimpse of Monsieur Petitdemange passing from one office cubicle to another. These days he was sporting the aggressive sideburns that were now in fashion. They unfortunately did not mask the fact that the locks he had fixed to his head like sculpted marble on a Greek statue had defied his efforts at immortality. He was losing his hair.

The bank, of course, was minutes from the rue de Verneuil, and as I walked out of it that day in April, I could feel my mother's presence in these streets as if she were right at my side. Before I could put it off yet again, I picked up the phone the minute I got back to Mélo-Vélo. With each ring, panic rose. After the fifth I was about to hang up, when I heard an irascible "*Allo*."

It had not occurred to me that Lisette might answer. She viewed phones as a nuisance, an interruption from the more vital occupations of the day, such as polishing the silver or scrubbing the bathtub.

"*Allo*," she said, even more irritably.

"It's Trevor," I finally got out, in not much more than a whisper. Silence, except for a heavy, wheezy intake of air. "Lisette?"

"Five years and four months."

"I know. I'm sorry."

"How could you do such a thing to me? Keep silent and away for so many years? Have you forgotten all our afternoons in the kitchen? Have you forgotten all the food I cooked for you? Have you no feelings for me at all? Or for any of us? Especially with your dear *maman*..." I heard the heave of her plump bosom and knew that the tears would be welling up, that the neat white handkerchief would be pulled from her apron pocket, the way it was when she'd been chopping onions.

"That's why I'm calling. Is *Maman* there?"

"I'm here," said a ghost voice. She must have picked up the

phone at the same time as Lisette and decided to stay silent, to let the words of reproach fall from Lisette's frank lips. Then again, her voice sounded so tired, maybe she had just been summoning the energy to speak.

"Mother," I paused. Lisette honked pointedly into her hankie, then let the phone clatter back to its receiver. "I . . . You . . . Edward told me. But I didn't know if it might not be better, if you wouldn't prefer, not to hear from me. If I might be less trouble that way." I felt like a little boy again, a very little boy, who had come home late from the neighbor's, with torn trousers and a filthy face.

"Please," she said in a tone that sounded like both a plea and a dismissal of my stumbling excuses. "I'm relieved you've phoned. That you got me." She cleared her throat. "I'm off early this evening," she added, as if about to depart on an ocean cruise instead of to the hospital.

"Maybe I could come around. Maybe later this afternoon?"

"Yes." She sounded so diminished already. "About four thirty would be perfect."

I had two hours. Piotr was still at lunch, and I paced the place like a caged animal. I looked at what was left to repair but was too agitated for tinkering. I paced some more, while Cassie wagged her tail and looked at me, head cocked. Piotr thankfully returned early, and I could leave. I needed to walk, to get out of this confined space. I took Cassie's soft ears in my hands and let her nuzzle my ear. Sensing that I was about to leave her, she gave me that look that said I was heartless and cruel. I agreed with her completely.

"Good to your mother," Piotr said, his pale-blue eyes as doleful as the dog's.

Outside I paused, looking across the street at the supermarket where until two weeks ago Michel would have been sitting. The store had a new manager who had forbidden him or any of his friends from lingering under the overhang for even an hour or two. Before moving on, he'd told me he'd be back to see me and the dog, to pick up the next installment of the money I owed him, but I hadn't seen him since. Just what I'd wished for, but now I almost missed him.

I turned right and started walking with no plan or goal in mind, and ended up at the Luxembourg gardens. Despite their proximity to the shop, I didn't come here often. Not only were they in the other direction from my daily commute, they also reminded me of my first miserable months in Paris, when we'd lived in a cramped, furnished apartment on the rue Jean-Bart. No sooner was I through the gates than those memories came rushing back to assault me.

How I'd hated everything about our new life, so unlike the one we'd just left behind in America. From the smallness of the apartment, to the fake-leather sofa that stuck to the parts of my legs not covered by the shorts my mother now dressed me in to go to the school where I felt so out of place. From the jaded eyes of the ponies in the gardens to the sight of Mother and Edmond ambling arm in arm down the shaded alleys of horse chestnuts, as if life were just one long Sunday walk in the park.

But worst of all was Mademoiselle Grimaud, the nanny Mother had hired to teach Edward and me French. She had a flat, round face, small eyes, and a tiny mouth. I thought she looked like the dish in Hey Diddle Diddle, and how I wished she'd run away with a spoon. Every day we had an hour's French lesson in the apartment, during which she would frequently express her exasperation by calling us, in English, "stew-peed boy-iz." Afterward she would take us to the Luxembourg gardens for our daily outing. She would settle on a chair near the fountains, where Edward and I watched perfectly modeled miniature sailboats with painted wood hulls and cloth sails being pushed around with sticks.

Mother, in an attempt to placate her scowling son, actually bought me a boat of my own. On the first day I carried it to the gardens, Mademoiselle Grimaud looked down at me disapprovingly.

She believed Mother spoiled and indulged us, especially me. When we got to the fountain, I put my boat in and gave it a push with my stick. The new white sail and fresh paint stood out among the dirtier, seasoned vessels around it. Edward wouldn't leave me alone, whining that he wanted a turn, pulling at my shirt. He did his whining in English, which had not escaped the notice of the other boys around the fountain any more than my new boat had. He grabbed my stick and ran off with it. I went after him, and by the time I got back, the boat was gone. I screamed in English at the boys to give it back, but they looked at me with mock incomprehension, just as they did at Mademoiselle Grimaud, when I had fetched her to intervene. Not that she made much effort to help. When I continued to demand my boat be returned, she looked at me, her message clear on that plate face: taking advantage of someone who can't even speak French properly is fair game.

I remember walking back to the apartment feeling utterly miserable, thinking that living was inescapably unbearable. It's the first time I remember feeling that it would be better to die. But not before I'd paid my brother back.

————————

The code at the rue de Verneuil had not changed: B1207, birthday of the dead duc de Coursault's favorite dead horse. Mother's Raleigh was still locked to the iron bar. The rearview mirror was misty with dust, the tires completely flat and the chain brown with rust. Despite looking gaunt and abandoned, it still had that Kryptonite lock tethering it to its post. "Just to be sure," I could hear her saying. I looked up at our windows, the old shimmering glass all closed.

I rang the buzzer with the discreet "H-L" still printed above and heard Lisette's short legs bustling across the creaking parquet toward me. The metal locks of the reinforced door clunked open.

"Oh, *Trésor*." Lisette pulled me across the threshold in a for-giving embrace. "How could you stay away so long, break so many hearts?" Though doughier and slightly more pop-eyed, Lisette seemed not to have changed since that first day we'd moved over from the rue Jean-Bart and she'd taken Edward and me into her soft arms. She still had the same smell of freshly ironed linen and whatever she was cooking. Today her eyes were rimmed with red from an afternoon of excessive emotion. "But you're back, that's what's important. We forgive you." She lowered her voice. "It's a bad business. Don't be too surprised."

Lisette waddled in front of me toward Mother's bedroom. The floorboards still creaked; a hushed, refined attention still touched every corner. Memories, sensations from long ago flooded through me as I walked down the corridor. I could hardly put one foot in front of the other.

The door was ajar when Lisette rapped cautiously.

"Come in." Lisette pushed it open and disappeared. I was left standing in the dark corridor, just outside the bedroom. Mother was bent over a small suitcase on the bed, a pair of white slippers in her hands. She did, as Edward and Lisette had warned, look terrible. The skirt and sweater she was wearing were loose. Her cheeks had lost their downy roundness. Her dyed golden-blonde hair was lank.

"Hello, T," she said without any of the zeal she usually threw into that one letter. We both stood frozen for a minute, then I walked forward to kiss her sallow cheeks, embrace her bony body. For a moment neither of us spoke. I looked down at her small suitcase, remembering how usually she was a big packer, always taking extra of everything. "Just in case." Now her needs were as reduced as her person. What just-in-case scenario could she pos-sibly encounter at a hospital?

"I didn't hear the bell," she finally said, "or I would have come out. Let's sit in the *salon*." I followed her slow, tentative step—at least her feet still splayed—down the corridor to the living room, which we had always called the *salon*, probably because it was such a Paris room. It hadn't changed at all. The tasteful reams of rich material still draped dramatically across the large windows. Two matching sofas had their cushions perfectly positioned along the back, not a dimple in sight. Each was still flanked by straight-backed chairs and antique tables, which in turn were still covered with Mother's boxes. The glass cabinet too. The Persian carpet covered just the right area of the uneven oak floor. I walked over to a window and looked through the wavy old glass at the inaccessible garden. The iron furniture had been replaced.

"New neighbors?" I asked.

"Yes. They have loud parties until all hours on their ugly plastic furniture," she said wearily. "Edmond phoned the police the other night."

"So the operation's tomorrow?" I asked, moving away from the window to a chair, near her.

"Yes." Lisette came in with tea and slices of her *quatre-quarts* cake, my favorite. She slipped in and out without a word, something I'd never seen her do. "Tea?" Mother asked. "Oh, that's right. You don't like tea."

"No, I'll have some," I said.

"So you no longer object to it as a bourgeois drink?" she asked with a faint and weary smile.

"No. It's good." I forced a sip down my throat and took a bite of the cake, which was still warm. "Why didn't you go to the doctor sooner?"

"You know how I am," she said, looking straight at me. I nodded, put down my teacup on the table, and looked away.

Then she asked me about the shop, and I forced myself to hold forth at length about Piotr, about Cassie, about the new popularity of bicycles that allowed Mélo-Vélo to survive in a world of hypermarkets and chain stores. Though we'd spoken by phone over the last five years, I had never provided many details about my life. Today I talked and talked because it spared her, and she was clearly too tired and preoccupied to talk herself.

"BP isn't here?" I asked just before leaving.

"No, he had some errands to run," Mother said, eyes fluttering, unable to hide the excuse. She may have been good at evasion, but she was a terrible liar.

I went to the kitchen to say good-bye to a still sniffling Lisette. To thank her for baking the cake, to tell her I'd be back soon, at which point, she dropped her potato peeler and flung her arms around me with a sobbing, "Oh, *Trésor*."

To Mother at the door, I said: "I'll visit you in the hospital, if that's all right."

"Yes, do come."

I walked back to Mélo-Vélo in a state of utter confusion and emotion. As always, we spoke about difficult matters in short, cloaked speech, more through our eyes, in fact, than with words. Yet hadn't it been better than no contact at all? Hadn't I enjoyed sitting in the *salon*, eating Lisette's *quatre-quarts*, the memories of other *quatre-quarts* tumbling over me? But what caused the most upheaval as I walked back to the rue de Seine was that I had been allowed through the front door at all. Their forgiveness was almost unbearable.

FOUR

"BAD?" PIOTR ASKED.

I nodded. "I'm going. You can close up."

"That girl phoned. The one you give the bike to." He handed me a chit of paper with a phone number neatly printed in a Polish school hand.

"Thanks," I said, stuffing it in my pocket and putting the leash on Cassie, who was still dancing with joy at my return.

When I walked into my studio, I threw myself down on my mattress, exhausted. Coming home from school as a boy, I'd stop in the kitchen, where Lisette would have prepared my *goûter*, my after-school snack, anything from a piece of leftover dessert to her *quatre-quarts* to a piece of baguette with a bar of chocolate wedged into it. It often seemed the best moment of the day, because I was starving, because school was over, because I was sitting in the kitchen with Lisette, while she prepared dinner. Edward must have been there sometimes too, but even as a small boy he was hyperactive and crammed his after-school time with tennis or swimming or ping pong or chess. And Mother was often out too. Like Edward, she was irrepressibly active, volunteering her time with abandon to various charitable causes.

After I ate my *goûter* and talked to Lisette, I would go to my
room and lie on my bed just the way I was lying on my mattress
now. I would look out my window at a little triangle of Paris sky
and daydream. Now I had no time for daydreams. Though Cassie
was a European dog, used to eating near eight when I usually got
home, she was also a creature of habit. Home meant food, and
she wanted her supper. She nudged me, whimpered, turned in
circles, and plopped her front paw on my knee. For some peace I
relented and fed her. I lay down again. But even then I couldn't
settle. My weariness had evaporated. I turned on the television,
but that quickly bored me. I tried reading, but after a few minutes
realized I hadn't absorbed a word. I had just seen my mother for
the first time in years. She was going to the hospital for an operation that was unlikely to save her. Concentration on anything
else was impossible.

I stood up and looked out the window. By now it was closing hour on the rue des Martyrs, and metal grilles were clattering
down for the night all up and down the street. Piotr would be
doing the same at Mélo-Vélo, I thought, putting my hands in my
pockets, leaning against the window frame. My right hand felt
the scrap of paper with Béa Fairbank's number on it. I looked at
Piotr's careful, Polish handwriting. I thought: why not call my
new friend. Curt, I remembered, was in the States. After I've asked
her about the bicycle, I can see if she wants to have a drink. So I
picked up my old phone, the same clunky grey phone I'd found
in the junk Nigel stored for half of Paris when I'd moved in here.
But I picked it up gingerly. Recently some colorful internal wires
attaching the springy cord to the receiver had become exposed.
I dialed, waiting patiently for the disk to return with a click after
each number.

The phone rang and kept ringing. As I was about to give up,
there was a breathless, "*Allo.*"

"It's Trevor." Classical music was playing in the background. "Am I bothering you?"

"No, I was just tidying up a bit. The bike's great."

"Good."

"Five hundred francs, right?"

"Yes."

"Then I'll take it. Can I come down to the shop sometime to pay you?"

"Of course. Or I could come up to you. I don't live far from Montmartre. In fact, I could come up this evening. You could show me your new studio. Maybe we could have a drink."

"I guess so. Sure. Why not."

Half an hour later, I was walking out the door, turning right toward the Sacré Coeur. When I reached the boulevard de Clichy, the tourist buses were coughing out visitors in search of the area's cheap bars, strip joints, and hookers. But on the other side, the Bohemian chic of Montmartre quickly took over. It was, in fact, hard to believe that I was still on the rue des Martyrs. At the end of it I had to stop and consult my grease-stained Plan de Paris, as I didn't frequent the warren of quaint streets crisscrossing the steep hill very often.

It seemed to take forever, getting to the address Béa had given me, but finally I was punching in the code on a nondescript Haussmann building. As instructed, I walked through the staid foyer, with its swirly dark marble looking lugubrious in the low-watt lighting. I pushed the door open onto the courtyard and stopped dead in my tracks. Béa had said "house," but I hadn't imagined anything like what stood before me, a beautiful old edifice that looked as if it belonged in the country. Its pale-yellow stone had green-shuttered windows and a slate roof. An ancient wisteria wound its thick, crooked trunk around the front door, its heavy flowers drooping, on the point of a lush first bloom. To the right were tall hedges and a wall, to the left a tree and grapevines. It looked as though house and tree and grapevines had been nobly holding their ground for the last two hundred years, while all around it the city had grown, unchecked, untended.

At the left side there was a small side door, as Béa had instructed. The bicycle was leaning right next to it. I climbed the stairs and knocked, and there she was at the door, letting me in with a guarded and distant smile that made me wish I hadn't come.

"You said house, but wow," I said, following her through a narrow passage into a large, sky-lit studio. "How did you ever find this place?"

"It belongs to antique dealers. The wife's father was a painter, and he had this studio built onto the side. Though he had been quite successful near the end of his life, he'd struggled for much of his career, and he told his daughter that this part of the house should always be rented to an artist, and cheaply. Since the Frochots are Anglophiles, they've been renting it to someone English for several years. It usually passes on just by word of mouth. The previous tenant is a friend of mine. The lease only lasts a year. So I'm savoring every minute."

At one end of the room was an easel, supporting a canvas I couldn't see, and facing an empty stool where a model had sat. There were brushes and bottles and signs of paint everywhere. The smell of linseed oil hung on the air with a pleasing sharpness. On the other side of the room was a sitting area, with two small sofas draped in sheets in front of a small fireplace, which had a guitar propped next to it. All one side was glass that slanted toward the sky, and along the walls, canvases were stacked one in front of the other.

"It's still a bit of a mess," she said.

"No it isn't. In fact, it's hard to believe you just moved in."

"The advantages of a furnished flat. Plus with all my moving around, I don't have much stuff. Just those," and she threw her hands dismissively toward the stacks of canvases. Then she turned to me. "I haven't been out all day. And I've got nothing to offer you to drink. I hope you don't mind if we go out."

"Aren't you going to show me some of those paintings?"

"No," she said flatly.

She grabbed an old leather rucksack, and we went downstairs, pausing at the bicycle, taking in the garden. Béa pointed out the three lines of grapevines, which were the only survivors of what had once been an extensive vineyard. Then she took me to a café-wine bar down the street. Classic Montmartre. Old-fashioned, unaffected, with simple bistro chairs and tables, a battered zinc counter, the day's menu and wine specials chalked onto a blackboard, run by young, hip people. At the back, an elevated platform had a drum set and a keyboard. "There's jazz here most nights," Béa said. "It's usually not bad. I used to come here quite a lot last year when I was in Paris for a commission and was staying with the friend who had the studio before me." She went up to the waiter and kissed him hello.

We each ordered a beer.

"So what about Curt. Is he going to move in when he gets back from the US?" I asked.

She sat back and didn't speak for a moment, letting her eyes wander around the room. She leaned forward in her seat, then leaned back. "He," she began and paused. The "he" sounded more like a hiccup. "That's finished."

"Oh," I said. "I'm sorry."

She shrugged. "The circumstances are a little hard to digest. He ran off with Connie."

"Oh."

"It was going on right under my nose for weeks. Certainly at Hautebranche that weekend. All the while he was talking about moving in with me—how we'd work things out in Paris, how he'd have to get another studio, how great it would be. Today was awful. A new model came—the first one since Connie—and I couldn't work. All I could do was think about Connie and Curt. She went with him to the States. I guess her novel's on hold."

Our beers arrived. "I really am sorry," I repeated, raising my glass.

"Cheers, I guess." She sipped her drink.

"How long were you together?"

"A year."

I nodded. "I probably shouldn't say this, but I'm not surprised." It had something to do with that half beard, his animal presence, and his pepper smell.

"Actually, I shouldn't have been either. He was with someone else in Aix when I met him." She rolled her eyes. "What goes around comes around, right?"

"Sometimes, I guess."

"You'd think at thirty-five I'd know better."

"I don't think that kind of mistake has an age limit."

"That's probably right. Anyway, at the moment my mind knows I'm better off without a serial cheater, but my gut is having trouble catching up. It will. My getting this studio is a sign that work and more work is the answer for me. And to hell with men."

"Come on. Just because Curt acted like a jerk . . ."

She smiled and looked at me with an ironic, knowing smile: "Do you want something to eat? I didn't have lunch. I'm starving."

"Sure," I mumbled, looking at the blackboard. Not only did I keep forgetting how much she knew about me, I kept forgetting what I knew about me. What *I* had done, peppery patchouli oil nowhere in sight. Then again, if Curt had been seeing someone else when they met, she wasn't exactly a stranger to the dark side either.

We ordered some food and a carafe of red wine. Someone came out on the stage to check the sound system.

"Do you play that guitar next to the fireplace?" I asked.

"I played a lot when I was teenager. At school, for assemblies, parties. That kind of thing. Mostly now I play for myself. It's a nice break from the easel."

She told me about how she'd been to art school in London instead of going to university, and that as soon as she'd finished, she'd run to Aix, where she'd met Viviane and Cédric. Since then, she said, she'd always felt the need to move around. She was hoping that this year in Paris, where she'd be staying put as much as she could, would actually help her work, focus on it as well as on herself. "But my life is boring. What about you?"

I was saved by the jazz trio. Béa knew them too; more kisses were thrown around. The pianist tried to get Béa to come up and sing, but she turned red and refused.

"You sing too?" I asked.

"Only when I'm in the mood," she answered, still flushed.

The musicians talked and made jokes between playing. Because it was a small space and they knew most people in the audience, we might have been sitting in someone's living room. It was intimate and relaxing, comforting almost. When there was no music, Béa and I talked about inconsequential things, and that I also found easy. By the time we left, it was after midnight. In front of the door of the drab building that concealed the beautiful house, we paused.

"I'd totally forgotten about the bicycle," Béa said, putting her hand to her cheek. "I'm sure I've got my checkbook in here." She opened the mouth of the leather rucksack and it was a spring box of old paper, odd pens, and plain junk.

"You don't owe me anything."

"No, come on." She was still rummaging through the mess.

"Remember I told you we got it for free. It was just a couple hours of work. Plus I owe you for my dog practically knocking you unconscious. I won't take a centime for it. Though it looks as though you've got plenty of those little coins running loose in that big bag of yours."

She stopped rummaging and looked up, hand still in the bag. Seeing my smile, she let go that laugh again, just as I'd hoped. I wanted to leave with it in my ears. "All right. I'll accept your charity. Thanks very much." And she reached up to kiss me on both cheeks. "Let's say I owe you a supper then."

"Okay."

"I'll ring you soon." And she disappeared behind the dark door, which closed with a firm click.

Making a wrong turn on the way back, I found myself walking along the side of Montmartre Cemetery. The tombs and mausoleums loomed in the dark. Though I had enjoyed the evening and found conversation with Béa effortless, I couldn't shed thoughts of Mother's illness and impending operation. On my way up to Montmartre, a haggard face on the boulevard de Clichy made me think of her. The hushed, grim building in front of Béa's house was like a morgue. During our meal and the music, I kept imagining my mother in the hospital, nurses coming in, getting her ready for the next day's operation. How lonely and scared she must be feeling, whether or not Edmond had been allowed to stay and help her settle. By now, in any case, she'd be lying alone, surely awake, with no food or drink in her, in preparation for the anesthesia. With my prolonged post-accident stay in the hospital, I could imagine it perfectly, right down to the crinkly noise made by the plastic bed pad under the sheet.

I picked up my step, walking as fast as I could to get past the chill that the tombs from the cemetery seemed to emanate over the wall. I didn't slow down, even once I was back into the lights of Paris nightlife, and by the time I reached my blue door I was out of breath. Inside, when I switched on the light, it looked as if a natural disaster had occurred. During my prolonged absence, Cassie had removed all the covers from the mattress, dragged my towel from the bathroom, and shredded a couple of newspapers that had been on the table. She greeted me sheepishly, but I couldn't scold her. I knew that she was frightened when left alone. That having changed owners twice, she was always afraid it would happen again. The same latent fear had haunted my childhood. People are there, then suddenly not, and your life is never the same afterward. I grabbed the dog, happy to feel her body's warmth and exuberance, but she wriggled away. Now that I was back, her anxiety had vanished and she just wanted to go out.

———————

The next day, late morning, I flipped through the pages of my small leather address book, a Christmas present from Edward in bygone days. Its green calf-leather cover was soft and smooth, the pages inside crisp and fine, cream-colored and gilt-edged. The best, even though the present was half meant as a joke. "Let's see if you can fill up a quarter of it," King Rolodex had laughed as I'd opened it that Christmas Eve. As for his *coordonnées*, I'd taken Tipex to the entry because of course everything had changed: his work number, his home address and number, the name of his wife.

The phone rang several times. Edward had in fact not moved far. He and Anne-Sophie now lived—"very comfortably," was the way Mother had put it—on the rue de Bellechasse. I imagined echoing halls and cavernous *salons* making passage to the phone a spatial challenge, until it suddenly occurred to me that I might get Anne-Sophie, or even worse, one of the children. It was Wednesday, and they would be home early. I hung up. I phoned his *portable* number.

"What news?" I asked.

"Nothing yet," I heard through background static. "It would be good if you could be there when she wakes up this afternoon."

"I'll be there by two."

"Caroline has a piano recital this afternoon. Then I have to stop by the office again, but I'll come early evening."

The clinic was outside Paris, in the leafy, swank suburb of Neuilly, and public transport was inconvenient. For the first time in many years, I took a taxi. It rolled down boulevards and avenues lined with imposing apartment blocks set safely back from the public thoroughfare behind black iron fences. The clinic had no black fence and was marked with a large cross; otherwise it looked just like the buildings around it. Behind some trees there was a parking lot, mostly filled with Jaguars and Mercedes, one of which must have been obscuring Edmond and Mother's little Renault. I paid the driver and walked up the path at the side to the entrance. The thick glass doors opened automatically with what almost sounded like a human sigh. The hushed lobby was paneled with light, cheery wood and adorned with a fake Chagall here, a fake Manet there. A pert woman with bleached blonde hair and a white coat that barely covered a short, tight skirt and tanned legs sat behind the front desk. After phoning upstairs to confirm I was really expected, she sent me up the elevator to room 33. It was not until I was walking down the corridor to Mother's room that I got my first pungent whiff of hospital, and I might as well have been right back in there myself, aching and bandaged after my bicycle accident. They could get rid of the harried staff and the yellowed walls of a public establishment, but ultimately they couldn't mask that smell of illness and death.

I gently pushed open the door to Mother's room. She was lying like a marble pillar under the sheet. Without the bleeping machinery and tubes attached to her, she might already have been stretched out in her coffin. Leaning forward in a chair at her side was Edmond. He looked up expectantly, obviously hoping for a doctor or a nurse. Somebody helpful. Anyone but his spiteful, disaffected stepson. Because his already sagging face fell farther at the sight of me. It was a look that confirmed beyond the shadow of a doubt that my long-term campaign had been an unmitigated success. But instead of being buoyed by victory, I felt punctured with shame.

"She hasn't woken up yet?" I asked quietly as he stood up. Since the last time I had seen him five years ago, he had shrunken noticeably, and his deeply set grey eyes had taken on a sad droop. Only his aquiline nose and the protruding, almost diaphanous forehead resisted the assault of aging.

"No. But soon," he said.

"How did it go?" I asked.

"As well as can be expected, I think. But you know," he paused and lowered his voice even more, then shrugged.

We both looked down at her pale, frozen face. Edmond gestured to the other chair, and I sat down too, putting my eyes right at the level of Mother's white shroud. The sheet was clean and still, but all I could think about was what lay underneath, what that body had been subjected to earlier today. How it would have been sliced open with a razor-sharp, sterilized scalpel, how the doctor would have peeled back her skin like his breakfast fruit, before sawing through the muscle wall and honing in on the murderous intruders, which he would have scooped out like peach pits. What did they do with the tumors? Did they plop them into a metal bowl, then cart them off for more slicing? It sent a nauseous shudder through me, and I forced myself to focus on the plastic drip suspended above Mother's head. For many minutes I watched the transparent liquid fall, pregnant drop by pregnant drop, regularly and relentlessly, at once soothing and tortuous.

After awhile Edmond said: "Edward will be here early evening."

"So he said."

I returned my attention to the drip and thought about how much more burdened than mine other people's lives were. Edward not only had a grueling job but also a sprawling family. Besides the three children with Stephanie and the other he'd had with Anne-Sophie, another was on the way, he'd told me. And here, I, Trevor so-proud-of-his-name McFarquhar, had shop hours and a dog to worry about, with help from Piotr on both fronts. And then there was Edmond, who'd had the prime of his life poisoned by me. What must that have been like? To come home every evening from a job he didn't much like to my scowl, to my disdain?

Edmond sighed and shifted in his seat. I looked down at my dirty fingernails, at the grease I could never quite get out of the small crevices in my hands. "I'm sorry, you know, for all the trouble I've given you, over the years."

His bushy eyebrows raised then settled again above the deep-set eyes. He exhaled, almost as if in physical pain, shifting on his chair. "Well. Yes. Thank you."

"I mean . . ." I stopped because his attention was elsewhere, back to Mother, whose eyes were now open. We both stood up, shifting into her line of vision so that she wouldn't have to move her head. "Hélène," Edmond croaked, putting his hairless, freckled hand gently on her shoulder. "Trevor is here," he said, and Mother's eyes turned slowly toward me, then closed again with reptilian languor. "The doctor said it would be like this for the rest of the day. Mostly sleep." We sat down again.

For the first time I could imagine what it must have been like for her, sitting at my bedside after the bicycle accident. How utterly terrified she must have felt at the idea that, after having already lost two members of her family, she might be about to lose another. While I was ruminating about how extraordinary it was that this hadn't already occurred to me at some point in my albeit solipsistic existence, the doctor swept into the room. He beamed energy and competence, and though it was hard to imagine maintaining such a friendly, confident air amid all that death and disease, his manner was reassuring. After checking Mother's machines and charts, he called us out into the corridor.

"The cancer has spread everywhere," he said, now serious and earnest. "I'm afraid there is little we can do except make her as comfortable as possible. She'll be heavily sedated until tomorrow."

"How long?" said Edmond, who seemed to have shrunk several more centimeters in the last minute.

"That's always hard to know. Probably not more than six months." BP shifted on his feet; I instinctively took his arm.

When the doctor left, we looked at each other but didn't speak. After awhile, he asked me in a whisper about the shop and the bicycle business. I asked him about how he was spending his time, now that he was completely retired. Mostly, he said, reading history. The First World War, "the last time the world as it had been was turned on its head," he said.

By early evening Edward still wasn't there, and I started worrying about getting back to collect Cassie before Piotr closed up the shop. Not wanting to disturb Mother, who was again sleeping, I asked Edmond if he had a mobile phone.

"No." He waved his hand as if trying to keep all of modernity at a great distance.

I walked down the corridor to look for a pay phone, thinking that we weren't completely at odds, my stepfather and I. We shared a recalcitrant relationship to time, a greater interest in the past than the present that meant we did everything in our power to resist the frantic age that was buzzing around us.

When I got back, Edward had just arrived. He and Edmond, previously almost exactly the same height, were whispering shoulder to shoulder. I could feel their intimacy, their complicity, and for once, instead of bristling, I felt envious.

"You two need to go home," Edward said. "I'll stay until closing at ten."

"I'll be back tomorrow," I said, leaving first.

And the next and the next, I thought, passing through the sighing glass doors of the entrance into a beautiful spring evening.

FIVE

––––

'"I HAVE NEVER been able to lie to your mother," Edmond said to Edward and me as we convened the next morning under a fake Picasso in the wood-paneled lobby of the clinic. "Even to spare her feelings," he added mysteriously. "We have to tell her the prognosis." I looked at Edward, but his mind was as always on how to proceed, the future rather than the past.

"If it would be easier for you, I'll tell her," he said. "Or we'll come with you, if that would be more helpful." He looked at me; I nodded.

After a moment, BP said: "You know, I'd planned to tell her myself, alone, but now I think it would be better if we were all there. Seeing her two boys together might give her strength."

"I agree," I said, looking down at the ground. "We should all be there."

So the three of us took the elevator upstairs and walked silently down the corridor to her room, gloomy as executioners. We stood around her bed. She was propped up now against the pillows.

"Hélène," Edmond said, taking her hand and smiling. "You look much better today." It was true, she did, and I could see him hoping, as we would all hope at some time over the next weeks,

Mother included, that she would defy nature and the medical profession and recover.

"I feel a bit better. Thank you." She looked at each one of us, but her eyes lingered on me. "And you're all here." Then the tears welled up and spilled over one by one, just like the drip I had watched so attentively the day before. Edward took her other hand.

"Anything can happen," he said, then looked apologetically at Edmond for such a misleading remark.

"Hélène," BP started again. "We have spoken to the doctor."

"You don't have to say another word, Edmond," she said quietly but firmly, perfectly in control despite two wet lines down her pale cheeks. "I know." And then she closed her eyes. The three of us exchanged glances.

"But . . . ," Edward started but stopped himself. The force of his optimistic nature made bad news almost impossible for him to accept. He was always sure a way out could be found, if the search was thorough enough and the effort sufficiently determined.

"What can we do for you, to make you more comfortable?" Edmond asked, looking up and down her bed, as if he'd lost something and was sure it was to be found in the folds of the bed covers.

"This is what I would like," said Mother, eyes still closed. "I would like to go home as soon as possible. You'll have to get a nurse. Don't let Lisette convince you she can do this on her own. But I want to be home. That's all."

I was searching for something to do or say, anything other than standing there like my usual sullen self. "Once you're settled at home, we'll have a big family lunch," I finally spluttered. Edward and Edmond stared at me in shock.

"Absolutely," Edward said, never disarmed for long.

For the next week, Mother stayed at the clinic. She was so uneasy, we took turns sitting with her all through the visiting hours. Being caught up in trying to make her comfortable, all of us pushed aside past troubles and resentments, and it was as if nothing had ever ruffled the seas of our domestic tranquility. But every day I thought a little more urgently that it was time for things to be said. That if I didn't try to chip away at that wall of silence soon, the opportunity would be literally buried forever.

On a clear, spring morning, Mother was wheeled down the corridor, into the elevator, through the hushed lobby and the sighing automatic doors. Edward pushed the chair, and I carried two plants that had been sent by friends. Plants that would certainly outlive the owner.

Edmond had pulled their small car out front. Edward and I helped Mother from the wheelchair into the front seat of the Clio. It was a horrible moment, her skeletal elbow poking into my hand, the effort required for her brittle, pained body to fold up and fit in. Once settled, she pushed the button to open her window and lifted her face to the two of us. "I'm sorry it always takes something unpleasant like a stay in the hospital, but thank you both for being here." Then Edmond moved slowly forward, as if he were driving a breakable antique, and Edward and I were left side by side, watching our mother and stepfather disappear down the leafy avenue. After a moment, I said to Edward: "Do you think she'll ever make it to another family lunch?"

"I'm afraid she probably will."

"The doctor said she's likely to be in a great deal of pain." More silence.

Finally Edward took a step forward and said: "At least she'll have all of us around her." He pressed the key in the direction of the car. The lights flashed and all the locks on his shiny silver BMW station wagon opened in unison. "Can I give you a lift?"

As we pulled out of the clinic, I wondered how much Edward knew. The few times I'd heard him mention our father's death, he'd said it was an accident as if he really believed it. I thought, as we passed the sign telling us we were back in Paris, I could tell him, tell him right here and now. Instead I said: "Are you ever going to let me meet Anne-Sophie?" Though she'd taken shifts with Mother at the clinic too, our paths had never crossed.

"You mean will I trust you?" He smiled.

"Sort of, yes," I said.

"Of course. There will be the family lunch, remember?"

"Right." And then I couldn't help asking what had been on my mind since our peace summit at the café. "What news from New York?"

"She's always swamped with work, though she did find the time to remarry. Bruce is his name. I'm surprised you don't know all this." He gave an arch look as he glanced at the side mirror and pulled out ahead of another car.

"Mother mentioned it once on the phone," I said. "Another lawyer, I understand."

"All they do is work and earn enough to acquire the necessary appurtenances of a successful Wall Street life. They have a roomy apartment on the Upper East Side and are building a large house for themselves on Nantucket." He accelerated too quickly at the green light.

"So you're still furious at her."

"No, no. After all, what's so different about my life? I work all the time too and live in a nice apartment in the *7ème*. It's her increasing disinterest in the kids that infuriates me," he said, a mixture of distaste and satisfaction on his face. "At first, she made noises about seeing them all the time, though she could never take them for the full school vacations. She used to call a lot. Now, she phones twice a week, always at the same time. Anne-Sophie says it's as if she's written it into her diary, like an appointment. And this summer, she can only take them for two weeks because she's working 'flat out' on a telecommunications merger and the house on Nantucket probably won't be finished. Even then, she's planning to get a nanny, because Bruce gets 'stressed,' was I think the word she used."

"She must miss Mother's services," I said but then wished I hadn't. My remark made me feel disloyal to everyone.

"The funny thing—the good thing, really—is that the kids still adore her. Even Henri, who remembers nothing of her in Paris. It seems to be built into the DNA. And Caroline can give Anne-Sophie a really tough time."

"Stephanie's never mentioned taking them back?"

"She mentions boarding school in America sometimes."

We drove the rest of the way in silence. Edward was in a hurry to get back to the office, so he swung around the place de la Concorde and dropped me at the entrance to the Tuileries. His silver car shot around the obelisk, out of sight, and I entered the gardens. Now that I walked the dog on the elevated terraces, I had become used to seeing the main section from a certain tree-level distance. Down here everything looked huge, magnified. The chestnuts towered over my head. The fountains and the statues loomed larger, and the expanse of white, chalky gravel seemed to stretch forever. I felt very small.

When my sister died, my six-year-old self was racked with guilt. I was convinced that if I hadn't insisted on going to Tom Rogers's house that day—selfishly, just so I could jump on his new trampoline—Franny wouldn't have died. If only I'd been a responsible child, had stayed with my mother, as she'd wanted me to that hot July day, I would have seen the car coming, put my hand up and stopped it, before it could flatten my little sister. When I got older and could think abstractly, the simple fact of my presence, it seemed to me, would have reordered events and avoided the tragedy.

A year later, I felt guilty again when I found my father lying on the driveway gravel. Though it was said he must have fallen during the night, when he went up to fiddle with the television antenna, I was convinced that if only I'd gotten up earlier, found him sooner, I would have been able to call for help in time to save him.

But in both those cases my guilt was that of the survivor. Even while my gut told me I could have done something to prevent the tragedies, my head knew that neither death was my fault. That my feelings of guilt were misplaced. In the Edward-Stephanie triangle, however, my culpability had been that of a perpetrator. I had been a full-blown actor, a catalyst, an antagonist, a villain. And that, I thought as I left the gardens to join the street traffic, was guilt I could never rationalize, much less shed. That what I had done would haunt me for the rest of my life.

When I walked into the shop, Piotr was busy making plans for a new tool rack. He looked up at me, pencil in one hand, ruler in the other. I collapsed on the stool.

"You look terrible," he said, squinting. "Go home. I close."

"You're the one who should go home," I answered. "You've been here day after day, with the shop and the dog to look after." Cassie was dancing at my side. It was hard to imagine that once upon a time, I'd seen Piotr as a stopgap, someone to help me ride out the transport strike before I closed up shop definitively.

"I'm good here," Piotr said. "I got to finish this job. Another day."

In the end, I stayed too, because I couldn't face an entire afternoon and evening alone in my cell. I went into an organizational frenzy, tidying the small desk that had grown into a mountain range of papers. I took an informal inventory of what was left on the shelves, making a list of supplies to reorder. By the end of the afternoon, I felt marginally better. Restoring practical order is a great palliative, even if its soothing effects are quickly eroded by the relentless return of more chaos.

When I returned to the rue des Martyrs early evening, Madame Picquot was just opening her door, dirty nylon shopping bag in hand, all stocked up for an evening alone. She leaned over and patted Cassie.

"I left a letter and a plastic bag for you at the bottom of the stairs," she said, putting down her bag inside the door and slipping Cassie the end of her baguette. "A woman dropped them off this afternoon." She looked hard at me, never having observed a female anywhere near me.

"Thank you," I said, thinking it was probably Jacqueline, in urgent need of something. She always seemed to pop up just as I was beginning to forget about her.

But as I picked up the off-white envelope, I saw immediately that it was not her hand. This writing was loopy, and the ink was a sepia tone Jacqueline never would have used. And in the plastic bag were my shirt and sweater. When I got upstairs, I placed the envelope on the table while I fed Cassie. I filled her water bowl and washed my morning's coffee cup. I collected a stack of old newspapers and put them next to the door to be recycled. I looked at some of my recent photos taken along the *quais* during my morning walks, particularly ones of the five-meter stone wall that masons had been working on all spring. Every day they chipped away another patch of the *crépi*, the roughcast that had been smothering the great slabs of limestone, probably since not long after the war, when the country slapped it on every surface they could find. The letter sat like an eye on the table.

Finally I took it over to the window, where a shaft of late afternoon sun slipped between two buildings into my room, and I slit open the cream-colored envelope with my kitchen knife. Inside was a postcard from which Béa's face stared back at me. It was a self-portrait, from the shoulders up, her face turned a quarter away from the viewer so that her prominent features—the broad, flat forehead above slightly bulging eyes and long nose that had a small bump at the top, her delicate chin—were outlined and accentuated by the wall behind her. The wall with straggling vines resembled the garden at Hautebranche, and she looked as if she were turning to leave, to go out the gate for a run, except that her hair was loose on her shoulders. The colors were muted, the textures thick. She had captured her healthy complexion well. I turned over the card, where it was printed in the corner: "Beatrice Fairbank, *Auto-Portrait*, 2000." Underneath was her swirling hand in the sepia ink: "Dear Trevor, The bicycle is great! I haven't taken the métro once and what a pleasure it is to live above ground. Many thanks for your kindness (clothes included!). Hope you enjoyed the jazz. *Amitiés*, Béa"

It was the handwriting that I looked at most closely. The hand that was able to produce such controlled extravagance seemed to tell me more about Beatrice Fairbank than the self-portrait or the words. I thought about her determined pursuit of a difficult career as a painter, and the chaos of her jack-in-the-box handbag, of her being late at the shop and forgetting an umbrella on a rainy day. Her trouble settling down, even at age thirty-five.

I opened the plastic bag and took out my shirt and sweater. I propped up the card on the table as I took a beer out of the refrigerator, slit the bread down the side, and slid in sausage, cheese, and tomato. After my sandwich in the company of Béa's card, I watched a bit of television. It helped get the morning out of my mind, the sharp medicinal smell of the clinic room mixed with the rotting flowers we'd left behind. Mother's clothes were now way too big and looked totally out of place on her. Her decline could almost be measured in hours, rather than days or weeks or months. Standing in the doorway of her clinic room, I'd found this so distressing, I'd offered to fetch the wheelchair. That rush away from death had surprised me, since most of the time I found living such an arduous chore.

When I took the dog out, it was still light; the towers of the Sacré Coeur were bathed in pink, a soft blue sky behind. It reminded me of Béa's complexion. Maybe she really was becoming a friend. That was a happy thought. I looked down at Cassie, who was intently sniffing the corner of the building. She made me happy too. My family taking me back made me both happy and relieved. On the other hand, my mother's slipping from the picture was both sad and terrifying and made me very unhappy. I looked back up at the towers and the fleeting evening light. It was all very intense and confusing, this happy-sad business. But at least, finally, I was feeling something other than melancholy and rancor.

———————

How do you talk to your dying mother about things that have been off limits for more than thirty years, I was desperately asking myself as I climbed the stairs at the rue de Verneuil the next day, the dog dancing around me. The answer was another question: how do you live for the next thirty without finally getting a few things spoken out loud?

Edmond answered the door for perhaps the first time ever, and it occurred to me that in the past, he'd probably actively avoided letting me into the apartment. His reading glasses were halfway down his nose, a book in his hand. It was an awkward moment because for the first time too, I felt we should kiss hello. The way I kissed Mother or Lisette hello when they answered the door, the way Edward kissed Edmond, in the filial way all French family members, male and female, greet one another. Fortunately, we were both spared by the dog, whose great excitement over a new place and a new person diverted our attention from one another.

"How is she?" I asked.

"Happy to be home. Better than she was in the clinic. But you know . . ." he trailed off. "When you called to say you were coming, she perked up. Go see her." Edmond took his book back to his study, and I walked down the dark corridor to the bedroom, Cassie lurching on her leash, right and left.

Mother was in bed, with books and magazines strewn about, as if she were having *une grasse matinée*, a fat, lazy morning. Except there was nothing *gras* about the scene. The room had the same sharp medicinal smell as the clinic, except here it mixed uneasily with the usual scent of her perfume. And it was afternoon, not morning. Her face was about the same color as the pillowcase behind it. And though it seemed impossible, she looked even thinner in the wide bed.

"Hello, T," Mother said with no bounce. Cassie now lurched toward the bed, and I followed to kiss her hello. Up close I noticed her streaked-blonde hair dye was growing out, exposing a few centimeters of grey, mixed with the odd strand of brown. Shortly after we'd moved to Paris, still living near the Luxembourg gardens, she had returned one day from the *coiffeur* with it dyed. I had gone into an uncontrollable rage, had locked myself in the bathroom for several hours, until she'd started to sob outside the door. Today, seeing the neglected dye was almost as painful. I sat on a chair next to the bed. "Hello, Dog," she said, letting Cassie lick her veined hand. "I hope you're not coming today to tell me you won't be here tomorrow for lunch."

"No, no. I just thought I'd stop by today too. I hope you don't mind I brought the dog." I'd let her off the leash, and she was sniffing every corner of the room. "Cassie is her name."

"She's sweet," Mother said absently.

"She'll calm down in a minute," I said. "What are you reading?" It had been a long time since we'd passed books back and forth, using literature as a code to communicate, a place to leave messages for one another.

"Something Tiffy sent me, apparently all the rage in New

York. I don't think much of it. Or I can't seem to get into it. I'm reading a lot of magazines." Aunt Tiffy was my godmother and my mother's oldest friend. They'd grown up together in New York, and since my mother was an only child, she thought of Tiffy almost as a sister. When I was a child, she'd been my subversive godmother, the person who had sent me books in English when my mother wanted me reading nothing but French.

As for Mother herself, she always had a book. She alternated between French and English, and in both languages she read quickly and with total absorption. Even a room full of people sharing a hilarious joke wouldn't distract her. Befitting her general approach to life, she would only talk about what she'd read in the vaguest terms, as if the inner workings of a book also constituted too private a matter for public discourse. She'd go no farther than suggesting I read this or that: "It's about a family. It's well written." And I'd gobble it up, looking for what she might be trying to tell me through somebody else's story. And today, just for a minute, she brightened, lifting herself slightly from the pillows, and said: "Actually, the last really good book I read, also recommended by Tiffy, is right there, on top of that stack." She pointed to her desk.

"Thank you," I said, taking *The Emigrants*, by W. G. Sebald, an author I had not even heard of. The cover photo was promising: a group of about ten schoolboys, around the same age as me when I arrived in France, around the same era. Some smiled, some looked blank, and some downright unhappy. "How is Aunt Tiffy?"

"The same effervescent ball of fire as ever. Age hasn't slowed her down one bit." We sat in silence for a moment. She looked at Cassie, who was sitting at my side, panting: "Do you remember this?" She pointed to a blue object on her bedside table.

"I certainly do."

"It's never left that spot." She looked down at Cassie, who was now lying attentively at my feet. "You finally got your wish."

Mother had enrolled me in a pottery class, and in preparation for her birthday, I'd made a dog out of clay because for the previous year I had been begging for the real thing. Thinking a clay one might help my cause, I worked very hard on it, and I painted it blue, her favorite color. The morning of her birthday, I came in the bedroom with my gift. As I handed it to her, she thanked me for the sweet lamb. At which point I burst into tears and delivered my final plea. She'd stroked it, tried to console me, saying over and over how much she liked it, how it would never leave her bedside. But no real dog.

"And when the wish did come true, she seemed like a curse."

"Really?"

"Just at first. Now I would even say Cassie was a stroke of luck." I leaned over and touched her now supine back. Her tail thumped.

"Good. Because I worry, you know." She paused and fiddled with the stems of her reading glasses. "I worry that you never see anything in its better light." I stayed silent. She went on: "Looking back on it now, I probably should have gotten you a dog. A small one. It might have helped you adjust. You had such trouble adjusting."

"A lot had happened," I said.

"Yes, a lot had happened." My heart beat faster.

Lisette pushed the door open with the tea tray.

"Ah, *Trésor*," she wheezed. "Why did no one tell me you were here? I must have had the vacuum cleaner on when you buzzed." She put the tray down on the table near my chair. I stood up to embrace her soft, round body, which today smelled like spice cake. "This is the way it should be," she babbled on. "You here with your *maman*. There is no better medicine, I'm sure of it. Do you want some tea and cake? I didn't bring a cup or a plate for you."

"He can use mine," said Mother. "I don't need anything right now."

"Oh, *Madame*," Lisette clucked. "Take some tea at least. Please."

"All right. A little tea then," Mother said.

"And I'll have some of the cake," I said as Lisette bustled the tea service into action. Sparkling silver spoons clinked against delicate porcelain, hot tea flooding the cup. A slice of cake was placed with a silver fork on a patterned plate. Once she'd finished with that, Lisette straightened the magazines on the bed and plumped Mother's pillows as best as she could without moving her. When she finally waddled out, we were back to flitting across the surface of the here and now.

"So you're coming tomorrow," Mother repeated, just as I was about to leave. She looked worn out by my visit.

"For whatever it's worth," I said, leaning down to kiss her good-bye. "Yes. I'm back."

Edmond came out of his study as I walked toward the door.

"How do you think she seems?" he said. "She's better at home, no?"

"She tires easily," I hedged. He nodded, a flicker of hope abruptly extinguished. "I'll be back tomorrow for lunch," I said as I headed down the stairs, the dog nipping at my legs. Edmond stayed in the doorway until I was out of sight, and that image of him stuck with me for a long time. An old man, still trim and smoothly dressed, but his elegant trousers pulled up on his shortened waist, his face haggard and lost, standing alone on the threshold.

———

Though our exchange had hardly caused walls to crumble, the first bricks had been loosened. That was something. And then I was surprised at how reassuring it felt to be back at the rue de Verneuil. Absence had given me a new appreciation of its hush, its familiar objects and smells. Much as I had tried to forget and deny them, there had been plenty of happy memories. There was sitting in the kitchen with Lisette or in the reading corner that Mother had set up for me in my bedroom, with its large, cushioned armchair and a standing lamp. I'd spent hours curled up comfortably, until I got too big to curl. Or there were the times I surreptitiously slipped into Edmond's study, which was lined with oak shelves and the old leather-bound history books he collected. How despite their belonging to my hated stepfather, I would pluck one from the shelf and smell the old paper and leather, turn the brittle pages, consult the print date, and try to imagine the first owner. Then, too, I remembered the frightened feeling I used to get, especially in the early days, if Mother were out for too long. I would fill up with terror, almost to the point of being sick, that she wouldn't come back and I'd be left an orphan.

The next day, the day of the lunch, I let Piotr close up the shop so that I would be on time. At just after noon, I washed my hands until I thought the skin would come off, put on the cleanest, newest clothes I had, and set off with the dog through the mass of last-minute shoppers to the rue de Verneuil. It was a late spring day, hot and sunny. The light was blinding and the air heavy, and I let Cassie pull me along as she nosed the grubby pavement. She lurched right and then left, but I was patient with her today because I viewed her as my protective shield against the encounter. Everyone together was not the same thing as one or two at a time. And there would be the new wife Anne-Sophie, plus I would have to face my niece and nephews. Did they know what had happened? Stephanie, modern, free-spirited mother that she was, may just have told them.

By the time I stood at the front door, I was prickling with the heat. The dog, tongue hanging in a pant, stood like an unwatered flower, her tail barely swaying as she heard the confident click of Edward's heels approaching.

"What a handsome couple," he said, stepping aside to let me in.

"She keeps me on a short leash, at least."

Edward shook his head. "How stupid we sound."

"You're right," I said. "Ridiculous."

As we walked into the front hall, Edward almost whispered: "Mother's in bed. Saving her strength for mealtime. It's a bad day. I almost wish we hadn't tried to pull this off."

I headed down the hall. Mother did look worse than yesterday, and the artificial color she'd added to her cheeks only highlighted what was missing underneath. She was propped up on her bed, dressed, but looking uncomfortable and out of place in her clothes. "Don't worry about me. Go join the others," she said. "You have to meet Anne-Sophie. And the children will love the dog." I stopped in the kitchen to give Cassie water and say hello to Lisette. Her eyes filled with tears as soon as she saw me. Out came the hankie from her apron pocket.

"Oh, *Trésor*. It's terrible. She won't eat, and she can't stand the smell of meat cooking, so look," and she pointed to the counter where a cold roast beef sat ready. "I had to buy it at the butcher like this, cooked by somebody else." She shook her head and dabbed her eyes with her hankie. "And *Monsieur* looks worse every day too. What will he do when she's gone?" She stopped to blow her nose. "*Et le chien*," she went on, looking disapprovingly at Cassie, who had slopped water from one of her mixing bowls all over the clean kitchen floor. "Why can't you bring home a human?"

And what about you, Lisette, I'd wanted to ask. You, whose whole life, except for a sister in Brittany, revolves around this house.

"Here's my elusive brother. I told you he was real," said Edward as I walked into the *salon*.

A youngish woman with glasses smiled at me. I almost couldn't speak—the idea that Edward could marry someone with even a minor handicap, and one displayed so boldly—it seemed impossible. And she was not stunningly beautiful, just okay-looking. "Nice to finally meet you," she said, standing up. It was hard to judge her figure in her pregnant state, but she clearly had nothing like the perfect body of her predecessor either. She was short, maybe that was it; she didn't rival Edward in height or age. "And who's this?" Anne-Sophie asked, bending down to the dog. "The children will love her."

"Cassie's her name. Don't be too nice to her or she'll bother you all through lunch."

"I don't mind," she said, stroking her head. "I love dogs. Someday maybe we'll have one," she added, looking at Edward.

"Not until the children are responsible enough to walk it," he said. "So never."

At which point children could be heard walking briskly, not running, down the corridor. Two boys stopped abruptly at the door. Matthieu and Henri had stretched like toffee since I'd last seen them. As with Edward and me, they had a brotherly resemblance, but not much more. Now Matthieu looked less like Edward—still the curly hair, the slightly rounded face—but around the eyes, he was Stephanie. Henri still looked like his own person. He had the curly hair, which seemed to pass to every male member of the family, but his face was longer and thinner, the features finer. Right behind them was a squat, roly-poly boy, dragging a white cloth diaper by the corner. He half hid himself behind Matthieu and stuck his thumb in his mouth. And then Caroline sauntered in. She crossed one long leg over the other as she leaned against the door jamb with a studied attempt at apathy. She looked more like Stephanie than ever. Just toned down. The hair wasn't quite as red, the eyes more hazel than green, the features less chiseled. But the body—long and lithe—was a nymphet's version of her mother. On some level, it must have been hard for Edward to look at her.

The boys came forward, little soldiers under orders to behave, be polite. After each one kissed me hello, he peeled away toward the dog, even pudgy little Paul. Caroline continued to stand in the doorway with such conviction, I thought: she must know. But after a glance at Edward, she too came to greet me. I said stupidly, in English: "Three brothers must be tough."

She answered me with a shrug in French: "You get used to it."

Edmond announced that it was time for lunch as if he were calling us to battle. Then he and Edward went to fetch Mother, while the rest of us shifted rooms. Anne-Sophie had to scold the boys away from Cassie, and as soon as they'd gone, Caroline sidled over to the dog.

"Stroke her ears," I said, making her look up and blush. Cassie now licked her ear. Her laugh sounded brittle, out of practice.

Edward and Edmond came into the dining room, one on either side of Mother, who despite the warm day, was dressed in a wool cardigan. Curved forward, as if she had a bad stomach ache, she barely lifted her feet as she shuffled to the oak chair brought in from the living room, one with arms and extra cushions piled on it. Even the boys stopped bickering as their grandmother was lowered into her seat. The rest of us sat down. After a moment the silence became awkward. No one seemed to know what to talk about. Usually it was Mother who guided us along the road to social intercourse. Without her we were lost. Then Caroline, who was not yet seated, walked over to Mother and kissed her gently on the forehead, saying simply, in English: "Hello, Granny." The graceful gesture somehow put everyone in the room at ease.

Platters of food were passed around the table. The children—even little Paul, next to his mother   sat quietly, and I was reminded of that lunch years ago when the children had joined the adults for the first time. How Henri had complained about his soup and had fidgeted with the books on his chair, until called to order by Mother. Today, they behaved like all French children, who from a very early age are expected to rise to the occasion of adult gatherings.

"What are you reading, Mother?" Edward asked, assuming the role of social motor. Since he was not a big reader himself, the question sounded forced.

"For the first time in my life," her eyes fluttered, "I'm having trouble with fiction." She looked at me. "I can't suspend my belief and get into the story. Maybe it demands too much concentration. Magazines are my limit. Anyway, Anne-Sophie—how's *your* book coming along?"

"I'm hoping to get the research done before the baby arrives," she said, putting her fork down and pushing her glasses up her nose, her other hand on her lump of a stomach. "But I'm not sure I'll make it." She had a high, light voice.

"What is the subject of your book?" I asked.

"I'm writing my dissertation on the Bièvre," she said.

"As in the rue de Bièvre?" I asked. It is a short street in the Latin Quarter across from Notre Dame, known to all of France because President Mitterrand had lived there.

"The street was named after an arm of the Seine that ran from the south and joined the main river near where the Gare d'Austerlitz stands today. An abbey diverted waters to what's now the street for its gardens in the twelfth century. I'm trying to reconstruct the history of the communities that developed along the whole river. Of course, not the original inhabitants, which were beavers. That's how it got its name. I'm starting from Gallo-Roman times."

"What happened to it?" I was astonished I'd never even heard of it.

"It was eventually covered up. Besides being full of junk—the rue Mouffetard, for example, gets its name from the word *mofettes*, which was what the residents called the stink that the river gave off—it flooded all the time. The last of it was covered over after the big flood of 1910."

"You see, there are lots of things you don't know about Paris," Edward said, crossing his arms across his chest with a satisfied smile that his wife knew more about the city than his weird wanderer brother.

"Where do you do your research?" I asked, refusing even to acknowledge Edward's mild taunt.

"Mostly in the national archives, in libraries."

"Have you been to that socialist monstrosity?" Edmond asked with disgust.

"Yes," Anne-Sophie said, putting a napkin to her heart-shaped mouth. "And I'm afraid to say the new national library is a nightmare, inside and out."

"The city of Paris," Edmond continued, "hasn't built anything worth its own cheap concrete since 1930." This was generous of him; usually his cutoff date was the war. The first one. But how pleased he must be, I thought, to have a historian for a stepdaughter-in-law. Edward had really hit the jackpot this time. Anne-Sophie had something for everyone.

But as social motor, my brother was sputtering. The conversation lagged over the salad and cheese without Mother's impetus. She made a few efforts at asking more questions, at maintaining her old job, but she couldn't seem to focus for long on the responses. It seemed, in fact, she wasn't quite there, as if part of her had already left this earth. So instead of covering politics and culture, our usual menu, we rambled from the weather, and how the relentless rain had given way to relentless sun, to comments on the food, something we never talked about, since it was always assumed that whatever Mother had planned and Lisette had prepared was good.

While the weather was being discussed over the peach tart, I watched my mother and niece. They obviously had a great deal of natural affection for one another, *une sympathie* that had been fed by much time spent together. Even before Stephanie left, Mother had mothered those children several times a week. And after the split, she was all they'd had in terms of maternal affection until Anne-Sophie, whom Caroline resented anyway. Which perhaps partly explained Caroline's particular affection for her grandmother. While I ate the very sweet, juicy peaches, I tried to look at Mother from Caroline's point of view, as source of succor. I tried to imagine what it might be like not to have that wall of unsaid things between us.

The children were excused, and it was obvious Mother needed to be too. I took one chicken arm and Edward the other, and we guided her back to her room. As we lowered her onto the bed, Edward said: "You shouldn't have stayed the whole meal, *Maman*. It's tired you out too much."

"I wouldn't have missed that lunch for the world," she said, looking from son to son, then closing her eyes.

"I'll come back on Tuesday," I said. "During my lunch break."

Each of us leaned over and kissed her on the forehead, then slid silently out of the room.

SIX

ON THE FOLLOWING Tuesday morning, just after I arrived at the rue de Seine, I got two calls. One was from Edmond telling me that Mother was still worn out by lunch and didn't want to see anyone that day. The second call was from Wanda, Piotr's wife, telling me that on Sunday afternoon, while they were taking a stroll along the Seine, he had been knocked over by a roller blader and was in the hospital with a concussion. Wanda told me breathlessly: "The doctor said that if he had been a smaller or an older man, he would probably be dead." She was silent for a moment, undoubtedly crossing herself and looking to heaven. "But he will be fine, after a week's rest."

Such an accident wasn't surprising. The city had been over-run with wheels in general since that same 1995 strike that had propelled Mélo-Vélo into solvency. Everyone had some form of nonmotorized locomotion, and roller blades were popular and dangerous, especially on weekends, when people tore through the city, oblivious to pedestrians. It was in fact more surprising that such an accident didn't occur on every street corner, especially now, late spring, as people emerged from their winter holes.

The May sky got hotter and hotter. Flags went limp, shut-
ters got shuttered. I had to pull my fans out of the cupboards at
the shop and in my room. It was so warm that everyone wanted
to be outside, and they often dug old, rusty bicycles that needed
repairing out with them. Or they bought new ones. Things were
busy, and with Piotr out, I was stuck at the shop most of the time.

Which meant my visits to the rue de Verneuil were quick
and limited. I had no time alone with Mother. When I went
during lunch, Lisette would be preparing a tray for Edmond to
eat at Mother's bedside. When I stopped by after closing, either
Anne-Sophie or Edward would be there. But while not managing to talk to Mother, I did get to know my new sister-in-law.
She was cheery, energetic, and, being from a large family herself,
undaunted by all the children under her care. Like Mother, she
was organized too, so she had her help lined up, allowing her a
few hours a day to work on her book. Though the next time I
saw her, she looked considerably less bookish: the glasses had
disappeared, and the contact lenses were in. Her unmasked blue
eyes, along with the heart-shaped lips, gave her a perpetual look
of pleasant surprise. Though she was not stunningly beautiful
like Stephanie, the whole package was highly attractive. Edward
hadn't gone that soft.

He and I, with Mother as our main topic of conversation and
often no audience to receive our wit, dropped the sarcasm entirely.
Because Edmond was too distraught to confront the practicalities
of Mother's illness, we unburdened him as much as possible. We
dealt with her medication and the nurses. We wondered about the
state of her legal affairs. Edward suggested that we ask about her
will and whether all was in order. At first, it struck me as typically
callous, but then I realized he was just being typically practical.

By Saturday evening I was exhausted and not in the mood
to go out. Plus I was riveted by the book that Mother had given

me. The inner rhythms of Sebald's prose mesmerized me, as did the photos and drawings he interspersed into his text. In fact, if the backdrop to the alienation felt by the narrator and the Jewish exiles he describes hadn't been the Second World War, *The Emigrants* might have been written for me. The sense of displacement, loss, and isolation resonated that strongly. But also shamed me. By comparison, my story seemed small and contained, completely personal, while theirs belonged to a tragedy of epic proportions, the tragedy of the twentieth century.

But Béa had followed up on her offer and invited me to dinner, so there I was again, walking through the gloomy foyer of the main building and into the magical space beyond. The wisteria was in full bloom now, the musky flowers hanging in heavy bunches from the twisted vine. The whole garden smelled of them. Two upstairs windows were flung open in sunny abandon.

As I knocked on the door, I heard a plaintive jazz saxophone.

"Hello," she said, swinging the door wide open with a flourish. "Come in." The studio caught just an edge of the late sun. Some of the lower glass panes were open, and warm air wafted in. Here it wasn't hot or stuffy, as it had been in my close quarters. She was wearing a loose silk top and a pajamas-like bottom, pale green on darker green, and bare feet. She was clearly in a happier mood than the last time I'd come.

"What's that song?" I asked, recognizing the tune though unable to place it.

"It's John Coltrane playing 'My Favorite Things.' You must know the song from *The Sound of Music*. Every American I've ever met grew up on that film."

"Maybe I saw it once at the cinema on Long Island, but I certainly didn't grow up on it."

She cocked her head with a smile. "That's right. You're not a real American."

"I'm not a real anything." I shrugged and handed her the bottle of red wine I'd brought.

"Who is?" She looked at the label. "Thank you. It looks better than what I've got. Shall we drink it?"

"Sure. I'll open it," I said. The kitchen was very narrow and lined with shelves that were crowded with herbs and oils and pots and pans. "Now you really look moved in."

"Most of this stuff isn't mine. It's what people leave behind. I guess no one ever cleans it out. The other day I was rooting around for some sage, and I found a pot of crystallized honey that looked as though it had been there since before the war." After handing me a heavy brass corkscrew, Béa lifted up on her toes and reached for two glasses. The sleeve of her pale-green silk shirt slid up her graceful arm, right in front of my face, and I could see blonde hair shooting up in all directions. The sliding silk and Béa Fairbank's gently curving, somehow vulnerable arm, made my heart give a little leap that it wasn't supposed to give. I quickly took the glasses from her hand and returned to the larger space of the studio. She followed me out, saying: "It's a little early for really good basil, but I've made pesto. Today felt so much like summer."

"It smells good." I walked to the window. Under a shady tree stood a chair and a small table. I could hear what sounded like a small party from some part of the garden I couldn't see. "Your landlords must have a nice life."

"I guess, though sometimes I wonder. I mean, they always seem a bit sad, disappointed, and I wonder if it's because neither of them had a real profession. Their antique dealing seems more like a hobby."

"You're sounding like Viviane, with her True Purpose talk. It seems to me they're lucky to live in a beautiful place and not have to worry about the next month's phone bill. Or to spend their time doing something they don't like."

"You mean like running a bicycle shop?"

"Sort of. I guess. It's not that bad."

"I'm not sure I believe you," she said. "Anyway, I need a reason to get up in the morning, and work gives it to me." She laughed. "I can say that today, after a decent sketching session in the garden this afternoon."

"Do I get to see some of that work this time?"

"Hmm," she said, taking a sip of wine, unfolding her legs from the sofa before going over to the wall and rummaging through a portfolio and the canvases. "Here are two I'm *quite* pleased with." She propped them up on chairs and stood back to reevaluate them herself. One was an ink drawing of a tree that reminded me of one of my photos, with its gnarled, arthritic branches.

"Did you do this at Hautebranche? I think I photographed the same tree."

"No." She laughed. "I did it in England last autumn."

"I like this," I said, now looking at an oil painting of a nude, a young woman with long, black hair. She was leaning on one arm, slightly off-center, on the sofa I had just left. The expression on her face was miles away.

"Here we have Connie's predecessor," she said tartly. "As a model, that is. She was a Portuguese waitress in a café I used to go to."

"You have a nice touch," I said.

"Thank you." She suddenly jumped up. "Damn. I forgot the pasta water." And she ran on her small, bare feet to the kitchen.

While she was gone, I peeked at a few more paintings against the wall. I saw a lush white flower, with one petal curled and ready to fall. A seemingly peaceful Paris rooftop scene, except the brick chimney was badly cracked. A bucolic landscape with one cloud painted a sickly, threatening yellow. Every one of them quietly found a way to remind the viewer of the dark side, of mortality.

"I'm not sure I want you digging that deeply into my work. There's too much junk." I hadn't heard her come back in. I was looking at a drawing of the wisteria over the door. The penciling was wild and loopy. A bit like her handwriting.

"If I didn't like it, I wouldn't bother. I think you got the weight of the flowers even without the color," I said as she walked over and looked from my side.

"Thank you," she said. "The pasta will be ready in ten minutes. Can you help me lay the table?"

So I sat down with Béa Fairbank at a round wooden table, adorned with three wine bottles, heavy flows of white wax already caked to their sides, just like at Hautebranche in the pre-baby days. What was hers and what others had left behind in the studio wasn't clear, and the uncertainty disturbed my usual system of observation and analysis. How many of the wax layers, for example, were formed during her evenings and how many had been left by others? Was the kitsch poster hanging in the entry passage hers or some previous tenant's? And what about these flowery plates, or the simple blue vase on the mantle? The pieces were impossible to fit together, and I was forced to abandon my usual critical self to the fading light of her studio, the food, and the wine.

The warm spring air wafted on us from time to time through the open panes of the skylight. Béa lit the candles. Whether it was this house that had survived all the razing and rebuilding of two centuries, or Béa's company, I didn't know, but I had a peculiar sensation. I felt safe.

She told me about growing up in a large house in Devon. There were five children; they'd had a very traditional upbringing. Though she remained close to her family, she'd always felt different. "Maybe I was just born that way. Or sometimes I think it has to do with my family history. My grandfather, you see, was a humble farmer who turned to business and made quite a lot of money. And my mother had grown up in Kenya. Her father was a gentleman farmer, but the colonial thing made her a bit different. I always think that made me feel a bit off kilter."

"What about your brothers and sisters?" I asked.

"I have one brother and one sister who are fiercely traditional," she said. "And then two brothers who are a bit like me. One's a filmmaker, the other a musician."

"Do you get along with them?"

"I do, actually. All of them. Obviously there are some personality clashes from time to time, different ideas about how to approach this or that, but we seem to get over it. Except for a time in our late teens, early twenties, when we were all establishing our identities, we've always stayed in touch. I count on them, in a funny way, even the two traditional ones." She paused, cocking her head. "There's a lot to be said for the no-questions-asked recipe for living, if you can manage it. I mean, wondering who you are every five minutes can be both exhausting and counterproductive." She paused. "Anyway, enough about me. Do you want some coffee or tisane?"

"No, thanks, but let's clear up."

I helped Béa take out the bowls and started washing the dishes.

"You really don't have to do the washing up," she said, putting a dented brass kettle on the gas.

"It's good to get it done."

I washed the dishes while she dried and made herself a verbena tisane. We settled on the sheet-covered sofas, the coffee table between us. Béa was sitting cross-legged and holding her mug between both hands, blowing on the hot liquid.

"How about your parents. Do you get on with them too?" I asked.

"Yes, even though it's all very English. We don't argue, but neither do we have deep discussions about feelings and the meaning of life." She sighed. "I don't know. For some reason I feel happier living at a distance from it all. In another country, in fact. As I said, I always felt different. From a very early age, and it only got worse as I got older. It didn't help that when I was a teenager I got, you know," and she blew up her cheeks, making her arms into a fat circle. She couldn't utter the word and she was all red, looking away, as if in having been overweight she had committed a crime.

"Cédric thinks you're the prettiest woman he knows," I said.

"Well," she said, even redder, "all I'm trying to say is that I'm one of those people who feels more at home away from home. But what about you? Where do you feel at home? Where *is* your home? It's hard for me to imagine having two bona fide cultures."

I shrugged. "I don't know. Here, I guess. It's where I live."

"That's not much of an endorsement."

"I can't really imagine living anywhere else."

She nodded, thinking. "But do you feel French?"

"In some ways, yes. In others not."

"Do you feel American?"

"I tried very hard to, for most of my childhood. But when I went there to college for a year, I felt like a total freak." I paused. "I don't feel one thing or another because I don't really feel comfortable anywhere."

"How old again were you when you moved here?"

"Eight."

"And you said your father had died the year before?"

"Yes. Which means I don't remember much."

"But you've had your mother to help fill in the blanks."

"Oh, no."

"What do you mean?"

"We never talk about my father. Or anything else about our life then."

"Ever?"

"Never."

"That's more English than the English," she said. "Surely your father's not an unpleasant subject just because he died."

I looked up at Béa, whose cheeks were no longer red in embarrassment but just a bit flushed from the wine, whose eyes were sparkling in the candlelight. I thought of her graceful arm and the chaotic hair it sprouted and of her own adjustment problems. "The circumstances were unusual." I stood up, walked to the table, and filled our glasses with the rest of the wine. Considered the risk. Telling Jacqueline had left me feeling stripped naked.

I put her glass on the coffee table, took a sip from mine, and walked toward the windows. Outside, the tree rustled and the early summer sky still had a glimmer of light to it. The chair underneath was now a forlorn silhouette, as were the vines. In the dim light they almost looked like huddled figures, old men crouching over the stony ground at their feet.

"A year before my father died," I finally said, "my sister died."

"Oh," Béa said, from behind me.

"She was run over by a car."

"Aie."

"The official story of my father's death," I said, "is that he went up to the roof one night to fix the television antenna. That he lost his footing and fell to the ground."

"It sounds plausible, though I guess it's a bit strange to be up on the roof in the middle of the night."

"Exactly."

"He didn't leave a note or anything?"

"No. I don't think so, anyway. I never understood it. It wasn't his fault."

"What do you mean?"

"My sister's accident. It wasn't his fault."

"What do you mean it wasn't your father's fault?"

"It was my mother who was with her. After dropping me off at a friend's house, she went shopping in the town, and while they were walking down the street, my sister pulled away from her hand and jumped in the street just as a car was passing."

"Ooh." Béa shuddered.

"That was the last time I saw Franny, when my mother dropped me off. I remember her waving at me from the back seat of the car while I rushed off. I was so anxious to try my friend's new trampoline, I didn't wave back."

"You hardly could have known what was going to happen."

"I know. But that's what you remember. What you didn't do, what you might have done differently. I guess that's why my father couldn't live with her death, even though he wasn't there either." I paused, shifted my weight, and felt as if I were on the edge of a high dive. I took a long breath. "When he died, we were at our house in Connecticut. I always got up early and loved the morning time before everyone else woke up. I was getting ready to go exploring. From my bedroom window, I'd seen a deer at the edge of the woods, and I was going to try and follow it. As I ran out on the front porch, I saw my father facedown on the gravel driveway, dressed in nothing but his pajamas. He was lying in a strange position, and even though I was only seven, I knew that lying on the gravel driveway meant something must be wrong. There didn't seem to be blood everywhere, and just as I was beginning to think I was mistaken—for some strange reason my father had decided to lie down in the driveway, half naked—I came to his face, which was twisted unnaturally to the side. It had three flies walking over it. Out of his mouth, there was a trickle of blood that made a path in the gravel."

"God." Béa's low voice was right next to me. I nodded, sickened all over again by the memory of my father's twisted neck, of those flies walking over his face, and that brook of blood. "It must have been terrifying," she said, both of us in front of the window looking out into the dark garden.

"It was. But the guilt was almost worse than the panic and fear. Terrible, irreconcilable guilt. For not coming sooner, for not having somehow prevented it."

"Your mother didn't wake up?"

"No. Often that year after Franny died, she didn't get up until late. Maybe she was taking sleeping pills." I shook my head. "Until I was fifteen or so, I believed my father's fall was an accident because that was the story I'd been told somewhere along the line. The truth came to me in a flash one day, unwittingly through Cédric. He was telling me a story his father had told him, about a friend who had always believed his mother had tried to slit her wrists by accident, until one day he realized that wasn't possible— wrists don't slit by accident. I felt as if I'd just been slapped in the face—the truth about my own father was suddenly so obvious. How could I have been so stupid, so gullible?"

"Because you were a child."

"I guess." The sky was now dark enough to allow a few insistent stars to penetrate the glowing orb of city lights. "In any case, I've spent most of my life angry and resentful."

"And now?"

"Not so much." I shrugged. "Viviane has undoubtedly told you about my unforgivable deed." She nodded. "That went a long way in humbling me, putting things into a different perspective. It made me able to see what all human beings, even my ever-so-superior self, are capable of doing." I took my last sip of wine and put the glass on the table. "Now my mother's dying of cancer, and all that anger is beginning to seem an unconscionable waste of time and effort."

For several minutes we just stood there, very close together. So close together that by the time she was in my arms, it seemed that neither one of us had moved, that it had already been that way from the beginning of my story.

"This isn't supposed to happen," Béa said as our lips pulled apart.

"Huh," was all I said, leading her back to the sofa. We lay there, stuck together, for a long time, talking in a whisper, though no one was around to hear us. I told her everything. About my mother and me. About my brother. About my banishment. About Mother's illness and the reconciliation with my family. It was so easy, lying in the half dark with my arms around this small woman. But then, just after midnight, I remembered Cassie. I never wanted to move from this spot, but Cassie the spell-breaker beckoned.

I couldn't ask her to come with me. I was afraid that she would say no, that in kissing me, she was only being kind and sympathetic. She had told me, after all, that she didn't want any more relationships. And then I was afraid that even if she said yes, seeing my room would quickly change her mind. So I left Béa—who did indeed seem happy to stay—at her door, small and smiling, and made my way back down the hill, through the warren of Montmartre streets and the Saturday hordes at Clichy, back to the rue des Martyrs and Cassie. As I walked, I felt strangely light on my feet. Telling my story had been a relief, as if with each sentence I had physically shed several grams. It hadn't felt that way with Jacqueline, but that was a different time and she was a different woman. Jacqueline's reaction had been to provide an analysis of my psyche, while Béa had responded with a kiss.

To reward Cassie for her long wait and because I wasn't in the least bit sleepy, I took her for an extended walk. At the little park on the avenue de Trudaine, I paused. It was here that one night during the strike I had repeatedly tried to reteach myself to ride a bicycle so that I could get to Stephanie faster. Since then, every time I walked by the park I was reminded of that hopeless effort made for the wrong reasons and felt foolish, ashamed. Now standing in front of its low gate and brimming with thoughts of Béa, I viewed that winter night with a sort of beneficent sympathy for a poorer version of myself.

My father used to make breakfast for the family on Sunday mornings. I remember running into the kitchen with Franny, shouting: "What's for breakfast?" He'd kneel down, grab one of us in each arm, and say: "Who knows but the nose?" and he wouldn't tell us what he'd made until he put pancakes or eggs and bacon on the table. Later I came to think of those words as an omen. Who knows but the nose? Today your father's making waffles; tomorrow he's dead in the driveway. Who knows but the nose? Today your sister has sticky syrup all over her face; tomorrow she's flattened in the street. It was the principle by which I'd lived my life: who knows when the next tragedy's coming. Even though my mother's illness could be viewed as further proof of my catastrophe theory, tonight, walking down the avenue de Trudaine, it occurred to me sometimes, something good might happen. Could happen. Even to me.

———

The next morning, I opened the shop late, but it didn't matter. This was Pentecost weekend, with Monday a holiday, and *les Parisiens* were elsewhere, visiting friends in the provinces or gardening in their own country houses. Some tourists who needed directions came in; that was it.

Instead of repairing bicycles, I spent the whole morning at my desk daydreaming about Béa Fairbank. I couldn't wait to see her again. I missed her already as I reran not just the previous evening but also all our encounters, even the first one with Jennifer. After all the women in my life, I wondered, what was responsible for these peculiarly urgent feelings? What was different, special about *her*? Shared friends and interests, a general unease with the world around us? The fact that I could talk to her forever? Or that she was gorgeous in an irresistibly discreet way? Of course she was also sensitive and funny and talented. Spirited, too.

What was I doing, sitting in the back of the shop, with compliments gurgling about in my head? By now you would agree unrestricted praise was not my thing. Maybe, I reasoned, it was just because she'd listened to me sympathetically without laughing or running away in horror. Or making me feel exposed, like Jacqueline. Maybe this was just a temporary rush of gratitude that would be gone by tomorrow. But when I considered the possibility that she might not be thinking happy thoughts about me, that she might be regretting every minute of the evening, I felt desperate.

Tired of sitting in an empty, dead shop, I closed early and set off to Piotr's, where I was invited for lunch.

He and Wanda lived in a tiny studio between the place de la Nation and the Père Lachaise Cemetery. They had resourcefully made the most of not much. Shelves and cupboards built by Piotr lined the walls, which reduced the space but meant that everything had a place. The table was a board that pulled down from the wall, the bathroom a miracle of economy, and the kitchen only big enough for one person at a time. The bed, I guessed, pulled out from the Ikea-style sofa that was tucked under the one window. I knew from an earlier visit on a cooler day that the window looked onto a large, light but noisy courtyard. Today the sun would have been streaming in obtrusively, but it was softened by the white cloth shade they had put up. The small space on the fourth floor would also have been stifling, but—as Piotr showed me, proudly pulling up and down on the cord—they had installed a ceiling fan. Its blades just missed the walls as they swished around.

Wanda greeted me with three Slavic kisses, her face swishing around mine with the same flourish as the ceiling fan. She was trim and tidy, dressed in slim-fitting jeans and a cotton pullover, a gold cross hanging around her neck. Her movements were brisk and able, and she never sat still for more than a minute or two. But there was something frustrated about all this efficiency, as if it needed more than these fifteen square meters to survive.

Except for the shaved spot behind his ear, Piotr looked recovered from his run-in. He had his usual air of half apology, the large hands dangling at his side, the head slightly lowered. Perhaps he looked paler than usual, though there was little color to drain from his white face in the first place.

They both greeted Cassie, who one minute lurched from corner to corner, assessing the place in her own canine fashion, and the next fussed around Piotr as if their separation had lasted several years instead of a week. She mostly ignored Wanda, which seemed to further put her out.

"She's a bit shy of people she doesn't know," I apologized, but Cassie's neglect still ratcheted up one more notch the existing tension in the small room. Tension that I assumed sprouted from the Poland Question, on which Piotr was holding firm.

"I thought we'd eat straight away," Wanda said. Her French was much better than Piotr's, covering the whole range of verb tenses and a more accurate use of idiom. "If that's okay."

"Just fine," I said cheerily.

The laminated wood board that served as the table was pulled down and set with three white plates, a wine and a water glass, and very shiny stainless steel, a mauve paper napkin folded under each fork. A plate of sliced cucumber and tomatoes in *vinaigrette*, with bits of thyme and feta cheese sprinkled on the top, sat in the middle of the table. A bottle of red wine was open, a jug of water already poured. "Please. Sit," said Wanda as she pushed her sleeves up to her elbows, straightened her watch. We took our places, and she passed the salad. "I made you some potato dumplings for the main course," she said. "I remember you liked those at the wedding." That recollection at least brought a wan smile to her face.

During the meal, Wanda watched every sip of wine Piotr took, as if readying herself for the moment when she would swoop in and snatch his glass away. Piotr seemed oblivious as he retold the story of his accident and his stay in the hospital. He also ignored her frequent interruptions to correct his French and did not amend a single one of his truncated sentences. Finally I said: "Don't worry. I'm used to it," and that only made her look more put out.

Over a dessert of a Polish-style cheesecake, Wanda asked me about my mother, but of course there wasn't much to say, except that she was dying, and by coffee the conversation had evaporated. For Piotr and me, silence was the norm. We spent hours without exchanging a word. But here at the table, with Wanda, it was awkward. The cups clicked on the saucers, children shouted, and a ball bounced in the courtyard. Though the ceiling fan helped, it was hot and stuffy, certainly too hot for a heavy lunch and red wine. But Wanda, who had eaten very little and drunk no wine, was still brisk and efficient. As she stood to clear the table, she once again pushed her sleeves up to her elbows and straightened her watch.

"Wanda still wants moving for Poland," Piotr said. Though he didn't have many words, he wasn't one to mince what he had available. Or to pretend that the tension I'd felt the moment I walked in—every bit as heavy as those potato dumplings—and now this ponderous silence, wasn't there.

"But you're going for July and August," I said, trying to sound enthusiastic. In fact, with Mother's illness, I'd begun to wonder how I'd manage without Piotr in July; August the shop would at least be closed anyway.

"The future here is a dead end," she said, face tightening while she stacked the dessert plates.

"And Poland?" said Piotr.

"Things are changing there. My sister told me so."

"A little, she said. A *very* little." Piotr folded his arms and looked at the white-shaded window. "It is a bigger dead end there."

"You've got a job here, at least," I said to Wanda.

She stopped fussing with the table and, standing straight as a bowling pin, said: "I *had* a job." She stared at me defiantly: "One night two weeks ago, I stayed late to help with a dinner party. While I worked for them in the kitchen, they talked about how we immigrants first drain the social security system, then take advantage of the unemployment benefits. One guest said: 'Even those Eastern Europeans—they just don't have the same culture, the same values, as we have here in France.' My employer answered: 'I know what you mean.' That's what they think about the person who takes care of their house and their children? I quit the next day. They can hire a French person. I'm only too happy to leave this arrogant country."

"Not everyone thinks like that," I said softly. "And maybe your employer was just saying that to placate the guest. She hired you, after all."

"Every day she condescended to me, and I wasn't going to put up with that," she said, stabbing her finger to her chest, making the gold cross jump on its chain. "I've had it up to here with this place." Her hand now flew above her head as she disappeared into the tiny kitchen. Piotr and I exchanged glances as she blew her nose loudly over the sink.

In a more limited way, he too had been exposed to xenophobic remarks, but he managed to remain unwounded by the animosity. He shrugged it off, saying people were stupid. Sometimes his lack of reaction made people like him, in spite of themselves. Michel, for example, didn't like immigrants even before he stabbed the Ukrainian, but he made an exception of Piotr. And of course, it was easier for Piotr to remain untouched by prejudice because he didn't work for a xenophobe, just a cranky misfit.

Anyway, I wanted to be able to give them advice, to provide a solution that would bring back that hopeful smile Wanda wore when she first came to France. But what could I offer? What did I know about marital affairs or patriotism? I used to have enough opinions on everything and everyone to span the globe, but if I had learned one thing over the last five years, it was that I had been full of shit.

As I was about to leave a grim Piotr and a brittle Wanda in their small, hot room, I did not have any answers, but I felt sorry for them. So I told Wanda to come to the shop on Tuesday morning. "The place needs a good clean," I said. "And I'll try and think of some other tasks to keep you busy."

———

When I got back to the rue des Martyrs, the room was unbearably stuffy. I opened the windows, turned on the fan, filled Cassie's food and water bowls, poured myself a glass of water, and sat down on my one hard chair. After a moment, with beating heart, I fished in my pocket for the crumpled scrap of paper with Piotr's angular numbers. I picked up the phone with its exposed wires gingerly and dialed, waiting impatiently for the dial to click back to the starting point. The phone rang. And rang. Not even an answering machine. I pictured the studio, the cold, solid wax fixed on the sides of the wine bottles, the smell of oil paint and the stacks of canvases. I hung up and dialed again, on the chance that I'd mis-dialed the first time.

Where could she be the Sunday afternoon of a holiday week-end? I told her I'd call, and she hadn't mentioned going out. She hadn't tried to dodge or dissuade me. And now she hadn't even put on her answering machine. This was a great disappointment. I wanted more than anything in the world to talk to Béa Fairbank. I wanted to go see her again that hot, stuffy evening, despite my exhaustion. Because like a bunch of brightly colored balloons, she had buoyed me through the entire day. Through a tedious morning at the shop, and then through the heavy, tense lunch with Piotr and Wanda. She had countered the painful thoughts of my mother, which surged and resurged in my head as I walked home. And I'd imagined telling Béa about everything I was seeing, every photo I'd wished I were taking, had I not stupidly forgotten my camera. She, in fact, made the prospect of taking those photos at all seem more urgent.

With the gentle air of the fan blowing over me, I lay down on my mattress and thought more about this woman and how lonely I suddenly felt without her. I imagined others on this holiday evening. Edward and Anne-Sophie, who had gone to Bordeaux for a reunion of her large family, I pictured in a huge house, surrounded by a crowd of people. Cédric and Viviane were probably in the garden at Hautebranche, fussing over their little Russian and talking in low but excited voices about what it would be like when the other baby was born, while the shafts of sunlight slanted lower and lower over the apple orchard. Then I thought of Mother and Edmond, and that was less idyllic. But at least for whatever time was left, they had each other. Tomorrow I was supposed to visit Mother. It was all arranged; she was expecting me, and I was determined to break the silence, no matter who interrupted us, no matter how tired she might be.

But where was Béa?

PART III

ONE

I WAS WOKEN up at six that Pentecost Monday by Cassie's tongue in my ear. Sometime during my pensive stare at the white ceiling I must have dozed off. Cassie backed off and took my shoe in her mouth. She fixed her eyes on me expectantly, ears cocked, tail wagging rhythmically. Having missed her late evening walk, she was requesting, urgently, to go out. I sat up. The air had cleared, the temperature had dropped, and I hadn't slept so long and so well in ages. It gave me a whiff of boyhood, of Connecticut, and of waking up before the rest of the house.

I remembered my plan for the day. The shop would be shut and I was going to see Mother. There was hope of being strong enough to talk, since no one would have visited this weekend. But last night's resolve seemed less certain, my plan more daunting in the light of day. What if I couldn't summon the courage to speak? Cassie had no patience for my inner struggles and started nudging me with her nose, so I put on some fresh clothes and left. The early morning calm, the bright sun and cool air, and Sacré Coeur lily white against the deep blue sky forced hope and energy on me. Cassie and I were the only living souls on the terraces of the Tuileries. I let her sniff around, while I tried to catch the light slanting through the powerful green of late spring, to transmit its essence on film, but I wasn't happy with what I imagined the results to be, and wondered, in fact, just what I was doing behind a camera anyway.

Le Relais was very quiet.

"You open today?" Alain said, giving the table a wipe.

"No. I'm just going to catch up on some paperwork," I fudged.

"The usual?" he said, starting to walk away.

"No. This morning I'll have that English breakfast you offer. You know, with the eggs and bacon. I'll have scrambled eggs."

"Are you sure you wouldn't rather have an omelette? Nicole makes a great omelette."

"No. I want scrambled." My father's best eggs were scrambled. When he fried them, he often broke the yolk. He didn't do omelettes. I wanted scrambled.

Once their special *"English breake-fast"* came, it tasted nothing like my Connecticut memory. The bacon was meatier, the toasted *pain de mie* slightly sweet. I nudged Cassie, who was at my feet. She wagged her tail without looking up from the bone she'd begged from Nicole. Lucky dog, untroubled by disappointed memories of earlier bones.

As I walked to Mélo-Vélo that quiet morning, I saw it in a different light. The metal grille was pulled down over the front. The sign, on top of the old *Poissonnerie* sign, looked out of date and forlorn, particularly in the company of the new Italian restaurant across the street. Its facade, all sleek lines and muted tones, bore no trace of the old cheese shop it had once been. The derelict end of the street, which had attracted me here five years earlier, was being buffed up and modernized, regenerated.

I pulled the grille up just far enough to let myself and the dog in, then pulled it back down behind me. Inside, it was eerily still—even Cassie sensed it—and instead of lying on her bed as she usually did, she stood at my side with her "so now what are we going to do?" look. "Nothing," I said to her. "Nothing at all."

What I wanted to do was phone Béa again, but it was only just after nine. I could do the books, always the wretched books. I could finish the repairs I hadn't done the day before. I could sweep the dirty floor, straighten a shelf, or put away tools, but then Wanda would have nothing to do tomorrow. Instead, I sat at my desk and picked up a book of photographs by Eugène Atget that Edmond had given me. It was just a small sampling of his Paris photos, and he had slipped it into my hand one day at the apartment, a small peace offering.

Looking at it carefully for the first time, I became completely absorbed. Atget's photos captured a disappearing nineteenth-century Paris. There was a cobbled street, empty but for one old cart, the building facades peeling and sooty; a dim entry with an elegant, neglected staircase; a street seller laden with baskets. The images jumped out of the page at me. He had created a quiet, eerie ambiance that avoided sentimentality because the photos were as much historical record as aesthetic composition. Indeed, I learned from the text at the back that Atget considered himself, or wanted to be considered, an actor. He thought of the photos mostly as documents attesting to a vanishing age and a source of funding for his acting.

The documentation idea was what I had been working on all those years ago at Bercy, where I had wanted to leave a visual memory of the wine warehouses before they were ripped out and replaced by a park and a shopping mall, a sports stadium and a new Ministry of Finance. And really what unofficially I'd never stopped doing as the twentieth century turned over to the twenty-first, whether it was capturing the interior of the old Mélo-Vélo when the early evening sun slanted through the window or photographing the Tante Louise sign, before the phone company stripped it off. Put this way—photography as a record, a document, rather than as art—seemed a much more compelling reason to pursue it.

It was almost eleven. I could phone Béa. By now I knew the number by heart and quickly punched it on the modern, wireless shop phone. It rang and rang and there was still no answer. Where could she be? I asked as I picked up the keys and Cassie's leash and got ready to go the rue de Verneuil.

———

Since it was a holiday and Lisette had the day off, Edmond answered the door. It was only as I stepped over the threshold that I realized I hadn't shaved since Saturday or combed my hair, which even I admitted was in need of cutting. Edmond, of course, despite his increasing disarray from impending grief, was dressed impeccably: a checked cotton shirt and grey flannels, tortoise-shell reading glasses in one hand, the weekend *Figaro* in the other. Mother would hate the fact I hadn't that morning used the shaving brush and bowl she had once given me for my birthday: "I thought you should at least be properly equipped."

"She's been having terrible nightmares. Visions," Edmond said, not seeming to notice my appearance.

"The nurse told me morphine can have that effect," I said, omitting the other half of what Solange had said, that morphine often caused nightmarish visions "in people who are not at peace."

"It's frightful. She says she has seen snakes coming out of the desk in her room. They slither right over to the bed and stretch their heads up toward her. Another time it was a large bird, like an eagle, that was swooping down to grab her head with its talons. She hears scratching in the walls. I don't know what to do to help her."

I followed Edmond back to the bedroom. Just as we were about to enter, he whispered: "She might be a bit drowsy."

Indeed, Mother opened her eyes slowly, taking a minute to focus and recall who was there. "Hello," finally emerged, as if through water.

"Hello, Mother," I said, bending down to kiss her forehead. Her eyes closed again.

"She doesn't speak French anymore," Edmond whispered, quickly adding, "But she understands me."

"Do you think she'll wake up?" I asked.

"You're a little early. She told the nurse who just left to plan the drugs so that they'd be wearing off when you got here. Give her another quarter of an hour," he said, looking at his watch. "Do you want to wait in the *salon*? Can I get you something to drink?"

"No, you go back to your paper," I said, trying to conceal surprise at this unusual display of attention. "I'll get myself a glass of water and wait until she wakes up." We walked back down the corridor, Edmond peeling off to his study, while the dog and I walked through to the kitchen. Almost nothing had changed here since I was a boy. The refrigerator had been replaced when the old one finally died, but that was it. Otherwise, the big stove was the most recent acquisition, bought when we moved in over thirty years ago. Every few years when I was a teenager, Mother would campaign for a remodeling job, but Lisette wouldn't hear of it. The tiled counters, the handmade wood cupboards, the painted table in the middle where I used to eat my *goûters*, were familiar and friendly, whereas she viewed possible modern replacements as hostile interlopers. "I know just where everything is, and everything works *sans problème*," she said with emphasis. "Why change what's already perfect?" Then she'd finish drying the bowl in her hand and put it back in its cupboard with a flourish. Mother would always admit defeat; the kitchen was unquestionably Lisette's domain.

When I was a boy, in fact, I hadn't liked coming in here on her days off. I'd found the clean surfaces cold, the huge stainless steel sink glaring, the whole place spooky. The kitchen needed Lisette. But today I found its unchanging surfaces reassuring. Edmond's breakfast dishes lay in the sink, where they would remain until Lisette returned the next day. The dented red tin that had held the coffee for as long as I could remember sat on the table, with a box of filters next to it. I opened the fridge for some mineral water, and there were the lunch and dinner that Lisette had prepared, as she always had. Except now, with Mother ill, each was also labeled, with instructions on how long and at what temperature each dish should be reheated. There was a large bowl of broth for Mother.

After giving Cassie some water, then cleaning the bowl and the slop she'd left, I took my glass of water and returned to the bedroom, taking my place on one of the two chairs that stood near the bed. Cassie, as if sensing the solemnity of the scene, lay immediately at my feet. Mother looked a breath away from death. Her hair, which was almost completely grey now, hung lankly around her gaunt, equally grey face, instead of being pulled back pertly in tortoiseshell combs. Her droopy skin, it seemed to me, had begun to look like an imitation of the real thing, already losing whatever it was that made it vital. I sat tensely, afraid that one of her visions would take hold right then and there, but instead she finally stirred, in slow motion.

"Hello, Mother," I said. She looked at her watch. "I'm a little early. Sorry."

"That's all right." Her voice had taken on the same half-departed quality as her skin. She pulled herself up, with difficulty. I leaned forward to help her, and she was so light. Just bones collected in a thin casing. She was beyond notice of my scruffy head. "Can you hand me some water?" she asked. I took a glass from the side table, next to my blue pottery dog.

"I finished *The Emigrants*. It's the best book I've read in a long time. Most original, too."

"I thought you might like it. It's the last novel—if that's what you'd call it—that I managed to read through to the end."

"It's interesting, the way he inserts photos and drawings," I said.

"Yes."

Normally this would have been the extent to our discussion of a book, but I continued: "They add, somehow, to the ache one feels reading about those displaced souls. People who have suffered and lost so much."

Hands tightly around the glass of water, she looked up at me, then back at the glass. "Yes."

"Maybe that's why you suggested it to me."

She gave something between a shrug and a nod.

"I have been wondering . . ." I paused, hoping she'd know what I meant, but she just stared at her glass. "Wondering about, you know . . ." I didn't even know how to refer to my own father. When he died, I called him Daddy, but that childish moniker had been buried with him. "About our own story. About what happened in Connecticut."

She closed her eyes, then opened them slowly, saying: "Yes, your father." She paused. Her veined, bony hands still clutched the water glass. She was staring into it like a crystal ball. "I'm sorry. I have been wrong not to talk to you more about him."

Silence again. For long enough that I began to worry that she wasn't going to say any more. Especially when I saw her eyes welling up, her chin trembling, and her lips pressing together, disappearing into her mouth. My heart was pounding, my skin prickled all over, but it was now or never: "He didn't fall, did he?"

"I don't know," she said, now shaking her head against the pillow, the tears running freely down her cheeks. "I can't know, for certain. There was never any proof," and she looked at me desperately, as if I might provide it, then looked back at her glass of water.

"But no, I don't think it was an accident. Or maybe it was half an accident. I've always believed that he didn't actually jump. That he maybe let himself fall." She took a short, half-choked breath and looked at me again, then at the ceiling. "He, he . . . he took your sister's death very hard. We both did, of course, but him in particular." She paused again and looked back at me. "He was never the same, afterward. There was also his career, which he believed was going nowhere. Since her accident, he hadn't been able to work, and he was afraid he'd never be offered a full professorship and tenure. He was not someone who took life easily. Like you," she said. I shrugged. "You are a lot like him," she continued, "in more than just looks." She took another sip of water; I could hear the gulp go down her throat. "Could you?" She held it up to me. I put it back down next to the blue dog. "For a long time I couldn't talk to anyone about all that had happened—couldn't even much think about it myself. But then your Aunt Tiffy made me talk. And Edmond too."

She took a deep breath that convulsed her whole frail frame as it turned into a sob. Her face contorted; tears streamed. Her voice came out almost a squeak. "But I couldn't find a way to talk about all that had happened to you." She looked at me pleadingly. "You were just a child. And how do you talk about such horrible, unresolved things to a child?" She was now fretting with the duvet cover. Her face was a mess—eyes and nose running—even though there was a box of tissues on the bed, right next to her, but she seemed oblivious. "And you were so angry, which created its own kind of barrier. I just didn't know what to do." Another tremor shook her. "So I did nothing, and eventually it seemed too late, too strange to speak about what had happened all those years ago." Then the sobs came again, with even greater force, and I thought they might kill her right here and now. "I'm so, so sorry."

I stood up, snatched a Kleenex from the box, and gave it to her, putting a hand on her trembling, bony shoulder. I'd never seen her in such a state. She looked up at me pleadingly: "Can you forgive me?"

"Mother, please," I said.

She blew her nose, wiped her face, took one more shuddering breath, exhaled audibly, closed her eyes, and laid her head back on the pillows. Again, I thought this is it, her sick and tired body can't take such emotion. But after a minute, more or less composed, she raised her head: "Have you ever talked to anyone? About your father? About all that happened?"

"A little, to Cédric. Once," I said. I couldn't bring myself to mention Jacqueline, whom she'd never liked, and she didn't know Béa, though it crossed my mind then that she wouldn't disapprove of her.

"Do you think, T," she said, fretting again with the duvet cover. "Do you think you are, you may be—I was going to say, 'growing out of it,' but I guess you're too old for that. Do you think you might be moving on?"

"It's possible," I said. Béa Fairbank, wherever she was, damn her, flashed through my mind again.

She took another Kleenex, blew her nose, and wiped her eyes again. Edmond tapped the door.

"Everything all right?" he asked my mother tensely.

"Yes," she said, pouring much relief into that one syllable. "Under the circumstances, things couldn't be better," she said, looking at me.

"Good," he said, visibly relaxing. "How about a little lunch. I've got the oven on one hundred eighty degrees and the casserole has been in for fifteen minutes. It will be ready in five." He consulted his watch, not wanting to stray even half a minute from Lisette's instructions. "What do you think, Hélène? Something besides that dreadful gruel today?"

"Yes, I think I will. I'll try at least."

"Excellent." Edmond smiled so that I could see his teeth, not something that generally occurred, at least not when I was around.

And it was here I had my flash of hope. Maybe Revelation was powerful enough to kill those cancer cells. She did look a little better, a little less grey. She was hungry. "Will you join us?" she asked me shyly.

"I will, but let me get it ready, BP. Where do we eat?"

"Here is best," said Edmond. "We have these new little tables. 'TV tables' Hélène tells me they are called. Dreadful name, but as with all things of American inspiration, they are practical. They do make life easier." He began unfolding the trays on spindly metal legs.

The two of us got plates and glasses and reheated casseroles laid out, and we began eating from our TV tables, while Mother tried to swallow from her bed tray. Edmond was practically chirpy. I felt so lightened, I even teased them: "If you two are allowing TV tables in the house, what will be next? BP's study turned into a family room?" Once on Long Island, Edward had come back from a friend's house and referred to what we called the library as a family room. Mother had informed him in the strongest terms that we did not nor never would have any area of the house carrying that name. "It's so lower class," she'd said, flaring her nostrils in distaste. "Next you'll be asking for reclining chairs."

We spent the rest of lunch remembering summers on Long Island. Today I found that even in these memories, which I had always viewed on balance as unhappy, there were salvageable moments. Swimming in the ocean, walking the long beaches. I had actually enjoyed playing tennis. The last couple of summers Mother and Edmond had had friends with horses, and I'd raced up and down the sand on Jelly Bean. How I'd missed that horse when we came back to Paris.

By the time I left, Mother could hardly lift her head from the pillows. I kissed her cheek, and despite her fatigue, she managed to wrap her bony arms around my neck. "I'm so sorry," she repeated, and I could hear the tears coming again.

"Please," I said. "But thank you."

She dabbed her eyes with another Kleenex and gave me a little wave as the tears rolled again. "Come back soon."

As Cassie and I walked out onto the rue de Verneuil, I too felt spent but in a loose-limbed, post-exercise kind of way. If Béa Fairbank had lightened my step after dinner that Saturday night, this exchange with my mother had practically given me wings. In no time at all, the great wall of silence had been razed, and the world looked a lighter, brighter place.

———

My euphoria didn't last long, though. It never does. Questions and more questions always start rearing their ugly heads. Though my mother's breakdown had moved me profoundly, by the time I was back on my mattress, staring at the ceiling, I was also wondering about what had been left in shadow, what had not really been discussed: Franny. Mother had not even been able to pronounce her name and had only obliquely referred to her death. Perhaps Franny was the real cause of those nightmarish visions. Or maybe those snakes and eagles were paying her back for another dark corner, our move to Paris and the quick remarriage. Maybe that was the real source of her guilt.

I tried Béa again, waiting impatiently for the dial to return to its place after every number. Once again, the phone rang and rang. Where could she possibly be? Why hadn't she tried phoning me last night? Doubt came crashing down. She must be avoiding me. There was no other explanation possible. Either she was there and not answering, or she'd gone out, most likely with another man, and left the answering machine off intentionally. That way she wouldn't have to feel guilty about not returning my calls. These thoughts caused me the most unusual agony. I did not want to be ditched by Béa Fairbank.

I put on the television for distraction, but it didn't help. My mind continued to careen between Béa and my mother, the inexplicable absence of the one and the encroaching disappearance of the other.

TWO

THE NEXT DAY Piotr was back, with his shaved patch like a full moon behind his ear. The rest of his hair was longer than usual, but it still stuck straight out like a brush. It now looked as though he had received an extreme scare, which I suppose he had. Cassie was ecstatic, as if she'd feared he was gone forever. I tried to think of nothing but bicycles, but this proved impossible. Thoughts of my mother and Béa continued to thrash around my mind, even as I calmly helped a customer or answered Piotr's questions about what had happened while he was gone. Midmorning, Wanda came in, and by the time she was finished, Mélo-Vélo was as clean as the day we'd moved in. Even better, Wanda seemed to enjoy the work. She hummed as she moved the broom vigorously across the floor and as she rubbed down the counters with a rag. I hadn't seen her this content since their wedding day.

I took them both to lunch at Le Relais. Just as we walked back in, the phone was ringing. I picked it up.

"Where have you been?" the voice said urgently.

"I might ask you the same question. I've been phoning you since Sunday evening. No answer. No machine. No word from you."

"I left rather precipitously. But I've been trying you at home since Sunday evening too. There was never any answer."

"I was there," I said piously. "So why didn't I hear you trying?"

"How should I know?" she almost screamed.

I thought back. I couldn't remember the last time I'd had a call at the rue des Martyrs, and suddenly, those exposed colored wires came to mind. The delicacy with which I'd been handling the phone so that they wouldn't break. Maybe the one that makes the phone ring had snapped.

"The baby died."

"What?" I said.

"Viviane's baby died."

"Who? André?"

"No—the one that wasn't born yet. It strangled itself on the umbilical cord, in the womb. She. It's, it was, a girl. Cédric and Viviane are at the hospital. I'm here with André." I could hear the tears rising. "Do you think you can come out? I hate to ask you, but I'm losing it a bit. And Cédric . . ."

"I'll be out by the end of the afternoon," I said.

Within the next half hour I arranged to leave the shop in the hands of Piotr and Wanda for the next two days. And, though I hadn't driven in years, to borrow one of Edward's cars. He actually dropped off his silver BMW so that I wouldn't have to walk over with the dog. When I arrived at Hautebranche, Béa answered the door, André on her hip, just as he'd been on Viviane's the last time I'd visited and their life had seemed brimming with hope and good fortune.

"Let's go outside," she said. We went across the large sitting room to the walled garden behind. Béa shepherded the dogs out the door to the apple orchard, where they could play without disturbing us. Cassie gave me a quick look, then disappeared behind Fyodor, the dog I'd walked almost six years before.

I made room among the toys on the blanket Béa had laid out and sat down. Béa started building a tower of colored plastic beakers to distract André.

"According to Cédric, Viv got very quiet and withdrawn last week. At first, he thought it was a normal letdown after the euphoria she'd been living for the last few months. Or that maybe the weight of two children under one was finally beginning to dawn on her. He asked her what was wrong, but she said she was fine. It wasn't until Friday that she admitted it had been some time since she'd felt the baby move. For a few days she'd tried to convince herself that she'd felt something—just less, because there was less room—but then she couldn't even tell herself that anymore. 'Suddenly it was as if I just had a big stone in my stomach,' she told Cédric. On Saturday they went to the hospital and the doctor confirmed that the baby was dead. She'd strangled on the umbilical cord. The doctor said it just happens sometimes. I can't get the vision out of my head of a little baby, totally formed at seven months, floating contentedly in her liquid home and then getting tangled in her own lifeline, until the blood is no longer circulating." She shook her head and shuddered; André took a swing at the beaker tower and burst into giggles. "I happened to ring on Sunday, just to say hello, and got Cédric, who was home with André. I dropped everything and left for the train station. I guess I'm helping, but I feel pretty useless. Viviane's shattered. You know she had to give birth as if the baby were still alive. Contractions, all that breathing she was practicing, the whole thing. Can you imagine going through all that, just to get a dead baby in the end?" She pulled her knees up to her chest. André was now trying to build his own tower. I shook my head, partly in shame, for all my selfish, distrustful thoughts.

"How long will she be in the hospital?" I asked.

"Until tomorrow." It was Cédric who spoke. He'd come in so quietly, not even André had noticed him. Now André began whining and stretching his arms toward the person he'd come to consider his father. I watched Cédric carefully, for traces of resentment that this was the one to live, but he had a stoic, resigned look on his uneven face. Melancholy, half-Hungarian Cédric had always believed tragedy was right around the corner. Now he was going to weather the storm he'd been mentally preparing for most of his life. I hoped he hadn't heard Béa's detailed vision of the dying fetus. "We've named her Marie," he went on, picking up André in his arms. The child had gone suddenly quiet and solemn, tucking his head in the crook of Cédric's neck, physically attaching himself as tightly as possible. "Viviane thought it was important that she have a name. I guess that's right." He shrugged and sat on the stool. "She wants to have a proper burial, even though she hasn't been to church herself in over twenty years." He shook his head. "'What if there is a heaven?' she asked me. How can I answer a question like that, after this?" And he looked from one to the other of us, as if he seriously expected an answer.

"If it makes her feel better . . . ," I said. He nodded.

The dogs were scratching at the orchard door, and I got up to let them in. It was a perfect early evening, the late sun slanting low between the roses, which cast long, jagged shadows across the grass. We went inside. Cédric fed the animals; Béa got some soup and milk out for the baby, and I made some pasta for us. But no one—not even the dogs or the baby—was at ease. Viviane's absence hummed through the air the whole evening. After dinner, Béa said she needed to go to bed. Cédric, with some difficulty, settled André in his crib in their bedroom, and then he and I sat down in the garden.

"I keep thinking: what could I have done to prevent this? Should I have questioned Viv sooner, instead of being my usual passive self? Because maybe there would have been time." The guilt, the tortured revisiting of the event and what we could have done differently. That state of mind with which I was doubly familiar.

"Of course you couldn't have done anything," I said, so easy to say and believe when it's not your story.

That night, as we sat in the dark, Cédric talked for a long time about how Viviane had been consumed by her inability to have a baby, how he'd find her in the middle of the night in front of the almost dead fire, or out pruning her roses in the early morning, tears streaming down her face. How nothing she could do made her feel worthwhile, as long as she remained infertile. How hard it had been to get her to admit defeat and adopt some stranger's child as her own. Even when they'd gone to Russia and she'd first held André in her arms, there had been no joy in her face. It was only when they'd left the orphanage and were the only people André had in the world that she'd melted. Her natural sympathy and good heart had taken over. When they returned from Russia, she'd worried about her own health. She felt funny. Her breasts hurt, especially the left one, and she went to the doctor expecting to hear she had cancer, only to find out she was finally pregnant. The prospect of two children in a short time didn't daunt her for one second. She'd finally succeeded; she was worthwhile after all.

"Now what's she going to think?" Cédric asked me, a note of desperation creeping into his previously monotone voice. "How will she go on? She sits there in her hospital bed, taking her medication so the milk won't keep coming, staring blankly, hardly uttering a word, except when she gets going on all this business about heaven and Catholic burials." He shook his head.

"You have to give it time," I said.

"But I worry she won't be able to bounce back from this. That it will be too much for her. She's almost forty. The doctor said there's now no chance of her getting pregnant again."

"She'll be all right," I said to Cédric, hoping I sounded convincing, as we parted. He went to sleep near the crib of his adopted son, in their ground-floor bedroom that overlooked the apple orchard, and I climbed the steep stairs with my dog to the alcove where I always slept, wondering if indeed Viviane would be all right.

I opened the door. The moonlight was coming through the colored glass of the bull's-eye window, leaving patches of blue and green and red on the tall bed that took up almost all the space in this small room.

"Hi," came a sad, defeated voice from the bed.

"Hi," I answered.

Cassie settled on the floor at the end of the bed, and I got in with my clothes on. Béa, dressed in a nightshirt, threw her arms around me. I could feel her begin to quiver. "It's so awful," she said as the tears rose and spilled over. She began to shake with sobs. I held on tightly, kissing her hair and her face lightly, while she cried and cried.

———

I woke up the next morning still fully dressed. Béa didn't move as I slid quietly out of bed and Cassie danced around. I looked down at her, the light-brown hair a messy mound around her fair face, and I didn't think I'd ever seen anything so beautiful. I could have stood there forever, but Cassie couldn't and Cédric was already downstairs knocking around the kitchen while he talked to a babbling André.

Instead of my usual start to the day at Hautebranche, a long, hot lie in the bathtub, I splashed cold water on my face and headed downstairs to help Cédric. André was propped up and contained in his high chair, and Cédric was feeding him baby cereal with a spoon. Caught up in the morning routine, he'd put aside his brooding of the night before.

"I've got to get this baby in his own room. He wakes up with the sun, which these days is about five," Cédric said as I poured myself some coffee.

"I thought you'd done up a bedroom for him."

"We did, but it's upstairs, and Viv's worried it's too far away."

"I thought you had one of those intercom, walkie-talkie things," I said.

"We have got one. But she won't let him go."

"Maybe we should move the bed before she comes home today. She's less likely to object to a fait accompli."

Cédric put down the spoon and wiped André's face, where most of the cereal seemed to have landed. "Maybe you're right. Just take control. I've never been very good at that."

"Would you stop talking as if only you'd been a better person, none of this would have happened? Neither you nor your character has anything to do with it." We sat there in silence for a few moments. I walked over to the French doors and looked at the garden where we'd been sitting in the dark the night before. It was still in shadow, though the sun would soon be above the trees of the forest beyond the wall. Cassie ran around, sniffing this and that in a businesslike manner. I always liked waking up here. The birds sang, the light grew. It was as close as I ever came to those Connecticut mornings before my world fell apart.

"It's time for our breakfast, and then let's move that bed," Cédric said as André let out a piercing scream when his cereal bowl was removed. "It's all gone, *mon ami*." Cédric leaned over André and planted a kiss on his soft white hair. "*Ter-min-é*. Now it's my turn to eat."

Just as we finished our *tartines* with Viviane's quince jam, Béa came down, dressed in running shorts and a T-shirt, her hair pulled back in a ponytail. Her eyes were slightly red and puffy from the crying, but she smiled and said good morning and tried to look cheery. She walked to the refrigerator for some orange juice. Her wrists and ankles were so delicate, it was hard to imagine her chubby.

"I hope you don't mind. I've *got* to have a run," she said, standing right next to me.

"Please," said Cédric, looking at the two of us with a little smile. I felt myself go red. "Have your run. We have furniture to move." She went out the front door, but that smile stayed plastered on Cédric's face as he watched her doing warm-up exercises through the window. I cleaned up the breakfast dishes. "What, exactly, were the sleeping arrangements last night?" he finally asked.

"You've obviously figured that out for yourself, Sherlock," I said.

"But Trevor," he turned to me, now speaking seriously. "You can't . . ."

"I'm not."

"This is Viv's good friend. You can't just add her to your list."

"I don't have a list anymore," I mumbled. "And this is different. I can't tell you how or why, but it's different."

"I hope you know what you're doing." He shook his head.

"Well, strictly speaking, I haven't done anything," I said.

"*That* must be a first," he said. "But please be careful. I like Béa, and Viv might never forgive you." He looked at me with his uneven lips pulled to one side, his slightly crooked nose, his soft eyes as stern as they could ever get.

"I can't make any promises about the future," I said. "But for once, at least, I'm thinking about it. Hoping, even."

"Okay." He nodded. "Now let's move that bed. I've got to get to the hospital, and you're right about just doing this. Otherwise André will be a teenager before he's out of our bedroom." We moved the bed, showed André his new room, and Cédric left, the brooding resignation back on his face.

André stayed in his playpen in the sitting room while I cleaned up for Viviane's return. The baby had an extraordinary capacity to amuse himself. Maybe it was his past in the orphanage, but he remained intent on the selection of toys I'd laid out for him and didn't make a sound until Béa, red and huffing, came in the door. She'd been gone for at least an hour.

"Do you always run that long?" I asked.

"No. But I needed it this morning. It's a gorgeous day. What are you doing inside? Where are the dogs?"

"In the orchard."

"Let's take André out there for a minute. While I cool off." She took a large glass of water from the tap, and I picked up the baby.

"You're not carrying a bicycle, you know," Béa said, her laugh rising and dancing. "Just put his legs around your hip." I tried to remember if I'd ever held a baby. I must have taken one of Edward's children in my arms, sometime, when no one else was available. But that compact, alert body against my side felt completely foreign.

We walked through the French doors to the walled garden, past the rose bushes in full flower and through the gate. The apple orchard, a large area surrounded by high hedges, actually contained several kinds of trees. Predominantly apple, but there were also quince, plum, chestnut, and walnut. On various weekends, I'd helped pick whatever fruit or nut was ripe.

"You see what you've been missing staying in the house?" Béa said, shading her eyes from the sun as she looked up at me. Nature was in peak form this June morning. The grass was thick and green and just beginning to look unkempt. The leaves had lost that tenderness of early spring and were a strong, chlorophyllic green. The apples on the tree near where I was standing were little nuggets, at the point where the link between fallen blossom and future fruit was clear. There was not a cloud in the sky, and birds sang lazily. The dogs had stopped playing and were lying in the sun—all except Cassie, who was jumping jealously at my side. I put André down on the grass to let him explore and took Cassie's ears in my hands, letting her lick my face. Béa lay down on her back next to André; I lay down next to her.

"Don't get too close," she said. "I must stink."

"No, you smell like the sun." Despite the lost baby and my dying mother, it was a sublime moment, lying flat on my back here on the early summer grass, looking at the blue sky, next to Béa Fairbank. Most unusually, I felt happy and lucky to be alive.

Cédric came home with Viviane, who looked broken in half. She moved slowly, tentatively, as if even the soles of her feet hurt, and hardly seemed to recognize where she was. We stretched her out on the sofa. The poor woman still looked pregnant, the bulging stomach a cruel reminder of what might have been. Béa brought André over to sit on her lap. At first, she hardly reacted, but then he began touching her face with his strangely unpudgy fingers. He had an intense look on his own face—as if he were part sculptor, part blind man. He might well have been modeling clay, because after a few minutes Viviane's taut muscles relaxed and a faint smile appeared. She pulled André very close, folded him into her arms, and exhaled.

"It's been hell," she said. "But coming home—it's a start."

Béa and I drove back that afternoon. We talked a bit about Cédric and Viviane and what might happen now, but mostly we were silent. Béa cried again, and I drove with one hand on her thigh.

"I'm completely drained," she said to me as I dropped her off that Wednesday afternoon. "Why don't you come for supper on Saturday. I'll have pulled myself back together by then."

Though Saturday seemed an unbearable wait, I just said: "I'll be there," and made our kiss last as long as I could.

⸻

Wanda and Piotr looked almost disgruntled to see me back. From the blissful smile on Wanda's face, these two days in the shop could have been the honeymoon they never really had. The place was spotless, and all the repairs were finished. I felt superfluous in what was supposed to be my own shop. Since Wanda lingered, so obviously loath to leave, I invented a chore and left myself. Like Béa, I needed a bit of time alone. I even left the dog.

For the first moments, I felt unfettered as a teenager when the teacher is absent and class is canceled. But then, when I got to the corner of the rue de Buci and the rue de Seine, I stopped, at a loss for what to do and where to go. Suddenly I felt more like a newly released prisoner, unsteady with the sudden freedom of choice and movement. The need to make up one's mind—even about whether to turn right or left—can be a terrible burden. I walked to the pont des Arts, where I could sit down on a bench and think.

About the future.

My future.

I considered the facts.

Fact number one: my mother would soon be dead.

Fact number two: I knew—had always known—that when my mother died, there would be some money for me. Mother had sold our house and apartment before moving to France, but she'd bought the Long Island house, which her parents had only rented. My grandfather, I believed, had made some bad investments in the 1970s. But the Long Island house was now to be sold, and the proceeds were to come to Edward and me.

Fact number three: that money alone would be enough for me to give up this bicycle shop business.

Fact number four: Piotr and Wanda were practically running Mélo-Vélo already—and loving every minute of it.

All this should have had me quivering with excitement. Bubbling over with plans. But all I could feel was apprehension. Wasn't it easier to live like a failure, doing a job I didn't much like, seeing women I didn't care about? The idea of picking up my camera as a profession, or thinking of Béa in the longer term—well, the longer term from any conceivable angle terrified me. Failing at things I chose to pursue was not the same thing as choosing failure.

But there was also fact number five: I was forty-two, and life was passing me by as fast as the waters of the Seine running underneath me at that moment. Did I really want to die the not-so-proud owner of a bicycle shop?

I got up and went to see Mother. The blip of improvement was gone. Not wanting to mention Cédric and Viviane, afraid that the baby would appear as her own angel of death, I couldn't think of anything to say, and what a relief it was when Anne-Sophie arrived. She had all those children to talk about. Though she too avoided bad news and did not mention that Caroline had been caught skipping school one day and was being sullen at home. Anne-Sophie brushed over her stepdaughter with: "She's rushing into adolescence headfirst, that Caroline." Throughout, Mother just lay impassively, as if she were already somewhere else.

On the way out, still thinking of Caroline, I said to Anne-Sophie: "Maybe she's acting up because she's losing the person who's acted like her mother for so much of her life."

"Maybe." Anne-Sophie shrugged, looking at the ground in a way that suggested she was no longer interested in explanations for Caroline's impossible behavior. She was just fed up with it. I recognized the look; it was the expression that Edmond had worn with me for the last thirty years.

Over the next few days I left the shop often in Wanda and Piotr's happy hands to visit Mother. They were good days when she needed little morphine, and I wanted to take advantage of her desire now to talk. She in fact talked so much that I suppressed the desire to take notes, to get the story down before the source was gone. Instead, as soon as I left, I went straight to the café on the corner of the rue de Verneuil and the rue du Bac and scribbled it all down. From scraps of paper the first day, I went to a notebook the second. My own memories started spilling out on the page. With the dog lying at my feet, one espresso led to two, and I kept writing until Cassie got impatient. Each day I walked out feeling released, relieved, but also unsettled as I reworded sentences I'd written in my head, as more memories continued to burble to the surface. On the street I started scribbling in the pocket notebook usually used for notes on photos.

My father's parents, she told me, had wanted him to be a banker. They'd lost most of their money in the Depression and hoped he'd reestablish the family's fortunes. But he had no interest or mind for finance. Literature was his thing, and he was determined to pursue it. When my parents met, Mother's mother had died a couple years earlier. She was working as a French translator and living with her father, who liked Gordon, my father, but worried about his ability to keep them afloat. The pressure from above weighed on him. When his parents left them that rundown house in Connecticut, as Mother called it, and moved to Florida, and her father gave them a small flat in New York, my father's sense of responsibility—almost guilt—only increased. He would go quiet for several days at a time, she said. Disappear into his study to work, work and only come out when she'd call him for meals. Occasionally Mother would look off, lost in some thought that she didn't want to share.

But she'd start up again, telling me that before my father died I was an easy child. Always an observer, she said, but a smiling one. Certainly—to my surprise—easier than Edward, who couldn't sit still or keep his fingers out of trouble, and Franny, who had colic and cried for months and months. Every mention of her daughter's name made her mist up, and she would quickly change the subject. Her death we didn't discuss, and I resigned myself to forever living with only my own re-creation of those events. Our move to Paris also remained off limits, and these gaps meant that however much information I gobbled up during each visit, I felt a gnawing hunger for more. But I told myself that's the way it is with starving people; they never feel quite full. Meanwhile, on I wrote.

And I was getting nourishment of another kind. On Thursday and Friday evenings, though I didn't see Béa, I spoke to her on my new touch-tone, cordless telephone, for over an hour each time. After the calls, I lay on my mattress with my head gently buzzing, my arms and legs a-tingle. It was funny in a way, given our geographic proximity, that I didn't just rush up there and grab her. But both of us needed to get some distance from little Marie's death, from Cédric's and Viviane's crushing sorrow. And I still questioned what would happen on that Saturday night. Because when we talked on the phone, it was quite superficial: what we'd done that day, how we thought Cédric and Viviane were getting on. Or we told each other stories about our younger selves.

What was or wasn't happening between us, just what these long calls did or didn't mean, was not discussed. Though she clearly enjoyed talking to me, I still wondered—okay, worried—what Béa really thought of me. Had she embraced me the first time out of sympathy? And then had she allowed me to embrace her at Hautebranche because she needed some comfort that night herself? I kept thinking, with a rising panic in my throat: she knows all about me; how could she ever trust me? When I said to her on Friday night, just as we were hanging up: "I can't wait to see you tomorrow," spoken with all the breathlessness of a teenager, she just said: "Good night. See you tomorrow."

We in fact ended up going to a restaurant. Béa said she didn't have the energy to cook, and anyway, she needed to get out. I of course wondered if this request wasn't a ploy to keep me as far away from her bed as possible. After much agonized reflection, I decided to leave Cassie behind. Although she was fine at the Relais, she got overexcited in restaurants she didn't know and took up too much space under cramped tables. And it was better not to assume that things would end up the way I wanted them to.

When I got to the restaurant at eight thirty exactly, she wasn't there yet. Béa would of course be late. I waited for twenty minutes. Finally she came rushing through the door, out of breath, the color high in her cheeks. When her eyes found me, a smile crossed her face—warm and wise and apologetic, all at once—and my pique at her tardiness dissolved.

"I know," I said, kissing her hello. "You're sorry you're late." Her hair was still wet from the bath.

"I—forget it." Up came the laugh.

From the first sip of wine until I put too large a tip on the table, I was enchanted, almost to the point of delirium. I didn't pay attention to what I ate, to anyone else in the restaurant. I couldn't get enough of her voice, of her eyes that lit up and went wide when she told a story, of her small, tapered hands that flew up when she was making a point. The whole dinner my head buzzed gently, my limbs tingled. And then we were out on the street and walking, locked arm in arm, and suddenly Béa stopped and asked: "Where are we going?" I said: "I have no idea."

This was the first pause the whole evening. Finally I said: "I have to walk the dog."

"Of course," she said with a mischievous smile.

"Would you like to come walk the dog with me?"

She hesitated but was still smiling, gently playing with me. "Okay."

And so we walked, still arm in arm, but quieter now, toward the rue des Martyrs. I only panicked when we approached the building. Though I had warned her my studio was "stark," a quick peek at my room might send her scampering back to the tasteful heights of Montmartre forever. In front of my door, I fumbled with the lock, as if I'd never opened it before. Cassie's nails clicked against the floor in a frantic dance on the other side.

"It can't be that bad," said Béa with one of her chortles.

"The dog can't wait," I said, opening the door just wide enough to let the dog out and my hand in for the leash hanging from a hook inside. On the street, I asked, trying to sound casual: "Can I walk you home?"

"No, I don't think so." She still had that damn smile on her face. But now I started to laugh and said: "So—what—has this been your strategy right from the start? A way to penetrate the walls of my cell? To join the ranks of Cédric and Piotr and become the third human being to have crossed my threshold?"

"No," she smiled, but thoughtfully, and then seriously, not smiling anymore: "I do, though, want to know what I might be getting into. I mean, I have no interest in a fling. And I don't think I could bear another Curt."

I didn't answer, just put my arm tightly around her shoulder and led her straight back to my room. With the dog walked and my excuses run dry, I opened the door all the way. Inside, the street lamps cast just enough bloodless light to highlight its emptiness. I turned on the low-watt lamp on my table, hoping that would cheer things up. Not much. Cassie had shredded a wrapper I must have left on the table and pulled the duvet halfway to the sort-of bathroom. I watched Béa run her eye over the flat surfaces. "Not big on knick-knacks, are you?" she said. "Or furniture, for that matter." We were still standing, the last two players in a game of musical chairs: one chair left and who would get it?

We settled on the mattress.

THREE

SUNDAY MORNING, ON a high that surely no drug could ever induce, I floated down to the shop, opened up, put out the bicycles, and waited in a sort of heavenly stupor for Piotr and Wanda to arrive.

"Are you all right?" asked Wanda as she slipped her bag from her shoulder.

"Oh, yes," I said through the haze.

And off I went again to gather more information about my father and our life in America from my mother. As soon as I left her early afternoon, I was back at the café, writing what she'd said and now, too, what I thought about it and how it had contributed to making me the adult I had unfortunately become. I found that the writing gave me a blessed distance from myself, an ability to take everything less personally. It was liberating. Thrilling, actually, especially with thoughts of Béa lingering in the background, the prospect of another night with her ahead of me.

I had never and have never since felt as charged with life as I did during those few days with my dying mother and those few nights with my first real love.

Then came Monday. I left Cassie with Piotr and Wanda, borrowed Edward's car again, and drove out with Béa to unborn Marie's funeral. Béa had her guitar with her, because Cédric had asked her to sing. Probably to fill his mind with something other than his dead child and grieving wife, he had organized the service like a professional. The little Romanesque church in the village next to Hautebranche couldn't contain all the mourners. Their families were there, Viviane's all the way from Aix-en-Provence. Friends from Paris drove out. Then there were people from Cédric's school in Vernon. His students had requested that a bus be hired so that they could attend. Many teachers had come along too. Except for the school group and Béa, it was just like their wedding.

By inviting so many, perhaps Cédric was trying to remind Viviane how much they still had in their lives. How important it was to carry on. Because Viv wasn't carrying on very well. Her face behind the large dark glasses that gave her a strangely ill-suited Hollywood look was drained of all its usual expressiveness. She walked as if she'd been wound up and pushed in the direction of the church. According to Cédric, she'd just disappeared. "It's as if all her insides had been scooped out," he said. "Except when she's talking about God. And that's even worse." Being Cédric, he didn't say anything to her. He just circled around her, silent or accommodating.

During the procession, where Cédric was the only pallbearer necessary for that shoe box of a coffin, Viviane's face finally woke up. She began to look reverent, an expression I'd never seen on her face. She listened to every word the priest said, sang the hymns with a force verging on anger, and took Communion as if she'd been receiving the body and blood of Christ every week of her life since childhood. In a matter of days, she had turned into a person I didn't recognize. I thought of Mother telling me how I'd changed from the smiling, loving child I'd been the day it sunk in that

Daddy wasn't coming back. My father's death had caused suffering capable of changing not only the course of my life but also of my very person. Or it had forced different aspects of my character to rise to the surface, while tamping down others. And the same thing was true with Viviane. The soft, generous person was still in there somewhere, but in her desperation, a pious and shriller self was emerging. The question was would the shift prove lasting.

After the priest had given his sermon, where he said that God had his reasons for "taking *la petite Marie* to his side" (just what those were, we were not informed), it was time for Béa to play. She had been rehearsing all weekend, though not when I was there. I hadn't, in fact, ever heard her sing. When I'd asked, there had always been an excuse. "I need to sustain the belief that I'm alone. So that I won't lose it in front of the whole church." I knew, too, that she was slightly embarrassed by Viviane's choice, which was a song that Eric Clapton wrote when his four-year-old son fell out the window of a New York skyscraper, "Tears in Heaven." "It's just a little, you know, obvious," she'd said, the wrinkles forming straight lines across her forehead.

"At least she's not asking you for a Gregorian chant," I'd answered.

She walked over to the chair with that delicate step of hers, toes pointing out. She sat down and crossed one leg over the other, rested the guitar on her thigh. After giving it a final tune, she looked up and in her English-accented French explained about the song she was going to play. "'Tears in Heaven.' '*Larmes au Ciel*.'" Then, with her eyes fixed on some point in the mid-distance, she started to play, and the entire world except for her in that chair melted into a blur. Her voice seemed to come from the same deep well as her laugh. It wasn't loud, but every word was clear. I don't think anyone in the church moved, all of us wishing she'd never finish, that we could forever be caught inside her beautiful song. Her cheeks became more flushed the longer she sang. Her big eyes glistened, but her voice never cracked. She never sped up or missed a chord. When she did finish, there were hankies out and noses sniffling all around. Béa returned quietly to the seat next to me, and I felt as if she were giving off a warm glow in which I had no right to be sitting. When she put her small hand on mine, it was shaking. I covered it with my other hand. She was still staring straight ahead, this time at the priest who was saying the final prayer before we walked out to the graveyard.

The lowering of that little box into the ground was unbearable. It had been arranged that only family and close friends would attend the actual burial, and with our reduced numbers standing around that small hole—hardly bigger than the one I'd help Cédric dig the previous year for a young apple tree—the tragedy of a dead child was undiluted. The scene was immutably final, womb to tomb, with nothing in the middle. Not even one breath. Cédric was now holding André, who until then had been held by Viviane's mother. Viviane stood next to him but side by side, not arm in arm. Not one of their body parts touched. They didn't look at one another, didn't seem connected in any way. It rendered the scene completely desolate, despite the sun that was shining in dappled spots through the trees, despite the birds chirping a lazy summer song and the breeze rising and falling. Despite another perfect summer's day, here were Cédric and Viviane, the couple I'd held up as inviolate, standing like two shards of a broken bowl over the grave of their daughter.

Back at the house there were canapés and wine. People moved around the garden, speaking in muted tones. Béa and I lingered to see if there wasn't something we could do—of course there wasn't—so we drove back to Paris.

"Give it time," Béa kept saying to my worries about Cédric and Viviane. But I was afraid of time, afraid of how it built up tensions and walls of silence and resentment that were hard to tear down.

During the service, while the congregation had been filing toward the altar to take communion, I was thinking of Franny's funeral. I remembered being in a church with my buttoned collar uncomfortably tight, with many grown-ups towering over me in dark clothes. I remembered how Franny had two pallbearers, my father and her godfather. Seeing that small box and thinking of my sister inside made me pull at my tight collar and gasp for air. Afterward, I remembered how the door to her bedroom was closed. Even though it had a knob, a point of entry that the coffin lacked, the room seemed as terrifying as the box. I avoided passing in front of it, and when I had to, I ran, took a leap, and held my breath. The weight of Franny's absence, the density of that black hole, sucked up our lives. For my parents, it was as if they had ceased to be human beings, as if they'd become a pair of my lead soldiers. Or at least they'd become lead on the inside. Because they walked and talked and put meals on the table for me and insouciant Edward, who continued to smile and babble, as if nothing had changed. But there was a heavy dullness to everything they did, as if their running red blood had been replaced by dense grey lead. No one had bothered to give me an explanation, to talk to me. Along with the guilt, I felt abandoned, cut off, confused.

After the first weeks, my parents began fighting, in a way they'd never fought before. As if the only thing that could make them come alive was an all-out row. Even in their grief, they were much too controlled to let their invectives hurl in our presence. They waited until Edward and I were tucked up in bed. But it was then that I began to have trouble sleeping, and I would creep out of bed, post myself in the corner at the top of the stairs, and spy on them. Through the bars in the banister, my ears would prickle at the sound of their voices distorted with anger, my nose would twitch at the air of strife that wafted up the stairs.

The only actual words that stayed in my memory were spoken not long before my father's death. I remembered them because he then stormed out of the house. "You should have married a banker," he hissed, just before the back screen door slammed shut like a mousetrap. Later, the words seemed oddly prescient, but at the time I was just sick with fear that he wouldn't come back.

And soon of course he didn't.

At Franny's funeral I remember calculating with great relief that the coffin was not quite big enough to hold me. My childish reasoning had been, as the service droned on and on, that if I couldn't fit in the box, I therefore couldn't die myself. Not yet, anyway. A year later I tried similar reasoning at the sight of my father's coffin, that it was too big for me, but it didn't work. Nightmares have haunted me ever since, dreams where I find myself in a space of suffocating proportions—a low-ceilinged room where I have to crouch, a closet so narrow I have to stand with my shoulders at an angle, a staircase so constricted that I have to slither up the steps like a speleologist in an underground passage of rock. The places are always very dirty and dark, and I spend the entire dream gasping for air, desperately trying to find light and oxygen.

As we entered a particularly long tunnel on the *autoroute*, I thought how little Marie's service was not just *déjà vu*. It was also a dress rehearsal for the fourth funeral I would soon add to my list: Mother's. I wondered who would be at that one. Who were my mother's friends, besides my godmother Tiffy in New York? Unlike Edward and Stephanie, Mother and Edmond's social life was almost exclusively French. Except for her spotty churchgoing to the American Cathedral and the work she did at the American Library, Mother had avoided the expat scene, had melted into

Edmond's world almost entirely. Maybe too many Americans, too often, brought back memories of the life she'd left behind and couldn't talk about.

I looked over at Béa, who had her arms folded across her chest and was staring intently at the road ahead. What made her different, I wondered for the umpteenth time, as the toll machine spat back my credit card? In a strange way, it seemed as if Béa had always been there. At least an awareness of her, of all the things I would need in a person. As if the sum of all those Casuals, plus Jacqueline, plus Stephanie equaled a certain latent knowledge of the right person. Without consciously picking apart the strands of each woman and each relationship, my mind had performed its own sorting job. And Béa was the sum of those parts. Right from the start, she'd seemed to understand me completely. At first I'd assumed it was because Viviane had told her so much about me, but maybe that was wrong. Maybe the pieces just fit, and there was no need to hold them to the light to make sure one side didn't have too large a gap, another too sharp an edge.

Maybe now, too, I was finally ready in a way that I hadn't been. I mean, how can a person who looks with arrogant disdain at the rest of the world love another human being? How is there room for love when anger and resentment take up so much space? Perhaps my humbling and the suffering that that mortification caused had added up in a parallel equation, to a new version of me that meant I was now able to love someone else. Then again, there was still no assurance I would meet my Béa. That had to be attributed to luck, a word I'd never held much stock in.

Of course being me, I couldn't help tagging on a caveat: perhaps what looked like luck today was just setting me up for greater sadness down the line. For Cédric and Viviane next to the grave of unborn Marie.

Now Mother faded, every day a little weaker. She was so thin, her body under the bedcovers just looked like extra wrinkles. The morphine doses increased and she was often not conscious. With the cancer having chomped its way into every vital organ, the incontestable victor, it seemed to me that the body should give up, elegantly accept defeat, and bow out. That through evolution, we should have developed some mechanism for knowing all was lost, some body chemical that would kick in and finish us off. But day after day, she hung on.

Whether she was aware of us or not, we never left her alone. A nurse did the nights, and one of us stayed by her during the days. The room began to feel stuffier and smaller, as if oxygen was being consumed but not replaced. Edmond rarely went out. He spent most of his time shuffling between the bedroom and his study, where Edward had set up a camp bed for him. He sat by Mother's side or read his books on the Great War. How he could have been dividing his time between the trenches and his dying wife, I don't know. Lisette wheezed around the apartment, a hankie constantly at hand. She resented the presence of the three rotating nurses. The bossy one she undoubtedly imagined would take her place. The second, young one she thought was "too pretty by half." And the third, Solange, the one who had told me about the morphine and who was actually the most helpful, reassuring, and quietly efficient, Lisette instinctively didn't like because she was black. She was so vociferous on the subject, we sent her over to help Anne-Sophie the days Solange was on duty. On Edward's new wife, she pronounced: "She's certainly better than the Other One." Then, her bulgy eyes staring at me portentously: "But the less said about *that* subject the better."

Edward, whose usual style was to take charge, pulled back, moving into the background. True, he had a lot of work at that time, and the banking business had no truck with personal problems. "Illness, death, divorce," Anne-Sophie said with an ironic smile on her heart-shaped lips, "are no excuse for leaving the office before midnight. Fortunately he seems to thrive on it," she added with a shrug. Having Mother thrown into Edward's already complicated juggling act of work, wife, and children must have been one too many balls in the air, even for him.

But there was more to the shift in roles than too much work at the bank or his large family. I was now dealing with the nurses, with both Mother's American and French lawyers, even with the formerly supercilious Monsieur Petitdemange who was still at the bank, still losing his hair. Now that my *situation intenable* was long over, now that I was speaking for my mother, he even showed me a certain amount of obsequious respect.

For the first time in my life, I was assuming the role of the older son.

Mother soon slipped into a constant state of semiconsciousness. But she lingered on day after day, for almost a month, until we all began to hope for death. There was no point, absolutely none, in her hanging on to life by a drugged thread. I began to wonder if my theory on the evolutionary mechanism that should have finished Mother off didn't work the other way around. Perhaps an excruciatingly protracted death was meant to help the survivors cope, by assuring that they would feel a certain relief when the person finally died.

At Mélo-Vélo, for my sake, Piotr and Wanda had put off their travel plans to Poland until August, and Wanda had slipped right into my place. One afternoon I spent a few hours showing her how to reorder bicycles and supplies, and from then on, she took over that job. The following week I showed her how to keep the books, and she latched on to that tedious task with more enthusiasm than I thought possible. She noted the numbers with careful, clear figures, caressingly running her pen up and down the columns, as if she'd be sorry to turn the page. Now all her quick, efficient movements—sleeves shoved above her elbows, watch adjusted on her wrist—had a satisfied rather than a sour snap to them. Although she still treated Piotr like an incompetent child, her fussing had a more loving tone to it. And I could see, too, that she admired Piotr's dexterity, his ability to fix anything that passed by his large, able hands. I often left Cassie with them, though that part I didn't enjoy. I missed her at my side, felt treacherous at her pleading looks when I walked away.

But it was Béa's absence I really felt. She was in London, staying with her brother and working on a commission, a family portrait, which she had at first hoped would only take a week but which she now saw would take much longer. I couldn't even complain out loud; she'd been very low on money. "It's divine intervention," she'd said to me when announcing her departure. "I'm not sure how I'd have made it through next month otherwise." My only compensation was speaking to her every evening on the phone. I lived for those calls and the sound of her deep voice and airy accent, the rising laugh. Partly, I suppose, because she was a lifeline, a world outside my dying mother and the rue de Verneuil. Mostly, though, because she was on my mind, either front and center or lurking in the shadows, every minute of the night and day.

FOUR

THE ARRIVAL OF Aunt Tiffy, my godmother and Mother's best, oldest friend in the world, ushered in the final scene of the final act.

Mother and Tiffany Marshall had been friends since they were girls in New York City. My grandparents, realizing their only child had a lonely life, allowed her to become as much a part of Tiffy's larger family as she wanted. "I was the Marshalls' fourth child," Mother had always said. They'd gone to the same girls' school in New York, to the same boarding school in Connecticut, and had only parted ways for four years of college, before ending up back in New York together. Both briefly worked—Mother as a French translator, Aunt Tiffy as a secretary—before getting married within a year of one another. They both had three children, and neither marriage had lasted. A few years after my father had died and we'd moved to Paris, Aunt Tiffy walked out on her husband, a handsome, trust-fund drunk who'd never worked a day in his life, except to gamble away the family fortune on backgammon and cards.

In my memory of my godmother, she had streaked blonde hair and always wore black clothes, adorned with an abundance of gold jewelry. Though tall, she loved food and had a tendency to "hip problems," as she put it. But roundness didn't stop her from wearing tight-fitting trousers and tops because Aunt Tiffy was unabashed about everything. I was always happy to see her; her self-confidence and easy laughter made the world almost seem a more manageable place. Her exuberance meant that she talked incessantly but without being dull or self-centered. Whenever I saw her, she immediately asked me twenty questions about what I was doing, who I was seeing, and how I thought other members of my family were doing. She never seemed to get depressed, though she had passed many difficult years with her soak of a husband, and then even more difficult ones when she'd tried to divorce him. He'd stayed sober enough to refuse child support or alimony, until the money was wrung from him by court order. Even then, the amounts were not generous, so she got a job that she ended up loving in real estate. Now she refused to retire.

She wafted into the rue de Verneuil the first week of August, after everyone else in the city had left. I'd offered to pick her up at the airport, but she'd insisted on a taxi. "Don't make me feel old," she'd said over the phone. I was at the apartment when she arrived. Even indomitable Aunt Tiffy would need warning about how bad Mother looked. The nurse had just left, Lisette was out shopping, and Edmond had taken their Renault Clio for a checkup. In the last week, he'd come out of his slump and had embarked on a frenzy of activity. He'd rewritten his own will, had the apartment revalued by the insurance company, and drawn up a list of his assets, as if he were going to die with Mother and wanted to tie up all loose ends first.

Though more subdued than usual and not wearing tight black but flouncing turquoise, Aunt Tiffy was still a breath of fresh air in a stifled household. Impending death was, in a sense, contagious; its imminence had sapped and dulled all of us.

"Paris in the summer is even worse than Paris in the winter," she said, dragging a suitcase on wheels behind her. It was a muggy, cloudy morning, the air sodden and cloying. "You're still as handsome as ever," she went on, pulling me to her perfumed breast and kissing one cheek. "Is she awake?"

"Not yet. Lisette's made up my old room for you. Here," I said, taking her suitcase and walking down the hall, "you can get settled first." All the doors were closed and the silence was ponderous.

"I'm longing for a cup of good French coffee, Trevor," said Aunt Tiffy, plopping down on the bed. "Would you be a dear and make me one, while I have a bath? Then I might feel human again. And your poor mother might be awake." Though she had quit some years ago, she had kept her smoker's voice; it was even rougher than I'd remembered. She also looked a bit stooped, and her face, which always looked tanned, was more lined. Age was gnawing away even at Aunt Tiffy. At least her limpid blue eyes still opened wide as a child's when she spoke.

Just as I was putting the old copper kettle on the gas stove to boil, Lisette returned with her caddy full of shopping. She was happy to have Aunt Tiffy here because she'd have another healthy mouth to feed.

"Is she here, Trésor?" Lisette whispered in the confidential tone she reserved for the non-French. Whenever we had an American visitor in the house, even if the person spoke decent French, Lisette acted as if he or she couldn't, as if communication were impossible. Foreignness went much deeper than the vocal chords in Lisette's mind. "You let me make that coffee. I'll prepare a little breakfast tray for her."

"She just asked for coffee."

"I know, but she'll be happy to have something to eat with it."

When it was ready and Aunt Tiffy was finished with her bath, I knocked on the door, tray in hand. "Lisette insisted," I said, putting down toasted baguette, jam, and a pot of yogurt on the desk.

"She knows me, even if she can't understand me," Aunt Tiffy said, putting on her glasses and looking over the food. She poured herself some coffee and sat on the desk chair. "Sit there on the bed," she said to me, "and tell me how bad she is."

"Very bad," I said. "She's wasted away to nothing. You'll hardly recognize her."

"I hope she recognizes me," she said, spreading jam on the bread.

"Most of the time, she's not really conscious of much. The morphine also gives her terrible nightmares." Though I had hoped that once our peace had been made, the snakes and birds would disappear, they hadn't. The higher the dose, the worse the visions. "Sometimes, when she's lying there, her face contorts, and her head starts rocking back and forth on the pillow. Then she'll open her eyes wide and look at you with such terror, you have to wonder if the drugs are worth it."

"Poor, poor Helen," Aunt Tiffy said. Her knee crackled as she stood up slowly, one hand on the desk. "Now that you've warned me of the worst, take me to her."

———

Mother had developed breathing problems, and when the doctor came later that morning, he quickly diagnosed pneumonia.

"It's actually a blessing. It will carry her off quickly, without any additional pain. I can't believe it will be more than a couple of days now." Pulling the stethoscope from his ears, he added: "You should get a canister of oxygen from the pharmacy. That will soothe her breathing a bit. And prepare yourselves."

After the doctor left, I went to the pharmacy and ordered the oxygen, then went back up to the rue des Martyrs with the dog. Madame Picquot had agreed to take Cassie for Mother's last days.

Despite her gruffness, which during the years had entrenched itself in every deepening crevice of her face, and her lack of sympathy for human beings, Madame Picquot liked dogs. She snuck treats to Cassie whenever she could, which meant I had to tug the dog by Madame Picquot's door every time we passed. Since I'd asked her to take the dog, she'd been waiting with baited breath for my mother to die.

Late that afternoon, with bed and bowl and food in hand, I rapped on my *gardienne*'s door.

"Don't worry," she said, taking the leash greedily in one hand, offering a slice of sausage to Cassie with the other. "You can leave her here as long as you like."

By the time I got back to the rue de Verneuil, my mother had tubes up her nose, and the oxygen machine was purring and spluttering at her side. The morphine doses were such that she was no longer conscious at all, though the nurse Solange assured me she could still hear what was going on around her. I sat in a chair near the bed reading a book I had found at the bottom of the same stack that had been topped by *The Emigrants*. Though she had not mentioned this book to me, I took it as her final message. Maybe I should say warning. It was Michel Houellebecq's *Les Particules élémentaires*, a literary sensation a few years earlier, about a guy who has crippling problems with the world in general but most particularly his mother and women. While pulled along by Houellebecq's no-fuss, ironic style, I was repulsed—there's no other word for it—by his undiluted nihilism. It was too close to home. Or too close to the persona I was trying to shed. Reading it also made me realize how easy it is to be negative, to cast aspersions on everything and everyone. The greater challenge is seeing the world in its truer, more nuanced form.

Every time her labored breathing became more strained, I looked up, stared at my struggling mother, and wondered if she'd been able to get through more than the first few pages of this story that must have reminded her of me. I imagined that I was getting the answer when her ashen, cadaverous brow grew worried and her breathing nothing more than coughing gasps, and I would administer the morphine under her tongue the way Solange had showed me. I found it impossible to stray farther than the kitchen or the living room, in case she died while I was gone. After everything I had put her through, the least I could give her was my presence when that lonely moment came.

It was also true that my way of coping with her death was to embrace it. Unlike both Edmond and Edward. The closer it came, the more they found reasons to be away, but for once—and this was a true sign of progress—I did not resent them for their coping mechanism. As for Lisette, she just cleaned and cooked; carrying on the routine was her method. Aunt Tiffy came and went but spent a good part of her time trying to distract Edmond.

The third day the nurse told us the time was near. That evening the whole family gathered around the dining room table, the children included. Though Edward had resisted, Anne-Sophie had insisted that they see their grandmother one more time. It was especially important for Caroline, who wrapped her arms around my mother and whispered something into her ear before kissing her gently on the forehead and marching solemnly out of the room, but in fact all four of them took the farewell to their grandmother in stride.

"I told you," Anne-Sophie said as we prepared to sit down for supper. "Children are tougher than you think. And they need to say good-bye as much as you do."

The meal that followed was surprisingly festive. We reminisced about Mother, already talking about her in the past tense, but this seemed normal, even healthy. We actually laughed, especially at some of Tiffy's stories from when they were girls.

That night, not long after I fell asleep, I heard a knock at the door.

"It's time," Solange said.

I woke up Edmond and Tiffy, phoned Edward, then Lisette in her room upstairs, and within twenty minutes, we were all gathered in the room. Sitting in the chair next to the bed while the others remained at some distance, I took Mother's hand and put my head very close to hers. Her breath, coming out in coughing spurts, smelled of morphine. I told her we were all there, naming everyone in the room. I told her about the weather and what time it was—I rambled, just so that she would die with the sound of my voice in her ears. So that she would not feel abandoned by the living.

After what seemed a long time, Solange said: "She's just expelling air. She's gone." Edmond gave a painful sigh.

"Really we have to thank God it's over," said Aunt Tiffy. That made Lisette heave a sob and bury her face in her bathrobe, a pink, frilly thing Mother had given her many years ago for Christmas. Anne-Sophie took Edward's inert arm.

It was too early to phone the doctor for the death certificate. Edward and Anne-Sophie went back to their children. I helped Lisette make coffee. Aunt Tiffy disappeared into her room. When I went back into Mother's room, Edmond was now sitting on the chair next to the bed. He looked just as he had when I came upon him in the clinic, after Mother's operation—slightly on the edge of his seat, waiting for her to wake up.

"*C'est fini,*" I said gently to my stepfather, putting my hand on his shoulder.

"Oh, I know," he said, standing and looking at me right in the eye. "I was wondering where she's gone. Can't you feel it?

Hélène is no longer there." He pointed to the bed. I looked down at my mother. Her mouth hung open and her eyes were slightly open, just the whites showing. The skin was waxy and bloodless. Edmond was right: the body of Helen Stanford McFarquhar Harcourt-Laporte was lying before us, but she was no longer giving out warmth, feeling, mood—all those invisible particles that fly through the air and constitute human vitality. Even when Mother was unconscious, they were still palpable. Now they were not. Her spirit had indeed gone.

"But where has she gone?" he asked. "Her spirit—the energy it gave off—cannot have disappeared into thin air. It has to have gone somewhere." He paused and sat down again, folding his hairless, spotted hands on his lap. "My faith, you know, has always been of a conventional, unconsidered nature. I have always believed in God because my generation, my world, believed in God." He paused. "Until my parents died, I did what they told me, believed what they told me." He shook his head. "Anyway, look here—she's been taken away."

"You're right, her energy's gone," I said. "But where?"

"Maybe to heaven," he said simply, his voice actually sounding stronger.

He left the room, and I sat there alone with my dead mother. I kissed her forehead and it was cold as stone. Maybe it was just exhaustion and a certain relief that her suffering was finally over, but I felt that early morning sitting next to her that I knew exactly where her spirit had gone: it had gone into me.

———

I really did feel a transformation after Mother's death. It had made me want to grab onto life and the living—to leave Michel Houellebecq's world far behind me—to run out in the street and make noise. It had made me feel like a bigger, more expansive person, one full of compassion, almost love, I would have to say, for the whole human race. I felt that I had experienced something so profound, that from one day to the next, I was changed forever.

There was, however, little time for reflection or even grief. Death means reams of paperwork, bureaucracy. There's a funeral to plan. Mother's was to be held, per her request, at the American Cathedral, where she and Edmond had been married. It was a ceremony that I remembered with funereal gloom.

Around that time, Mother had made Edward and me attend the Sunday school and I hated every minute of it. Many of the other American children went to the same school; their parents were friends. I felt doubly miserable at being excluded where I believed I should still fit in. Edward, of course, was too young to be aware of fitting or not fitting. I remember him sitting at the little table with a large grin on his face, a Crayola crayon gripped in his fist like a scepter, while I sat slumped across from him, counting the seconds until Mother came to rescue me.

Being August, it was a small service. With the help of the reverend, we'd chosen a couple of hymns we thought she'd have liked and a Bach organ piece. Being the older son, I was designated to read something. I spent hours looking through the Bible but finally decided on a Shakespeare sonnet.

I was so nervous about the reading that I remember nothing of the service until I was standing in front of the mourners, focusing on the page in front of me, trying to master my quaking voice: "That time of year thou mayst in me behold, / When yellow leaves, or none, or few, do hang / Upon these boughs which shake against the cold, / Bare ruin'd choirs . . ."

Then the words took me over; I could feel my voice getting stronger, and by the time I got to "This thou perceiv'st, which makes thy love more strong, / To love that well which thou must leave ere long," I was able to look at the people seated in front of me. There were wet eyes all around, though at least half the mourners wouldn't have understood much of what I'd read. So maybe the words meant nothing. Maybe it was just seeing the intractable and impossible Trevor McFarquhar read a poem for his long-suffering mother that brought tears to their eyes. For my part, it felt pretty monumental to be eliciting some other sentiment than annoyance, exasperation, or shame at a family gathering.

Since no one else was able to face the idea of Mother's body being cremated, as she'd requested, I had volunteered to accompany her to the flames. Edward lent me his car again, saying it was undignified to take the métro on such an occasion. I'd been to Père-Lachaise many times—not surprisingly, walking among the dead was an activity I enjoyed—but had always skirted the crematorium, which sits in the middle at the top of the hill, two big smoke stacks jutting to the sky. I was greeted at the door by a man in a charcoal suit who spoke in a hushed voice and looked fittingly grave. The body had arrived, he said, and led me downstairs to the incineration room. It had rows of chairs, like a church, but instead of the altar, there was a metal grille and a screen. My mother's casket was in the middle of the room, draped in a purple cloth.

"Are you waiting for anyone else?" asked the man.

"No. I'm alone."

"Have you prepared any kind of ceremony? Readings? Music?"

I shook my head; a couple more men appeared from nowhere and removed the purple cloth, lifting the casket onto the conveyor belt where an altar might have stood. The machine was put into motion and the coffin moved slowly, like a piece of luggage at the arrival area of an airport, except here it descended and disappeared into flames, visible now behind the plate glass. Some music began to play, but it was impossible to catch more than the odd note over the powerful noise of the furnace that was enveloping my mother's body. I endured the flames by imagining the alternative: her cold, chemical-filled body being eaten by maggots underground.

After it was over, back in the foyer, he said the ashes would be ready in about two hours.

So I meandered around the cemetery, under majestic trees that towered over abandoned mausoleums with broken locks and rusted doors, while the tree roots, having run out of space, grew at right angles around and between the cobblestones. And amid hundreds of tourists, who helped create an odd energy: life humming through the corridors of death.

Suddenly there was a large group in front of me. It was Oscar Wilde's tomb, covered with lipstick kisses. Minus the crowd, I might have walked right by it. There seemed to be no rhyme or reason to the placement of bodies; the names of those who made up the indexes of French history books were littered randomly amid the concierges and the taxi drivers. The tombs might vary in size and grandeur according to the occupant's stature on earth, but underground everyone was humbly jumbled together.

Just beyond Oscar's tomb, a cluster of people was facing an arrangement of bushes on a narrow lawn. The bushes formed a semicircle around a tombstone that read *jardin du souvenir*, garden of memory. A cemetery official had placed a canister on a marble circle that stood in front of the tombstone, and the couple was taking photographs. They stood there for quite some time, until finally the official picked up the canister and moved to a patch of grass at the side. As the group of mourners watched, the official swung the canister, releasing the ashes, presumably of the loved one, as if dispensing lawn-care product. When I got a bit closer, I saw that the narrow strip of grass in fact had line after line of ashes. That this garden of memory was a mass grave of sorts.

I stared and stared at two of these lines and somehow was reminded of the day Béa and I had lain on our backs in the grass at

Hautebranche, just after Marie had died. How despite the circumstances of a dead baby and a dying mother, it had been a sublime
moment. And then I started thinking that if I ended up as a white
line in the grass, I would like Béa's white line next to mine, and
in the meantime, I wished she were here to witness this curious
scene with me. Experiencing it alone was, well, lonely. And that
no matter how well I described it to her, or described it later on
paper, it wouldn't be the same as her actually being here at my side.

The sound of lawn mowers and the friendly, summery smell
of the fresh-cut grass roused me from my reverie. Part of the garden
of memory, I could see, had been cordoned off. For all the signs
telling people to have some respect and not walk over all these
dead people on this *lieu de mémoire*, two municipal employees
were leaning dutifully into their lawn mowers, and ashen bodies
were flying through the blades by the dozen. One minute you're
lying in the grass on a sunny summer's day; the next you're a line of
ashes, about to be mown over in the garden of memory. There's no
more to it than that. I wasn't sure if this was reassuring or terrifying.

When I picked up my mother, the urn was still warm.
Although the man who handed it over to me apologized for this,
I was happy for the heat and clutched the thing to my chest, sitting
with it on my lap in the car for quite some time before strapping
it into the passenger seat and returning to the rue des Martyrs.

Later, lying on my mattress, the urn sitting on the table,
I could not get the line from "To His Coy Mistress" out of my
head: "The grave's a fine and private place but none I think do
there embrace." My room, in its rejection of life, certainly had
something of the grave to it, and until Béa, no one had done any
embracing in it. As I thought again about those lines of poetry and
those lines of ashes in the garden of memory, I realized that I was
lying flat on my back. In a brusque, almost violent movement, I
turned on my side and bent my knees.

———

Edmond was going to return to New York with Aunt Tiffy and Mother's ashes. She had requested that her remains be placed under a particular tree next to the house on Long Island. Edward objected: "He can't just put the ashes there."

"You're not worried about scaring away prospective buyers, are you?" I asked with a smile.

"No," he said. "I'm worried about just leaving her there. I mean, how do we know there won't be bits of bone or something?"

"I can assure you," I said, "that there are no bones. But you're right. We should consider whether to bury or scatter them. She didn't specify, did she. The trouble with burying the urn is it might be dug up by a stranger years from now. She wouldn't have wanted that."

"You're right." Edward nodded.

"BP should scatter," I said. Then, thinking of those white lines and the lawn mowers: "Over a large area."

This was a strange reversal of roles, having me suggest solutions to problems, but around the time of Mother's death, the first in his living memory, Edward was at times almost befuddled. It was actually heartening to see that death at least could rattle him.

A couple days before Edmond and Aunt Tiffy's departure, I had just gotten off the phone with Béa in London. It was the first evening where practicalities had not been crowding my mind. I took a beer out of the fridge, sat down at my table, and there were the notebooks I'd been writing after talks with my mother. I started leafing through the pages, and all I could see was what hadn't been said, what was missing: the story of Franny's death and the reason why my anything but whimsical mother had decided to move herself and her remaining two children across an ocean. "A fun year in Paris," plus a few years as a translator just didn't add up to a plausible motive.

There were of course two people who might know the answers to these questions, and asking Aunt Tiffy somehow seemed cowardly, inappropriate.

I got up and paced the room with such agitation that Cassie got up too and stood wagging her tail at me in perplexed sympathy. I looked at my watch. It was too early to walk her. But not too late to make a phone call. I looked at my new phone. Sighed. Picked it up and punched in the number that when my mother had made me memorize and repeat to her in French was 705 52 57, but had over the years been stretched to 47 05 52 57 and finally 01 47 05 52 57.

———

Late the next morning, Cassie at my side, I was once again ringing the brass buzzer, next to the discreet "H-L." As I'd hoped, the approaching feet wore the soft rubber of my stepfather's crepe soles.

"*Entre*," he said, standing aside. Now that Mother was dead, he had regained most of his old composure; he even seemed less stooped as he led me to his study, saying that Lisette was out shopping for lunch and Aunt Tiffy for presents for her grandchildren. Following him, I felt for the first time that Mother would never be coming back, that Edmond was there alone for good. That any time from now on when I came to the rue de Verneuil, I was entering his territory and his alone.

"Please," he said, pointing to a chair before seating himself on the leather-covered swivel chair he must have brought back from Frères Laporte when he'd left for good, after the merger.

"Thank you," I said, looking at his blue cotton shirt, his perfectly creased grey-flannel trousers, and his soft-soled brown-suede loafers, not a scuff in sight. I shifted slightly in my chair, uncomfortable at being alone with him, though technically, we did have company. Not just Cassie, who was sniffing around with ill-mannered curiosity, but also Mother, whose ashes were on the desk.

"Well," he said, crossing his arms defensively. "You wanted to speak to me."

"Yes," I said. The camp bed that had been set up in the corner for him since Mother's illness was still there, and it gave the place an air of a military headquarters. Though I had requested the meeting, it felt uncomfortably like a father-son chat.

"I am all ready to go to New York tomorrow," he said, breaking the awkward silence. "To carry out your mother's wishes." He placed his hand on the urn.

"Yes. Well. As you may know," I cleared my throat, "Mother and I spoke about certain things in the weeks before she died." Edmond's evasive nod told me I'd come to the right place. "About our life in the US, before we moved here, about my father." I paused. "But there were some things Mother did not talk about." My stepfather now crossed his legs too and stared at the floor, transfixed by the pattern in the carpet. "You know obviously that I had a sister. That she died a year before my father."

He nodded.

"It seemed very painful for my mother to talk about her death, I assume because she was with her when the accident took place. But it has occurred to me that I don't really know what happened." He glanced at me for a split second. "And that you might."

For a moment he sat very still, eyes back to the carpet, but finally he sighed, unfolding arms and legs. Then he looked me dead in the eye. "It was your father who was with your sister the day she died."

He might just as well have hit me over the head with a board. My ears were ringing. "But it was Mother who dropped me off. Mother who went shopping and who let go of her hand." Beyond the shock, I did indeed feel enraged at him for telling me. And I felt betrayed all over again by my mother for not telling me, for her telling Edmond instead. It felt as if he were trespassing on my story.

"No." Edmond shook his head. "It was your father who was with her."

"Why wouldn't she have told me that herself?"

"You know why." He looked at me with pained defiance. "She didn't want to tarnish your image of your father."

"But you're only too happy to."

"You asked me the question, Trevor," he said very quietly. "I'm giving you the answer."

I nodded.

"And it shouldn't tarnish anything. An accident is nobody's fault. I told your mother that, I don't know how many times, right from your first days in Paris."

"What do you mean?" I asked, feeling a tingling at the back of my neck. "Our first days in Paris? You didn't know her then."

"You didn't really think that your mother just picked up and moved to Paris on a whim, did you?"

"But there was the whole year abroad thing, the translating work . . ."

"She moved to Paris for me."

"For you?" I half screamed. Cassie slunk out of the room, tail between her legs.

"Your mother and I met when she was a student here. The family Hélène was staying with were friends of my parents. I was just a few years older and was asked to escort your mother on certain evenings. For some reason, it never occurred to anyone that something might happen between us. When it did, when I told my parents not long before she left that I wanted to marry her, they forbade it. They were very, very old-fashioned and wouldn't hear of me marrying an American. And I obeyed." He shook his head. "As I always did. Anyway, your mother went back and finished her college, met your father, and married him. We did not speak for quite a few years; she had been very hurt. But I came to New

York for a visit once, after my parents' death. I had dinner with both your parents."

"You met my father?" I had completely lost control of my voice.

"Yes. A lovely and gentle man. You *look* very much like him." He paused again. "Anyway, your mother and I also had lunch. Several lunches, in fact. All innocent, of course. We always had such an easy time talking, your mother and I." He took a deep breath. "Then not long after your father died, she contacted me to tell me. It just seemed so obvious what should happen," he said, shaking his head, as if still stumped by such inexplicable forces. He looked right at me, now almost pleadingly: "Do you know what I mean?"

If my stepfather had asked me that question several months earlier, it would only have fed the crackling flames of my fury and resentment; I would have sneered at two cowards running into each other's arms, once the coast was clear. But several weeks ago, I had met Béa Fairbank. In the meantime I had experienced my mother's death. Now indeed, I knew exactly what he meant. My anger evaporated, and in its place I felt a pang of sorrow and longing for my mother. Sorrow that she had tried to keep my father's image untarnished in my eyes, even at the expense of her own. And longing for the lost chance to tell her that it was okay, I understood that she had moved us across an ocean for love.

Aunt Tiffy came back, and Lisette too. We talked about checking the ashes at the airport, the prospects for the sale of the house. Aunt Tiffy, of course, would take care of everything. "That place will be sold before I push the send button on my computer," she said. "You have no idea how desperate people are for a house on Long Island. The life of a successful New Yorker these days isn't complete without one."

They asked me to stay for lunch, but I needed to be alone with this bruising new information. With the added twists to my story that made such perfect sense. I wondered, in fact, if my sub- or semiconscious hadn't already sensed the truth because after my meeting with Edmond, I had a strange feeling of having just woken from dream. My imagined version of events had targeted my mother partly because she was the one to drop me off at Tom Rogers's, but partly because I wanted to blame her for everything. Of course, that's why my father couldn't live with Franny's death; he was the one to let go. And of course, now that I looked back carefully, Mother already knew Edmond. He was walking with us in the Luxembourg Gardens right after our arrival; it was obvious even then the two had not just met. I remembered too the argument after which my father had stormed out, the line that had dangled in my memory: "You should have married a banker." Maybe I had misunderstood, or misremembered, the article. Maybe he'd said: "You should have married *the* banker."

For the first time ever, I felt sympathy and a certain admiration for my stepfather. Not only had he stoically put up with me over the years, he'd also sustained a misperception that had fed my spite toward him. After all I had put him through, how had he resisted the temptation to shout the truth at me?

And I realized that he was not trespassing on my story; it was his life too.

Despite this newfound sympathy, I doubted that I would ever feel any real closeness to him. But I also thought, so what? Just because I don't adore him doesn't mean I have to hate him. I can like him well enough, do what I can to help him get used to life without his beloved wife, my mother.

Maybe I was growing up after all.

FIVE

HAVING VOLUNTEERED TO sort through Mother's things while Edmond was gone, I spent the last week that Béa would be in London at the rue de Verneuil. First I saw Lisette off to Brittany for the holiday she had not taken as usual at the beginning of August. I helped her on to the train, placing her small bag on the rack above the seat. In a way, she was the most bereft; she had so little in her life already.

Mother's bedroom, the logical place to start, was both eerie and comforting. It looked as it had before her illness: medicine bottles had been removed, and the bed was made up without a wrinkle. The closets and chest of drawers were still filled with her clothes. Her belongings meant that even if her spirit was gone, her presence could still very much be felt. But she wasn't there and never would be again. And once I had removed all trace of her, wouldn't her presence disappear too?

Wandering the apartment, shadowed by Cassie, I couldn't bring myself to touch anything. Until I got to her collection of boxes. Edmond had instructed me to leave them in place; in them my mother would fittingly live on at the rue de Verneuil, and I could get started on the clean-up job that would take me the whole week to accomplish.

At night I would lie in my old bedroom and look at the triangle of sky that I had first seen when trying to wish myself back to Connecticut and a complete family. The bit I'd stared at many afternoons after school, and subsequent nights when I couldn't sleep, and again as a teenager, dreaming about my future in the US where I would rediscover eternal happiness. And finally, in my last days at the rue de Verneuil, bashed in body and soul, that triangle had been there for me to stare at for hours at a time, while I convinced myself that the word Future had been stripped of any meaning for me.

That whole week, in fact, my mind flooded with remembered events, impressions, and sensations of the place, and it occurred to me that that is really what we mean by home: our private garden of memory.

I got some relief from Edward and Anne-Sophie who, between Mother's illness and Anne-Sophie being too pregnant to go anywhere, were stuck in Paris and on their own. The older children had gone for two weeks to the not-quite-completed house in Nantucket, with Stephanie, Bruce, and a Danish *fille au pair*. The youngest, theirs, had been sent to Biarritz with cousins.

In my cupboard-airing mode, I asked Edward if he knew about Franny's death, about Mother and Edmond. He did not, but being Edward, he of course had a completely different reaction.

"I guess it's good to know what happened, though I can't say I've ever lost sleep wondering about all that stuff."

"About the death of your sister, then your father? About the relationship between your parents?"

"Come on, Trevor," he said. "You know I have a terrible memory and certainly can't remember anything before the rue de Verneuil. Even then . . ." he trailed off. "I remember BP picking me up from Boy Scouts one Saturday."

"And you're married to an historian?"

Anne-Sophie shrugged her shoulders and smiled her heart-shaped smile; Edward got that weird, misty look in his eyes. The effect of her natural sweetness and composure on my less than sweet, driven brother seemed nothing short of a miracle. Though I still didn't feel a great *sympathie* with either one, I admired their easier approach to getting through the day, now that I'd dropped the unreasonably rigid requirement that everyone in my family be just like me.

Near the end of my clean-up, I opened the drawer of my mother's bedside table. Amid the nail scissors and pens and coins and other junk lay what I first thought was a book.

Photo albums from our first life were kept in the bottom drawer of Mother's oak desk in the bedroom. These albums had not been thrown away, but neither had they been left out in the open, placed next to the French photo albums, for example, which sat on the bookshelves lining the corridor. This meant consulting them was a clandestine activity, one which I had indulged in somewhat obsessively at different times in my childhood. As far as I knew, this was all there was in terms of a photographic record of our previous life. But there in her bedside drawer was a little album of only a dozen or so pages. The leather cover was darkened from much fingering, and many of the inside plastic sheaves were cracked near the binding from much leafing. Every photo was of Franny, starting when she was a few hours old. In the second-to-last photo, Franny was sitting in Mother's lap on the front porch in Connecticut. Mother had her arms protectively around her and was kissing her ear. It almost looked as if she were whispering a secret. The sense of intimacy between mother and daughter was so strong, I couldn't pull my eyes away for some time.

The last picture in the book was a family photo, taken of the five of us outside the house in Connecticut, at the time of

Edward's christening, which meant it must have been taken not so long before Franny's death. Edward was in Mother's arms, trailing a white gown. To her left stood my father, with Franny in his left arm. I stood in front of my parents with one hand raised, in a wave or a salute, as if I had just conquered the world. We all looked smiling and victorious, a big happy family.

I stared hard at my parents in that photo, trying to get underneath their smiles. My father's was always a little tight, like mine. I'd thought it was a result of our apparently similar natures or his feelings of professional inadequacy. But now I wondered if it didn't have something to do with my parents' relationship. I looked at my mother. Did her smile have something sad and frustrated in it? Or uncomfortable, not quite satisfied, as she stood next to my father? Had she loved him at all, or was Edmond her only true love? And what did my father really know about all that? Did he feel unloved—did that explain the melancholy my mother had talked about? Looking at that photo, another question suddenly struck me: had Edward been named Edward because it was only three letters away from Edmond? His name certainly didn't have any family significance, as mine did. These were things I would never know, things that even if Edmond knew, I would never be able to ask him.

The image of her poring over this album at night—thumbing its pages as religiously as a Bible—haunts me to this day. How could I ever have presumed to judge the depth of my mother's suffering?

———

While I was rendering my first favor ever to my stepfather, he was doing the same on the other side of the Atlantic. Or Aunt Tiffy was. The Long Island house, as predicted, had sold immediately, and even she was surprised by the huge price it had fetched. Edmond was staying into September "to tie up loose ends," but from phone calls, I gathered that Aunt Tiffy was doing most of the tying.

The house proceeds alone would easily allow me to go ahead with the plan I had outlined on the pont des Arts that day, including the bit about handing over the shop to Wanda and Piotr. With my long and frequent absences, they were already doing most of the work, and that, Piotr told me, had completely cured Wanda of any *mal du pays*. And I liked the symmetry of it: the shop had fallen into my lap, and now it was time for it to fall into someone else's.

As for the other part of my plan, I already found myself taking more photos. Of Mother during her illness and in the hours after she died. Of the rooms at the rue de Verneuil while I was cleaning up. Of the empty city during my morning strolls with the dog.

And Béa in all this rummaging through my past and planning for the future? I had the disembodied version on the phone daily and at length, but I was missing the real thing sorely. For once in my life it had very little to do with sex. I wanted to absorb her spirit, her human energy, the quality that had abandoned Mother when she died. To touch, feel, smell her. To hear that laugh without the help of France Telecom. On the other hand I still worried (I hadn't changed that much) that once life was less emotionally charged and demanding, once it had settled back into the humdrum—well, that that's how she'd view me—dull and dreary.

Still, I was desperate for some uninterrupted time together and had figured out how to get it. We would dog- and house-sit at Hautebranche while Cédric, Viviane, and André went to Aix for a holiday. It had not been easy to convince Viviane. In her state of guilty mourning, she was refusing to do anything that might improve her outlook. She had a million reasons why she should never budge again. Being intimately familiar with this frame of mind, I eventually managed to persuade her she might as well try a change, for her husband's sake if not her own. From what Cédric told me, she was still catatonic, except when talking about God, but I held out hope that a combination of being away from her house, where every corner held a trove of painful memories, and breathing the sunny air of her beloved Aix would help the old Viviane resurface.

The day of Béa's return I had one more task: removing Mother's bicycle. It was still down in the courtyard, attached to the iron bar and in a sorry state. In the course of our conversations, she had mentioned that since "that business five or six years ago," she hadn't ridden it. I'd left it until last because in all my cleaning up, I had not come across the key for the Kryptonite lock she'd insisted on buying with the secondhand Raleigh. Edmond didn't know where it was. Neither did Lisette. "*Etrange*," she said, when I phoned her at her sister's. Needing more than a sturdy pair of cable cutters to remove a Kryptonite lock, I eventually called in the locksmith Jean-Baptiste. Just back from his holiday, he came with his young son and equipment to remove the intractable lock.

"What a lady," he said gravely. We—Jean-Baptiste, his son, Cassie, and I—were standing over the bicycle as if gathered around her coffin. "There's no sense, no justice."

I nodded. After a moment of respectful silence, I said: "I hope you can break this lock. They're made to be indestructible."

"There are few problems concerning a lock that I cannot resolve," Jean-Baptiste said. He looked and spoke more like a hippie professor than a locksmith, with a mop of blond hair, thoughtful blue eyes, and a thick beard surrounding a serious mouth. "*On y va, mon grand*," he said to the boy, who must have been about seven. He stood in the shadow of his father as metal met metal in a piercing whine. The sparks began to fly, and the boy put his hand on the back of his father's hip, peering around, both wanting and not wanting to witness the scene. Cassie jumped back and forth, expressing her canine version of the same conflict. The breaking of a lock is indeed an ambivalent—and in this case a violent—act. Whether it represents a release or a rupture is open to interpretation, and I wasn't at all sure what was being accomplished here. For the first time in the last weeks, I felt the tears pricking my eyes.

After many minutes, having drilled the mechanism out entirely, Jean-Baptiste pulled apart the lock. The rusty bicycle was free, and my work at the rue de Verneuil was finished. Jean-Baptiste, who refused to be paid, wound up the long electrical cord he'd dragged across the paving stones and walked away solemnly with his drill in one hand, his other around the shoulder of his young son. I was left alone with the dog in the courtyard. In fact, the whole building was empty except for Cassie and me. Even the Morales were away. I stood there gripping the handlebars on the bicycle that had been my mother's, that I couldn't even ride, and the tears were streaming down my cheeks. I didn't think I could stand so much emotion. It was too painful, too confusing.

Eventually I took a deep breath, wiped my eyes on my sleeve, and looked at my watch. It had taken Jean-Baptiste longer than I'd expected, and I still needed to get the bicycle back to Mélo-Vélo and myself up to the Gare du Nord for Béa's train. I pushed the airless tires forward. Stuffing the bike in the back of the small car was not easy—I had to contort the wheels and twist the rearview mirror on the handlebars—but I finally got it in. Cassie, in the front next to me, sat at full attention at these unusual proceedings. I pulled out into the street with a bump. The bicycle clattered, and Cassie almost lost her balance before regaining her alert posture at my side. I looked at my watch again. The train was arriving in half an hour. Amid my turmoil, there was one certainty: I wasn't going to be late.

About the Author

MARY FLEMING, originally from Chicago, moved to Paris in 1981, where she worked as a freelance journalist and consultant. Before turning full time to writing fiction, she was the French representative for the American foundation The German Marshall Fund. A long-time board member of the French Fulbright Commission, Fleming continues to serve on the board of Bibliothèques sans Frontières. *The Art of Regret* is Fleming's second novel. She writes a blog called *A Paris-Perche Diary* at http://mf.ghost.io.

Author photo © William Fleming

Selected Titles from She Writes Press

She Writes Press is an independent publishing company founded to serve women writers everywhere. Visit us at www.shewritespress.com.

A Drop In The Ocean: A Novel by Jenni Ogden. $16.95, 978-1-63152-026-6. When middle-aged Anna Fergusson's research lab is abruptly closed, she flees Boston to an island on Australia's Great Barrier Reef—where, amongst the seabirds, nesting turtles, and eccentric islanders, she finds a family and learns some bittersweet lessons about love.

A Cup of Redemption by Carole Bumpus. $16.95, 978-1-938314-90-2. Three women, each with their own secrets and shames, seek to make peace with their pasts and carve out new identities for themselves.

Anchor Out by Barbara Sapienza. $16.95, 978-1631521652. Quirky Frances Pia was a feminist Catholic nun, artist, and beloved sister and mother until she fell from grace—but now, done nursing her aching mood swings offshore in a thirty-foot sailboat, she is ready to paint her way toward forgiveness.

Shelter Us by Laura Diamond. $16.95, 978-1-63152-970-2. Lawyer-turned-stay-at-home-mom Sarah Shaw is still struggling to find a steady happiness after the death of her infant daughter when she meets a young homeless mother and toddler she can't get out of her mind—and becomes determined to rescue them.

What is Found, What is Lost by Anne Leigh Parrish. $16.95, 978-1-938314-95-7. After her husband passes away, a series of family crises forces Freddie, a woman raised on religion, to confront long-held questions about her faith.

Tzippy the Thief by Pat Rohner. $16.95, 978-1-63152-153-9. Tzippy has lived her life as a selfish, materialistic woman and mother. Now that she is turning eighty, there is not an infinite amount of time left—and she wonders if she'll be able to repair the damage she's done to her family before it's too late.